LiT
Part VI – Impasse

I0642829

Maxwell F. Hurley

LiT
Part VI – Impasse

FICTION4ALL

This book is dedicated to

Family & friends

Past, Present, and Future

A special thank you to all

who are reading this series

Prologue

The experiences of the past, big or small, shape the impact of the future. The choices of how to react to these occurrences leave an impression on the world around them. Values mold the way to choose which pathway to travel. These choices can test to ignore the ideals of the Lite for the false promises of the Dark. Tough decisions are made every day, some without even knowing the consequences. There are some impasses that should not be placed on anyone.

Introduction

It hurt too much to be a dream; it was more of the rawest form of a nightmare. One so intense, so painful, no movie or story writer could ever properly describe. It was as if there was no time lapse. Kameron couldn't remember how long he was being tortured before his rescue. Standing was difficult due to the slimy substance below his feet. Breathing the air felt like tiny rocks of burning sulfur tumbling down his lungs, but he couldn't cough them up. His rescuer, the young light brown-haired woman dressed in renaissance clothing, was trying to hold him up. There was a sense of honor in her focus as she concentrated on the surrounding blackness. Kameron tried grasping onto the slippery ropes that once bonded him to the wall, but the wall was no longer there. His legs turned to jelly as he started to drop to the ground.

His liberator caught him from crashing onto the ground. "Be careful. Watch your footing. If you are to fall, I do not think I could find you again." She quickly snapped her head back as if something caught her attention.

There was something oddly familiar about this woman. Was it a familiarity of a person? It seemed to be more of an emotion. Why couldn't he remember? His mind was in constant movement of scattered confusion. Nausea started to overtake him, but again, he wasn't allowed to do anything about it. "Andre? No, Alec."

The girl was starting to get irritated. "I am not a man." Her mannerisms mimicked an animal having a predator on her trail. "We must continue to move about."

Kameron couldn't keep his chaotic mind in check. Why were her glowing blue eyes and hands comforting to him? He gently pushed her away to show he could stand on his own. "I'm fine."

She cautiously let him go, still keeping her hands close to him. "Are you certain? Please, if you fall…"

Kameron gave off a false sense of confidence. "I'm good." The light from her eyes vanished, but she kept her hands lit with a neon blue light so they could see each other; otherwise, there was complete darkness. Kameron gazed down at his suit; it was dirty, full of holes, and soaked in blood. He frantically checked his stomach, where he'd been pierced with an iron prod. There was a faint scar where that white-faced creature had shoved the burning spear into him. "How am I alive?" The black business suit he was wearing was familiar, though it didn't feel accurate. The tie was black with a single speck of a bright blue metal tie pin.

"You are not alive." The young woman kept her eye on Kameron. There was a moment, where she had a facial expression of unbelievable hope, but it quickly vanished as a faint sound of evil came from the depth of the overwhelming shadow.

"I'm dead?" Kameron lost all feeling in his legs as he started to fall again. The lady caught him again with both hands. She gripped him so tight out of pure fear. The strength in her grip was unprecedented.

"You cannot fall." She stood him on his feet, followed with a nod to confirm he could stand on his own power. "No, you are not alive. Although, the Dark will not let you properly die."

"The Dark?" Kameron took a second to process everything. "The Dark? The Lite?" He turned to her. "Alex?" He squinted as he studied the girl. There was no shaking of the constant reminder of the person in front of him.

"No, my name is Cara. Daughter of Lord DeTronous." She leaned in with curiosity. "Who is Alex?"

A deep sense of emptiness overcame him. It was like having a melody stuck in your head but not knowing the words or name of the song. "I don't know."

"Well, whoever he is, that is the second time you called for him." Cara moved her hair back. "We must move. He will find us if we stay still."

"To where? Where can we go?" Kameron scanned the vastness of pure blackness in the area. "My skin, it's burning, I'm cold." He lifted his sleeve from his blazer and shirt. "There is something in my arm." A cylinder underneath his skin to wave. It seemed to poke through a hole near his wrist. With his fingers, he pulled out a worm. "What the hell?"

Cara hesitated before answering. "That is where we are."

Kameron's eyes widened with fear at the realization of his situation. "Can we escape?"

11

"You are the key." That ghostly sound returned from the distant deep.   Whatever it was, it caused Cara to flash her eyes. Her demeanor changed to a mounted expression of seriousness.

"Well, I'm ready to leave." Kameron's fear and anxiety were not contained. "How do I unlock it?"

"I cannot tell you that." Cara dropped the unfortunate news. "If I tell you, it will not work. But what I can tell you is…" Cara turned around into a fighting stance.

The Lite generating from both her hands and eyes showed a creature with the face of a bear with glowing red eyes.   It lunged at the girl, but she elegantly counterattacked the beast.   The fight continued until she deemed it necessary to form a knife to stab in its back. The monster seemed to disappear into the ground. "Time is short." She quickly turned to Kameron. "Give me your ears."

The intensity of the position they were facing became clear. Cara's eyes had a mixture of distress and ineptness. "What is it?" Kameron fixated on what she was about to say.

"He is coming. If we are to separate…." Cara grabbed on to his shoulders.   "Hopefully, I find you. You will not know me. I cannot tell you who you are. Listen to me now and try to remember my verse…" She was suddenly yanked away from Kameron by her feet. Her eyes glowed blue, and the only thing Kameron could see was the Lite moving from a frantic battle.   She could only manage to yell, "Stay true to your…." Then it was dark, silent.

The burning breathing had stopped for a moment, and there was no feeling of anything whatsoever. Fear overpowered his mind and body. There was nothing, complete blackness. There was no sound, no light. He couldn't even hear himself breathe or move about. There was nothing around him. Kameron was now alone. It seemed like an eternity before he could even start to move. The only thing he could do was stare forward into the nothingness of his prison. What was he to do? The air seemed to start to burn again as he reminded himself to start breathing. The small, razor-like cuts were scorching the flesh on his skin while he was getting colder. He needed to move; it was the only option–but where?

The only direction he could think of was the direction where his rescuer was taken. He took a single step forward when a sudden red light appeared from nowhere. An evil figure with a white face now stood before him as he grabbed Kameron's chin to pull him closer. His tilted black hat shadowed his black eyes behind his long, greasy hair. "I remember you and your pure heart." Contempt could be heard in his voice. "I have something special in mind for you." He picked Kameron up and, in an instant, slammed him downward. Only the echo of Kameron screaming into a constant fall could be heard.

Chapter One

Alex moved her head in the direction of the distant scream. It almost sounded like it was coming from within the fire that engulfed the building before her. This former clothing store has been burning for quite a while, and any person caught in the blazing fire would have died long ago. Plus, the cry for help was far too faint. The main support pillars of the structure had finally started to collapse. Little fireflies of burning embers floated into the sky before disappearing into the blended stars of the night. The fire was giving off massive waves of heat. It was disheartening that she enjoyed the sense of warmth on this cold early spring night. At first, Alex was reminded of snow from the ash of the fire.

The quarantined area of CopperTop Mountain seemed to be a war zone. The curfew set by Gron, our soon-to-be, Demon-possessed mayor, Roger Somberson, had been in effect since the riot. That night, the Conduit of the Dark, Vandor, briefly returned. Alex's heart sank from the memory of that night. The image of her fiancé, Kameron, tackling the Dark Master back into the Conduit just made her stomach turn. Regardless of what she was going through, she had to conduct her hunts to try to bring back the Balance. The Dark Harridan had somehow managed to take away her ability to sense both the Lite and the Dark. Doing so made her job a lot harder. On top of that, she had to avoid CopperTop Mountain authorities. That was

14

something she couldn't deal with right now. She could only control what was happening now.

The scream came again, but this time it sounded different. This was closer and didn't sound like the original one. Regardless, it broadcasted as a cry for help. She and Komptin, who was in a German Shepherd state, approached a boarded-up supermarket. There was a small hole someone had kicked into the boarded-up windows. Alex motioned for Komptin to go around before she approached the jaded entryway.

She flashed her eyes a quick neon blue burst before easily ripping off the board to scout the abandoned market before entering. Normally, she would have gone through the hole already there, but she didn't know what was on the other side. She wanted to do a small recon. Shelves were toppled, unworking light fixtures were barely hanging, and small amounts of traces of food could be seen. Alex did notice a faint outline of a human figure in the rubble.

Alex quietly made it through the window, waiting for the imminent attack. There was no sound as she landed inside the supermarket. After a quick survey of the rampaged area for Infiltrators or Demons, she cautiously approached the body. Her heart felt heavy when she saw a young male with dark skin; he was gripping a damaged package of dinner rolls. His breathing was slow and heavy; the marks of Demon claws on his chest were oozing dark red blood.

"I just wanted to get food for my mom," he muttered with the sound of blood gurgling in his throat.

All she could do was wipe the blood from entering his eyes. "Shhhh," she said in a quietly caring fashion. It was all she could do.

"Am I going to die?" The fear in his eyes told Alex he already knew the answer.

"Yes, I'm afraid so," Alex scouted the area to make sure she wasn't going to get blindsided. "In a short time, you will never know what fear or pain is anymore." Alex grabbed his hand for comfort. She kissed his hand and placed it on his chest. She gently placed the other one on top of it.

"Please, make the pain stop," he tried to hold in the mixture of crying and fright.

Alex checked the wound, but she already knew there was nothing that could be done. It would be a long twenty minutes for the boy before the inevitable. "I can make the pain stop."

The boy tried to smile. His body showed evidence of losing color. "Thank you."

"Close your eyes," Alex tenderly whispered to him. "I want you to think of your happiest time...and remember, in your heart, He loves you. Okay?"

The boy slowly closed his eyes in anticipation. Alex placed her fist on top of the boy's heart. Alex closed her eyes, prayed, and then quickly formed a spear. The boy's body quickly tensed, but then relaxed as his eyes became lifeless; the pain now gone. The Lite Sentry wiped a tear before standing up. Behind her were three figures standing upright, with glowing red eyes and claws extended. Alex remained still while continuing to stare at the boy as she lit her fists to the same neon blue as her eyes.

"How'd it feel to kill someone so young, Sentry?" The Demon in the middle hissed.

"I ended his pain." Alex peeked over at an Infiltrator outside the window she climbed in, staring at her.

"After I'm done with you, I'm going to dump the body to his mother." The Demon started to laugh. "I'll be sure to watch the whole thing. I think I'll record it for all to see."

"You are so sick." Alex was disgusted. "But I do find it funny you think you're leaving." She cracked her neck in anticipation.

Komptin jumped at one of the side Demons in his purple-skinned gargoyle form. The Demon screamed as he knew the fight of his life had just begun. The Infiltrator in the window was about to join the fight, but it was dragged from behind, preventing it from entering the building.

The remaining Demons attacked Alex. She grabbed one of the shelves and swung it across the side of the head of the first Demon. That sent the possessed man sliding on the floor into the wall. The second Demon screeched as it charged Alex. She dodged the punch; normally she would've met it with an uppercut to the chin. But she wanted to make this Demon suffer. She instantly kicked its knee. Like dry kindling, the sound of the snapping leg brought it down to the ground. There was a bottle of briquette lighter fluid on the ground. Alex grabbed the container while holding the Demon in a headlock. She squeezed his head until he screamed so she could dump the fluid into his mouth. She threw the Demon off to the side. The Demon could only stand on one leg as the two stared at each other.

"Now what?" It asked her sarcastically.

Alex flicked a match from a box lying on the floor and tossed it at the Demon as she squirted more lighter fluid. A trail of fire followed into its mouth. The soldier of the Dark started burning from the inside out. He frantically screamed in pain, flailing about. Alex decided to let him suffer while she took on the other Demon. He tried to run, but she shot him with a Lite Beam to the back of the head. The possessed man somersaulted over into a pile of rubble. Alex ran over to him and angrily stomped on his head until it caved in. She picked him up and threw him into the wall. Then followed with a knee to the gut. She dropped to the ground, using her leg to flip him over. The Demon barely stood up, with black blood dripping from his body. "You suck."

Alex formed a knife with her Lite and ended the Demon's existence. She slowly turned to the body shell of the burnt Demon. He could barely stand. Alex swiped the Demon's knees, keeping it on the ground. "Stay down." She forced the weakened, burnt Demon to the ground.

Komptin finished killing the Demon he fought. He limped over to Alex's side as she stared at the body of the young boy. The Lite Sentry checked over a small wound on her hunting companion. "You okay, boy?" The gargoyle dog enjoyed a small scratch behind the ears. Alex knelt at what once held the life of an innocent child with his life ahead of him. The sound of an Infiltrator being diminished brought a small grin to Alex's face, but it didn't last long. The burnt Demon rustled as he stood back up. "I said stay down." She shot another Lite Beam at it. It screamed in pain as it fell back to the ground.

Tristan, the new Lite Sentry who was waiting for orders from the Council, joined Alex inside the supermarket. His face had a bloody nose and lip. "I got him," he said with half confidence.

Alex smirked and continued to stare at the boy's body. "Good job." She barely spoke.

Tristan saw the small shell of a lifeless boy. "That looks like a Sentry burn on his heart, was it Gron?"

Alex just stared over the boy's body. "I needed to end his pain."

A realization of what Alex did hit Tristan. "Alex, I'm sorry."

"You didn't know." Alex stood up. "Tristan, being a Sentry, you are going to have to make decisions; decisions that will affect people who you know, and those who've you never met. Some of these choices are going to suck and others are going to be flat out gut-wrenching." Alex turned to Tristan. "This is gut-wrenching. Call this in anomalously. The boy's mother will need closure." Alex turned to walk out the door. "Let's call it a night." Suddenly, the charred Demon stood back up with his eyes glowing red.

"What the hell is that?!" Tristan jumped back with his fists and eyes glowing.

"Come on, let's go home." Alex and Komptin started towards the Demon with no sense of urgency. She formed a knife and nonchalantly cut the Demon's head off without breaking stride.

***

Anne decided to spend the night at the church. It wasn't that she didn't want to sleep in her own bed; far from it, she was just way too tired to drive home. The feeling of not wanting to get into a car accident or hit a deer didn't seem appealing to her. It seemed her duties as Council Historian were pushing a little bit more every day. Luckily, the plumber was able to switch out the hot water tank before the contractor quit. The Freedom Off Religion, aka - the F.O.R., destroyed this church before the Catholic Council was able to retain it back. Every step forward to get the church open was a major cost increase. But the key part was proceeding. The sun wasn't even hinting to start the day when she finished showering. This gave her some time to finish up some work before everyone got here, including her handwritten weekly journal.

As the same as last week, there really hasn't been any change. Though, I really wish that wasn't the case for the start of the next seven days. A leader of evil will be sworn in as mayor of CopperTop Mountain tomorrow. Roger Somberson, whose Demon name is Gron. He will be in another top position of power. The Dark-possessed leader of the F.O.R. will oversee the well-being of the oblivious citizens of CopperTop. It was almost a landslide victory when he was voted as the youngest mayor in the history of the state, might even be the country. The scary part is that the majority of the citizens are welcoming him into office. Fortunately, we who follow the Lite are still making our presence known. Even though I have found peace in my husband's death, it still isn't easy watching the man who murdered him being paraded around as a hero.

Though it hurt, knowing he is in Heaven with no pain is comforting. I wish Alex could feel the same. Alex's fiancé, Kameron, sacrificed himself to close the Dark portal that brought Vandor, the Conduit of the Dark, back for a very brief time. No words could describe the pain our Lite Sentry felt as she watched the only person she ever fell in love with, throw his body into Vandor, pushing him back into the Dark Conduit. I have never seen her in such emotional turmoil.

Alex tries hiding her pain by acting as if nothing has happened. She isn't fooling anybody around here, but we all play along until she's ready to talk about it. Right now, her focus is the new Sentry, Tristan, by taking him on some random hunts. Although she still prefers to go herself, well, with Komptin at her side. There still hasn't been a way to bring back her inability to sense the Dark, or what Alex needs the most, to restore her connection to the Lite. The only progress we made was finding out her link was taken by something called the Dark Harridan. We still don't know who it is..."

21

"What are you doing?" Megan came into Anne's office with a stack of folders. The church's secretary came into Anne's office with a little caution. "Father Carl wanted me to give these to you." She placed them on her desk, in clear view of Anne's work. There was no hiding the fact Anne closed her journal for privacy.

The Council Historian peeked out the window to see the sun had made itself known. Time seemed to have escaped her. "I was just journaling; it helps with everything, kind of a stress reliever." Anne calmly put the journal into the opened file safe behind her desk. With a quick spin of the dial after closing the door, it was locked away. The pile of folders Megan brought showed Anne she had a lot of work ahead of her. "Thank you."

Megan intentionally sat down on the seat where Alex normally sits. Her black and red streaked hair was tied nicely behind her with a maroon bow. "I get that, the journaling thing. I've been doing a lot of writing myself lately."

Anne got up to get some much-needed coffee. "Really? Is it something you hope to have published, or is it just for your own personal release?" She showed Megan the pot. "Want some?"

Megan waved off the offer. Megan grabbed a book from Anne's desk to start thumbing through the pictures. It was an early renaissance book of church literature. Megan was disgusted holding it, but she needed to hide it. "Oh, I already have a publisher."

22

Anne found herself pleasantly surprised for Megan. "Really, who picked it up?"

"Well, we're in talks right now. I don't want to jinx it by saying anything." Megan quickly retreated. "But if they accept it, it's ready for worldwide distribution."

Anne smile at her sweetly. "That's fantastic. I understand why you would be leery. What's the context?" Anne leaned on the heater in the room to warm up.

"It's about life-changing perspective." Megan got up to join Anne in leaning against the heater. "It's a bit chilly down here."

"The furnace is on its last leg." Anne savored the sip of hot coffee. A quick feeling of warmth trickled down her body. "I can't find anyone to fix it." Anne and Megan just sat there in silence for a bit. "You know, I would love to read your book as a beta reader."

Megan just turned her eyes towards Anne. "Oh."

Megan sat there, didn't really know how to answer. "I really hope one day you do read it." Her phone chimed, letting her know of a message. "Oh, Father Carl needs me to grab some coffee and doughnuts for Bible study." She got to the doorway to head to the store for Father Carl's request.

"The offer to read it is always open." Anne's chipmunk cheeks seemed to emphasize her genuinely caring nature.

Megan turned to Anne with a grin. "You know, I may actually take you up on that." Megan spun around to see Alex standing right next to her. Megan screamed. "You scared the hell out of me."

Alex chuckled as she joined Anne by the heater. "Hey Anne, do you have any of those note pages?"

Anne waited until Megan left to grab them from her filing cabinet. "Starting your report early?"

"You know me, Ms. Punctuality." Alex received the approved blank Council report papers. "You think they will ever go to at least a typewriter."

"Nope." Anne knew the pain of writing reports for the Council. They didn't want any machinery used for Council reports in fear of hacking or copying their official correspondence. Anne handed her the report pages. "Have fun."

***

Alex didn't want to stay long in Anne's office. It didn't miss Alex's attention on how tired Anne had come off; it was mostly Alex who couldn't put up this front for much longer. Part of her wished she could sleep again, or maybe she was sleeping. Perhaps Sana actually killed her upon that stabbing. This was her Hell—to find the meaning of true love for another person, only to have it ripped from her. This nightmare she was currently living had no foretelling of any closure. Alex was exhausted, tired of the hate, so drained from losing. Was the Dark that strong? Could the Lite not defeat them? The Lite Sentry had to quickly check herself. That was the dangerous path Sana decided to travel.

That particular dead-end road did not have a pleasant destination. Lately, it seems that a constant reminder was needed that she was a Lite Sentry. Her job wasn't to defeat the Dark. It was to help keep the Balance. And she was doing a piss-poor job at that.

On her way up to her own secluded office to write her report, she noticed Tristan basking in the sanctuary of the congregation room. The young man always wore a conservative sweater when he sat in the middle of the room on the far end of the wall. It was an odd place to sit. Alex either liked the very back when she went to mass or the very front when she was alone or nestled up with Kameron.

"Alex?" Father Richard was coming by with his coat still on. The overweight priest was coming in from the back parking lot. He was a good man, caring. Alex knew he wished his Lite Sentry would open up to him. For some reason, she felt that would betray Father Tom. His death never should have happened. Neither should have her brother's, Sarah's, or Kameron's.

Alex shook her head to get rid of the thoughts of Kameron. "Sorry, Father. Just thinking of a song in my head. Can't think of it, but the tune keeps playing over in my head. Don't you hate that?"

"Yes, it's almost as annoying as being lied to." Father Richard gave a caring smile. "Do you want to talk about anything that's on your mind?" The shiny bald man took off his coat. No matter what, it always seemed like he was sweating.

"Nothing to talk about," Alex lifted the unfilled Council report paper. "Gotta get to the writing."

"You know where I'm at; completely confidential." He joked as he pulled on his collar.

"I'm good," she went down the hallway, whistling a song. "Can't get that song out of my head. Ugh!" She gave out a fake laugh.

Father Richard watched his Lite Sentry put on a false sense of confidence and emotional expression as she started her day. "Hey, Alex."

"What up, padre?" She bounced as she turned around.

"*Tears in Heaven.*"

"What?" Alex stared at him in confusion.

"The song you're whistling: *Tears in Heaven* by *Eric Clapton.*" He pointed out.

Alex just nodded as she turned back around to head upstairs. "If only he was crying in Heaven." She slowly found solace away from everyone when she opened the door to her private office.

The only other living soul was her faithful hunting companion. Komptin was asleep by an open window in the wooden bed made by Kameron. The colossal protector had peace to him as he slept, regardless of what form he was in. There was a clipboard inside her desk drawer, which she quietly grabbed. She slowly made it up to Komptin to sit next to him on the floor underneath the window. The smoke from the fires still gave the air an unwanted scent. The riots were all but gone, but their damage took a toll on the town. Alex stroked her dog's fur before starting her report. How she envied him as he laid down in peace. With a gentle kiss on top of his head, she started to write her account from last night.

***

Gron salivated over the fear and power he had as he strolled through the F.O.R. compound– his compound. There was such tenseness emanating from members of each level of the F.O.R. He couldn't be happier, and why shouldn't he? They were so close, so close to finally having the Dark tip the Balance permanently. During his last fight with Alex, he caught a glimpse of how the Conduit of Lite couldn't keep up with might of the Dark. The look of defeat was written all over her face. Gron loved it.

Though, his plan didn't go exactly as he commanded. With his leadership, Vandor did return for a moment…before he was unexpectedly tackled back into the Conduit. He didn't understand how Kameron was able to manhandle the Conduit of Dark so easily. His erogenous Dark Harridan, Misluna, suggested crossing the portal had him weakened. Next time, they will have Pure of Hearts on site ready for consumption.

"My Leader." The father of the social diva Scarlett Roberts approached him. Geoffrey was a loyal member of F.O.R. He provided financial security to the organization's mission success. His loyalty was getting him closer to infiltration. Still, one little item still loomed; he had no contact with his daughter, who was being hunted by the F.O.R.

If Scarlett Roberts were to testify, it could be quite damaging for the F.O.R.

"This better be good news." Gron's attention was distracted by an overweight Serf tending the rocks. "Maybe that fat ass could lose a couple of pounds." He whistled to one of his supervisors. He motioned with his arm to the fat kid, then pointed to the rejuvenation chamber. In an instant, the kid was hauled off, screaming towards the mandatory weight loss program. He turned back to Geoffrey. "What is it?"

"Merik's assets have all been transferred to the F.O.R. Beneficiary." The man gave his report. "Apparently, Merik had a hefty amount on his life insurance that we inherited."

"Suggestion on what to do with it. Didn't you say we needed a quick tax write-off?" Gron watched an attractive girl bending over, tending a garden by the Compound.

The big black man pulled out his electronic pad to show him a picture of the Coppertop Historical Building. "We put a down payment on purchasing this building here in town. It can be written as an investment in the rebuilding of the quarantine area. The historical donation can be used for taxes, and since it's guaranteed to lose money, we can use that to our advantage."

"That's fine. Plus, it will be a public relations investment. Send me the report on the building and the benefits of this purchase." He checked his watch when Misluna came through the gate. She was right on time to continue her translation of the Dark Text. The double agent of the F.O.R. had to

28

burn the sacred writings to prevent her cover from being blown. The text inhabited her body upon burning, thus becoming the Dark Harridan. There was only one focus on Gron's mind as he approached this high-ranking slave to the Dark. Her short skirt enabled Gron to stare at the curvature of her body. The sexual kiss was just a prelude to what he wanted. The inside of her thigh rid up his body. "You almost done with the book?" He asked her in between his actions of his desire.

"Almost, I have time for a distraction," Misluna whispered back in his ear before biting it.

"Later, get done what you can with the texts. I have to talk to Azrael." Gron gave her a look that they were going to finish this sometime tonight.

Misluna was excited, but she wanted to play now. "I will, after I check on the children."

Gron inspected the Compound on his way back to his office. He went to his secretary's desk as she handed him a sealed envelope with a wax seal of the F.O.R. symbol. In his gut, he knew this wasn't good. He sat down in his chair before cracking the seal. Inside was a report from the secret complex in Las Vegas. This secretive compound was in charge of performing the darkest research to find a way to open the Dark Conduit. It seems as if it was destroyed. Along with it, the Dark Sentry Gron kept secret from everyone. He had planned to use him to fulfill the duty that Alex prevented Gron from completing.

Gron stood up and grabbed his computer, smashing it onto the wall. "I thought I had it.

Damn it." He hit the button on his secretary's intercom. "I need a new computer."

The secretary didn't skip a beat. "Tech is bringing one up now."

Gron went to the bar to grab a drink. Inside the massive room, he could sense the Dark Angel named Azrael was nearby. The presence of the blackened angels was Dark, but it felt different, almost a bitter hate. Gron turned around to shut the door to his office. A cold draft hit the back of his neck when Azrael entered the room. "And?"

"I can't find her scent." Azrael solemnly stood in the darkness of the corner.

At first, Gron was worried about Azrael's arrival from the Dark, and that his master would prefer him over Gron. That was quickly diminished after a week of him entering the land of the primates once again. Azrael only lived to serve Vandor; that's it. It didn't matter where he stood in the pecking order. Gron on the other hand, had to be next to his master's side.

Azrael stood tall in his angelic body armor. The black misty fog formed wings and the shape of horns instead of a halo like his Lite siblings. He morphed into a black suit that draped down to almost his knees. The dark red button-up shirt was almost camouflaged by his fat black tie.

From the window, Pytho landed on Azrael's shoulder. This little pure black figure reminded Gron of a demonic bird. It perched on Azrael's shoulders as a loyal servant. He whispered something in Azrael's ear. "Pytho had located one of the Sentries."

Gron grabbed a drink, "Want one?"

"No, the sentries must be extinguished." He flashed his dark eyes with a quick burst of red.

"In due time." Gron ensured him. "Tomorrow, I am granted the main leadership role in this town. That will be just the beginning. My plan is something our master will be quite proud of. The best part is the town will welcome it." Gron started snickering before sitting down at his desk. He turned his chair to face the Dark Angel brooding in the corner.

"What must I do?" Azrael remained perfectly still.

"I need a collection of Pure of Hearts to have ready for our master's next return." Gron put his feet up on his desk. "There would have been no way Alex's boytoy could have tackled our master back into the Dark if we had one available."

"The failure of collecting pure of hearts is something that will not be repeated." Azrael gave his assurance. "Pytho will be able to seek them out."

Gron turned his head to the Dark Angel. "Does he have the same abilities as Salamar?"

"Do not compare me to that traitor's name!" Pytho hissed.

Without missing a beat and with relative calmness with a touch of annoyance at the bird, Gron asked again to Azrael. "Does he?"

"Not as strong." Azrael scratched underneath the bird's chin. "Failure is not an option. The collection will begin."

"While you're doing that, kill some of those damn sentries as well." Gron stood up to refill his drink.

"All their blood will be a gift to our master," Azrael lifted his chin with pride.

Gron stared at his drink. "Speaking of which." He went to the shelf to grab some empty glass orbs. "Do you mind filling this up with their blood?" He tossed the Dark Angel the glass globe.

***

Alex was returning her usual lack of detailed report to Father Richards when she saw Tristan still basking in the warmth of the Lite in the congregation, something Alex envied about him. He was just getting up from the pew in the middle of the room near the wall. There was a glow to his face as he gave a reluctant smile when he caught Alex spying on him. She cautiously asked, "How are you feeling?"

"I'm fine," Tristan would have made a lousy poker player. His face could be read from across the room. Shame was almost written all over his face.

Alex recognized the aching he must have been feeling; she had had it many times herself. "There's nothing wrong with being sore. God's little reminder to you that you are still alive." She playfully punched him in the arm.

Tristan flinched a little as she hit him just in the right spot. "I suppose you're right."

"But there is something else bothering you?" Alex leaned on the wall as she sipped her Apollo.

Tristan was a little squeamish at first, but finally broke down. "Me." The rookie Lite Sentry couldn't look her in the eye.

"What's that supposed to mean?"

Tristan peeked back into the congregation room to see the big stained-glass window that just finished getting repaired from being shattered. "Seems like every time I start to gain confidence in myself or start feeling like I'm good at something, I get a reality check that I'm actually nothing special."

"Excuse me? What the hell are you talking about?" Alex now stood up to give Tristan her full attention.

"When I accepted to become a Sentry, it was the proudest moment of my life. It's not the abilities or what we are able to do; it was being part of something much bigger than me, protecting and helping people from the Dark." Tristan gave a minor insight into his internal battle. "I trained; I thought I was ready. Then I met you."

Alex shyly turned her head from him. "Don't compare yourself to others. You will always see a version that isn't true." Alex saw Father Richard coming down the hall. He motioned that he needed to see her. She just lifted her finger, signaling that it would be a minute. The bald priest silently let Alex know he would be in his office.

"The first day I met you, you put a garbage can over my head." Tristan pointed out.

Alex smiled at the memory. "Yes, but it was a lesson you needed to learn. You thought you were going to die; you needed to remember that feeling."

"I get that, reality check. Then, after the riot, even though the night ended horribly, we completed our mission. I was feeling confident in my abilities, and I was on my 'A' game. Never felt so good about myself."

"You did good that night." Alex had no idea where this was going, but it sounded like he needed that reinforcement.

"But last night, I struggled to kill one Infiltrator. For a second there, I thought I was going to the stars." Tristan almost seemed humiliated by his next statement. "I got him. Then I come to see you killed three Demons by yourself. You hardly had a scratch on you. You've got to be the best that ever lived."

"I'm far from the best one that ever lived. I should be dead, many times over. I had to fight the best one that ever lived and lost and lost badly. Alex lifted her shirt to show her the scar from Sana. "I've failed multiple times." She put her shirt down. "It cost me a lot: my brother, best friend, and fiancé." Alex had to take a moment to get back on track with her point. "Look, I don't know where this stems from." She put her finger on his forehead. "But stop it." She gave him a little push with her finger. "You are Lite Sentry; stop comparing yourself to others. The other person more often is not the person you perceive them to be." Alex got a message from Kameron's sister, Janelle, but she ignored it. "And trust me, the rate CopperTop is going, you'll have plenty of opportunities to fight a Demon. Just keep in mind–they're a lot stronger than an Infiltrator."

Tristan gave a not so confident nod. "Thanks, Alex. I'm going to go train."

Alex stopped him from going. "No, you need to relax. How do you do that anyways?"

"I can't remember the last time I was able to." Tristan rubbed his neck.

Alex handed him her car keys. "The next town over, in Westington, there is a small little diner that makes the best Monte Cristo. Why don't you go and get us all lunch?" She handed him her church bank card. "Just grab some cash."

"Lunch isn't for five hours. Westington is ten minutes away." He took the card.

"Exactly. Go find something fun to do, go for a walk, go to a movie, go find a willing girl." Alex teased him.

Tristan shyly laughed. "Alex."

"What I'm trying to say is, you need to learn to relax." Alex thought about how she should take her own advice.

He was about to leave, but then stopped himself. "Hey, what's the pin?"

"He protects the paths of justice and guards the way of those loyal to him." Alex tested him.

Tristan smiled. "Okay, 0208. Proverbs."

"Nice." Alex was quite shocked he knew the answer.

He retaliated with his own quiz, "But be sure to fear the Lord and serve him faithfully with all your heart; consider what great things he has done for you."

"I have no idea. I had to Google the Proverb one for my card." She winked at him. "Go enjoy your day. Just make sure to be back by lunch. God help you if you don't have my Monte Crisco on time." She winked at him before going to Father Richard's office.

On her way down, she peeked in at Anne, who was on the phone trying to find another new contractor to fix the church. By the sounds of it, it wasn't going well. She just rolled her eyes at Alex before trying to convince the contractor to take the job. Alex made it down the hall a couple of steps when she heard Anne scream at the phone. "You want me to pay $2,500.00 just to come look at the job!" Alex found herself moving a little bit faster to Father Richard's door.

"Come on in, Alex." He was going over some of the notes from his meeting with Cardinal Joe.

"I'm having Tristan pick us all up lunch." Alex sat in the black leather chair she normally sits in. She put one leg up on the arm of the chair as she rested her head on the back of the chair.

Father Richard kept his head down at his desk as he went over some paperwork. "Even Megan?"

Alex sarcastically answered, "Yes." But it did click something in her head. She texted Tristan to pick up a vegetarian meal for Anne.

"How was your night?"

"Three Demons, two Infiltrators dead." Alex had a quick second panic. She quickly turned her head to make sure she remembered to see they were secure after she said that.

Father Richard chuckled at his Lite Sentry. "Who got them?" Father Richard leaned back in his chair.

"Tristan got an Infiltrator, Komptin got the other, and I killed the three Demons." Alex handed him the report. "There was a collateral."

Father Richard closed his eyes. "Tell me about it."

"I heard the boy scream in the distance. He was trying to get some food. The Dark just killed him. Do they ever need a reason?" Alex blatantly told him the truth.

"Unfortunately, they don't. How are you doing?" Father Richard was studying Alex.

"I'm actually not that sore, Tristan is. Komptin is upstairs sleeping, again." Alex was knowingly avoiding the true question he was asking.

Father Richard took off his hat. The lights seemed to reflect off his bald head. "You know that's not what I meant."

"I know, I'm fine." Alex's body language told him she wasn't having this conversation.

The priest wasn't going to force the issue. Father Richard knew there was no point in pushing until she was ready. If she talked to him, it was going to have to be on her own terms. "Okay, if there isn't anything else, take some time to relax. We can't have you making mistakes. Especially since you have a young Sentry in training."

Alex gave him a thumb's-up as she got up. "Anything else?"

"Yeah, Gron's inauguration is tomorrow. I think we should attend. We are not going to be hiding, waiting for the Dark to make their moves. We should be on the frontline, showing we are not afraid."

Alex was taken back a bit by this revelation. "Holy shit, I love it!"

Father Richard got up from his desk. "This town needs us."

"Awesome, can't wait to see his face when we show up." Alex was about to leave before Father Richard stopped her.

"Alex, there is more."

"What's up?"

Father Richard took a deep breath. "Since we are doing this, you're going to have to be there."

Alex thought that was a stupid statement. "No kidding."

"As a Sentry in case something happens."

"Obviously."

Father Richard rapidly tapped his fingers on his desk. "Father Carl will be there as well."

"Yah, I know." Alex was getting confused. Father Richard just stared at her until she put it together. "What?" Then it hit Alex. "Oh man, you mean…"

"Yes." Father Richard was studying her reaction. He was actually taking in some pleasure in her annoyance about his news.

"When?"

"Well, it has to be tonight." Father Richard thought that the answer was obvious.

Alex just shook her head in disbelief. "Fine, I'll tell Tristan." Alex left the office and closed her eyes when she shut the door behind her. It took all her strength to keep it together. For a second, she felt like she had a hard time breathing. After she took a moment, she went to her office to see Komptin still on his bed, enjoying the sunlight. The smell of fire continued to fill the air. She quietly knelt next to him as she hugged her dog. "We'll get him back. I don't know how, but we'll find a way."

***

The crowd was a rapid-flowing river of rage. The angry mob that surrounded Kameron was now becoming increasingly violent. Trash flying through the air included a tirade of vulgarity spewing from their heated faces. All Kameron could do was grip the wooden handle of the axe. His fingers turned white from squeezing the wooden handle so tight. He had to remind himself to breathe. Up on the platform, leading the gathering, was the host of tonight's retribution. Roger was in a position of authority, riveting his followers. Off to the right, mixed within the crowd, was Megan yelling with outright anger, telling him to get it done.

The night was clear, but the stars seemed to be dull with sadness. Kameron was continuing to be encouraged on by the crowd. He gripped the axe tighter as he thought about what must be done. Kale and Anne stood together, throwing trash at the young lady in the metal pillory. They joined the

39

populace in chucking insults as she remained immobilized. The small-natured prisoner was bent over with her hands tied behind her. Only her head was on the other side of the iron wall, with a clear exposure of the back of her neck. Kameron slowly approached her left side with a heavy heart. The young lady managed to turn her head towards Kameron with tears in her eyes. The fear in her pale face was soon to be alleviated. At the peak of the raising of the axe, Kameron locked with her big brown eyes through her black, weaved-in braided hair. It seemed like an eternity before the release of the swift swing, and then she saw no more.

Chapter Two

Alex rubbed the back of her neck as she leaned on a tree. Her phone provided an escape from the boredom until everyone got there. The spring nights were still cold. Anne couldn't get warm even though she wore a thick white jacket. Tristan came out from the obscurity of the forest from securing the perimeter, rubbing his hands together.

"You're not looking forward to this, are you?" Anne put on some thin white gloves.

Alex was studying Tristan as he made sure he wasn't followed. "That obvious? I can't stand him." Alex was annoyed about the situation. "He's an ass."

"Maybe he will understand you better. Mend some feelings." Anne never had a problem with Father Carl. There were good qualities to the future Council priest. The Council Historian suggested as she opened her thermos. The steam from the coffee gave a quick little warmth. "Want some?"

"No, I'm good." Alex peeked over at Tristan as he kept looking into the woods. "Anything?"

"There's a sense of something Dark, but I can't find it." Tristan was on edge from his lack of experience. It was starting to take a toll on him.

Even though Alex was still handicapped by her inability to sense the Dark, she recognized the details of the night. Komptin wasn't leaving Alex's side. He was on edge as they both knew what Tristan was sensing. She wanted to tell Tristan, but this provided an opportunity to grow his confidence a bit. "No tracks or anything?"

"Nothing, but a sense of the Dark. But there is so much Dark in this town. It could be just that." Tristan zipped up his coat before heading to the two girls.

"Perhaps," Alex leaned into Anne. "Why are you here?"

"I have to record this." Anne was sipping her coffee with both hands.

Alex attempted to try to get rid of her. "I can tell you about it tomorrow."

"I'm fine, Alex. Besides, I kind of like this." Anne tightened her coat a little bit snugger. "I just wish it wasn't so cold."

Alex put her phone away as vehicle lights were seen coming down the muddy trail road. "Here they come. Let's get this over with." Alex tied her long-weaved hair in the back. She whistled at Tristan, who still was looking back at the woods. Alex motioned to the young Sentry of the coming car.

Father Carl came out of the car in his combat boots and black tactical pants. Alex was curious where he got those from. Father Richard was wearing some jeans and a red flannel shirt and vest. He wore a baseball cap that had a logo of *Redcat Racing* on it. "Nice choice, Alex."

Alex moved her eyes from side to side. "Maybe it'll be better than expected, or worse, depending on what is going to happen in the next few minutes."

The two priests found their spots next to the girls. Father Carl was the first to talk. "This is a little weird. Not really what I was expecting when Rick told us we had a night op."

Father Richard could still see that Alex wasn't keen on this reveal. "Well, what we need to talk about affects all of us."

"Where's Megan?" Father Carl noticed the church secretary was not there.

"This is a Council matter," Father Richard pulled out a piece of beef jerky to snack on.

Father Carl nodded. "I understand." He may have said he understood, but he still had confusion written all over his face. "Is Tristan part of the Catholic Counsel?"

Tristan corrected his assumption. "No, I'm actually Methodist."

"What are you doing at a Catholic Church?" Father Carl was trying to piece it all together.

Father Richard took advantage of this opportunity to explain, "Carl, the Council is comprised of all the major religions of the world: Baptists, Catholics, Lutherans, Methodists, Muslim, Jewish, etc." Father Richard bit off another piece of jerky. "Each major religion has its own respective Council. They all convene about once a year. Their primary responsibility is to house the Sentries if one is activated in their respective sanction." He made sure to motion at Anne. "And employ the Historians."

"Thank you." Anne appreciated every time she was verbally included as a member.

"Sentries?" Father Carl veered over to Alex, who was keeping uncharacteristically quiet.

Father Richard signaled to Tristan. "Go ahead."

"Our job is to keep the Balance from tipping in Dark control. We battle the Infiltrators and Demons the Dark sends." Tristan turned his head toward the woods as the sense of the Dark was getting stronger. He wanted confirmation from Alex, but then he realized she couldn't sense it.

"Infiltrators?" Father Carl shook his head as he was trying to wrap his head around everything.

Anne chimed in. "A bear-like creature sent from the Dark. Their only job is to kill on command or possess willing humans to become Demons. Once a human is possessed, they infiltrate society to try to sway mankind to the Dark."

"And that's when the Sentries step in, to protect the Balance." Tristan finished the creed.

Komptin nudged Alex, as she made eye contact with him, he flashed his eyes. Then, she scanned the area with her eyes as she was still on her phone. She just motioned for him to stay, even though she knew what was coming.

Father Carl snapped his neck down at Komptin. "Did I just see his eyes light up?"

"Yep," Alex nonchalantly moved closer to Anne.

"When you told me evil took physical form, in the back of my mind, I actually thought you were just being passionate." Father Carl turned to Tristan. "Are you one of these…Sentries?"

Tristan flashed his eyes and lit his hands to show him.

"And the dog?" Father Carl pointed to Komptin.

Komptin then morphed into his purple-skinned gargoyle state with glowing neon blue eyes.

Father Carl really wasn't expecting that, causing him to jump back a bit, but he was able to regain his bearing. "Oh, shit."

Alex snickered at Father Carl, swearing at the sight of her faithful hunting companion.

"So, you're a sentry." He pointed to Tristan. "Anne records everything; Alex is here because of Komptin, and Carl is the priest to house the Sentry."

That got Alex's attention. "Excuse me, I'm just here because of Komptin?"

Komptin startled everyone, but Alex, as he gave a vicious roar as a black mist started coming from the woods. Tristan was frantically scanning the surrounding area. Alex resisted the urge to take control. The black mist started to take form into a bear-like creature with glowing red eyes. Its vicious snarl eyed Alex, who calmly stood behind Anne.

"You, okay?" Alex whispered just close enough for Anne to hear.

"Alex." The fear in her voice was evident.

"You're fine." Alex was studying the situation. "Komptin, make sure there aren't any others." Komptin flashed his eyes before heading off into the woods.

Tristan shot a Lite Beam at the Infiltrator, knocking it onto the ground. Then Father Carl ran over to the girls. He pulled out a gun from his back. "Stay behind me, girls."

"You know, that's only going to piss it off." Alex calmly advised as she pointed to the little pistol.

"It's better than nothing." Father Carl was acting on his military training background.

Alex gazed over at Father Richard, who just motioned for her to be patient. Alex didn't really care anyway, she wanted to see how Tristan was going to handle this. Which he was able to get a couple of good hits in before the Infiltrator got angry. The beast flashed its nasty red eyes before tackling Tristan to the ground. The Lite Sentry in training grabbed the beast's mouth from tearing out his throat.

"Either Beam him or flip him over; get out of that situation," Alex mumbled under her breath.

Father Carl turned to her. "Did you say something?"

"Nope," Alex was evaluating Tristan's fight.

"We need to help him somehow," Father Carl stepped forward, but Father Richard stopped him. "It will be fine. Trust me."

Tristan was able to roll over as he tried to get an advantage over the now fully formed Infiltrator. He managed to free one of his hands to grab the throat of the creature and land a punch. The creature swung its free claws at Tristan. The sentry guarded his face, but the cost was a major scratch on his arm.

Alex made a cringed face. "Ooooo, that's going to bleed."

Father Carl turned with anger. "He's out here risking his life, and all you're doing is making smartass comments." Father Carl put his hands on Anne and Alex. "We need to leave."

Alex pulled her arm away from Father Carl to continue watching the fight. It didn't escape her notice of the set of red eyes in the woods. Another Infiltrator was about to jump in, but a pair of blue eyes came behind it. The sound from the Infiltrator announces he was now in a fight. Then, Alex heard another one try to sneak up from behind the group.

Alex sighed as she twisted around and grabbed the arm of the Infiltrator before it killed Father Carl. The highly experienced Lite Sentry's hands were glowing along with her eyes. She flipped the black creature to the ground. It growled as it kicked her under the chin. "Ow." It flipped up on its legs and charged Alex. She bent over, avoiding its claws, which provided an opportunity to counter with a hit to the stomach. Then she was able to get a quick punch to its side. The Infiltrator elbowed her on the side of the head. It charged her, Alex kicked it in the stomach. It bent over from the pain. She grabbed the head of the creature, then she jumped in the air, driving the head into the ground. She leaned back on the creature while holding onto its head. The sound of the neck snapping gave her a clue that it was time to dispose of the creature. Alex formed a knife with her Lite and jammed it in in the side of the creature's head, coming out the other side. It then disappeared into the ground.

Alex got up to wipe the mud off her clothes. "Damn it." She checked the blood on the side of her head. "That hurt." Her attention went to Tristan, who was bleeding under his lip. "Tristan, feel the creature's weakness. Look for the opening."

Tristan must have heard Alex. The creature swung at Tristan, but he dodged out of the way. He punched it on the side of the head, it dropped to the ground.

"Watch the arms, good. Now, if it's weak and on the ground, give it a couple of hits, and then…" Alex instructed. But before Alex could finish, Tristan formed a knife and dropped it on top of the Infiltrator's head. That one too disappeared into the ground. "That works as well." Alex proudly helped him up.

Father Carl just stood in complete shock. "Alex is a Lite Sentry as well."

"She is the one the Dark fears." Anne had to control her breathing a bit as she pulled out her inhaler. Komptin came out of the woods with a couple of scratches, but nothing serious.

Father Richard watched Alex give Tristan some pointers as she went over the fight. "Hey Alex, we're taking off."

The female Lite Sentry just gave a thumbs up. "We'll meet you at the church sometime tomorrow." She continued to go over the fight with Tristan. She whistled for Komptin. The massive gargoyle dog joined her side to use him as an example of the position in a fight. Then she started laughing out loud as Komptin was licking her face.

Father Carl just watched her laughing on the forest floor as Komptin played with her. "She's a sentry. Why would God give her such a responsibility?" He shook his head. "This is a lot to process."

"Are you good?" Father Richard studied his confused colleague.

He made it up to his friend. "Honestly, I couldn't thank you enough for this. For the first time in quite a while, I feel like I'm part of something special again."

Father Richard watched as Alex give pointers to Tristan. "Good. I'm hungry, Anne, let's go eat. Alex, we're leaving.

"Later!" Alex said as she was lying on the ground with Komptin on top of her.

"Good job, Tristan," Father Richard yelled to him.

"Thank you. Drive safe!" He replied and then turned to listen to what Alex had to say.

Father Carl made a scan around the black forest. "You're just going to leave them here?"

"She'll be fine." Father Richard took a last look with pride at the warriors for the Lite. "Should we go get midnight breakfast?"

"That sounds good." Anne headed towards her vehicle. "Lumberjack Inn it is."

"That's music to my ears." Father Richard said, getting his keys. "Carl."

Father Carl shook his head from disbelief before he went to join the other members of the Council. "Are they the only ones? Are there others?"

***

Reginald ended up in the deep swamps of Louisiana. The swamp air was humid with the smell of wet laundry that was forgotten about in the washer. The Baptist Council sent him down here because there had been rumors of a black swamp creature with glowing red eyes. This would be his virgin hunt. He had killed an Infiltrator before, but Kafziel had weakened it prior.

Kafziel was the angel assigned to prepare him for his life of putting the Balance back in order. The training was far more intense than any football practice ever attended. He was asked to become a Sentry right after his graduation from college. Even though he was slotted as the third-round draft pick as a safety to Detroit; the answer was obvious when he was asked to join this war. Though, to get him ready, Kafziel didn't keep it easy on him.

The swamp didn't really make him nervous. The glowing red eyes of the alligators and other creatures reflected in the moonlight didn't bother him. Kafziel remained back to make sure the Infiltrator didn't circle around to escape. He assured Reginald, this was his hunt. This is what was asked of him; this was his divine duty: to destroy Infiltrators.

Reginald quietly rowed his little boat through the still water. Some fog was starting to form above the surface. Then he noticed there was no sound. The humid staunch of the swamp was replaced by the staleness of the Dark. He wiped the sweat off his chiseled brown face. He peeked around a tree to see if he could see anything. Up above in the distance, he saw a big bird fly before camouflaging itself into the leaves of a nearby tree. He couldn't really see what kind it was, but it was perched on the branch, staring at him. The focus was the Dark beast before it could cause any damage or, worse, possess a willing person.

There was a spot on the shoreline to anchor the boat to a stable tree. A small snake slithered in front of him into some vegetation. He continued forward, the sense of the Dark getting more intense with every light step. Over the hill in front of him, he saw the faint outline of the bear-like creature. It seemed to be hunting something as well. That evil creature sent by the Dark probably caught the sense of his Lite. Now, they had become each other's prey.

Reginald took a moment to study the immediate area. A route opened to flank the Infiltrator. Soon, this creature would meet the power of Lite. A sense of the Lite was suddenly behind him. Kafziel stood before him with angelic body armor. His neon yellow hair was down to his shoulders. His misty gray fog as wings and halo were in battle-ready position. Normally, he had calm in his eyes, but not at this moment. There was panic embedded deep within them.

"Kafziel, what are you doing?" Reginal murmured. "I can take this monster."

"We must go. The both of us are in great danger." The angel of Lite turned his hand in the opposite direction of the Infiltrator. "There is not much time."

Reginald felt the Dark, but it wasn't any Dark he had felt before. "What is that?"

Then with almost no sound, something landed behind Reginald. The Lite Sentry flashed his eyes and lit his hands. Before him was an angel like he had never seen before. He had blackened eyes. His wings were made of black fog. The same black mist formed horns on top of his head instead of the majestic halo like the angels of the Lite.

"Azrael," Kafziel greeted his former brother with caution in his voice.

"Kafziel. You look as when I left." Azrael calmly took control of the area.

"And you can still ask for forgiveness, my brother." Kafziel stepped back from Azrael to defend from a sudden attack.

"What do I do?" Reginald frantically was hoping his mentor had a way out of this situation.

Kafziel put his arm on his Lite Sentry. "The only thing we can do."

Reginald turned to his angel. "What?"

"We proudly die with our heads held high." Kafziel turned his eyes towards Azrael. The Dark Angel formed a sword and axe made of a dark red light.

Reginald took a deep breath and attacked Azrael. With no effort at all, Azrael killed Reginald as he stepped towards Kafziel. The angel saw the Sentry disappear into light particles as he joined the others as a star. "Upsetting the Balance is wrong. The Dark was never to take over humanity."

"The primates need to be ruled over. They are a parasite on the land that was meant for us." Azrael remembered Gron wanted Lite Sentry blood before they went to the stars. The next would have to bleed before entering the sky with his brothers and sisters.

"Azrael, the primates were not given this land. We are meant to share it. We are meant to enjoy it as much as they do. He just needs us to help them in moments of need." Kafziel lectured him.

The Dark Angel came alongside his brother, who was staring down at the night swamp. "They are meant to be ruled over. So much free will should never have been given to such unevolved animals. I argued against giving such a young creature that much knowledge."

Kafziel turned to where his Sentry once stood. "He gave them just as much free will as He did us."

"And look what happened to them. They need to be ruled to save them from themselves. My master knows this." Azrael put his hand on Kafziel's shoulder. "Brother, look at me. You know this, we both know this, we've discussed it."

Kafziel kissed Azrael's hand, which was still on his shoulder. "I wish I could have saved you from losing your faith, brother. Your master is serving the Dark One who is destined to lose."

Azrael tapped the shoulder of his brother. "And I wish I could open your eyes from the blindness of your arrogance." Azrael formed his axe and sword. The two fought briefly before the echoes from the angel of the Lite were silenced by the darkness of the swamp.

**

Father Carl couldn't help but stare at the crucifix hanging from his office wall. He had never felt so much closer to God than he did now.

Unwillingly, his eyes were convincing him that a quick nap was needed when the Council Historian peeked in his door. "Hey, Anne."

Anne remained outside his office. "I can come back." She pointed out the door.

Father Carl rubbed his eyes. "No, I'm just trying to take a power nap before the inauguration."

"You wanted to see me?" Anne sat down in the chair in front of his desk.

"Am I allowed to read the history of the Sentries?" He opened the drawer to his desk to grab a power bar.

"You can have the files on the history of them, but not specific missions or hunts." Anne let him know. "But if there is a specific instance you want that links something we are researching, we can do that."

"No, it's okay. Just the basic history is all I'm interested in. I would like to know who I'm working with." Father Carl mixed his peanut butter and chocolate bar with a sip of his coffee.

"I'll have the Vatican courier bring them over on the next trip. Should be in a couple of weeks." Anne let him know.

"Thanks." He tried to hide his yawn. The priest's youth had left him because he was much more tired than he thought he should be.

"Anytime," Anne was about to leave when he called her back. "Yes."

"May I ask you a personal question?" He got up from his desk to refill his coffee. Father Carl offered Anne a water that she generously accepted.

"Of course," she sat back down. "What is it?"

"What was it like at your first encounter?" Father Carl tried hiding his yawn.

Anne innocently gave a sweet smile. "Hard wrapping your hands around it?"

"You could say that." Father Carl wiped his face, trying to wake himself up.

"Well, my first encounter wasn't as controlled as yours." Anne thought back to that life-changing event.

"That was controlled?" Father Carl chuckled under his breath.

"Well, for Alex, it was. Back in our senior year of high school, my husband and I just started dating. He was riding home from my house when he was attacked by the Demon Gron, Roger Somberson." Anne clarified.

"The Demon who is going to be mayor?" Father Carl verified.

"Yes, unfortunately. Anyways, Roger really hurt Kale. Bad. Broke his legs, one of his arms, and messed up his back." Anne started to feel her eyes start to tear from remembering that frightful night. She accepted a tissue from Father Carl.

"If it's too hard to talk about…" Father Carl offered her a way out.

"No, it's okay." Anne blew her nose. "Roger was going to kill us, that is, until Alex arrived. She and Komptin came out of nowhere, glowing eyes and fists."

"Why didn't she kill the demon then?" Father Carl couldn't help but think they wouldn't be in the situation they are currently in if Alex had killed the Demon right there and then.

Anne answered, "One of her best friend's dad was possessed as well. Roger told her that Sarah was going to die. Alex left Komptin behind to protect us while she went to try to save our friend. She didn't make it in time."

"I understand living with that guilt." Father Carl's own memories started to overpower his train of thought. "Thanks, Anne."

"No problem, I'll get the file ordered." She wiped her tears as she left the office.

Father Carl got up from his desk to stare at a picture of his squad during his time in the desert. This picture was taken just prior to his last mission. It was his fifth time in charge of patrol. They got word the enemy combatants were mutilating bodies a couple of roads over from the market. He stayed in the patrol vehicle to coordinate the entry and clearance of the building. There were four lieutenants under him leading the teams. Another team was coming in from a helicopter, and another was approaching from the ground. They were told the combatants were in this building.

Captain Carl Gray sent them in. Unfortunately, only two of them returned home that day. After he sent them in, it wasn't long before shots were being heard. Carl wasn't certain, but for some reason, he thought the only firepower was that of American weapons. With sudden gun fire from the rooftops and building next door, the chopper started taking fire from above, so they had to vacate the premises. The radio was chaos, people screaming. Captain Gray was trying to coordinate the efforts, but it was futile. He grabbed his weapon and told his driver to stay put and prepare to vacate the area.

He entered the building entryway. Inside, it was an eerie quiet. The only thing he heard was Islamic praying over the loudspeaker coming from the center of town. Sweat started to blur his eyes before he saw the first body of one of his men. It was shredded as if the insurgents used machetes to tear apart the body. The cold stare of death from the soldier's eyes just remained still. He shut the young man's eyes before continuing his rescue. In another room, there were more bodies. Each one shredded just as the first.

Captain Gray cursed the people who could do this to another human being. How could someone do this? There was a special place in Hell for whoever would do this to another person. Each room he entered was the same; his men's bodies were all butchered. There was a young private who grabbed onto his leg. "Captain, they were pure monsters." He kept on crying, "But God, He sent someone to get rid of them. After he killed them, he rushed over to me. A man…he just told me that my faith would get me through anything. His kind eyes glowed..." Then he died in his arms. That was the last mission of Captain Carl Gray. It was right then he knew his new mission in life was to ensure people kept their faith through the worst life has thrown at them.

"Father."

Father Carl's travel to the past was disturbed by this girl who possessed the power of the Lite. "Yes, Alex."

She studied his face. "You, okay? You look pale."

"Well, the last twelve hours don't happen to me every day." Father Carl turned to face her.

Alex couldn't make eye contact with the priest. "Well, there are times I wish I could say the same thing."

"I'm glad you're here. There is something I need to get off my chest."

"What's up?" She sat down in the chair.

"I did not say you could sit down." He gave her a stern look.

Alex took a second before standing up to face him. "Look, before we get into this. You realize, while in college, I was doing this job. I had no choice but to hide it from you."

"I don't care about what you can do. Frankly, it doesn't impress me. Don't think my viewpoint of you is going to change. You still need to prove yourself." He wasn't backing down.

"Bullshit, I have to prove myself. I risk my ass almost every night; I'm pretty sure I don't need to prove myself to anyone, least of all you. Oh yeah, and I volunteered for this. And FRANKLY speaking, fighting Infiltrators, Demons, and whatever else the Dark throws at me is far easier than putting up with your stupid ass!" Alex left the office, and Father Carl could hear down the hallway. "Jackass!"

***

58

Father Richard just rubbed his eyes in disgust. "Why can't you two just get along?" Alex was just about to speak her case in front of the two priests in the basement cafeteria of the church. "Stop, you know what. I don't want to hear about it anymore. You two figure it out. Leave me out of it." He checked his watch. "We have to go. Look, we'll all ride together."

The three of them collected Anne and Komptin as they headed upstairs. Megan was in the hallway with her coat. "Are you heading to the inauguration?"

Komptin was rubbing against Alex to get some attention. "Yep, joy." Alex hit the right spot behind his ear.

"Can I come? I think it would be neat to see?" Megan invited herself for the ride.

The group all looked at each other before all of them turned to Father Richard. "Okay, come on." They all got into the van. Alex sat in the very back seat with Komptin lying on her lap. Father Carl was driving with Megan in the front seat. Anne was in the second row with Tristan. Father Richard stayed by himself in the third row. "Okay, now remember. We are all there to show we are not backing down from F.O.R. ideology." He turned around to Alex. "Peacefully."

Alex rolled her eyes. "What?" The truth was, Alex didn't really feel like going. Anne was deep into reading some history book. Tristan was playing a game on his phone. For some reason, Alex reached into her backpack to pull out her Christmas picture of her and Kameron. She did everything in her power to suppress that nauseous feeling in her stomach. This false wall of strength she was portraying couldn't last much longer.

"We'll have to park down the road and walk. Looks like it's all blocked off." Father Richard pointed over to the barricade.

"There's a parking garage down a couple blocks from Redwood. It's the next right," Anne gave directions to Father Carl.

The group got out of the van parked in the public garage. Alex was the last of one to get out of the van. She straightened her clothes, hid the wiping of her eyes, and noticed Komptin flashing his eyes at her. He pointed with his snout in the direction behind a structure to see Devine hide behind a pillar. Alex didn't take her eyes off her surrogate sister. "I'll catch up to you."

The two priests turned around but didn't say anything. Tristan had confusion written all over his face. "Want me to stay or go?" He full-out knew the angel of the Lite was here.

"Go on, keep them safe. I'll catch up." She waited until they were down to the ground level. "I'm here, alone."

Devine emerged from behind the concrete column. She was in civilian clothes, but she still had some reservations about her. "I apologize for hiding. I'm still working on wanting to be seen."

"I get it. Can I give you a hug?" Alex was still making sure she was okay.

Devine opened her arms to hug Alex in a sisterly embrace. "I welcome it."

"How ya feeling?" Alex didn't hesitate in hugging her surrogate sister. Alex was still a little cautious about the angel's state of mind.

"I should be asking you that question. There is much sadness in your eyes." Devine stared at her.

"I'm fine," Alex tried to hide her true feelings. "I'm more worried about you."

"I am improving. The support from my family has been very helpful." The purple-haired angel was trying to put up a wall herself. The woman's trench coat was white, and she was wearing a neon green shirt. "Celestial is upstairs. She would like to see you."

"What are you doing here? Extra security?" Alex inquired, gazing around the area.

"There is some stuff I need to check on." Devine started in the direction they went. The angel of Lite put her hands in her coat, slowly making her way to watch a Demon become the leader of this town. Her movement was almost as if she was in deep thought.

The amount of Dark here must be thick. Alex didn't need her ability to sense it. It is no surprise Celestial is here to counteract the Dark being dispersed during this event. Alex made it to the top of the parking lot structure where Celestial was overlooking the town. Arome and Omelia turned upon her approach. They both parted away from Celestial a bit so Alex could see Celestial. It was nice to know they had learned to trust Alex enough to know she wouldn't hurt her.

"Pretty bad down there, isn't it?" Alex mentioned to her.

"It is worse than what is shown." Celestial's face was like a hurt mother as she watched over the crowd. It was as if she knew her children were about to make a big mistake, but she could do nothing about it.

Alex watched the city employees set up for the swearing-in of Roger Somberson. "I don't know if it could get much worse."

"We lost a Sentry and an angel last night." Celestial informed her.

Alex stood there in shock. "I stand corrected. Who?"

"Reginald and Kafziel." Celestial answered her Lite Sentry.

Then, Alex seemed to look away in embarrassment. "I didn't know them, or hear about them."

Celestial calmly expressed, "Tonight, their stars will be the brightest for members of the Lite to see." Celestial herself took a moment to remember. "We have lost more in the past one hundred years..." She stopped herself from remembering the past. She sharply spun to Alex. "That Dark Angel who came through the conduit, he is dangerous to us all. More so than that Demon."

"I faced danger before." Alex didn't really take it to heart.

"Not like this." Celestial had to put her Sentry into reality.

"I'll be careful." The crowd below started to cheer as the precursor of Roger's inauguration started. "I have to go." Alex was almost thankful Kale wasn't alive to see this.

"Alexandria," Celestial called out to her.

Alex turned around to see the blonde-haired angel all in white. Her wings and halo vibrant. "Yes."

"Azrael hates Sentries. His passion is to destroy them. It is the only way he knows how to deal with what he hates about himself." Celestial motioned to her guardians. "We must go." A blinding light came behind her as she entered the conduit.

Alex caught up with Anne and the rest of the group. Anne leaned over to Alex, "Everything okay?"

"A sentry and his trainer got killed last night," Alex whispered low enough so no one would hear. "Celestial was freaked out." The crowd started to cheer at the sight of Roger entered the stage. He was holding the hands of the twins Devine gave birth to after her rape from the Demon, Merik. They were dead faced, no emotion to them. They just stared out at the crowd as Roger waved to his supporters.

"This will be interesting," Father Richard had a certain strength emulating. "I wonder how many in the crowd are F.O.R."

"There's enough Dark around here not to pinpoint; it's all surrounding." Tristan zipped up his coat. "It's cold."

Alex skimmed the crowd. "Well, there is good news."

The two priests along with others turned around to Alex. "Like what?" Anne asked.

Alex took a moment, "It's not raining out." She pulled that one out of thin air.

"Shh, it's starting." Megan pointed to the stage.

Roger faced the judge and put his hand on a book. He started repeating the oath of office with winning smirk that only Alex could see.

"I wonder what he has a hand on; you know it's not the Bible." Alex was studying the situation.

Anne answered, "The State Law Book."

"...solemnly, sincerely, I truly declare and affirm." Roger turned to the crowd as they cheered. He kissed the children on the side of the cheek before passing them to the nanny. The mass of people applauded as he waved before taking the podium. The roar of his supporters was truly disheartening to those who follow the Lite.

"Well, this should be good," Alex prepared for the deceitful speech ahead.

"Ladies and gentlemen. Let me begin by saying, I didn't take this job for myself. I did it for my town, a town that is my home, a home that holds all of you, and as far as I'm concerned, all of you are my family. And I protect my family!" The crowd started to cheer. "My first order of business is to open up the quarantine area. We need to show everyone, that CopperTop Mountain will be a city that everyone should look up to high on the mountain. And how am I going to do this? My administration will be transparent; I hide nothing." Roger saw Alex with the group of Lite followers. He gave them a quick wink. "I will be creating a special division of the police force. They will directly report to me, and their sole job will be cleansing the town so we can live free from any persecution. Effective immediately, we are going to open the quarantine area. To show it is safe, there will be a concert held in the old Purch-Mart parking lot. Go, find your business. We are going to be envied by all who look upon us!" The crowd cheered. "Now, if you excuse me, I need to get to work."

Alex watched Roger take the twins' hands from the nanny to escort them off the stage. The small boy and girl stopped as they both slowly turned their heads to the crowd but in a specific direction. Alex turned to see Devine on the rooftop across the street, staring down at her children. The angel took a moment before she slowly turned away and disappeared.

***

The crowd was screaming louder with every passing moment. The screaming voices were so loud, Kameron couldn't tell what they were saying. Unfortunately, their intention was very clear. The hardest part was each moment seemed to be longer than the previous. Kameron was getting scolded by Roger about loyalty, dedication, and following the Trinity of the Fallen Star. It wasn't clear what was happening. His mind still couldn't believe how things got so bad. Behind him were Kale and Anne, both giving him a look of disappointment. They stared right into him with dissatisfaction.

"You do what you need to do, Kameron," Anne could barely be heard over the crowd.

"It's the only way. The alternative sucks," Kale added in as he stepped closer to Anne.

Megan came rushing to Kameron with far-reaching anger at the fact he hadn't finalized his charge. "You listen to me. You do this. Do it now!"

Kameron stared down at his service pistol in his hands.

"What are you waiting for, Kameron? Finish this!" Anne gritted her teeth as she pointed in the direction before him.

Kameron saw a young woman tied to a cemented post. Her head was hunched over, almost as if she was beaten. Kameron studied her before staring back down at the gun. The young, beautiful, tied-up woman slowly lifted her head with what little energy she had left. In between the blood and bruises, her pale skin with dark make-up reflected the glow in the moonlight.

Megan angrily rushed over to Kameron. "You show your loyalty to me and to the Fallen, right now!"

Kameron locked eyes with the woman who had her arms tied around the pole from the back. He raised the weapon, pointing the gun at the woman. With a single pull of the trigger, he put a hole into her forehead.

Chapter Three

Alex rubbed her forehead. This day was nothing but one big headache. She knew it was going to be bad, but not this bad. The sight of the pain Devine displayed after seeing her children with Roger stuck with Alex. Even though they were pure evil, they were still her children. The van ride home was quiet. No one was really saying anything. Even Megan was keeping quiet; she was just on her phone texting. Anne was quietly reading her book while Komptin was sleeping on Alex's lap.

It was so silent; the only thing making noise was the humming of the tires contacting the pavement. The phone inside her pocket vibrated from Janelle calling again. Alex didn't know what to say to her. She declined the phone call with a canned message: *Can I call you later?* Within a second, there was a reply. *Please do. We haven't heard from Kameron for quite a while. We are all very worried.* Multiple replies ran through Alex's mind, but none of them made it to the phone. So, she just put the phone back in her pocket.

Alex put her hands on the seat in front of her where Father Richard was sitting. It provided a barrier from the tears that were coming. Father Richard turned around to see her struggle. He didn't ask. He didn't pry. All he did was put his big, gentle hands-on top of hers. With a couple of slow and gentle taps, he turned back around–for some reason, that made her feel a little better, but not enough. Nothing could be enough.

Komptin lifted his head as something caught his attention. He looked up at Alex and gently put his head back on her lap. Alex slowly scratched his head a bit. "Father, there are some things that just talking about won't fix."

Father Richard just leaned his head back. "But it's a step to making it feel better."

Alex knew the place she felt the most comfortable was the congregation room, but that room was too open for her to be truly alone. For some reason, she didn't want to spend the afternoon in her office. She would go out to the woods, but she didn't want to be interrupted if the Dark happened to appear. Being all alone in a vast, empty church was all she wanted.

Upon their return, Father Richard and Father Carl treated everyone to lunch. That left the church completely empty, just what she secretly wished. Just Komptin and Alex remained in the church. Alex led the way into the main worship hall, holding a can of Apollo. She went to her spot in the front pew to stare at the stained-glass window. There was slight hope she would feel the warmth of the Lite again, but there still was no connection.

"The night I lost Kameron." The Lite Sentry just started to talk to the empty room. "It hurt so bad." She took a sip of her Apollo. "He asked me to marry him." Alex smiled a bit, "I didn't even hesitate." Alex, for some reason, found humor in her next sentence. "Then he shot me." It was a bit before she was able to speak again. "He's gone forever, isn't he?" Alex waited for an answer, but there was none to be found. It wasn't that He didn't care; it was because He couldn't hear her. Now, the tears started streaming. "Why do I even bother? You can't even hear me. He's suffering in Hell, and there is nothing I can do about it." She got up to face the alter. "All I can do are my duties. Osiah told me my life wouldn't be easy, but nothing like this." Alex walked out of the congregation room, mumbling, "This sucks."

Celestial was in the front corner of the congregation. Her guardians were standing on the other side of the hallway. Along with Komptin in his hunting form, she watched her Lite Sentry leave the chamber. A small golden tear dropped from Celestial's face. The Conduit of Lite gazed down at Komptin. She generated something to eat for him and knelt to kiss him on the forehead.

Devine was in the next candle room off to the side. There was something she could not help but feel. It was a confusing mixture of sadness and guilt as she saw the pain of the Sentry. It was also strange to see Celestial in such sadness, Alex so vulnerable. It was her job to protect the Conduit of Lite for so long. Maybe now, it was time for Devine to find a way to safeguard all that she loves.

***

Gron quickly pawned the kids back to the nanny once the public relations portion of this event was completed. His young Latina secretary stood up from behind her desk as he entered the waiting area to his office. The young kid, who looked straight out of college, felt uneasy as he approached, as she should. She was clean, professional looking. He noticed she had a crucifix on her necklace. "Congratulations, Mr. Somberson. I'm Jennifer Rodriguez. I cleared your schedule for the next thirty minutes. Just to get your bearings. Then, there's a meeting with your immediate staff for a half-hour briefing. After that, each department has blocked fifteen minutes for the rest of the afternoon. I apologize for bombarding you with this, but I just went off the last mayor's first day."

He snatched the schedule from her hands. "First, that's Mayor Somberson. Second, follow me." He stopped but waited for a bit. Then, arrogantly looked at the door and then at her.

"I'm sorry," she quickly opened it for the new mayor. It was a decent-sized room for the mayor of the town. It was smaller than his office at the F.O.R. The office had a picture of Moses with the Ten Commandments. There was also a crucifix hanging on the wall. Roger put on a pair of gloves before ripping the cross off the wall to throw it in the trash. "Get anything with a religious symbol out of here."

The secretary took a breath in. "I'll get a box."

"You fail to understand, the whole damn building. If it's painted on the wall, paint over it." Roger went to the bookshelf. On the shelf, he grabbed a copy of the Koran, Bible, and T'orah. An uncanny thud sound echoed in the room when the new mayor threw them all in the garbage. Inside his pockets were some wipes to clean his hands. "Does that bother you?"

"You have a right to your religious beliefs." The secretary tried to hide her disapproval.

"Yes, we all do." He sat down at the desk to see a rosary in the drawer. "What was with this guy?" He broke it as beads went flying all over the floor. "Clean this up, then get the attorney prosecuting Moses Grossman up here."

"Attorney Michael Johnson." She continued to write her notes.

"Send out an email to get all religious artifacts out of this building by the end of the week, to include painting the walls. We are not pushing any religious propaganda, or separation of church and state. That is to include employees; we are not influencing anybody who comes in here as a representative of the state." He pointed to her necklace. "You have one chance to prove yourself. If you do well, perhaps you can gain absolute power."

"I'm good." She bit her bottom lip as she tucked in her necklace. "Is there anything else?"

"If that accidentally pops out, you're fired." Roger waived her off. He couldn't help but grin behind his new desk. This was a big victory. He laughed as he flashed his eyes red. "This is too good." In the top file drawers was a renovation proposal for the museum the F.O.R. had invested in. This was the historical building the F.O.R. put Merik's insurance money into as an investment. Inside the plans for renovation, there was a listing of artifacts. Gron pushed a button on the intercom. "Set me up sometime tomorrow to tour CopperTop Historical Museum." The secretary acknowledged just before she told him the prosecuting attorney was outside his door. A knock on the door interrupted Roger's thought. He quickly closed the book and put it back in the desk drawer. "Come."

His secretary announced the District Attorney.

"Mr. Johnson, how's the family?" Roger grinned.

"Mr. Somberson," he extended his hand.

"That's Mayor Somberson." He didn't offer his hand in return. "Where are you with the Moses kid?" Roger just stared at him before motioning with one finger to sit down.

"That's a federal case; we aren't trying it."

"No, it's a local matter. We are going to try it." Roger continued to write some paperwork. "Here you go."

Michael read it over. "How? You have no right to seize all the evidence to that case."

"Yes, yes, I do. As the official representative of the Town of Coppertop, I need to review all official correspondence going to the state and federal level to ensure all information is presented accurately." Roger showed him the order from the Federal Court.

Michael was in complete shock. "How did I not know…? How did you…?"

"Hit you like a semi-truck, didn't it?" Roger arrogantly taunted the attorney. "I also need all the details regarding the attack on the power station."

"The officer is still in recovery." Michael put the piece of paper in his pocket.

"She's a terrorist." Roger wanted her dead. He just stared at the man who prevented him from killing her.

"We got notification she was under orders from the CIA on a task force operation. Other than that, the file is labeled 'classified' as a need-to-know basis." Michael was studying Roger's reaction, which could be read like an open book.

"I need to know." Roger was not happy. "What's her condition?"

"Coma. Not allowed visitors per her agency." Michael could almost see his eyes change from anger.

"I'm assuming at that Catholic hospital." Roger sat back in his chair, trying to calm himself down.

"Yes."

"That is all. You can go." He waved him off.

Michael got up with pure agitation. It took everything in his power not to tell this kid what he thought. "You're not going to ask if she was working alone or not." He couldn't help but study the newly elected mayor.

Roger gazed up at the attorney. "I'm sure she wasn't, but that doesn't concern me."

Michael couldn't help but test the waters of this new mayor. "I hope you realize you don't have the same authority as mayor as you do in the F.O.R."

Roger stared at the lawyer, leaning back in his seat. "I am F.O.R. My authority follows me everywhere."

***

Alex decided to freely move about in the newly opened quarantined area. It was amazing how many posters were up thanking Roger Somberson. The only escape from the sea of posters thanking the evil mayor was Janelle's persistent messaging. It was starting to get to her. Sooner or later, Alex was going to have that painful conversation. Though, she had no idea what she was going to tell Kameron's sister. How could she tell her the truth?

The former quarantined area had dreadful peace to it. There had been no sign of Qawi since the riots had stopped. It was like he just disappeared along with Mack Righteous. Even though Righteous was shot in front of everyone, Alex knew he was still alive since he was a Demon. It almost seemed like overnight; CopperTop was becoming a wholesome city.

Komptin was leading through down the sidewalks area in the direction of Kate's supper club. Inside were business owners looking at the damage from riots. Some were starting to clean the mess, and most were crying over the devastation. It was a different perspective as they made it through this area in daylight. It was truly demoralizing. Then, what she feared came true. There were charcoaled remains of the supper club. All that was left was the burnt, rickety framework. To her shock, there were outlines of three people standing in front of the rubble. Alex approached to see that it was Kate, along with Dan and Jessica.

"I'm so sorry," Alex hoped the sympathy in her voice only matched to what she was actually feeling.

"This blows," Dan just stared at the ash that was once his future.

Jessica held his hand in a supportive fashion. "We'll be okay, baby."

Kate just stared at the rubble. She didn't say a word. What could she say? This woman had lost so much in the past couple of years–her business, her son.

Alex was debating on even saying anything. "What are you guys going to do?"

Kate just stared forward. "I don't know. I called the insurance company. They said it didn't cover riots because there was no single person to pin it to or some bullshit like that." Kate's voice was evident about how disgusted she was at the situation. "And to make matters worse, found out the insurance agency was purchased by a company owned by F.O.R."

Dan chimed in. "And there it is, bastards got what they wanted." Jessica leaned onto Dan's arm.

Alex felt a wave of guilt come over her. Maybe all this was her fault. What would have happened if she hadn't accepted the responsibilities of being a Lite Sentry? Would her friends be alive? The town still stand, would the Dark not be here? "Are you going to try to rebuild?" That question stemmed from a hopeful relief of guilt.

Dan was just agitated. "Sinking money into this town is just throwing it away."

Alex turned to Dan. "You're moving."

"Do we have a choice?" The irritation in Dan's voice was evident.

Jessica leaned over to see Alex. "We're going to move to my hometown in Connecticut."

"Her dad got me a job as a food delivery dispatcher. God, this sucks." Dan clenched his fists. "You wanna hear the icing on the cake? The F.O.R. called me yesterday to see if I wanted to run their compound cafeteria. Free room and board with private schooling for Big D."

Alex held her breath. "What did he say?"

Jessica laughed. "He told them to kiss his fat, organic, grass-fed, ass." Her phone beeped. "Your mom wants to know if we're going to be home for supper."

Dan nodded. "We gotta go. Alex, if I were you, I'd leave this hell hole." Dan headed towards the car, still obviously upset.

Jessica hugged Kate and then Alex. "Please, come over for dinner before we leave."

The two of them nodded. Kate was the first to speak after Dan and Jessica left their dreams behind smoldering. "His future just drastically changed."

"I'm afraid so," Alex felt hopeless in helping Kate. Almost like she failed to protect Mole all over again. "What are you going to do?"

"It'll be tight, but I'll be okay. I'm going to move to Missouri. I have a friend who got me a job as a school secretary. I'll be fine. If I get my insurance check, I'll be really fine," she gave a small chuckle. "But, not holding my breath on that one."

"I understand." The two of them hugged before Alex took off to the church.

Alex took a small amount of enjoyment munching on her overly preserved, manufactured chocolate cupcake with a white creamy center as she joined others in the church. They were all in the reception area, outside of Father Richard's office. Her nerves shot up as she saw her dad in the middle of the group.

"Alex," her father came up to her to give her a hug.

Very cautiously, she accepted the hug. It was weird; she saw something in her dad she had never seen before: Vulnerability. "What's going on?"

"Don't know, your dad just came here and asked to see us?" Megan continued to work on her computer. It was almost like she didn't have a care in the world.

The two priests entered the lobby, discussing Council matters. They immediately stopped when they saw the audience. "Where's Anne?"

"I just got here," Alex finished her cupcake from her packet. Her dad pointed to the chocolate and cream mixture on the side of her mouth.

"I'll go get her," Megan got up with her phone. "I have to go to the bathroom anyways."

Komptin laid down next to Alex as she leaned on the windowsill. Tristan came into the room. He made sure to get eye contact with the priests as they silently told him there was no news. Alex leaned into him so only he could hear. "What's all that about?"

Tristan whispered back. "I'm just waiting for word from the Council on my next trainer and mission."

"There's not much more training you need." Alex acted as if it was common knowledge.

"I don't know. I don't think I'm there yet." He put his hands in his coat pockets as he stared at the ground.

Alex tapped him on the shoulder. The new Lite Sentry turned to her. "The only thing stopping you is this." She tapped her finger in the middle of his forehead. "You are a Lite Sentry, a damn good one, and everyone knows it but one person."

He just smiled as Anne and Megan came into the room. Anne found a spot on the other side of Alex. "I lost track of time."

Michael didn't waste any time. "Look, I apologize for this, but I really need to tell you guys something."

"Yes," Father Richard made sure no one was coming.

Alex noticed that Megan was still here. Why was she still here if they were discussing Council matters? Was she being considered for the Council? She tapped Anne on the leg to get her attention. She moved her eyes over to Megan. In a direct nonverbal communication, Anne knew exactly what she was asking. All she did was nod. Alex shook her head.

"Look, the only reason I'm telling you this, is that you guys helped with the hiding of Scarlett Roberts." Michael made sure no one was out the window. "My trust in Roger Somberson doesn't exist."

"Trust me, you're not alone on that one," Alex murmured.

"He was very interested in the status of Agent Midnight Solis' condition over at the hospital." Michael silenced his phone.

"Is she still in coma?" Father Richard was hoping for some status change.

"I lied to the mayor. I told him she was, but she's been in and out. She's tubed and can't talk."

Alex realized Midnight had no idea what happened to Kameron. "What was she doing out there?"

"We can't ask her any questions until she's cleared by the doctor," Michael told Alex. "Anything she says would be inadmissible due to the trauma and narcotics she's on."

"What is it you want us to do?" Father Carl was almost militaristic in his voice.

Michael started to answer. "I was hoping you could…"

Then Komptin started to bark aggressively. It was the meanest Alex had ever heard; it actually made everyone in the room jump. Out of nowhere, Roger Somberson came into the room. He was followed by Azrael and two other people who were no doubt Demons. Everyone in the room was on edge and instantly kept their mouths quiet.

Both Father Richard and Carl grabbed their rosaries. Roger just snickered at the sight. "So, this what goes on in the House of your Lord; conspiracy, treason…" He picked up the cupcake wrapper from the garbage. "…and gluttony." He threw it on the ground instead of back in the garbage.

Azrael was staring at the two Sentries leaning on the window. The Dark Angel's presence reminded Alex of a vampire. He didn't look comfortable being in a church. The big man seemed to float as he approached the two sentries with contempt. "You are Alexandria Johnson and Tristan Yarrow."

Tristan broke eye contact with the Dark Angel, but Alex stared right into his dark eyes. "And you are …a piece of shit." Alex grabbed onto Komptin's collar to make sure he didn't lunge.

Azrael moved his dark eyes down to study the dog. "Is that Komptin?" He started to calculate how she came into possession of him. "My master told me Osiah died like an earthling baby–crying and flying about like the coward he was."

Alex stood her ground. "The next time I see you; you will regret those words."

"No, I will not," Azrael had a stoic confidence to him.

Gron was enjoying the show. "Okay, Azrael." The Dark Angel backed off, but only at Gron's request. "Please don't let me stop you from your little meeting. What are we all discussing?"

Anne could only see the Demon who killed her husband. No one had ever seen such negative emotion come from her. "You're a monster," she finally spoke with raw emotion.

Roger turned to Anne, "Oh Anne, such harsh words with such a heart as pure as yours." He studied her a bit. "Speaking of pure hearts, haven't seen your boyfriend around, Alex? Is he out of town or something? Weather is still cold here; I hope he is somewhere warm."

Now it was Komptin who was holding Alex back.

"Is there a reason you're here?" Father Richard stepped up to address the Demon.

"Well, professional courtesy, I guess you can say. You see, after this week, I'm going to…why, who are you?" He focused on Megan, who was sitting at her desk, where he calmly approached her.

"I'm Megan," she extended her hand to greet him.

"I'm Roger, Roger Somberson. Are you new to CopperTop?" Roger gently placed his hands on top of hers.

"How'd you know?" She acted smitten by his approach.

"Because you have something special about you. Look, I'm looking for a new personal assistant if you're interested." Roger could tell Megan was trying to play it off.

"I'm happy where I'm at," she pulled her hand back for her audience.

"My door is always open," Roger faced the group. "Michael, as district attorney, you really should separate yourself from religious influence."

"I'm here to see my daughter," he quickly retorted.

"Sure, you are. Be prepared to have a very short day tomorrow." Roger sat down on top of the desk. "I don't know why you all would oppose me. I'm trying to bring peace to CopperTop. I just want what's right for the pri…people of this town. I know about the sacrifice needed for order."

"Slavery," Anne spoke out.

81

"Careful, Anne, that could be slander," he warned her. Then, a low thunder and flash seemed to come from outside the building.

Azrael just moved his eyes to see where she was coming from. Then, out came Devine from around the corner. "I thought there was foul stench emanating from this place."

"Sister," Azrael greeted her. "We'll talk later, but for now. I need to go see our brother." Azrael turned to leave the building.

"Tensions in families is so heartening. He lost a brother recently. So sad for him. Can you imagine what that feels like?" Gron stared directly at Alex.

Father Carl had enough, he moved to stand in between Alex and the mayor. "You need to leave; you are not welcome here."

"Oh, take a look across the street. That is where I'll be standing when my statute takes effect. Now, if you will excuse me, I have messes to clean up." Gron left the church with his other two Demons.

"That was pleasant." Alex watched as he got into his car with his driver.

"Looks like I'm getting fired tomorrow." Michael rubbed his eyes.

Father Richard stated, "We need to get her out of there."

"Who?" Megan inquired.

Alex continued to stare out the window. "Midnight."

***

82

Lakota Redwood always loved this time of year in the Badlands. Life was starting to birth from the Earth. Even though Lakota was a Lite Sentry for the Lutheran Council, he always felt a pull from his grandfathers to address the Great Spirit. Lakota didn't mind; he had never thought it was conflicting. All the Lite religions basically give thanks to the same spirit, regardless of the terms used.

Last night was not a good day for a patrol as his trainer told him that one of the Lite Sentries and a Lite Angel was taken by the Dark last night. Lakota stared at the skies to see the stars shine bright of his comrades.

A sudden strong sense of the Dark appeared from nowhere. The earth was telling him danger was afoot. This couldn't stop Lakota from eliminating the Infiltrator he was stalking. What was it doing out here, in the middle of nowhere? It made no sense. This was just a training ground for Lakota. Even though he was confident in his duties, he wished his trainer was present.

A sense of the Lite was a welcome relief as he sensed the Lite Angel coming near. "Ask for and answered." He laughed to himself. The massive male angel landed in front of him. "Raguel." He greeted his trainer.

"Lakota," the angel addressed his mentee.

This angel had bright, light blue hair. It reminded Lakota of anpetuwi. The strength he possessed was only matched by the warmth of his heart. Lakota only wished he could be half the man this angel showed him to be. He stood before the

Lite Sentry in his angelic battle armor. A sense of urgency was written on his normally stoic face.

"I'm glad you're here. This Dark I sense is different." Lakota noticed it had become quiet. He had a sense, a sense as if the Great Spirit himself was telling him to run.

"We should not be here. This night is filled with death." Raguel was keeping an eye on the skies along with some of the cliffs that lay ahead of them.

"We will live to see the morning, Akicita." Lakota turned and saw a small shadow figure perched on a rock. "What the hell is that?"

The bird-like creature tilted his head in a manner as if he were studying him. It almost stared into his soul with disappointment. "He will be here soon," it spoke.

Raguel eyes opened wide. "We must go. Now. Run, do not look back."

Lakota turned to his trainer. "Why? What's going on?"

The eyes in the angel were full of worry for his Sentry. It was a level of fear Lakota had never seen before. "Your feet need to be moving, now!"

The emphasis of the Lite Angel caused Lakota to realize it was a dire situation. He nodded in acknowledgment. As soon as he turned around, a man stood before him. His blackened hair was only matched by the evil in his eyes.

"Too late," the bird-like creature stated as he remained settled on the rock.

Raguel immediately pushed Lakota behind him. "Do not run. You will not make it."

84

"What do we do?" Lakota regained his footing, ready for whatever Raguel instructed him to do.

"Raguel, my brother," the Dark Angel stepped back a bit in case of attack.

"Azrael, you should not have come back," the angel of Lite made sure Lakota was at a safe distance. Raguel quickly glanced to ensure there was no other attack coming in any direction.

Azrael moved his head a bit to see the Sentry. "He's scared."

Raguel turned to his Sentry. "If you know you are going to fall, do not use your powers; you will go to Heaven."

"We can beat him," Lakota quietly whispered.

Azrael stepped back a bit more. "No, you can't." His attention turned to his former Lite comrade. I don't want to fight you, brother." His black, misty wings were not in battle position. The foggy horns were slowly protruding the shape, but it was clear they were prominent.

"Then why are you here?" Raguel cracked his neck for the imminent assault.

"You know I'm right; we've talked about this before." Azrael motioned for his minion to vacate the area. The loyal servant took off to the skies.

"What's he searching for?" Raguel watched the little underling leave.

Azrael stared at the sky along with Raguel. "So many brothers and sisters."

"Some at your hand." Raguel didn't know why his brother was waiting to attack.

Azrael turned to his brother. His stare became hypnotic with his soothing voice. "Aren't you tired?

There can be no more killing. Join me. The Dark will ensure this war is over."

"We must keep the Balance," Raguel refuted.

"That's Celestial talking. Even she knows the NEWS will be reporting soon." Azrael commented. "But if we rule over the primates, then they have no reason to be here. There will be stability."

"He wants the primates to be free." Raguel contested, but it was falling on deaf ears.

"He is just unwilling to be wrong."

Raguel came back with, "He is never wrong."

"Really, explain the duck-bill platypus." Azrael pointed out.

Raguel thought about it. "Leftover parts."

"Brother, please." Azrael approached him. He put his hand on his shoulder. "The primates kill each other over the font of the book but ignore the message. I know you are tired; we're all tired. The primates need to be ruled. They are just children. Undisciplined, selfish, ignorant, children."

"Raguel," Lakota softly called the name to his mentor.

Azrael just peered at the Sentry over his brother's shoulder. "Come over to the Dark, join the Fallen Star."

"There are Sentries out there. I heard you even lost one rather quickly."

"She will not be seen again." Azrael peeked over at the Lite Sentry, who was waiting to see what was going to happen next.

"Maybe, but there is another who is, well…she is unique." Raguel let his brother know.

"I've met her. I'm not impressed." Azrael focused on his work. "She will die just as easy as the rest."

"What do you mean by rest?" Lakota stepped back a bit.

Azrael ignored the Lite Sentry. "Join me, brother. You know this world is lost. This world belongs to the Dark. Together, we will rid it of all who oppose us." Azrael pulled Raguel in with a hug. "Yes, brother, together again, we will ensure the primates are ruled over."

"Akicita?" Lakota cried out in fear.

Raguel turned around with his blackened eyes. His halo was replaced with the same horns as Azrael. The now blackened wings stood proud. He formed a sword with a look of determination Lakota knew too well. The Sentry ignited his fists, but before he could act, Raguel thrust his sword into the stomach of his former trainee. Azrael smirked as he slowly came to the back of the dying Sentry. He formed an axe, and with no time at all, he removed Lakota's head from his body. Parts of Lakota fell to the ground before joining the sky as a star.

Azrael turned to his brother after enjoying the disintegration of another Sentry. "Now, brother, tell me where I can locate the Sentry who guards a carrier."

***

In this town of darkness, the only available light was from the torch that Kameron was holding. The angry mob around him was loudly chanting her destruction. Kameron held the wooden handle with the fire blazing on the other end. The illumination of the flickering flame showed a woman tied to the windshield of the car. Her hands were bound by a rope that was knotted around the mirrors of the BMW. Ropes bounded her legs to the point where she couldn't move them. The only thing she could move was her head as she cried for Kameron not to do it. Kale and Anne continued to pour the gasoline from the red containers over her body and head. She closed her eyes to prevent the gas from entering her eyes. The ignitable liquid dripped from her hair onto her bruised and cut face. Roger was standing on the roof of the car telling them to drench her more.

"You do this!" Megan appeared to Kameron's right with scary determination as she gritted her teeth. She got angrier as Kameron hesitated. "Prove yourself to the Trinity of the Fallen Star! You're embarrassing me– in front of Roger Somberson, of all people! Now, for Dark's sake, don't be such a creampuff and do it already!"

Kameron slowly made it towards the car, gripping the torch in hand. Roger smiled as he hopped off the car. Kale and Anne backed away from the car, tossing the gas cans at the small girl's body with anger. The paleface, beautiful, woman lifted her head with a mixture of gasoline and blood dripping from her black-weaved hair.

"Kameron," she softly pleaded.

He took a deep breath before he gazed at Megan, yelling at him to do it. Kameron turned to Roger Somberson, who suddenly had a figure standing behind him with a white face, greasy hair, and a big black hat.

"Watch as he upholds his oath to the Dark Trinity," Roger motivated the crowd. The mob responded to his words in an erupting thunder of hate towards the bounded woman.

With a sudden cold emptiness of determination, Kameron threw the torch on the car. Flames engulfed the petite woman's body as her screams were mixed with coughing. She couldn't even flail her body around as a distraction; she had to take it. The crowd cheered as the smell of burning flesh filled the air. Kameron closed his eyes, but it only made it worse as he only heard the suffering of the woman he loved.

Chapter Four

"Son of a bitch." Alex waved her hand up and down from burning the skin on her fingers. It was a quick pain, but then it started to alleviate. The match head dropped on her hand while it was lit from lighting a candle for prayer in the votive station. She sucked on her finger to further ease the pain. Luckily, Father Carl didn't hear her. He would've yelled at her for swearing in a such holy place. She would hate to admit it, but he'd be right. She took a deep breath as she stared at the candle. Hopefully, tonight would go smoothly. Even without being able to feel the warmth of the Lite, she needed this moment alone.

"Alexandria." Celestial's voice echoed in the congregation hall.

Alex felt ill, not because Celestial interrupted her alone time, but because she was calling out to her to find her. It hurt Alex's heart every time she was reminded the Lite couldn't sense her, which was quite often. Alex appeared from the corner room. "I'm right here."

Celestial had a sense of guilt to her. Almost embarrassment for not being able to sense her Lite Sentry. "I am glad to see you."

Alex tried to put up a false front. "Thanks. Is everything all right?"

"Things have not gotten worse, but far from getting better." Celestial seemed to glide to the front pew. She did a quick bow to the altar before sitting down. Her guardians gracefully took their leave of their mistress before going before the altar to pray. "Join me, please."

Alex always welcomed an invitation to sit next to Celestial. Alex leaned a bit after she sat down, realizing she sat on her phone. "The council would be pretty pissed off if I broke another phone," she chuckled, showing Celestial her phone. As she moved her phone, the screen showed a picture of Kameron and Alex together.

"May I?" Celestial requested.

Alex handed her the phone, but the screen went black. Celestial got scared, but Alex just smiled as she tapped the phone to show her the picture on the lock screen. "There you go." Alex got a rush of sadness as she saw the picture.

"Tell me about this day." Celestial studied the picture.

Alex got a little shy with Celestial. "Well, not to go too far into details, okay?"

"Of course," the caring angel handed her back the phone.

Alex began to tell her how Kameron took her on a trip to meet up with his family at a cabin in the woods. They rented it right next to a lake. They all laughed and talked by a campfire. On one of the nights, Kameron took Alex on a boat with Komptin. He had some blankets as they just anchored in the water, watching the stars with a storm coming in from the far distance. Alex felt so secure. She took a picture of themselves just before the storm forced them to leave.

"In that perfect moment, I was embraced by the man I love under a blanket. Komptin, sleeping soundly next to me. Minus the storm interrupting us, it was the perfect moment in time. Is that what Heaven is like…a constant state of that feeling?" Alex probed her godmother.

"In a way," Celestial assured her Lite Sentry.

"But as a Sentry, I won't enter Heaven; more than likely, I will fall as I'm using my powers, becoming a star." Alex was sad as she realized what her fate was more likely to become.

"Most Sentries fall in battle," Celestial reluctantly told her the truth.

Alex put her head on Celestial's shoulder. "There is so much hate and Dark. I may not be able to sense it, but the Balance is shifted, isn't it?"

"It has been tipping slowly for quite some time. Slow enough for most not to notice." She seemed to stare forward in a blank store of thought.

Alex joined her in the stare of hopelessness. "Like a frog in a pot."

Celestial just moved her eyes down at her Sentry. "We have only been able to prevent a mass slide, but people are ignoring the Lite with blind repercussions." Celestial wiped a tear. "They are slowly fed Dark propaganda, before they realize it, they are nurturing off of it."

"Sometimes I think humanity needs a reset?" Alex just shot that out there with a feeling of defeat.

Celestial's body tensed up. "You do not realize the consequence of that action or train of thought."

"I'm sorry, I didn't mean anything by it, I'm just saying, sometimes when things get so bad, it's better to wipe the slate clean and start over." Alex defended her statement. "Has anything like that ever been done?"

"Once," Celestial reluctantly admitted. "The Dark found a way to close off humanity to accept the Lite. It was necessary to find out how, so after forty days of torture, the man sent had found a way. A sudden burst of Lite was needed to open humanity for acceptance. His sacrifice allowed humankind to forever choose the Lite for themselves."

Alex drew attention to the crucifix sitting on the mantle in front of the church. Her watch beeped, notifying her that she needed to head out. "I have to go."

"Be careful. Remember, just because the Lite cannot see you, does not mean you are out of their love." Celestial kissed her forehead.

**

Megan soothingly sang a lullaby as she tucked in the red and black blankets on each of the kids' beds. "Just remember, when you get old enough, you will accept absolute power. You'll be top generals in the army of the Fallen Trinity." The children didn't give any emotion to their caregiver. All they did was lay on their backs and close their eyes. Megan caressed their cheeks with her hands, then slowly shut the doors for them to enjoy their peaceful slumber.

Gron was outside the thick wooden doors, peeking in as Megan snuck out of their room. "Are they destined to become generals?"

"Just a feeling." Megan took in this small taste of home life. She made it a point to stand next to Gron. It was heartwarming as Megan felt like she and Gron were two proud parents watching their children sleep. This was a sentiment she could hold on forever, but then the wall hanging of Vandor quickly caused it to vanish. "I'm almost done translating the texts."

"Good." Gron grabbed his phone. "I have a meeting with the chief of police and attorney general tomorrow. We're going over plans to introduce the SI program to City Council." Gron had a bit of excitement in his voice.

"Will they vote it in?" Megan went to grab Gron's hand as they walked down the hall. He rejected the gesture as he continued to read his phone. Megan tried to keep face as she pulled back her hand, almost not knowing what to do with it.

"I'm not that worried," Gron stopped at the balcony over the mainhouse lobby, overlooking some Serfs cleaning the house. "We have two board members whose kids are on the Map, and another who is a Host." Gron snapped his fingers to get in touch with one of the supervisors. He pointed to that overweight Serf he had seen earlier. "Put him in Rejuvenation. I can't have a fat ass like that represent the F.O.R."

The Supervisor grabbed the kid by the arm. "Yes, my Leader." The kid asked what he had done wrong as he continued down towards the locked Conex.

Megan watched the kid almost faint as he went towards his imprisonment. "Well, that's good.

Should we celebrate?" Megan bit the bottom of her lip. Gron flashed his eyes with his sharp teeth on display. He grabbed Megan by the throat just as he threw her against the wall with his raw power of the Dark before kissing and biting her neck.

"My leader," his elderly assistant interrupted. "I apologize for intruding, but I have an important phone call for you." She handed him his red phone.

He angrily grabbed the phone from his assistant. "This is Gron." He listened for a bit. "Okay, send a Host to take care of that." He hung up the phone. "One of the nurses at the hospital said that the agent is actually awake. That bastard lied to me, so it just gives me more grounds to get his ass fired." He handed his phone back to his secretary.

"Playtime over?" Megan pouted.

"Just postponed." Gron playfully slapped her kind of hard across the face. "Let's go check on our guests."

Megan rubbed her cheek as she loyally followed Gron to the bottom of the blackened basement of the F.O.R. Compound. It was dark and dingy; the smell of mold sat stagnant. It was mainly just because he wanted to keep the guests in fear. He opened the heavy steel door to see seven random people standing in distress. "You shouldn't be scared." Megan tried to come off as a gentle person. "While you have no idea why you are here, you should feel honored."

"What do you want with us?" One of the men stood up, almost taking charge.

"Just growing our crops," Gron motioned for some of the F.O.R. members to bring in some food.

He whispered into Megan's ear, "I thought I told you, only Hosts to feed them."

"I told that to Nadize." Megan was irritated. "Shall I dispose of this Serf?"

"No, I'll do it. This presents an opportunity." Gron had the F.O.R. member bring the food into the room. Gron came up behind the young man and snapped his neck with ease. He flashed his red eyes at the group. "Eat up." The people screamed as they watched Infiltrators enter the room to ravage what was left of the body. Gron had the door shut. "Okay, shall we go see our new friend?"

The darkness was interrupted by the slow opening of the door. There were two figures standing in the blinding light. The man, bound up on a wall, lifted his bloody head up. "Please tell me I'm dead," the man pleaded to his captors.

"Not quite, dear." Megan turned on the overhead lights. Before her and Gron was one of the agents that tried to foil the bombing of the electric transfer station. Megan grabbed a washcloth and gently wiped the blood off his forehead.

"How are those wounds treating you?" Gron snickered as he studied the man.

"Where's Midnight?" Scotty could barely get out.

"Every time we come down here, that's one of the first things you ask us." Gron was getting irritated. He grabbed his hair to pull his head back. "What if I told you I had my way with her before I tore her body into shreds of human flesh? Would you like that?"

"You son of bitch!" Scotty tried fighting from his standing chains.

Megan kept herself from laughing as she wiped the blood from his lip.

Gron continued to grill him. "You know the best part, you were fired from the federal government, so there is no record of you even being on that little mission of yours. No one knows you're here, not even the Sentry." Gron was keeping himself from laughing.

"Kameron knows," Scotty managed to say.

"Oh honey, we killed him long, long, ago." Megan gave him a little kiss on the cheek. "He didn't even have a chance to tell his little girlfriend about me." She slapped him on the other side of his face.

Azrael entered the room with Pytho perched on his shoulder. "I have the location of the sentry who carries a pure of heart."

"Good, see if you can get the location of that little Diva bitch before you hurt her too much?" Gron studied Scotty.

The bird-like gargoyle flew off the Dark Angel's shoulder to study the human chained to the wall. "He has much hate for the Lite."

Gron turned his attention from the gargoyle to Scotty. "Really? Not a fan of religion, are you?"

"You're an asshole." It was the only thing Scotty could come up with.

Gron snickered at his feistiness. "Who brought him here?"

"Shantaree." Megan watched the bird fly back to Azrael.

The master of the F.O.R. studied Scotty. Almost debated on killing him or not. "Have her work on him." The three of them left the room as Azrael briefed Gron on the whereabouts of the Sentry guarding a pure of heart. They left Scotty alone with his wounds in the darkness of the confinement.

*　*　*

Midnight could barely see when she tried to open her eyes to the doctor, who was also a priest. "Midnight," he greeted her. He always made it a point to pick up her hand as he was checking her vitals on the machine. It was always the excuse he was double-checking the machines, but it was mainly because he just wanted to give his patients a human touch. "Looks like everything is stable." He gently squeezed her hand after a couple of soft taps. Midnight still couldn't speak; she could barely keep consciousness.

The priest was greeted by his nurse. "Doctor Smithon, the transport is on its way to meet us downstairs."

"Midnight, we're going to take you to a safe location. There, you'll be protected by a sentry during your recovery." Dr. Smithon brushed her hair out of the way of her eyes. He placed his hands on top of her head to tell her it would be okay. "Carol, can you wait for the transport to make sure it has everything?"

"Yes, doctor." Carol left the room to meet up with the transport team sent by the Council.

The intercom came on over the ceiling speaker, calling for Dr. Smithon to report to the nurse's station. Dr. Smithon glanced at the speaker in the ceiling. "Really? Isn't Dr. Swanson on duty?" He gently palmed her on the head one more time. "I'll be right back."

Midnight tried to focus her blurry eyes. Things were fuzzy and disoriented, worst of all, she couldn't keep her thoughts in a straight line. She couldn't talk, as if there was a tube down her throat. A figure in a surgeon's outfit came in. She couldn't make out the doctor as he came into the room.

"Agent Midnight Solis," he called for her. "I'm here for your transfer." He gave her a gentle smile. "Straight to Hell!" His eyes became a steady glow of red, and his teeth grew as he slowly approached the helpless patient. The incapacitated agent could see her life about to end as she was held hostage by her wounds. As the Demon started to choke Midnight. The patient's monitors started giving alerts of her racing heart.

"I swear, that nurse is as useless as caffeine-free diet soda." Dr. Smithon was mumbling to himself as he entered the room. He saw the man in the surgeon's scrubs over Midnight's body. "What are you doing with my patient?"

The surgeon turned around with glowing eyes. Dr. Smithon managed to get in between the Demon and Midnight. He placed his hands out to protect his patient. "You will have to go through me before you get to her." Dr. Smithon stood his ground for his patient's life.

"That's my plan, go right through you," the Demon hissed. There was eagerness in his body language as he cocked his arm to swing. As he went to thrust his arm, something caught it before he could lay the damage. The Lite Sentry was behind him with glowing eyes of her own.

"Thank God, we're in a hospital because that pun just had me in stitches." She twisted his body around and pushed him out into the hallway. She stepped out of the room with a confident prowess. A hospital floor full of visitors and hospital staff stopped to witness the event. Among those were Tristan and Komptin in his service dog harness. Alex confidentially stared down the Demon. "I'm ready whenever you are."

The Demon fixed his outfit. "When we meet again, you'll need more than a doctor when I'm finished."

Alex rolled her eyes. "How many stupid doctor puns are you going to throw at me?" She turned to see the nurse down the hall on the phone, no doubt calling security.

Dr. Smithon came out of the room. "Code Gray!" He yelled.

Once they arrived, they immediately started ensuring everyone was safe. The hospital staff rushed to secure their patients until security arrived. The surgeon-dressed Demon ran to the exit staircase. Alex turned to Tristan, "Do you want him or Midnight?"

Tristan nerves shot up in him. "I'll take the doctor."

"Go get him," Alex motioned with her head. It was nice to see Tristan allow himself the opportunity to take the Demon. Though, it made Alex a little nervous about whether he would return or not. The young Sentry tensed up but then took a deep breath as he reluctantly started to go after his first Demon. Alex gave him a confident nod as he started his next-level hunt. Komptin joined her at her side. "I hope I did the right thing. He has to face one sooner or later by himself." Komptin rubbed up against her in support. She scratched his ears before she turned to Dr. Smithon, who was now looking over Midnight. "How is she?"

"She shouldn't be transported." Dr. Smithon got concerned over her vitals.

"She can't stay here," Alex stated the obvious. "She'll be dead in a couple of days." Alex watched Midnight as she just lay there with a bunch of tubes attached to her.

Dr. Smithon knew the Sentry was right. "I'll prep her."

"Transport is downstairs," Alex put her hand on his shoulder. "I'll have Tristan escort you and her to the location. You'll be fine." Alex couldn't help but wonder if he would make it back.

Alex went downstairs to watch over Midnight as she was put into a transport van. Dr. Smithon was clarifying with the nurse on the systems. Alex recognized the nurse; she had been with the good doctor every time Alex needed stitching. So, she knew the nurse was cleared by the Council. Father Richard was going to drive the van while Tristan rode shotgun.

The inexperienced Sentry came to Alex's side. "I couldn't find him."

"No big, I'm sure we'll see him again," Alex reassured him. "Nervous?"

Tristan shook his head quickly.

Alex laughed, "It'll be okay there, stud." She patted his back in support. "This should only take five or six days." Alex got serious for a moment. "Listen to me."

Tristan turned his attention to Alex, but his mind was focusing on the trip at hand. "Yes."

"You are a Sentry. Don't let this get in your way." She pushed her finger on his head. "Use your training, your experience, and you'll be fine."

He nodded. "I will."

"Now give me a hug." The two of them hugged goodbyes. "I'll see you in a week or so."

Tristan jumped into the van's front seat when Father Richard approached Alex.

"He'll be fine."

"Now I know how you guys must feel every time I go on a hunt. Not knowing if I'm going to come home or not." Alex scratched Komptin's ears next to her. She then took this opportunity to hit Father Richard on the arm. "And why the hell are you going, and I have to stay with the jackass?"

"For that *exact* reason. I need a break from you two." Father Richard rubbed his shoulder. "We should get going. We have a long drive ahead of us. Which I'm actually looking forward to." He teased the Sentry by hitting her back, but she didn't even budge.

102

Anne came up to the two of them with a yellow envelope to give to Father Richard. "Here is the paperwork that will get you through customs."

"Thank you. Well, ladies. I'll see you in a week." He hugged the two of them before approaching Father Carl to discuss some things before getting into the van. Father Carl looked in Alex's direction as he was given last-minute instructions from Father Richard.

"This is going to suck," Alex predicted to Anne.

Anne just smiled. "Just stay out of each other's way."

Father Carl joined Alex and Anne as the transport took Midnight, hopefully, to a safe location. Alex texted her dad that Midnight had just left. He replied with a thumbs up. The newest priest to join the Council was the first to say something. "The hardest part of command was watching a convoy depart. I always felt as if I didn't go on every single one, I wasn't doing my part."

"I get it," Alex admitted. "You feel as if you're not doing all you could."

"But it's worse when you do go and survive an assault, and you have to live with guilt you didn't die with your team." Father Carl stood with a cold stare. He didn't move; he just had a blank expression as if he were lost...

"Father," Anne put her hand on his shoulder.

He jumped out of his trance with a shake of his body. "Sorry." He wiped his face.

Anne met Alex's eyes; for the first time, the Sentry seemed to have sympathy for the priest.

Father Carl quickly changed the mood of the conversation. "Do you think they will run into trouble?"

Alex shook her head. "No, the Dark has no idea where they're going. They probably have other things on their agenda."

***

Zeke escorted Kaylee out of the movie theatre. The film was a welcoming doorway to some relaxation for the two of them. The Lite Sentry assigned to protect her had noticed some tension between the two of them. There was no sense in lying to himself. He liked Kaylee. He liked her a lot, but she was pregnant by a man who killed himself for her freedom from the F.O.R. It was too soon to tell her how he felt, but he had only known her for about five months. Perhaps it was just a crush. It would probably fade; at least, he hoped it would. Regardless, he was pretty sure she knew about his feelings.

"I needed that." Kaylee took the popcorn Zeke handed to her.

Zeke took some chewing tobacco from his back pocket. He carefully put some into his mouth to make sure he didn't spill any. "It was a funny movie. Normally, I don't like those romance comedy chick flicks, but that one wasn't bad."

Kaylee rubbed her stomach. Her baby didn't really like the nachos she ate while watching the movie. "Do you want to get some ice cream?"

"It's getting late. We really should get back to the church. You have to be getting tired." Zeke was scouting the area around them.

Kaylee noticed his posture change. The only thing she saw were people going to their cars. "What's wrong?"

Zeke rolled his eyes. "Dinah is nearby. I swear that girl doesn't trust me for no-how."

"Come on, let's get ice cream on the way to the church. Sweet Tooth should still be open." The two of them made it to the little ice cream shop just before they were going to close for the night. Zeke got cookies n' cream, while Kaylee got a mixture of ice cream, candies, and caramel.

"Want a lick?" Kaylee offered before she started to devour her treat.

"No, I'm good," Zeke had a sense of relief himself, as he felt that Dinah wasn't near anymore. "Thank God."

"What's that?" Kaylee was catching bits of her caramel chunks out of her ice cream.

"Nothing." The two of them strolled by a closed plant nursery. The smell of the flowers was pleasant and welcoming. Then, a sense of stale air came with a feeling of dread. "Oh shit. How'd they find us?"

Kaylee stopped. "Who?" Frantically, she was trying to find what got her protector so nervous.

Zeke grabbed her hands. He lit his hands and eyes in neon blue. He ripped open the chain-link fence to the nursery. "Come on." He broke into the main building to locate the cooler, where they store some of the plants. He took off his jacket to wrap it

105

around Kaylee. "Look, be quiet. Stay put. I'll be back for you."

"We can make it out of here," Kaylee only could think of was the life of her baby.

"No. There's something out there I've never felt before." He gave her a quick wink. "I'll be okay, don't worry."

Zeke closed the door to the refrigerator to the nursery. He didn't know why he did it, but he kissed his hand and placed it on the metal door. He made it to the display area. The only thing that was nice was the aroma of the flowers. Other than that, this was not a good situation. Movement through the aisles of flowers and plants had a weird mixture of calmness plus terror. Zeke jumped as the shadow of a very large bird flew across the room at a distance. A welcoming, familiar feeling arrived when he turned around to see his bright orange-haired trainer. "What are you doing here?"

"We need to leave. We are not safe." The angel had a sense of urgency in her voice. "Where is the carrier?" Then, her mood changed from hopelessness to determination.

"What is it?" Zeke flashed his eyes.

"I am going to call him out; lead him away from you. Get the carrier out of here." Dinah took to the air, screaming out the name "Azrael."

Zeke watched her take to the sky. Then, he saw a man straight ahead of him, with a confident stance that only a person possessed would have. The tall, blonde man just stood there, staring. The dark maroon shirt with an upside-down number four only confirmed he must have been a Demon. "Are you

106

going to tell me how the road to Absolute Power changed your life?"

The man flashed his red eyes, while simultaneously growing his claws. "No, I'm just going to kill you." The man rushed Zeke. The Sentry stood his ground as his first fight with a Demon was about to take place. As the Demon approached him, Zeke picked him off the ground. He instantly threw him down onto the table full of flowers. Then, with a snarl, he grabbed him by the shirt and tossed him to the adjoining table. The Dark soldier smashed a flowerpot across Zeke's head, causing the Sentry to stagger back.

The Demon went on the offensive. It got up off the ground and landed a massive punch to his opponent. The Demon twisted the Sentry around, grabbing the dazed Sentry. "I bet you always wanted to fly like an angel." The Demon threw him through the glass of the nursery. "Who says I don't give last requests?"

With a very bloodied face, Zeke managed to stand up to see Dinah talking to another angel with black wings. With tears in her eyes, she turned to see Zeke. All she did was shake her head. The other angel just pointed to Zeke as he was talking to her. He had contempt written all over his face.

The Demon attacking Zeke came up from behind. He spun him around to connect a knee to Zeke's stomach, causing him to bend over. It then pushed Zeke onto the ground and onto the broken glass. Zeke managed to twist around as the bottom of a boot was about to hit his face, allowing him the opportunity to push the Demon off him. He got up off the ground, grabbing a piece of glass. As the Demon faced him, he tossed the glass at the possessed man. The glass stuck in the chest of the Demon. It screamed in pain. Then Zeke generated a Lite Beam, pushing the glass further into the Demon's body. Zeke was able to sense the Demon's weakness. He formed a knife made of the Lite and stabbed the creature in the neck. The Demon dropped to the ground, disappearing forever.

"I got him." Zeke had a moment of pride in himself. He limped over to the two angels.

Dinah's eyes got bigger as another angel dropped from the sky. This angel also had black wings and foggy, misty horns instead of a halo. "Raguel, brother, why?"

"You of all of us know we are right. Stop this blind allegiance to His wish. These primates are not worth the mud on our feet. Join us, sister." The angel next to Dinah looked to the stars as a small bird gargoyle landed on his shoulder. "Did you find her?"

The creature wrapped his body with his wings. "Yes, she's in the cold box."

Azrael nodded before turning his attention to Dinah. "So many of your brothers and sisters have died."

"A lot of them because of you," Dinah sharply pointed out.

"Sister," Raguel stepped forward. "You need to realize the clarity Azrael has shown me. The primates are a horrible plague on this living rock. We should rule over them. We are superior. You and I have even talked about this."

"Do not construe my words, Raguel. Every species has talents over the other in different ways, Raguel." Dinah snuck a glimpse to Zeke. The innocent confusion on her Lite Sentry only hurt her more.

"What's so special about an evolved monkey?" Raguel started to argue.

Azrael nonchalantly started to move towards the Lite Sentry as Raguel and Dinah continued their debate. "Dinah, you yourself disagreed with His decisions regarding these primates. Then He punished you for your opinion. He forced you to train the disgusting mutation of the Lite and Primate." Raguel pointed to Zeke. "I know your true thoughts about His people. Deep down, you know they are vile creatures."

She turned to Zeke with a tear in her eye. "Zeke, I am sorry. I should have been a better teacher for you."

"What's going on, Dinah?" Zeke lit his fists as he felt a fight was coming from this confusing situation. Then, without even knowing what was happening. Zeke felt a burning, sharp object enter from his back. He looked down to see a glowing red sword protruding out of his chest. His eyes grew big as he dropped to his knees. The last thing he saw with his glowing eyes was the Dark angel form an axe and swing it at his neck.

Dinah just closed her eyes as the head of her protégé rolled on the ground before disappearing to become a star. The Lite warrior angel pushed her brother away for some maneuvering room. Dinah formed two short swords as she stood in a fighting position.

"Dinah," Azrael continued to admire how he caused the death of another Sentry. "You can't defeat me, let alone with Raguel at my side. Your only choice is to give in to your thoughts. I know you don't like them; I don't like them. Join me, and together, we will make sure they are ruled over with the sheer might of discipline."

Dinah put her swords away. With Raguel behind her and Azrael in front, she was surrounded. If she were to die, there was no way to save the carrier. She opened her wings to head towards the sky. Azrael and Raguel watched her take off to disappear into the night.

Kaylee was shivering in the refrigerator. She couldn't tell the difference between the cold of the refrigerator and the shiver of fear. The red light inside the cold box didn't help to calm her nerves. It reminded her too much of rejuvenation. She heard the door start to open. For some reason, she felt relieved as she knew Zeke was the only person who knew where she was hiding. The door opened to an actual angel. The problem was–Kaylee didn't feel secure. This angel had black eyes to match his black wings. There was no halo…just a misty fog in the shape of horns.

**

Alex returned the van to the church after dropping Father Carl and Anne off. For some reason, Father Carl didn't look like he was in the mood to drive. He didn't say much in his very cold tone, "Be sure to fill it and wash it by tomorrow." Alex gave him a very sarcastic salute; luckily, he didn't see it. She hated driving that thing. The only good part about filling it was that she was getting an ice-cold Apollo and packaged cake treat.

Anne didn't really say much either. She just went to her parent's house to go to bed. At the carwash, she surprised Komptin by giving him a bath in the bay. He didn't really appreciate it, but he was starting to stink a little. After she gave him a bath, she ordered two dinners to go. They ended up eating dinner at the church downstairs in the kitchen area. Alex just tossed him his steak like a frisbee. Watching him catch it was always a guilty pleasure for her.

After dinner, Komptin went up to the office to go to sleep while Alex roamed the church. It still needed so much work. The F.O.R. really did a number on it. She didn't know what time it was when she literally almost ran into Celestial as she turned a corner. However, her guardians prevented Alex from running into her. "Sorry," Alex said, as she did a quick bow before her inevitable hug.

"It is quite alright. It reminds me of the first time we met." Celestial was almost shocked to see the Lite Sentry. "Taking the night off?"

"Yah, if you call it that. We got Midnight out of the hospital and sent Tristan on his first mission by himself. He has the potential to become a good Sentry. Lord knows we need all the help we can get." Alex and Celestial both went into the congregation room.

Celestial stopped in the room to take it in. "That is truer of statement than you may realize."

Alex turned to Celestial. "We lost another one?" The silent concurrence was all Alex needed. "Who?"

"The one you met the night you saved the one you love." Celestial sat down on the pew.

"Zeke." Alex softly spoke his name. "Wait a minute. Kaylee?"

"She was taken," the Conduit of Lite almost had ineptness in her eyes.

"I'll rescue her," Alex went to stand with determination.

Celestial put her hand on the gritty Sentry's shoulder to keep her down. "Not yet. Promise me you will wait until I say so."

"But, I can…" Alex started to say.

"Alexandria, promise me."

Alex succumbed to Celestial request. "I promise." Alex spent the rest of the night trying to figure out why Celestial was so adamant about her not going to find Kaylee. Alex didn't realize how long she was thinking about it when her thoughts morphed into thinking about Kameron. Kaylee may have been taken, but she still had a chance to enter Heaven. Kameron: he was stuck in Hell, and there was nothing she could do about it. Anne's coming into work interrupted her thoughts. The time was a bit earlier than she normally came in.

"Couldn't sleep?" Alex greeted Anne in the church lobby.

"Not really." Anne put her keys in her purse. "How was your night?"

112

"I didn't go out, but I got some pretty disturbing news last night from Celestial." Alex escorted Anne to her office.

"Oh, what was that?" Anne started unbuttoning her coat while Alex escorted her down to her office.

"Zeke fell last night trying to protect Kaylee. The Dark took her." Alex dropped the unfortunate news.

Anne stopped in her tracks. "More than likely, she is going to be brought here to CopperTop."

"That was my thoughts, but Celestial made me promise not to go rescue her until I get her 'go-ahead.' It was really weird." Alex thumbed through her phone, coming across another picture of Kameron. "I thought I deleted all my pictures, but they all came back."

"Maybe they were backed up on the cloud." Anne stopped on the way to her office. "I'm hungry. Do you want to go get something to eat?"

"Ah, yes," Alex teased as if it was a stupid question.

They decided to stop off at Mrs. Clark's Bakery. It was always a nice place to visit, even though some F.O.R. members were in their uniforms having coffee. They were talking to some other people talking about the benefits of F.O.R. Road Map to Absolute Power. Anne ordered her pumpkinseed muffin, while Alex ordered a cream-filled Bismarck with cereal sprinkled on top. "There you go, darling." Mrs. Clark gave her the breakfast pastries. She gave her a wink and a loving smile as she handed her the bag. "I'll bring your coffee to you."

"Thank you," Anne returned a smile, almost embarrassingly.

Alex turned around to sit at an open table as she ran into an obese man. He had a Social Security Administration Tech Support polo shirt on and smelled like a candy store, but not obnoxious smelling. "Sorry."

"Not a problem, Alex," the man said, winking at another young twenty-five-year-old sitting down drinking coffee while reading her book.

"Do I know you?" Alex asked the man, whose black hair he'd tried to use to hide the baldness. Alex tried not to laugh at some long hair he'd tried to use to cover the top of his shiny head.

The man quickly retorted, "I used to work tech support for your cell phone company before I got my new job." He pointed to the lady's coffee and motioned to Mrs. Clark that he wanted to order two. "Now, if you will excuse me." He went to join the young woman who was smitten with the man.

"That's some memory," Anne found an empty seat for them to talk next to a window. It wasn't long before Mrs. Clark came by to give them their coffee. "Thank you." Anne was almost embarrassed.

Alex didn't miss that. "You know what happened to Mole back in high school during one of his drinking binges and Mrs. Clark, don't you?"

"I do," Anne smiled. "Kale told me that night at the lake."

Alex took a sip of her hot coffee. "I'll never forget that night you two first kissed. I knew you two would be together forever."

"That wasn't our first kiss," Anne nonchalantly said as she read her email on her phone.

"Wait, what?" Alex was a bit offended that she didn't know. "You're telling me the end of that race...wasn't your two's first kiss?" Alex was in shock as she watched her sister-in-law just shake her head as she continued reading. Then she watched the overweight, balding man leave with the attractive woman as she was smiling and laughing. Alex shook it off as she got a smell of Kameron's cologne he used to wear.

Anne turned her head around her as she smelt something familiar. "No, that wasn't our first kiss. I'm surprised he didn't tell you."

"Maybe it was something he just wanted to keep between the two of you, but I gotta know." Alex peeked out the window to see some small children in F.O.R. uniforms petting Komptin.

***

The charity bike around the lake organized by the high school went better than Anne expected. They helped raise a decent amount of food for the shelter. She was a bit sore from the ride; she forgot that the route the local bike shop helped her plan was mainly uphill. She had time to kill since her dad messaged her that the car would take longer to fix than expected and her mom would have to pick her up.

Anne texted her mom to say she was ready to leave the library. Her mom replied about an hour later that she would get her after her yoga class.

Anne decided to take hold of this advantage and go for a walk. The town was so peaceful at night. She would just tell her mom where she ended up. Anne just thought to let fate decide her destination. Anne was just in a good mood.

Tonight, the town was different; it seemed a bit colder than usual for being springtime, almost a bit darker. Anne lightly strolled for about fifteen minutes when she saw Mole lying on a local park's swinging bench. A sudden rush of blood came to her face. They didn't really talk after that night at the lake. He had driven her home, she guessed, illegally; then he escorted her up to her door while Robbie and Sara were left in the car. The two of them just stared at each other. Her nerves were going crazy as she was expecting him to kiss her, not just expecting, but giving every signal in welcoming it, but nothing ever happened.

Now, there was this weirdness. They were total opposites; she could understand why he didn't see her that way. Either way, she at least should go over there and thank him for riding the race. He actually was in the top ten of the finishers. It kind of impressed Anne. Mole didn't seem to know she was standing next to him. He was just lying there, almost sleeping. Maybe he was passed out from drinking. Anne didn't smell any alcohol or see any bottles. A sudden sense of worry hit her as she hoped he wasn't drinking again. Then Mole opened one eye at her.

He smiled at the sight of Anne. "No, I'm not drunk," he chuckled.

Anne was a bit shocked; did she say that out loud? "What are you doing?"

Mole took a moment to get up. He was halfway chuckling as he spoke. "I'm really sore," he embarrassingly admitted. He got up to scoot over to have her sit down.

"From the bike ride this morning?" Anne went into her bag and offered Mole a water.

"Thanks." He opened up the water. "No, I went swimming, and frankly speaking, I'm not the most graceful in the water."

"So, you're telling me you're not a beautiful swan on a calm lake," Anne teased him a little.

"More like a bulky gorilla falling into a river," Mole joked about himself.

Anne laughed, and she shyly turned her head. She could feel her face start to turn red. "Let me ask you something."

"Go ahead." He chugged down the bottle of water in one attempt. He got up to throw away the bottle.

Anne watched him as he made sure he put it in the recycle bin. He checked on his bike, which was leaning on the big tractor tire for kids to play on in the park. "Are you training for an Iron Man?" Mole turned around to look at her. He seemed a bit embarrassed as he nodded. "You should be proud of that. It's a rather strenuous tasking."

"It is." Mole went back to the bench swing where Anne was sitting. He grabbed one of the chains to lean on.

"You just seem a little reserved about it, that's all." Anne just stared at him. The sun setting behind him emphasized his gentle eyes.

"The swim got me a bit nervous. What if I fail? I don't think I could handle everyone ripping on me for not finishing, especially Shawn." Kale stared off behind Anne, trying not to make eye contact with her.

"Who cares what Shawn or anyone else thinks? The mere fact you're going to do such a race shows you aren't afraid of hard challenges," Anne confidentially told him.

"Well, trust me when I tell you, there are sometimes when fear has gotten the best of me once or twice," he softly admitted to her.

Anne wanted to know what he was talking about, but something told her not to push the issue. "We all have." She scooted over, inviting him to sit down. He took the offer as he closed his eyes, trying not to show he was sore. The two of them just softly swung as the sun went down behind the trees.

"You know, this race means so much to me. It's almost like if I don't finish it, then I won't be able to beat my alcoholism." Mole just stared at the sun disappearing.

Anne was a bit shocked he'd brought that up to her. "The two are not related. Alcoholism is a lot tougher to live with than any race. And it looks like you got that beat."

"I miss it," he tried to bring a little levity to the conversation. "But I'm such an obnoxious jackass when I drink. I can't take back the things that come out of my mouth. I'd become such a jerk."

Anne grabbed his hand, holding it. "How'd you quit?"

"Well, after the car crash and Alex's dad sent me to juvey, I didn't really have a choice." He squeezed her hand. He then turned to her. The two of them locked eyes. "While I was down there, I saw my future. What some of those kids looked like, how they acted, what they did due to drugs and alcohol; I just vowed that if I got out one piece, I would do something that my mom would be proud of."

"Well, it seems like you're already making her proud." Anne's phone rang as she answered it. "Hey, mom. I'm at Sachiel Park. Okay, see you then." She turned to Mole. "My mom is on her way to pick me up. Do you need a ride?"

"No, I need to loosen up my legs. The ride home usually does it." Mole got up to stretch his legs. "You got a big heart, Anne. I hope that never changes."

Anne's mouth got dry. She was trying to fight the blushing from Kale telling her that. "You are a welcoming, pleasant surprise."

The two just stared at each other. Leaving her on the bench swing, Kale got back up to lean on the chain. She saw her mom's car entering the parking lot. "My mom is here." It was almost as if she wasn't in control of her body, like she was allowing her feelings to control her actions. She stood up as he helped her off the swing. She stood on the tips of her shoes as she kissed Kale Moler. "I have to go."

***

"You kissed him, and then you just left?!" Alex was smiling ear to ear. This story of Kale and Anne was far too enjoyable to end.

"What was I supposed to do? We didn't really talk about it; it was something we just kept to ourselves." Anne admitted rather reservedly. Alex offered her a tissue so Anne could catch a tear forming in her eyes. "Thanks."

"I can't believe I never knew that! Oh my God!" Alex said a little louder than others around them.

"He doesn't exist." A member of the F.O.R. yelled from across the bakery. His buddies were praising his ignorant comment.

"Shut up," Alex shouted from across the bakery. She shook her head in disgust. "Anyways, so then what happened up to the race?"

"Well, we just didn't talk about it. It was out there, but each of us was so scared to see where the other one was at. We would talk almost every night. He would send me updates on his workouts; I'd send him some news on what was going on with me. Then, when Joseph died, he just shut off. I was so worried about Kale; that's when I knew I had very strong feelings for him. Then the Shawn thing happened."

"Yah, well, that didn't end too well for him." Alex teased Anne.

"No, it didn't." Anne agreed. "How are you doing with, well, you know?"

"As well as expected, I guess." Alex was watching the F.O.R. table talking to some other girls with their propaganda. "Losing him is so much harder than I realized."

***

The community of the Fallen Trinity's screaming was echoing inside the church. The anger was pointed at Kameron, but the hate was pointed at the one who followed the Lite. Inside the church was Roger Somberson preaching off to the side. Kameron was facing the crowd, standing behind the Martyrdom. It was an old circler horse troth that represented what the Lite used for baptism back before the Fallen began their appropriation. It was on some locked wheels to prevent it from rolling away during the Atonement.

Roger was screaming the word of the Fallen Trinity from the Dark Texts. Megan was sitting still in the front row. Disappointment was written all over her face. She gritted her teeth as she stared at him, telling him to do it now. Anne and Kale were off to the side, yelling at him that he couldn't wait forever. He turned to them as they both held a small, petite girl with a pale face and long black weaved hair. She had a cut on the side of her head and a wound bleeding from her neck. The white shirt she was wearing had evidence of blood protruding from her side. "Alex," he softly said to himself in a state of confusion.

121

"Kill her!" Megan finally stood up, pointing to the Martyrdom.

Kameron nodded as he motioned for Kale and Anne to bring her forward, and the crowd cheered even louder. The small girl who had her hands tied behind her back shook her body to prevent Kale and Anne from escorting her to the pool of water.

"I won't give you the satisfaction," she spit in Kale's face. She confidentially marched up to Kameron without Anne and Kale. She met Kameron with teary eyes. "I don't blame you. I just want you to know that. To show what you mean to me, I'm going to make this easy for you." She turned around and went to her knees. The water reflected her beaten face. She closed her eyes, mumbling the words of the Lite to herself before she forcefully put her own head under the water.

The crowd was shocked. They didn't know what to do. Roger got off the podium and pulled her up by the hair. "No." He turned to Kameron. "You must do it yourself!" He lifted Alex around as she was coughing as water dripped from her head. "Prove yourself. Look her in the eye as you do it."

"It's okay, Kameron." Alex calmly told him. "Really, it's okay."

Kameron watched Roger return to the podium as he smiled at Megan on the way up. Kameron wasn't sure, but he thought he saw a man in black behind Roger as he started to lead the Dark Madrigal. He turned back to Alex as he leaned her back over the water. He hesitated as he looked into her beautiful brown eyes.

"Kameron, I love you," she whispered, just before he forced her body into the water. He continued to hold her by the throat. The crowd cheered as he kept her submerged as her body started to thrash about. It seemed like an eternity before her body was starting to slow down in the movement. Her face had become lifeless under the water. Kameron's body came into shock on what he had just done. All he could do was stare at the body of the woman he cared for so much. Then she opened her eyes as they glowed a neon blue. He quickly stood up in shock as he turned to his right to a girl in renaissance clothing.

"There you are," she said out of relief.

Then everything went black.

Chapter Five

Alex choked on some water from her water bottle. "Son of bitch." The water dripped from her mouth, falling on her clothes. She realized that everyone at the city council meeting was staring at her. She met eyes with Roger. He gave her a dirty look after he had just finished giving his speech about the importance of the Pure Freedom Act.

Roger knew it wasn't intentionally aimed towards him, but Alex just took advantage of the situation. He motioned for the chairman to continue. The chairman spoke, "One more outburst like that, we'll have you removed." Alex just gave him a single snide crinkle of her face as a response. "Now that we have some order, we are going to vote on the motion of implementing the 'Pure Freedom' clause."

Father Carl leaned over to Alex. "This is the one that will remove all religious connotations from public purview. If this goes through, we may not survive the taxation. We'll have to close the church."

"But what about…" Alex was about to say until the priest put up his finger to have her keep quiet as the bill was put up for a vote. Alex recognized other clergy present; she saw the reverend of the Baptist church and a couple of other pastors. They all had worry written all over their faces.

The crowd was silent as the chairman read the bill and then called, "All in favor, say 'I,'" the sleazy-looking chairman ordered. All around the room were a bunch of confirmations from counsel. "Okay, effective immediately, the Pure Freedom taxation will be enforced. Mayor Somberson."

Father Carl just sat there stoically. "Damn it," was said under his breath.

Roger was applauded by over half the crowd as he took position in the center of the council. He raised his arms as he took it all in. "Thank you, thank you, really, stop," He paused for a second. "No, on second thought, keep going," he joked. The crowd laughed at his humor.

Alex just rolled her eyes to Anne. It was amazing how this crowd accepted his deceiving role in this town. Alex saw the overweight man from the bakery in the crowd as he had a different girl on his arm. He had the demeanor that he wasn't enjoying this meeting as well.

Roger began his speech. "I have a special police force in the planning stages who will report directly to me. If these special Sentinels get out of line, I will personally punish them to the full extent. They will not judge you on race, religion, sex, creed, or sexuality. Unlike the so-called churches in the area. We will become the bedrock of absolute power in this state." The audience cheered his decree. "Already, we are starting to see positive efforts in rebuilding the quarantine area. People, flourish in the fruit I offer you. CopperTop will be the piercing spear in a new direction. Don't fear the dark that lies ahead of you. I will be there right with you."

Alex's mouth dropped wide open at the fact that he bluntly stated his intention for everyone to hear. They were all deaf to his creed to them. Alex could have sworn she saw that man's eyes get darker as he stated his intentions.

"This is bad." Father Carl got on his phone to text Father Richard of the passing of the bill.

Alex couldn't stand it anymore. With a boatload of nervous energy, she stood up in the room. "I have a question."

The Chairman immediately slammed his mallet down. "Sit down, young lady. We are not taking questions at this time." The mass of people who supported the bill told her to sit down.

Roger hushed the crowd, "Quiet, please. I would like to hear what Ms. Johnson has to say."

All the eyes were fixated on Alex as she stood alone. Anne just closed her eyes in fear of what she was going to say. Father Carl was stone-faced as he just stared forward. Alex glared with vengeful hate. "Isn't that little cult of yours considered a religion according to this new law?"

The hissing of the crowd was volatile. The Dark was present in some of the people besides Roger as one of them flashed his red eyes at Alex. Still, she couldn't sense them. "I'll be seeing you soon," Alex thought to herself as she saw the man stare at her. "Well?" Alex gave Roger a little attitude.

"Oh, Alex, this is hardly the venue to air out old hurtful feelings." He turned to address the crowd, who were all focused on the two of them. "You see, back in high school Alex and I dated briefly. She never got over when I ended it with her."

"What?" Alex felt Father Carl forcefully tug her down before she did anything rash.

The crowd gave a low chuckle. "But to answer your question," Roger continued. "My organization is not a religion; it's a self-help program to absolute power. The self-help of the F.O.R. gives people the absolute power to get off drugs, find a good home from dangerous living conditions, and they are free to leave anytime they want." He motioned over to a group of F.O.R. members standing on the wall.

One of the boys stepped forward. "I have had the privilege of being with the organization for over three years now. I can say I was lost in life. The Road Map to Absolute Power has given me focus. I have to publicly thank Mr. Somberson for showing me what I can become." The boy stepped back as the crowd applauded.

"Alex, I'm sure you have more questions." Roger stepped closer in her direction. "I'll make sure you talk to a representative who achieved such power."

"I look forward to it," she yelled from her seated position.

The Chairman closed the meeting as the crowd started to leave. Father Carl leaned over to Alex. "What did that accomplish?"

"To show that we are not backing down from his bullshit," Alex grabbed Komptin to head back to the church. Tonight, she was going hunting; she was going to dispose of a Demon tonight, and she didn't care which one.

***

It was dark outside by the time Jennifer was finishing up the mayor's schedule as he was attending the city council meeting. Working for this Roger Somberson was so difficult. Not only did she have to work with the man who beat up her brother on the night her father died, but he was so secretive. He had her on pins and needles. It was a mistake to move back here after college. It was late, and the work was going to have to wait until tomorrow. She shut her computer off and grabbed her jacket. Underneath her jacket was a packet from the museum that he was waiting for. Her nerves shot up because she forgot all about it.

Out in the hallway, she heard the janitor removing a lot of the religious pictures in the hallway. "Hey, Larry," she called for the service custodian.

"What's up, Jen?" He stopped what he was doing to come talk to her.

"Can you get me into the mayor's office?" Her nerves were riled up, and Larry was her only saving grace.

"I'm not supposed to," Larry turned around to get to work.

"Larry, if the mayor doesn't see this first thing in the morning, I'm screwed," she pleaded.

"I don't know, Jen. I could get reported on if I do this." Larry was contemplating if he should or not. "I was under orders not to let anyone in there."

"Please," she begged.

He took in a deep breath. "Okay." He got out his keys. "Don't tell anyone I did this." He unlocked the door and made sure no one was in it. "This room gives me the creeps." He turned to leave. "You're on your own. Be sure to lock it."

"You have my word," she just stared into the office. It was generally plane inside, nothing really out of the ordinary, but it did feel creepy. She gently closed the door to the office and went straight to his desk to place the package. On his desk were the plans for funding the Sentinel program, ancient museum studies, and educational reform. She quickly skimmed through it to kind of see what his agenda was for CopperTop's future.

A book, the Road Map to Absolute Power, was on the shelf behind the desk. She took it off the shelf to open it up. Inside was a key that just fell out. She picked it up off the floor and stared around the room. This key was very old and heavy. There wasn't anything around that this would go to. The desk didn't have any locks that would fit this. Jen couldn't see anything around this key would open. Then, a cold breeze seemed to come from the wardrobe in the corner of the room.

This was stupid; she should have just left, but her curiosity got the better of her. She slowly crept over to the massive black coat closet. There was no lock on it, so the key didn't go to the doors. She opened the dual doors to see an ancient black book with writing on the cover she couldn't understand. Her body shivered as she went to touch it. It was warm to the touch. A bird flew by the window that made her jump. "Jesus," she said to herself.

The book smelled like burning sulfur. There was a metallic lock keeping the book together. She held the key in her hand, staring at it as she put the key in the lock. It seemed to guide itself into the hole at the eerie sound of it unhinging. The lock dropped to the ground, but Jen couldn't help herself; she didn't want to pick it up. This book: what was it? The writing seemed to be written in a black liquid–pictures of monsters inhabiting people who were standing in a circle of people in black robes.

Jen just flipped through the pages as her crucifix on her neck was starting to burn a bit. It looked as if the pages weren't finished yet. There was still writing that needed to be completed. "What are you into, Roger?" Jen said to herself. In the back of the book were some other loose pages. These were official reports from the museum. He circled item listings I0988 and F2322. They led to a word circled in the corner. "Misluna"

Then, there was another piece of paper folded in the back of the book. It was a list of names. Jen had seen these names before. They were names of the individuals who have been disappearing. Her heart rate started to sputter as she picked up her phone to look up the number of the local church. Her heart was pattering too fast to think. The only person she thought to talk to about what she had found was a priest. What should she do?

The phone ringing stopped. "Yes hello, I'm Jen…" but then she realized it was the voicemail. "This is Jen Rodriguez. I really need to talk to a priest. Meet me at the diner off of Weber and Moore…" Jen felt her phone get taken out of her hand.

Roger Somberson was behind her as he gently hung up the phone. "I knew I should have brought my personal assistant from the F.O.R. compound."

Jen stepped away from Roger, who was just staring at her. As she slowly backed away, she bumped into somebody. She turned around to see a man in a long black suit with a weird bird-like creature sitting on his shoulder. "I don't know what you're into, but you're not going to get away with it." Jen started to step to the back of the room, further away from the door.

"Yes, I am," Roger grabbed his phone from his pocket to call someone. "I think Larry's services are no longer required." He put the phone back into his pocket. "Jen, Jen, Jen. You have no idea the shit storm you just opened yourself to."

"Why do you have a list of all the people who disappeared, and what's in the museum?" Jen put her hands on her hips.

"Oh, that, that's nothing. I'm just into ancient artifacts." Roger turned around to flip through the Dark Texts. He knew that she saw what was in the book. He picked the lock off the floor to lock it back up. He gently closed the door before turning around. "Now, I have a choice to make."

"Are you going to fire me?" Jen asked him in fear.

Roger laughed out loud. "No. Don't worry about that." He turned to the man with the bird creature on her shoulder. "Is she one of them?" The bird creature shook his head. "Too bad, you might have had a small chance."

Jen was scared. "I want a lawyer or an HR representative."

That made Roger really laugh. "Yah, that's not happening." He started to slowly approach her, scanning her body up and down as he licked his lips.

"Well, there is something you should know about me," Jen said as she started backing up from Roger. The tall man continued to stare at her. "Something that may change your mind on what you're about to do."

"What's that?" Roger stopped his advancement.

"I'm a fan of the second amendment." She took out a small pistol and pointed it at Roger. "My dad was a cop, and I know my rights."

"Wait, were you Joseph Rodriguez's daughter?" Roger was starting to put it together.

"Still am," she kept the gun steady at Roger's body.

"That means you're Robbie's sister. Man, I really messed him up in high school, didn't I?" Roger sat down on the chair in front of his desk. "That takes me back." He stared off a bit and then turned his attention back to Jen. "That was the night I had your dad killed in the parking lot."

Jen's eyes grew big, then she shot Roger three times in the center of his body. He closed his eyes and held his breath. He let it out slowly as he slowly pulled the bullets out of this chest one at a time. "I liked that shirt." His eyes started glowing a neon red.

Jen went to scream but was muffled by the big man, who now had dark, misty wings attached to his

132

back. The bird creature was flying in the air with glowing red eyes. Roger stood up with his red eyes and sharpened teeth. She tried to escape the clutches of this evil, but she knew deep down, this was going to be the end.

* * *

The bridge walkway wasn't the most ideal place for Alex to grab a hold of the Demon's head. This hunt ended up on the dam where the river was raging due to the mountain run off. Alex couldn't help but flashback to falling in the river from the train. This dam was part of the running trail the town uses for bike riding and walking, but tonight, it was going to be a bridge to death. It was good fortune, though. The Demon she was fighting was the one from the council meeting. His head was met with a smash against her knee. Komptin was off hunting an Infiltrator that was paired up with the Demon. She tossed him in between the posts holding the railing.

The Demon was trying to get its head out as Alex kept on wailing on the man. She continued to punch the sides of the evil Host. She felt the ribs crack as she continued to hit it on its side. The Demon screamed in pain just before Alex jumped in the air and landed on its back. There was no doubt Alex broke it. She formed a knife, jamming her weapon straight into the back of the Demon's head. It screamed in pain before it dissipated into the ground.

Alex turned around to see two Infiltrators try to sneak up on her. One lunged at her, but it missed, and it fell over the railing. The other Infiltrator tackled Alex to the ground. It went to bite her head, but Alex dodged out of the way. Unfortunately, it got a hold of her shoulder. She screamed in pain as she jammed her finger into the beast's eye.

The Infiltrator put its sharpened claw on its eye, causing it to let go of Alex. It stumbled back as Alex ran at it. She ran past it, simultaneously grabbing its head, to forcefully drive it to the hardened ground. The second Infiltrator climbed over the railing to tackle Alex as she almost fell into the water. She managed to grab a hold of the railing to prevent herself from going over. In a desperate move, she kneed the Infiltrator in the stomach. It let go as a roar came over the top of the Infiltrator. The other went to finish Alex off, but she ducked onto the ground as the beast scraped the concrete railing. Sparks flew from the contact of its nails; Alex rolled out of the way. She immediately stood up to face her opponents.

They both flashed their neon-red eyes before running after her. She screamed as she charged them as well. They both went for her legs as she jumped over them. She immediately turned to Lite Beam one of them. It pushed it back far enough so she could attack the other one, pouncing it on top of its head when it charged her, driving its head onto the hard surface. Alex immediately started stomping on its head. Her foot caved its head in. She figured it was weak enough to dispose of, and she was correct. It disappeared into the ground. The other Infiltrator had a bit of black blood dripping from its nose.

Alex put her hands up and motioned for it to attack. It obliged. She managed to block the first swipe of its claws but got the second hit across her side. It then head-butted her in the nose, causing it to bleed. Alex stumbled backward as she felt a hit across her face, sending her twisting in the air. The landing hurt as she hit her head on the concrete.

The Infiltrator went for the kill with its claw, but Alex grabbed the creature's wrist. She used her free forearm to break the arm just before she flipped it over her back onto the ground and dropped her knee onto the Infiltrator's head. She formed a knife with her Lite to easily shove it into the Infiltrator's chest, causing it to disappear.

"That was fun." She checked her wounds to see how much blood was dripping. Alex quickly turned around as she hit an angel across the face. He had wings and black horns made of the black misty fog. She went to knee him in the crotch, but he blocked it, and he countered with a punch of his own.

Alex had never felt a hit like that before. He immediately kicked her in the side, sending her flying in the air. She crashed hard into the railing. She generated a Lite Beam, but the Dark Angel side-stepped. He charged her, but she moved out of the way, kicking the back of his knee and sending him to the ground. She generated another beam and shot him in the back of the head. It pushed him down, scraping his face into the concrete.

He immediately stood up with no markings on his face. She didn't cause any damage to him. "I told you we would meet again."

"Oh, Boy, am I the lucky one?" Alex put her hands on her cheeks, eyes wide in mock surprise.

The angel calmly walked toward her. "Malkaroy knew he would die at my hands; does it scare you knowing that you will die tonight?"

"Oh, shut up," Alex went on the offensive.

Azrael blocked every punch and a kick intended for him. He grabbed Alex's wrist with one hand; the other grabbed her throat. He head-butted her in the face, causing Alex to bleed more. He picked her up off the ground and slammed her back into it. He studied her face, looking at the scar on the side of her face.

"That is a from a Sentry." Azrael studied Alex as he was squeezing her throat. He picked her up and punched her on the same side of the face the scar was. "I know that hurts."

"Get it over with, will you?" Alex spit in his face. She then kicked him in the stomach, but it had little effect on him.

"I'm going to regret killing you. You would be an interesting one for Conversion. I can see why my master, Vandor, wanted to choose you." The Dark Angel went to give Alex a fatal blow but was tackled by Komptin. The massive gargoyle dog ended up on top of the angel. He immediately went for the throat to end Azrael's existence. The Dark Angel grabbed Komptin's by the neck before he could tear into him. Azrael still stood up while still holding onto his throat. "Komptin, my dear boy.

You should have gone home after my Master killed Osiah." He pulled him closer as if he were studying the massive gargoyle. Azrael took a moment before slamming him onto the ground. Azrael formed his axe, made of pure red light. He went to swing but was stomped on from above.

Dinah grabbed Komptin to get him out of the way while Devine tossed Azrael. The darkest of the angels didn't hit the ground. He caught himself in the air, and slowly descended to the ground.

Alex moaned as she got up, "That did not feel good." She slowly got up to turn to the battle. She had a splitting headache and was already starting to get sore. That didn't stop her from igniting her fists to face her adversary.

The four defenders of the Lite stood ready in their battle stances. Komptin was ready to leap with blood dripping from his nose. Alex's eyes and fists were lit as she was waiting for the next move. The two Lite Angels showed their skills with their respective weapons before getting ready for Azrael to attack.

The bird-like creature landed on his master's shoulder, and it whispered something in his ear. He nodded to it as he stared down his opponents. "Devine, I really look forward to talking to you."

"Azrael, what you are doing is wrong. Your defection from the Lite does not exclude you from forgiveness." Devine dropped her weapons. "She knows this, she saw something in you."

"Shut your mouth, you un-pure Lite whore. I know what you let them do to you," Azrael shouted at Devine. "You have no room to talk."

Alex turned to Devine to see the hurt on her face as her wings drooped with sadness. Alex's eyes flashed as she went to charge Azrael, but Dinah grabbed her. "You son of a bitch! I'm going to rip your black heart right out of your hollowed chest!"

"Quiet, hybrid," Dinah was having difficulty holding the Lite Sentry back. "He will kill you easily, and that will accomplish nothing." Dinah turned to her brother. "You are outmatched. You know this."

Azrael dissipated his weapons. "Perhaps, but you know me sisters. I'm always looking six hundred and sixty-six steps ahead." He disappeared into the night sky.

Komptin took a big breath before trying to relax. Alex came in front of him and wiped the blood from his nose with her thumb. She smiled at him, giving him a silent 'thank you' as she kissed him on top of his head.

Alex turned to the two angels. "Not that I'm complaining, but what are you doing here?"

Dinah went to check on her purple-haired sister, who still had a look of shame on her face. "I am tired of being a failure."

***

"What in the hell?!" Kameron sat up in bed. Beads of sweat dripped down his back, and it took him a minute to catch his breath. The hope that the Falling Trinity would stop these nightmares slowly diminished after each one. He wiped the crust off his eyes as he realized Megan was still sleeping. The time on his watch, charging on the nightstand, told him he had another hour before he had to get up. Going back to bed wasn't going to be an option.

"Get up or go back to bed," Megan mumbled as she turned over. The pull of covers meant she wasn't getting up with him.

"Sorry," he leaned over to kiss her.

"I'm trying to sleep," she shrugged him off.

"Okay, sorry," he quietly got out of bed. His bathrobe was on the back of the bedroom door. It was July, but he was still cold for some reason. The temperature was fine; it was just a sickly, empty feeling.

The house was dead quiet this early in the morning. It was a rare occasion that Megan had spent the night. Probably because Kameron was still at his parent's house. After he graduated college, he got the job with the Sentinels. Staying with his parents was only temporary until he saved up enough to put a down payment on a house.

The sky had a sense of a storm coming, but a bit of blue peeked through the clouds. Hopefully, this would pass before the barbecue they were hosting after the church services today. There was no point to worry about that time. The time was quickly approaching to get ready for work. Luckily, he would be able to make the service right after he left the office. He just had to go in to finish his report for the Supervisory Sentinel about the arrest he made just before his shift ended.

Kameron had detained a suspect of this mis-practice of religion last night. Hence, the reason he had to go in this morning. The prisoner kept refusing he wasn't a Lite Follower, but he had one of those underground pamphlets in his bag during a random Ideology Check. He claimed he got it from someone on the street, but during the investigation, he couldn't identify who did it. Kameron took him in for transfer to rejuvenation.

He shivered at the thought of being sent there. Most people returned from that program with multiple injuries. They had to cleanse the Lite out of them. It was a necessary but painful process. Kameron will never forget arresting that guy. The fear in his eyes as the Chariot arrived was something he would never forget. It was necessary for their purge of the wrong ideology.

There were rumors of unfounded religious movement of Lite Worshipers in the area. They preached fabricated stories about a forgiving Lord. It was pure blasphemy and dangerous. The fear of the Fallen Trinity is what people needed. There was a pecking order to keep people in line. The more you worshiped the power of the Fallen, the more you rose in the ranks, keeping power over the ones below you.

After Kameron showered, he put on his uniform and utility belt and ensured all his equipment was accounted for: cuffs, pepper spray, and his gun. The reflection in the mirror was of him standing in his uniform. The patch on his shoulder was black with an upside-down star with three lines on top of it. On his right side was a red armband sown onto his uniform. The image of two horns coming out of the silhouette of the badge. Inside, were the red eyes of the Fallen. A constant reminder that he's always watching.

Megan was now in the kitchen, staring at the house across the street. He peeked to see what she was intensely staring at. "Looks like someone finally bought that house." He leaned in for a kiss.

"Maybe they will clean it up." She kissed Kameron. "You need to be quieter in the morning. If I'm not on the top of my game for Roger Somberson, then I might not get the job as his assistant."

"You'll get it," Kameron grabbed some coffee. "You know, I was thinking, if you get this job, maybe we should look into moving in together."

Megan half chuckled. "So, you'll finally move out of your parent's house?"

Kameron took that sarcastic tone. "Well, we should start our life together, don't you think?"

Megan looked at her watch. "Ooo, I gotta go. Bye." She gave him a quick kiss before heading out in her convertible.

Kameron finished his coffee as both his parents came down. "Morning."

His dad showed his cup to his wife for some coffee. "Did Megan leave for work?"

"Just a little bit ago." Kameron grabbed his keys from the rack. "You look tired."

"Dog had its puppies last night." His dad rubbed his eyes.

"Really?" Kameron peeked outside at the doghouse. "I'm going to check on them on my way to work. I should be back in time for service and the picnic."

141

"You have to go in this morning?" His mom gave him a kiss on the cheek.

"I have that report to turn in on a guy I arrested during the Ideology Check," Kameron told her.

"Such horrible, wretched people. Spreading lies and not understanding the meaning of absolute power." His mom grabbed some eggs from the kitchen.

"People like should be hung in the middle of town after a severe beating." His dad grabbed the morning paper from the front door. "I see someone is moving in next door."

Kameron started to head out the door behind his father. "Apparently. I gotta go if I want to make it in time for service."

Kameron stepped outside to see the movers hauling in some furniture. Kameron went to check on their German Shepherd, Hinsdale. The tired new mother just peeked her eyes at Kameron as she was nursing the puppies. "Hey, girl." Kameron petted her. "Wow, seven little puppies. Congratulations." Kameron gently rubbed behind her ears. "I gotta go to work. Nice job, mommy." The tired new mother just fell back asleep.

Kameron walked out to his car, which was parked on the side of the street, where he met the new neighbor. She was telling the movers where the boxes needed to go. He politely waved to the girl with the long brown hair, who was a bit reserved waving back. The movers grabbed the box from her before she came over to Kameron. "Welcome to the neighborhood."

"Thanks. My sister and I are just renting this place." The brown-eyed girl was a bit hesitant to approach Kameron. "I'm Cara."

"Kameron." The two shook hands.

"I see you're a Sentinel," she saw the patch on his arm. "That must be rewarding."

"It does more than pay the bills," Kameron's watch beeped. "I need to get going to work. Welcome to the neighborhood. If you need worship today, Roger Somberson puts on a great service at the Alter at eleven. Then we are having a picnic here for a late BBQ. You and your sister are welcome to come."

"Maybe we will," Cara studied him. "Do you need me to bring anything?"

"Just you and your sister. I really need to go." He went over to the driver's side door. "See you around one." Kameron stopped as he saw a figure in the window, but he couldn't make it out. It must have been her sister. The time was escaping from him. He really needed to get that report done before the service started.

Chapter Six

Alex turned to the window, her peripheral vision thought she caught something in the reflection. "Ow," she snapped her head back to Father Carl, who was giving her medical care. His demeanor changed a bit when she came into the church, all bloodied. "You're surprisingly good at this."

"Not my first patch job." Father Carl finished stitching Alex's arm. Then, he studied Alex's finger, which was a bit crooked. "Something I've been dying to say to you for a while, Alex, you're out of this church and out of CopperTop."

Alex's eyes widened as she could feel the blood rush to her face. "You have no right, you son of a...." Then, with a sharp pain, Father Carl pulled on her finger to put it back into place. "Ow, son of bitch, that hurt."

Father Carl tried to hide a little snicker. "I had to distract you. Is it better?"

Alex moved her fingers. "Yes."

"Does this happen often with you?" Father Carl changed out the gauze from her forehead.

"It's not my first time getting combat aid from a priest." She couldn't help but think of similarities between this situation and when Father Tom was treating her.

The small cut on her head was stingy when he put some sort of medical stuff on the gauze. The small pad on the side of her face was starting to leak blood. Father Carl wiped the blood off the side of her face, unveiling her scar. He then unsnapped her collar to remove it, revealing the evidence of her first battle with a Demon. "I need to check to see if you have any broken ribs." He looked around the room. "We can wait until Anne or Megan arrives for a witness."

"We are in trouble if I can't trust a priest," Alex took off her shirt, still in her sports bra. Father Carl helped her. He studied her charred skin before he touched it. Alex winced as he pressed and prodded on charred skin, checking for broken bones.

"I don't feel anything broken; where does it hurt? Does it feel near the surface or like internal damage? It's hot to the touch." He immediately felt her head for a fever.

"It's always hot, just as it's always hurting." Alex rubbed her scar with her fingers to feel the heat radiate from Sanah's stabbing. "A departing gift from a former coworker."

Father Carl moved to the other side. "There is some bruising, but it doesn't look broken." He went into his closet and grabbed a zipped-up sweatshirt. "Here. Put this on." He threw it to her.

"Thanks." Alex put on the sweatshirt.

"Let me ask you something," Father Carl leaned back on the wall. "Why'd you accept being a Sentry? You're young, full of life…a future ahead of you."

Alex smiled, "Why did you join the Army?"

"Marines," Father Carl corrected. "But I get it. You think it's something cool at first, but then the reality of war hits you like a ton of bricks."

"I lost my best friend the night I got this," she pointed to the scar on her neck. "Her dad accepted infiltration. I killed the bastard that same night. Still, the memories don't go away." She pointed to her scar.

"Emotional memories are a far, much deeper scar." Father Carl had a blank look as he stared out the window. There was a pause for a moment, almost like he was debating what he would say about what was on his mind. "I've seen wounds and losses on both sides; I've murdered enemy combatants, men, women, and children, all by my hand. The aftermath is still the same: parents crying over their dead children. We justify our actions to ourselves so we can sleep at night. There is no reason for God's children to fight each other like that."

Alex didn't say anything. It wasn't the time. She just stared at the man who she never realized was fighting his own inner demons. Alex was about to say something until Father Carl's attention went to the church phone line as there was a message on the machine. "Did you forward the phones to me before you left?"

"I swear I did," Alex saw the blinking message indicator.

Father Carl didn't hide the disappointment on his face before he picked up the receiver to play the message on the phone of a frantic girl. "I have to go." Father Carl grabbed his jacket. "Are you good?"

"I'm fine. Do you want me to come with?" Alex gasped as she hopped off his desk.

"No, this is a priestly matter." Father Carl grabbed his keys to take off to the location of the frantic phone call.

Father Carl didn't have any trouble finding the diner where the scared girl was going. It was empty, with only one waitress and a cook cleaning up the restaurant. He looked around but didn't see any customers. There was no hiding the disappointment on his face.

"What can I get you, father?" The waitress grabbed her notepad.

"Did you see a girl in here by any chance? Maybe looked upset?" The fear of missing the young woman had him frantic.

The waitress put her notepad down. "There was one girl who sat over there by herself waiting for someone, but then she left maybe ten minutes ago."

Father Carl bit his lip. "Okay, thanks." He left a couple of dollars on the counter before he left to see if he could track down the young woman.

"Father," a girl's voice came up behind.

Father Carl turned around. "Thank God, I thought I missed you."

The young blonde girl smiled. "I thought I missed you too." Her eyes slowly turned to glow a neon red.

***

Roger enjoyed being able to sit back in his chair at the F.O.R. Compound. He closed his eyes to feel the power behind this desk. Absolute Power.

147

What he wanted, he got, no one questioned him. Unlike when he sits behind the mayor's desk. People didn't respect or fear him there, but that would change very soon.

There was a knock on the door. His older secretary, Beatrice, came in with a sealed document with a wax sealant of the upside-down number four. "I have the listing for the Sentinel Command."

"Oh, give me." Roger broke the seal to the list. It was mainly made of Demons and Provisionaries. This was good. "Fetch me, Sorol."

"I have him waiting outside, sir." She said with such pride.

"We're going to add to your duties," Roger continued to scan the list. "I need someone I can trust."

"Of course, my Leader," Beatrice nodded with complete obedience.

"Send Sorol in," Gron leaned back in his chair, reading the list. "Oh, and get me..." He started to say, but his secretary already handed him his drink. He was a little shocked as he took the drink. "Ever think of gaining absolute power?"

She turned around to her leader in shock, "Excuse me, sir?"

"We'll talk later," Gron told her. "In the meantime, send Sorol in here."

The Demon entered the room with the new Dark Angel, Raguel. He was a tall man, proud. "Yes, my Leader."

"Once I implement this in the town." He held up the Sentinel Command list. "I want the quarantine cleaned and secure the rebuild construction crews. Then I want you to issue citations to anyone that displays anything that promotes the Lite."

"Yes, my Leader, what about the churches?" Sorol stood in his new Sentinel uniform.

"Wait a bit on that one. I need the town's backing before we start our offensive." Gron leaned to the side as he saw Misluna glide into the room. She didn't look happy. "Excuse me, one second." The Dark Angel and Sentinel Commander bowed as they left the room.

Misluna waited until they shut the door before she snapped. "Where the hell is my book?"

"Watch your tone. Let me remind you who you are talking to," He got up from the desk as he slammed his drink. "Your book is safely stored in my office in town."

"Why?" She was still obviously upset.

"Was it done?" Gron leaned on his desk trying to hold in his temper.

Misluna was nervous about that question. If she told him it was done, he could dispose of her; he wouldn't need her. "Well..."

"Answer me!" he commanded with a thunderous tone.

"Yes, my Leader," she instantly answered with trembling fear. "Of all I know, but there is always more that can be added."

He got up from the desk, staring her down before he kissed her. "Don't worry then. I'm not going to get rid of you. Did they ask you yet?"

"Not yet," Misluna shamefully admitted.

"They will," Gron turned around to sit down on the couch. "What do you know about the Demophrims?"

"Just the theory, really, an offspring of a Demon and human, but none have ever been created since Demons can't produce children with primates." Misluna was confused.

"Is there a symbol of them?" Gron sat back, twirling his drink.

"Yes," Misluna cautiously approached his desk to grab a piece of paper. She drew a symbol of two triangles facing down diagonally. They hovered over a human on a straight line. "Something like this. Is that why you took my book, to research this?"

Gron slightly nodded.

"It's a fairy tale, they can't exist." Misluna reminded him.

"Is it in the book?" Gron tested her. This answer would see if she lived or died at the moment.

"Of course, but it's only one line because that's all they know. There's never been one." Misluna was getting nervous over this line of questioning. "I wouldn't get your hopes up."

"I'll keep you around. There's something I need to show you. In the meantime..." he patted the seat next to him.

Misluna knew exactly what that meant. She smiled as she stared at Gron. "Show me your teeth." Gron grew his teeth as he flashed his eyes. She seductively stalked towards him as she started unbuttoning her shirt. She straddled him as he bit onto her neck. Laughing in sexual pain, she tightly grabbed his hair.

Gron turned his head to see that bird-like creature on the sofa staring at him. It startled him enough to throw Misluna on the ground. "What the hell?" His drink also spilled all over the floor.

Misluna cringed with agony as her tailbone hit the floor. "That hurt. Do it again." She twisted her body to see Azrael standing in the corner.

The master of the F.O.R. didn't like he had to refill his own drink. "Enjoying the show? Care to try it?" Gron offered Misluna to the Dark Angel.

The Dark Harridan showed him more of her cleavage as she got up from the floor to lie on the couch. "It'll be an experience like you never had."

Azrael turned his back to Gron. "Not again," then he faced the Leader. "We obtained another Pure of Heart. The Sentry here did not perish."

"Phooey," Misluna pouted.

"She is a lucky one," Gron took a sip while staring at Misluna with lust.

"There is something you must see, though." Azrael watched as his Pytho landed on his shoulder.

***

Father Carl had nothing but black in front of him with the smell of a used potato bag over his head. His survival and P.O.W. training instantly kicked in upon his capture. For the most part, he was just keeping quiet as he tried to listen for any clues on his destination, but he pretty much knew where he was headed. The rope around his neck and

151

hands was just so tight that it was going to leave marks. It made it easier for the Dark to control him. All he could do was start planning his escape. He was trying to count how long he was riding and if he could recognize the turns, smells, and sounds of where he was going. If they wanted him dead, they would have killed him already. There was no logical reason he could think of why the Demon didn't kill him. She had the opportunity, clearly the means to carry it out. Father Carl felt steps as he felt cemented stairs below his feet. Why did they want him alive? The sound of the heavy steel door opening signaled his journey's end. Multiple hands caught him as he was shoved into his prison.

"It's okay, we got you," a man gently told him in the most calming voice he could muster.

Father Carl heard the door lock as the man started to untie the rope from his neck along with another, setting his hands free. "Thank you. Where are we?"

"I don't know," the man lifted up his hood.

Father Carl was now in a room with cots and wool blankets, and a small room in the back that was obviously a lavatory. There was a small pile of bowls on a crate. "I'm Father Carl Gray,"

"I'm James, and this is Sam." He pointed to the man holding the rope from his hands. "We were all taken to this place with no explanation."

"Is anyone hurt?" Father Carl felt his need to start setting up a chain of command. He started to assess how his people were.

"No, there are no injuries. They just feed us, that's it." James just showed him the bowls on the table.

"Have we established we are who we all say we are?" Father Carl surveyed the room.

"Meaning?"

"We should all be good, Father," a female voice said from the background.

The crowd departed to show Kaylee walking up to Father Carl to give him a big hug. "It's so nice to see a familiar face."

He returned the hug. "Kaylee, what are you doing here?"

"That seems to be the million-dollar question," Kaylee held her stomach.

"How's the baby?" Father Carl put his hand on her stomach after silently asking permission. He was feeling around for any damage.

"He's fine," Kaylee assured him. "At first, I thought they were going to kill me, but all in all, they left me alone. They are more interested in someone else for some reason."

"Who?" Then, the doors were unlocked before the steel door opened. The guards threw a man in a white jumpsuit, covered in dirt and blood. He landed on the ground as he was kicked one last time before the guards left.

"This is Scotty," Kaylee felt ill seeing the bruises he endured.

James and Sam gently helped him up to the nearest cot. "They only take him," James said as he carefully checked his wounds.

"They really worked him over this time," Sam went to grab a bowl to fill it with water from the wall. There was a button that gave them water from a hole. They started to wipe the blood from a torn piece of blanket soaked in water.

"I know this man. He's an agent with the federal government," Father Carl joined James. "Is there anyone with medical training here?"

"My name is Rachel. I'm a dental assistant," one girl came up. "But that's the closest we have."

"Well, I guess you'll be my assistant." Father Carl stated. "I have combat medical training."

"I was in the 501st Infantry, Army," James shook his hand.

"I was just an admin troop in the Air Force," Sam chimed in. "Other than that, that's all the military we have in the room."

"Marines, third division, Capt," Father Carl shook the hands of the men. "Obviously, we are not in an active-duty situation, but we'll have to maintain some sort of command here." He turned to Scotty. "Scotty, this is Father Carl. I'm a friend of Alex Johnson, Anne McClure, and Megan Rofush."

Scotty started opening his eyes, "No, you can't trust her." Scotty started to try to get away from Father Carl.

"Rachel, hold him down. He's going to get himself hurt." Father Carl tried to calm the tortured man down. "Scotty, it's okay. I'm not here to hurt you."

"You don't understand, she's not who you think," Scotty tried to get up.

"Who?"

The doors opened to the Mayor of CopperTop Mountain. Father Carl stood up standing in front of Scotty. Gron was the first to speak, "Well, this is interesting."

"Why have you brought us here?"

"Shut up," Gron slapped him across the face with the back of his hand.

Father Carl held his face when he saw Megan behind the lead Demon. "Megan."

Megan started to fake cry, "Oh Father, help me, will you? This man still hasn't had his way with me." She laughed as she kissed Gron on the cheek.

Father Carl was dumbfounded. "How could you betray us like this?"

"Betray? I was never on board." She started to laugh.

Gron leaned over to see a bleeding Scotty on the cot. "How's he coming along?"

Then, an attractive lady came from behind. "He's got a pure heart but hates Him with a passion."

"Continue working on him," Gron studied the man lying down.

"Why are we here?" Father Carl demanded.

"Don't worry about it." Gron turned to Misluna. "Prevent the Sentry from looking for him."

"I will," Misluna assured him. They both left with the sound of the door slamming shut.

***

155

Alex was impatiently waiting by the window. It didn't make sense why it was taking this long. She looked at her watch again, then back out the window, but there was no sign. "This is getting ridiculous." Alex impatiently voiced her opinions to her sister-in-law.

Anne just sat down, watching her friend pace back and forth. "Alex, he'll be here."

"He should be here by now. It's not that far away." Alex's heart stopped when she heard a car pull up. But it turned out to be Megan. The time on her watch seemed to be ticking backward.

"What's going on?" When Megan entered the church, she got a little nervous staring at a pacing Alex. She turned to Anne. "Who is she looking for?"

Anne was about to speak until Alex yelled, "Finally!"

Both Megan and Anne watched Alex run to the door. Alex was annoyed, "Where were you?"

The young sixteen-year-old boy got nervous when he saw Alex. It was obvious he was a bit smitten by her. "Sorry, that's a double pepperoni, sausage, thick crust."

"Yes, thank you!" Alex went into her wallet to tip the kid, then shut the door. She immediately opened the box and took a bite before offering any to the others.

Megan also took a slice before sitting down at her desk. "Sorry I'm late. It was a rough night."

"It's slow, no big." Alex looked around with a mouth full of food.

Anne picked off the meat to give to Komptin, lying on the ground. "Sweetie, something dropped out of your wallet." She pointed to the floor.

Alex had a mouthful of delicious pizza when she saw Kameron's Secret Service Access Card lying on the ground. "Oh, thanks." She picked up the card and took a quick second before putting it in her pocket.

Megan could see the hurt on her face. "Alex, it might make you feel better if you talk about it. Why did he leave?" She tried to say with as much fake empathy as possible.

Anne was waiting for "high school" Alex to go off, but to her surprise, it seemed as if she was about to answer Megan. Then she just came out with, "Has anyone seen Father Carl?"

Anne shook her head while wiping the sauce off the side of her mouth.

"He took a call and hasn't returned." Alex was already going after her second piece.

Megan acted like she was waiting to swallow before answering. "He told me to let you know he had to go out of town. Something about his old unit and one of his friends."

Alex dipped her end crust into some pizza sauce that dripped onto the box. "Whatever. Vacation." She did a little dance of happiness now that he was gone for a bit.

Anne tapped her coffee cup with one of her pinky fingers. "So, Roger will be implementing the Pure Freedom Act tomorrow."

"You think we should remove the crucifix from the steeple." Megan was reading her email.

"Roger Somberson can kiss my ass," Alex got up to grab an Apollo from the fridge.

Anne actually came to Megan's defense. "We'll never survive the fines. We'll have to close the doors, and what good would that be."

Alex shook her head with annoyance. "It's just wrong."

"It won't last long," Anne told her. "All we need is a lawyer to sue; it will go to the State Supreme Court, and then they will rule it goes against the First Amendment."

"The town voted on it," Megan played Devil's advocate. "He convinced them it was a good idea."

Anne got up to refill her coffee. "This is just the beginning of Roger's plan. Who knows what he plans for the future?"

Alex chugged her Apollo. "Too bad we couldn't get close to him, take the offensive to him."

Anne snickered at the obscurity of that suggestion. "Who would we send? He hates you. Pretty sure I stick out in his mind." Then Anne got serious as she saw the determination on Alex's face. "Alex, no. You can't."

"Watch me. Hey Megan, Roger seemed to be a little smitten with you." Alex yelled across the room to her.

"He did seem a little preoccupied with me." Megan fluffed her hair a bit. Then, she acted innocent. "Why?"

"When was the last time you went on a date?" Alex grinned.

Kameron snuck into the church service, where he found Megan sitting next to his mom and his sister, Michelle. His baby sister scooted over to let him sit next to Megan. She leaned into him. "You're late, naughty, naughty," she teased. "The Fallen Trinity will not be happy with you."

"That report took longer than expected." He felt a hit on his leg as Megan gave him a combined annoyed look with a nonverbal telling him to be quiet.

Michelle rolled her eyes as she sat there listening to Roger Somberson preach about Absolute Power. Kameron disciplined himself to take in the rest of the sermon without interrupting. Once the preaching ended, there were four children who were ceremonially given the Road Map to Absolute Power. The pride in their faces as they received their study material was truly an amazing sight.

Roger Somberson led the way out of the church with the choir in their black robes, holding red candles with black flame. He quickly turned around, which shocked everyone as he yelled, "Absolute Power!"

The crowd cheered as they stood up to leave the service. Kameron's dad grabbed his coat. "Go get the car, and make sure the air conditioning is on." He gave his keys to Kameron's mom. With his presence, there was no doubt he was in charge of the family. Kameron only wished he could have that kind of power. Though, in the relationship

159

between him and Megan, it's truly noticeable the power is going to go to her. There was no doubt that the assistant job to Roger Somberson was going to her, and that would bump her status not only in society but in their relationship.

They left as a family, with Megan following Kameron's dad leading out the front. She stopped in front of Roger to shake his hand. "Truly a remarkable ceremony."

"The fear of the Fallen Trinity is not something you should take lightly." The Leader smiled at Megan. "I can see you know that already. That's why when you report for work Monday, I expect the best."

"You mean I got the job?" Megan joyfully cheered.

"Just one little thing we have to cover, then yes, it's yours," Roger held her hand. Megan couldn't help but grin ear to ear as everyone congratulated her accomplishments.

"All that work you've been putting in paid off," Kameron went to kiss her, but she turned so he would only get her cheek.

Michelle was the first to say something. "Maybe now you can write off those knee pads as a business expense." Everyone immediately turned to Michelle in horror. "For all that praying to the Fallen you've been doing. What were you guys thinking?"

"We'll see you at the picnic, Leader?" Harold asked him. "I made sure the food spread is well worth your presence."

"Of course, I'm sure it is. I have a meeting with the governor regarding the upcoming movement those Lite bastards are pushing, but after that, I'll be sure to make myself known."

"We'll get those Lite Followers," Kameron vowed to the Leader. "They'll pay for their defiance."

"They will get what they deserve," Roger waved to some other people. "I have to go. I'll see you there."

Megan turned to Kameron. "I can't believe you embarrassed me like that." Kameron was following a clearly upset Megan to the car.

"What do you mean?" Kameron got into the driver's seat.

"Arriving late to service. Everyone was looking at me as you sat next to me." Megan started to get into him. "What was so important anyways?"

"I had to finish that report. I needed to verify he was guilty of Impurification." Kameron started the car.

"What more proof do you need? All you did was waste time and arrive late." Megan put her makeup on using the mirror. "Now, let's get to your parent's house for the get-together."

They arrived at his dad's house, where the food was already prepped to go. It just needed to be cooked and served. He got out of the car to see a girl come out the doorway of the house across the street. She was small, pale-faced, with long, weaved-in black hair. She wore dark makeup and wore a collar around her neck. She waved to Kameron and Megan.

"Who is that?" Megan asked with disgust.

"I'm assuming the new neighbor," Kameron answered back the wave that brought the small girl to them.

"Hi, I'm Alex," She shook the hands of the Kameron and Megan. Megan didn't really seem thrilled with it.

"I'm Megan. This is my boyfriend Kameron, who has to help set up for the picnic." Megan went inside the house, leaving Kameron.

"Wow, she has some Power," Alex tried to hide her impression of Megan, but failed miserably.

"And doesn't mind showing it," Kameron replied and then realized what he said. He frantically made sure no one heard it.

"You're safe with me," Alex teased. "My sister went to town to get some food. We were so busy unpacking we forgot we didn't have anything to eat."

Then, a car came up behind Kameron's. Kale came out of the vehicle with Anne. They both approached Alex and Kameron. "Hi. I'm Kale. This is my wife, Anne."

"How's it going?" The chipmunk-cheeked fiancé of Kale shook Alex's hand.

"Oh, I'm sorry, this is Alex," Kameron told them. They all greeted Alex.

"My sister Cara and I are renting this place." She pointed to the house. "She's a managing director to the Read Readers." Alex let them know.

Anne had shock written all over her face. "That's a very prominent book franchise."

Kale grabbed Anne's hand. "What do you do?"

Alex laughed, "Trying to get my life in order."

"Well, the Fallen can definitely give you the Power to do that." Kale kissed Anne on the cheek. "I'm going to go to the backyard."

"I'll join you in a minute." She blushed as she watched her fiancé go to the picnic.

There were a lot more guests starting to show up at the house. "I should get going," Kameron told her. "Why don't you and your sister join us? There will be plenty of food."

"Just give me a bit, and I'll be over. Is there anything I can bring?" Alex offered. "I have, well, paper cups."

"No, just yourselves," Kameron smiled as he walked back with Anne. "She's nice."

"I like her," Anne said as the two of them went around to the backyard.

The house and backyard were now full of people laughing, playing, and grouped about. The food was almost ready as the meat on the grill was sizzling, with Harold attending the food. Everyone was greeting Roger as he came in, waving to everyone like a politician at a rally.

Alex came to the party with Cara behind her. She found her way to Kameron. "Hi, Kameron. This is Cara." She motioned to her sister.

"Yes, we met." Kameron shook her hand. "How's everything going?"

"Interesting. There's stuff I've never thought of in a place like this?" Cara studied the area. "Nothing I could never dream of."

Kameron didn't understand what she meant, but he just blew it off. He turned to Alex. "All moved in?"

"Not even close," Alex told him. "Who's that?" She pointed to the Church Leader.

"That's Roger Somberson, he's the Leader of the area. His Power is unmatched around the state." Kameron watched as he was greeting the people.

"Ah," Alex studied the red-haired religious man. "Makes sense." The two sisters had a silent conversation with each other.

Roger came up to shake hands with Kameron. "Place looks good."

"It's my parent's house," Kameron clarified to his religious leader.

"Well, I'm hungry. Are we ready to eat?" Roger eyed Alex. "Who is this?"

"Alex and my sister, Cara," Alex put her hand on her chest.

"I'm the Leader, Roger." He pointed to himself. "I don't recall seeing you in service."

Kameron quickly jumped in, "They literally just moved into their house this morning."

Roger just stared at Alex. "Then we'll see you at the night service."

"I'm sure it would be interesting," Alex answered him back.

Harold came up with a plate full of cooked meat. "Foods ready!" The crowd cheered and applauded. "Leader, it would be our honor to conduct the Offering."

Kale and Anne approached Kameron on the other side. The two of them holding hands tightly. "Are we going to eat soon?" Kale was just staring at the food. "My stomach is growling."

"Shh, honey, we still have the Offering, then we can eat." Anne kissed him on the cheek.

Roger addressed the crowd. "I think the Fallen would be upset if the Offering didn't take place." The crowd parted so Roger could make his way to an empty table. He was just about to start but was looking around. "What will you be the Offering?"

Harold was looking around frantically. "I guess I could grab something from the house."

Megan came in front of the crowd. "An occasion like this, the Offering should be something really special."

The guests were trying to think of something. Kale's stomach rumbled in hunger. "The dog had puppies." Kale nonchalantly offered as he chuckled.

Anne gasped loudly as she hit Kale. "It's a symbolic ceremony."

"No, I believe an occasion like this deserves an old school Offering," Roger demanded. "Fetch me one."

Megan took that as a command from her new employer. She grabbed a male dog from the litter. It was shivering in fear when she placed it on the table.

"He wouldn't?" Alex stared at the table. She turned to Cara, who had a look of disgust on her face that she was trying to hide.

Roger began the ceremony. "The Fallen Trinity is Power. There is nothing but to obey the Fallen."

The crowd chanted. "Fear the Fallen."

Roger continued, "In this Offering to the Fallen, we show how Lite is weak by the taking of the children. The Fallen is Absolute."

The crowd followed with, "Absolute Power."

"Now, this blade will take the life, just as it took the life of the Conduit by the Warrior Prophet Osiah. The Dark Reigns!"

"Forever the Trinity of the Fallen!" The crowd cheered as he drove the knife into the puppy on the table.

A quick, high-pitched sound came from the small puppy, causing Alex to turn her head into Kameron's arm to shield her eyes. He just looked down at the young woman, who seemed paler than before. "Was that your first live Offering?" Alex just nodded as she stayed in Kameron's arm. "First one is always rough."

Roger studied the bloody knife. "Nothing like the control of Absolute Power." He then turned to the crowd. "Let's eat."

Chapter Seven

Alex threw her hot dog on the plate. The blood from her face seemed to drain. "Yuck, this is disgusting." Alex pushed her plate away from her. "Seriously, gross."

"Didn't like that one? The other two seemed to go down well," Megan continued to eat her chicken sandwich.

Anne sipped her iced tea as she picked out all the ham from her salad. They were sitting outside of the mall in the former quarantine area. Clean-up crews and volunteers from F.O.R. were helping local vendors get their shops back up and running. "Alex, this isn't a good idea."

The Lite Sentry just returned from throwing her hot dog away. "He was all over her. What is one date going to hurt?" Alex washed the remnants of her hot dog with an Apollo.

"He could kill her if he finds out." Anne turned to Megan, who seemed unfazed by the possibility. "You don't have to do this. It's dangerous."

"Dramatic, aren't you, Anne? Like the mayor of CopperTop is a murderer. I'm not too worried about it," Megan winked at her. "Besides, the Council can't prevent me from seeing who I want. Might as well get some good information out of it." Megan put the pieces of ham on her chicken sandwich. "Cordon bleu."

"Can we wait until Father Richard comes back? Promise me you'll tell him tonight before I have to write it in a report." Anne just shook her head out of disapproval.

"Yah, yah, I'll tell him," Alex finished her drink before leaning into Megan. "Could you find out anything about a harridan, by any chance?" Alex did not miss the look of disapproval from Anne.

Megan took a sip of her drink. "A what?" She asked, acting in a state of confusion.

All the girls finished their meals, so Alex gathered their garbage. Alex saw that overweight man again from the bakery. Now with a different girl from the previous two times she saw him. This girl was laughing as she was rubbing her fingernails on his arm. "Man, that guy really gets them, doesn't he?

"What?" Anne tried to see what Alex was talking about.

"Nothing." Alex saw her parents coming out of the mall. They approached the table. Her dad had bags underneath his eyes. "You look horrible."

"Well, I read the tea leaves." Michael hugged his daughter

"What do you mean?" Alex returned her dad's silent cry to hug his daughter.

Michael put his arm around his wife. "I retired this morning before that son of a bitch could fire me."

"Wow," Alex sat there and thought about it. "Can you afford it?"

"We'll be fine," her mom told her. "I'm kind of glad we ran into you. Can we talk to you in private?" She motioned over to the side.

Alex got up, with Komptin following suit. Her dad looked around before speaking. "You're not going to leave CopperTop, are you?"

Alex shook her head. "I'm needed here."

"What about Kameron?" Her mom had concern written all over her face about her daughter.

"What about him?" Alex couldn't help but feel the blood rush to her face.

"Any chance of rekindling?" Her mom just came out to say it.

"Not a chance in hell," Alex told her, not making eye contact. "Why?"

Her dad said, "I want to ask you before I ask you; do you want to buy the house?"

"You're moving? Where are you going?" Alex was in shock.

"A little town in Wisconsin. Our offer was accepted on a lake house." Her mom had a smile on her face. "I'd like you to come with us."

Alex shook her head. "I'm needed here, but I'll take the house."

"Can you afford it?" Her dad asked. "Obviously, I'll give you a deal."

Alex smiled, "It's okay dad, I'll pay what you would sell it for. I have enough."

Her dad sat back with a jolt. "How much do you make a year?"

Alex just grinned. "Enough not to worry." She hugged her mom and dad. "When are you leaving?"

"The end of the month." Her dad told her. "I'll have everything out and finalized by then."

169

"Sounds good. I'll have my people talk to your people." She winked at them. She went to rejoin Anne, but after a couple of steps she went running back to her parents. "I love you."

"Love you too, honey," Her mom hugged her with a loving embrace.

"I'm so proud of you," Michael put his arms around them both.

***

Gron had to sell their first date, so he decided to bring Misluna to a fancy dinner date. They made sure to play it off out in public in CopperTop. He escorted her up to the office in city hall where Megan was grazing her finger across the secretary's desk. "She didn't last long."

"Killing her actually felt like a family legacy." He went over to his desk to grab the key inside the Road Map to Absolute Power book. A creaking noise filled the mayor's office as he opened the wardrobe. "Sexy, isn't it?"

"I know, I wrote it." She went over to rub her fingers on the binder of the book. "What was it that you wanted to show me."

Gron unlocked the book, which seemed to echo throughout the Godless room. He took out a paper and handed it over to Misluna. "It's here...in CopperTop."

Misluna read it over. "This is a lie. How?"

"My backup plan. I didn't know it even got here." Gron admitted. "Do you want to go take a look?"

"Do I?" Misluna couldn't contain her excitement.

They both eagerly left for the museum. Gron told one of his Provisionaries to have Azrael meet them at the museum.

Azrael was already waiting for them in the nearest parking lot of the historic building. They walked up the steps to be greeted by the night security guard. "Sorry, sir, the museum is closed until Monday." Azrael snapped the guard's neck with no remorse while Infiltrators took care of the body.

"Don't tell me no," Gron just continued on into the building. The three of them confidently made it past the main hallway. They went to a side door that led to a spiral staircase in the lower basement. The room was an artifact-holding area filled with older scrolls, bibles, witchcraft books, and a multitude of occult paraphernalia. Off in the corner of the room was a mirror that stood well over nine feet tall. It seemed to be made of concrete and iron, with multiple trinkets infused in the borders of the mirror. There were also carvings within the concrete. "Can you read this?"

Misluna was vigilant as she approached the mirror. She was hesitant to even touch it, but her curiosity overtook her. "Symbols are familiar, but nothing I've seen before." She turned to Azrael. "How about you?"

The former angel of the Lite approached the mirror. "There is a symbol here about the Amalgam, but for some reason, I can't read this."

171

"But it's most definitely Dark?" Roger studied the mirror as he approached. "What's that concave up on top?"

All three of them leaned their heads closer to it as they studied it. "Looks like a plus sign with an arrow pointing down." Misluna put her finger in it. "It's got a circler indentation on the bottom, just before the arrow."

Azrael fed his bird-like creature sitting on his shoulder some of the blood from the guard he killed. "Where did you retrieve this?"

"The manifest said it came from Lithuania," Gron studied it more. "Šiauliai, to be exact."

"Underneath the Hill of Crosses?" Misluna was trying to put it together.

Gron opened his folder from his briefcase that a Provisionary was holding. "According to the report."

"It explains why the symbol of the crucifixion is in abundance at that location." Azrael studied the structure. "It was meant to be hidden from both the Lite and Dark."

Gron wiped his face from excitement. "How heavy is it?" Both Gron and Azrael tried to move the object, but it wouldn't budge. "Damn, how'd they get it in here?" He studied it a bit more. "We can't bring it to the compound. We'll have to bring them here."

"Who?" Misluna turned to them.

"Perhaps the Hybrids this is talking about are the twins." Gron continued studying the artifact. "The offspring of a Demon and Angel kind of fits the bill."

172

"I'll have them ready to go tomorrow." Misluna got a text from Alex ensuring she stayed safe, and to let her know if she needed help.

***

Alex nervously sat upstairs in her office. She felt guilty about thinking she had made a horrible mistake. She lied to Anne when she sent Megan on a date with Roger. It wasn't to see if she could find out what Roger was planning for the town. It was to see if she could find a way to bring Kameron back. She felt as if something was tugging her to find Kameron. The time was going on noon, and Megan still hadn't reported to work or answered anyone's text. Then she jumped when her phone rang, but it was from Janelle.

For some reason, Alex answered it. "Hey." Janelle was asking her if she had heard from Kameron. With much hesitation, Alex came out with it. "I can't tell you what happened, or where he went. All his supervision told me was he would never be returning." She could hear Janelle start crying uncontrollably as her kids and husband asked what was wrong in the background. "If I could, I would tell you more." Alex started to cry into the phone as she hung up the phone. Alex closed her eyes, imagining the pain Kameron's family must be feeling. In between her wiping her face, she checked to see if Megan had texted. Then, a disgusting feeling hit her stomach. Komptin came up to her at her desk. "Komptin, what have I done?"

173

A sudden rush of guilt for putting Megan in danger overcame her.

Then Alex heard a car door slam. Alex rushed to the window in hopes it was Megan coming into work. But, to her surprise, it was Father Richard. Alex came downstairs to greet him. Anne showed up to see how the trip went.

"Hey, how'd it go?" Alex saw Father Richard come into the church. She saw Tristan shaking his head as he mouthed. "Watch out."

"Come with me, Alexandria." Father Richard headed straight towards his office.

Alex's stomach got a bigger turn of anxiety. She cautiously went into his office and shut the door. Even before she could turn around, Father Richard started.

"What the hell were you thinking sending Megan on a date with the demon-infested, powerful leader of the F.O.R.?" He slammed his hands on his desk. His head turning red with anger.

"I was just thinking..." Alex was starting to plead her case.

"You weren't thinking! Damn it, Alex!" Father Richard's face was now sweating from emotion. "I had to find out from Megan about her date last night and how it went. The best part, I had no idea what she was talking about."

"So, she's safe," Alex had a sense of relief.

Father Richard slammed his fist onto the desk again; that time, it hurt him. "Yes, she's safe, but she shouldn't have been put in the situation to begin with. What in God's name was going through that head of yours?"

"I was, just thinking that he was smitten with her, and that she might find something out." Alex was actually starting to feel a little overwhelmed with remorse. Not that she was getting in trouble, but that Father Richard was actually disappointed in her that she willingly put someone innocent in real danger.

"Now, I have the Council jumping down my neck about sending a non-council member on a non-sanctioned task. Did you at least run it by Father Carl?" He stared directly at her.

"He went home on an emergency." Alex stated softly under her breath.

Father Richard's body actually tensed from trying to figure out what to say. "Alex, just get out of my office," he finally said out of frustration as he sat down at his desk.

"But I..." Alex managed to speak, with some great difficulty.

"Get...out." Father Richard gritted his teeth.

"Yes, Father," Alex turned around and closed the door. She put her head on the door and closed her eyes. Taking a deep breath, she whistled for Komptin to join her. Anne and Tristan were in the main hallway of the church. "I'm going for a walk."

"Alex, are you okay?" Anne asked out of concern.

"You didn't hear that?" Alex was trying to hold her tears in. Judging from Anne's reaction, she knew her answer. "How would you take that?" Komptin came to Alex's side as they headed towards the woods.

Alex wasn't on a hunt. If an Infiltrator came across, she felt as if she would let him take her. She had never felt so low. She'd been yelled at before, but never by Father Richard. He was legitimately upset, almost ashamed of her. Her legs needed to rest as she sat down, putting her back against a rock. Komptin was in his gargoyle state as he lay down next to Alex. She gently scratched his ears as he fell into a deep slumber. She closed her eyes, praying for some connection to the Lite. It was still cold, still no connection at all.

"Alexandria," Devine's voice came from the darkness of the forest.

She peeked one eye open to see the purple-haired angel leaning on her bo staff, staring at her. "Hey."

"You do not look good." Devine vanished her bo as she sat up on the rock next to the Lite Sentry sitting on the dirt floor.

"I'm not." Alex shook her head in disbelief. Then she looked up at the angel. "How'd you find me anyways?" She had a slight hope her Lite could be sensed.

"The Pure of Heart told me you went hunting in this direction." Devine looked around her surroundings. "Your hunting style is quite peculiar."

"I don't feel like hunting. Honestly, I feel like I hate life." Alex put her head against the rock and then rubbed it because it hurt.

"You primates confuse me. He gave you the choice of free will, to enjoy the gift of the world. You choose to hate what He gives you," Devine seemed in deep thought before she shook her head to get out of it.

"I lost him forever," Alex stared off into the distance.

"You will get your connection back to the Lite," Devine stated with uneasy confidence. "You will feel the warmth again."

"It's not His warmth that I'm talking about," Alex dropped a tear. "What're your thoughts of my chances on getting Kameron back."

Devine hesitated. In a most sympathetic tone, the angel replied, "You cannot lose hope."

"You didn't answer my question," Alex fought back from showing she was about to break down.

"I only know of one who entered the Dark willingly that did not die on Earth," Devine let her know.

"What happened?" That caught Alex's attention.

"Dark-worshipping primates found a way to open a portal without Vandor. To cut a long tale, Osiah reversed it to send evil back to the Dark." Devine stopped herself. "He sent evil back...," she murmured.

"Devine," Alex snapped her fingers to gain her attention back.

The angel again shook her thoughts away. "No one knows why, but Osiah took the gateway and hid it from both the Lite and Dark. He made a deal with the NEWS."

Alex stood up with excitement. "Well, if the NEWS knows a way to get the portal open to get Kameron out...let's go find him."

"Stop your thought, Alexandria," Devine quickly shot her down. "The NEWS is the delivery message to destruction. The NEWS must not report the message of revelation."

"Well, if the NEWS knows how to get him back?" Alex was confused about the purpose of the NEWS.

Devine tried to stop her little sister's hopes from rising. "They are only to report the status of the Balance when it is shifted to the point of dangerous proportion."

Alex sat there confused, "Well…if neither side controls them. How are they summoned?"

"All I know is that the Primates control their invitation." It was all that Devine could tell her.

***

It was nice now that night was coming later in the evening. Anne finished her request for Father Carl to get the general history on the Lite Sentries. It was weird that he took off like that without telling anybody. There was no word on where he went, or when he would return.

There was a sound coming from the end of the hallway. It was no doubt Alex returning from her walk. She was pretty upset when she left, causing her to be gone for quite some time. The yelling must have upset Father Richard because he had left immediately afterward. Anne closed her folder and locked her files in the safe. She heard another noise as if someone was coming towards her office. The memory of her kidnapping back in D.C. flashed through Anne's mind. Anne grabbed her purse to grab her pistol. She placed the holster in the small of her back, just in case. She locked her office after she shut the lights off. Anne turned around to see Megan next to her. Anne jumped with a small gasp of air, reaching at the small of her back.

"Are you okay?" Megan was peeking around.

Anne immediately hugged her. "Thank God you're safe."

It took a split second for Megan to react to Anne's hug, but then she accepted it rather cautiously. "Okay, what's going on?"

"Where were you?" Anne asked in a protective inquiry.

"I told Father Carl before he went out of town that I needed to take some time off," Megan told her. "I just came in because I left something in my desk drawer."

"We tried calling you. We thought the worst with Roger," Anne double-checked her door.

"Oh, that. He may be one of the most powerful men in town right now, but he's kind of a dweeb." Megan laughed. "He took me to a museum." Megan rolled her eyes. "I was like, really, a museum?"

"Oh, I'd find that interesting," Anne thought about it.

"Ah, no," Megan emphasized. "After a fancy dinner, only highlight of the night, he brought me to that museum, I thought at least he would try to make a move on me. He was a scared little boy. Kind of pathetic actually."

"I'm glad you're safe," Anne pulled out her phone to text Alex and Father Richard that Megan was in the church and was alright. After she double-checked to make sure her pistol was in the small of her back, the two of them headed down the hallway.

The two of them made small talk as they made it to the lobby together. Megan explained to her what had happened on her so-called date. "Do you know a lot about mid-evil artifacts?"

"I'm more of an event historian," Anne explained. "With a minor in Sociology, how society interacts with each other, causes and effects."

Megan turned to her. "Really? I always thought you had some psychology or counseling degree with a minor in history."

"Why do you say that?" Anne escorted Megan into her office.

Megan went into her desk drawer to grab a ring. She stared at it for a bit before putting it on. "Oh, just because you have such a big heart. Sometimes, I wish I had one half the size of yours."

"Well, thank you," Anne shyly smiled as she thought about how her heart almost got her killed. Then she noticed how Megan's demeanor had changed as she was eyeing the piece of jewelry on her finger. "There are memories attached to the ring; someone special?"

Megan nodded. "Not a boyfriend or anything like that. My cousin." She continued to stare at the ring. "She was…"

Anne saw something in Megan that she didn't expect or ever see before. She had the true emotion of sorrow. "What happened to her?"

Megan took a second, she opened her mouth, but then she stopped. There was only one thing she could come up with. "She died when we were in high school." She stared at the ring for a bit longer, then fought back a tear.

"I'm sorry," Anne told her. "I lost a friend in high school as well, but I know what it's like losing someone close."

"How'd you know we were close?" Megan looked at Anne, who was leaning on the radiator.

Anne gave her a comforting look. "I can tell when you look at the ring. What was she like?"

"Madison had a flare about her," Megan started to talk. "Our friends nicknamed us 'M and M.'" Misluna got a text from Gron. *Does she know anything about the artifact?* Misluna replied as she talked to Anne. *Nothing.* "I really should get going."

"Do you want to go get a cup of coffee or something?" It was no secret Anne could see the memory of her cousin was upsetting her coworker.

Megan got cold and distant look in her eyes. "No, I gotta go."

Anne searched her purse and her pockets. "I need to double-check my safe."

"Well, I can't wait for you. I need to go." She came off callous.

"I'll lock up. It will just take me a second." Anne went back downstairs to go to her office. She unlocked the door and went straight to her safe to pull on the drawer. It was obviously locked. Anne felt her phone in her pocket vibrate. Alex was telling her that she was going for a "walk." *Be safe* Anne replied back.

She checked her safe one time before leaving. There was a sweater draped on the back of her office chair she needed to get cleaned. When she opened the door, an older woman stood within in a big overcoat.

Anne jumped and stood back. Behind the woman was a smaller person. Anne couldn't see who it was; the person was hunched over with a hood that hid their face. Anne went to turn the light on, but the older woman prevented her from turning it on.

"Please, light, keep off," she said in a deep Russian accent.

"Okay, can I help you?" Anne took a step back. Anne nonchalantly put her hand at the small of her back.

"Anne McClure," the older woman spoke. "Me, Yelizaveta."

"Yeli?" Anne's mouth dropped. "I thought the worst. I haven't heard from you for a couple of years. Ever since you went into hiding. Why are you here?"

Yelizaveta turned to the person behind her, who still remained hidden in the shadows of the hallway. "We not here. You no tell. Give word."

Anne was taken aback. "If you're in danger, we can protect you."

"Give word," she forcefully asked. "Or we leave."

182

"I promise," Anne promised.

Yelizaveta went into her satchel and pulled out an old Russian Orthodox Bible. "No Council report, no tell we here. Yes. Swear on Bible."

Anne, without hesitation, put her hand on the Bible. "You have my word; I will not tell anyone you were here."

The big Russian female elder turned to the person behind her. With a nod from the mysterious person, Yelizaveta put the Bible back into her satchel. As she pulled her hand out of the bag, it held something inside a rag, folded in a wax seal in the shape of a compass holding it together. There were strings around the rag binding it together.

Anne was amazed at how heavy it was. "What is it?" Yelizaveta hesitated as she pulled out some old papers from her satchel. Anne glanced over them. "These are Dark Texts but written in modern English."

"Keep safe," Yelizaveta told her. "The Dark must not know."

"But, what is this?" Anne held up the item in the rag. "What's going on?"

Then the mysterious person put her hood down. She was a small blonde woman in her twenties with bruises and multiple cuts on her face. "Look, don't tell the Council about that." She pointed to the rag. "Those Dark Texts cannot fall into the Dark's claws. We can't protect them." The woman seemed to look around as if she heard something. "We need to go."

Yelizaveta nodded. "No tell Council where got, no?"

"I swear," Anne reaffirmed. "I won't say anything. You can stay here; we can protect you. Do you need a doctor?" Then, something caught her attention. The beaten-up blonde's eyes flashed a neon blue. "You're a Sentry?"

"I don't have much time," The mysterious girl told Yelizaveta. The two of them started to walk away until the unnamed Lite Sentry turned back to Anne. "Do me a favor; tell Alex I'm sorry. I wasn't going to do anything."

"Do you know Alex?" Anne was trying to figure out who is this Lite Sentry.

"No, we never met, but I just wanted to make sure she knows. I wasn't going to do anything," the young lady told her. She slowly turned to Yelizaveta. "I don't have much time." The young lady slowly limped with the help of the older woman.

Anne hurried to put items in her safe. She was fumbling with her shaking hands as she dialed the combo. After ensuring it was locked, she ran after Yelizaveta and the Lite Sentry. She frantically searched the church but couldn't find them. Then she saw two figures outside in the fenced-in backyard near the woods. Anne slowly came outside as the older woman was now helping the hurt Lite Sentry walk until she fell to the ground in complete pain. Anne ran up to Yelizaveta. "Is she okay?" Yelizaveta had tears running down her face.

The Lite Sentry grabbed her face. "Don't cry." She twitched as if it was her last attempt to hold onto life. "We will see each other in Heaven."

Then, her body twitched a couple of times before going limp as her eyes became lifeless.

Yelizaveta broke down in tears as she held the young woman in her arms. Anne turned around to see Celestial with her guardians. The Conduit of Lite nodded to her guardians to take the young woman's body.

"Wait, what about her family?" Anne was confused.

"No family," Yelizaveta broke down in tears.

Celestial knelt down to the saddened Russian lady. "She had you." Celestial put her hand on the old woman's face.

Then, the woman spoke Russian to Celestial. The angel listened and repeated something back in Russian. The woman nodded. Celestial put her hand on top of the woman's head as she said something Anne couldn't understand. Yelizaveta's body dropped to the ground. Arome was the angel who picked her body up from the ground. The two guardians carried both bodies into the doorway. Celestial turned before walking into the doorway. "Anne, speak not of this."

"You have my word," Anne assured the Conduit of Lite. "It will not be recorded."

Celestial approached Anne, and she put her hand on Anne's shoulders. "Kale loves you. His only wish is that you are happy."

Anne wiped a tear from her face. "Please tell him that I love him, and there isn't a day that I don't think of him."

Celestial kissed her forehead. "Your heart is pure love for all that comes across your path." The caring angel went back into the doorway.

***

Megan was probably driving faster than she should have. She couldn't tell how fast she was going, but it was well above the legal speed limit. There was no care for her life or anyone else. For some reason, the pain of thinking of Madison was hitting her hard. Then she turned on the radio to hear that damn song, the song that sent her into a deeper rage.

"Megan," her dad yelled for her from downstairs. "Let's go! We're going to be late."

"Coming, Dad," Megan brushed her dark blonde hair. She just couldn't get it right. For some reason, it never worked out on the days she had to go to church. She went to grab a clip but accidentally grabbed her sister's curling iron that was on. "Damn it." Megan freaked out in case her parents heard her swear. She didn't feel like getting twitched before church.

"Let's go, Megan, don't make us tell you again." Now her mom was getting on her case.

Megan unplugged the curling iron that her sister, Alora, forgot about doing.

"Daddy, we need to go." Megan heard her sister complain. "If I'm late because of Megan…"

"Megan, now!" Her dad yelled.

"I'm coming. I'm coming," Megan repeated as she came down the stairs. "Alora, I unplugged your curling iron."

"I only left it on to help you with your hair. I see you must not have had time to use it. Are you going to put makeup on?" She judged her sister.

"I did. Thanks for noticing," Megan snottily replied.

"Oh, well, okay, sure," Alora grabbed her mirror to check her makeup. She held up the mirror to check her long, jet-black hair. "I hope Jordan likes it."

"I'm sure he'll love it, sweetie," Her mom reassured. "And when you sing, it will be like he is listening to angels singing His praise. God gave you a gift for all of us to cherish."

Megan rolled her eyes. "I'm ready. Can we go now? I don't understand why I have to go. It's her deal. Besides, I went to church already this morning."

"One, there is no harm in going to the afternoon service. Besides, your sister will be singing His praise for all to hear. Pastor Chad brought in a music producer his brother knows to hear her sing." Her mom was so proud.

Her dad looked at his watch. "We need to go for sound check." They all rushed to the car to give Alora her time to be in the spotlight…again.

Megan arrived at the church in her plain dress with her hair clipped back. Her sister was all dolled up in dark makeup to emphasize the white in her wide eyes. Megan's only saving grace was her cousin Madison was there. Madison made eye contact with Megan and made a gun out of her hand from across the congregation. She pointed it to her head as Megan's aunt and uncle talked to Pastor Chad's friend. Megan could only assume that was the all-powerful record producer.

Madison and Megan managed to break away from their parents to meet up. "This sucks," Madison told her.

"I got to be here to support my perfect older sister," Megan wanted to leave.

"Come on, let's go up to the balcony to get away from the P.R. of Alora," Madison grabbed Megan's hand. They went up to the balcony and passed one of the ushers. The young man shyly turned away.

"What's with Carter?" Megan asked Madison.

"Oh, during coffee after the service last week, I took him into the storage closet." Madison found their seats.

"How far did you go?" Megan looked around to make sure no one was listening.

"Let's just say, he's not the innocent little choir boy he pretends to be," Madison laughed. "Do you want me to set you up with anyone? What about David? He's cute?"

"I don't want to date anyone; my parents wouldn't approve." Megan thought about the possibility. "Not in God's plan for me." She fingered quoted. "They actually told me I should be my sister's assistant when she goes on tour with that Christian rock band this summer. Can you believe that?"

Madison rolled her eyes, "They are pieces of work. My parents aren't much better. If they found out about me stealing that jewelry from the Purch-Mart, they'd send my ass to that camp they keep threatening me with. You should have seen my mom's face when she saw my hickey."

Megan looked at her neck. "I don't see anything."

"It's under my bra," Madison laughed.

"Ah," Megan saw David with Carter handing out programs. "You think David would go out with me?"

"Why not? You're cute. And you're far better than that two-faced sister of yours," Madison unclipped Megan's hair to fluff it out. "Besides, you don't have to date him. Just do him. I doubt he'll say no."

"I don't know, I never…" Megan was ashamed to speak about her virginity. "I'm not as confident as you are."

Madison leaned in, "Look, you are beautiful and talented; I've read your writing. Your parents are in the falling pit of Alora and unable to see you are something special. You need to get on the Road Map to Absolute Power I told you about earlier."

"The what?" Megan leaned into her.

"Don't you remember? Anyway, I'll tell you about it after church. Your precious sister is about to grace us with her voice," she said sarcastically.

After Alora sang her song, the church exploded with applause. After the service, Madison stood up, "Let's go get lit."

Megan saw everyone praising Alora on God's special gift to the singer. Megan couldn't stand it. "Where?"

"Really?" Madison was shocked. "Let's just go behind the dumpster." They managed to sneak out to start smoking some hand-rolled joints. Madison ignited hers first. She inhaled the smoke and closed her eyes with bliss. "Oh, that's it." She went to hand it over to Megan, but she quickly hid it. "Shit."

One of the cops picked her up by the arm. "And now that's a drug charge, Madison."

The other cop picked up Megan by the arm. "Let's go, sweetheart."

"Wait, she didn't do anything," Madison yelled, trying to get away from the cop. "She was trying to stop me, I swear."

"Sure, let's go," the cop holding Megan said.

"Madison," Megan cried for help.

A crowd started to form around the two girls, with the cops starting to handcuff them. Their parents watched, disappointment written across their faces, as Alora started crying. "Really, Megan, on this of all days. Why did you do this to me?" She started to cry into her mom's arms.

"Let's go. You can bail them out from the station," the cop escorted the girls to their police car.

Madison acted as if she was trying to get free, but Megan was just going calmly. Madison dug her feet into the ground, "Wait, wait, you let her go, and I'll tell you about the jewelry stolen from Purch-Mart."

"Madison, no!" Megan cried out.

"I'm listening," the cop who was holding Madison stopped.

"Let Megan go. She didn't smoke anything; she was trying to stop me." Madison lied to the police.

The cop holding Megan got close to her. "I don't smell any smoke."

"Okay, let her go," The cop holding Madison told his partner.

The cop uncuffed Megan. "Okay, she's free."

Megan begged Madison, "Don't."

Madison shrugged one shoulder. "What are they going to do? I stole the jewelry from Purch-Mart. These are the items I took: one ring, three bracelets, five earrings, a shit load of necklaces." She winked over at Megan. The crowd gasped as she admitted to her crimes. Madison looked back at Megan as she remained handcuffed to be taken away.

About a month passed when Megan was finally allowed to come out of her room. Her parents didn't talk to her, only to initiate the drug tests by peeing on a stick. Alora was still able to go on tour with that Christian rock band as the opening act or something like that. Megan came downstairs for the first time in quite a while to see her parents with their aunt and uncle holding a letter. It looked as if they were crying.

"What's going on?" Megan asked, with a deep feeling of hurt. It seemed as if darkness filled the room on this sunny afternoon.

"Megan, Madison's body was found at the Juvenile Ministry for Trouble Teens. She had slit her wrists before jumping off a banisher with a rope around her neck."

Megan didn't say a word, "When?"

"Three days ago," Her uncle fought back his tears. "This letter was addressed to you under her mattress."

"And you're just telling me this now!" Megan shrieked.

"We were organizing the funeral," her aunt failed to hold back from crying.

"And we were talking with your sister to get her over here to sing at the funeral. We thought this would be best." Her mom wiped tears from her face.

Megan approached the table, "Give me the God damn letter." She snatched it out of the hands of her dad. "You better make sure your precious little angel gets her spotlight at Madison's funeral." She stormed out of the house while her parents called for her to get back there.

Megan broke into her aunts and uncle's house. It really wasn't that hard since she knew where they hid the key. Madison's room had music posters hanging up and a computer on her desk. There was a bunch of stuff that a typical teenage girl would have. Megan sat down on the bed to open the letter.

Megan,
This place sucks. You have no idea. I have to get up at five in the morning for morning prayers. Then we have a physical education, breakfast, clean up, Bible study, chores, lunch, then talk about our feelings, then bible study, dinner, clean up, and then team building. After all that, bible study and then

bed. We do that every freakin' day! I don't know how much more I can do this. I'm being told I'm a disappointment to my parents, my church, and God; just because I asked one of the guards if he wanted a truly religious experience. Anyways, they put me in this box thing for two hours, but it felt like a week. This place sucks. I don't know if I'm going to make it out of here. I talked to a lawyer, and you're the only one who will be able to read this letter. So, if I don't make it out of here, there's something for you. It's in that place...where I keep that thing. In that box, you will see something that will change your life forever. Be sure to never come to a shit hole like this. I love you, M&M, forever.

Madison.

Megan went into Madison's closet, where she knew the location of the model of a church made of wood buried in a box of junk. She opened the roof of the church. Inside was a pamphlet for the Freedom Off Religion. A small book about the Roadmap to Absolute Power. Inside the steeple of the church was the ring she had stolen from Purch-Mart. She held it in her hand as she stared at it.

A week later was the funeral service for Madison. Megan was wearing black, and the ring Madison had given her. She sat on the balcony of the church, away from all those hypocrites down in the congregation. Her sister was singing some song about the praises of God. She sang this as her cousin lay in the coffin, but all attention was on Alora, not Madison.

193

Megan grabbed a piece of her hair and pulled it out. For some reason, the relief from that quick release of pain felt good. So, she did it again. She did it three or four more times while the service was going. After the service, Megan decided to walk over to the wake at her uncle's house. She decided to cut through the park, where she heard a growl. She wasn't scared. For some reason, she welcomed death. She sat down on the bench, hoping whatever made that sound would tear her to pieces. But a man a couple of years older than she was sat next to her. He had red hair and dark circles under his eyes. He had a bruise across his face, as if he had just gotten into a fight.

"I'm Roger," the boy said as he handed her a pamphlet with an upside number four on it.

Behind the two stood a man all in black, with long, greasy hair and a white face.

***

Kameron was patrolling the streets with his supervisor, Legion Commander Grossman. It was a nice day, but it still seemed a little gray. They made it down the street looking for any infraction in accordance with the Fallen Trinity Doctrine. The people of the town were going about their business. It was weird as they were always on edge to see what the Sentinel guards were going to do. That was because the market street was the best place to find the illegal solicitors.

"It's a nice day," Grossman adjusted his utility belt.

"If you say so." The streets were quiet; people seemed like zombies going through the motions of life while still keeping an eye out.

"What's on your mind?" Grossman grabbed an apple from a vendor. He just pointed at the badge, and the store owner just nodded. The vendor tried to hide his irritation as he went about his work.

"Megan got a new job as the personal secretary to Roger Somberson." Kameron picked up a piece of garbage from the street. He unraveled a pamphlet for Lite solicitation.

"Damn it," Grossman gazed down at the pamphlet. "They are like roaches."

"Should I log it?" Kameron nicely folded it back up.

"No, just get rid of it. Everyone knows they are here. It's just so weird no one is turning them in." Grossman pulled out his electric tablet. "Come on. Let's log our checks early so we're not in a rush to get them done later on in the day."

Kameron got a sickening feeling in his stomach. "Okay, first one we see."

"Sounds good to me," Grossman bit into his apple.

"I hate these," Kameron thought to himself. The opinions were so loud that he was afraid he said them aloud. It just so happened that Michelle and her friend came out of the store, bumping into Kameron. "Can we skip this one?"

"No," Grossman denied Kameron's request. "This is a test now. What are you going to do if you catch her with Lite?"

"Hey, Kameron," Michelle was happy to see him. "You want some ice cream." She showed him her ice cream cone. "I'm telling you; it tastes especially good today."

He took the ice cream and tossed it to the ground. "I'm sorry about this."

"Oh, come on," Michelle was annoyed. "Really, now?"

"Michelle, you know the rules," he pushed her against the wall while Grossman took care of her date. Kameron took her purse and started to go through it while putting stuff on the ground. "Purse is clean."

Michelle rolled her eyes. "This is embarrassing. Are you done?"

Grossman finished going through the wallet of her friend. "Wallet on this one is clean."

"What's going on?" Alex came out of the store eating a double chocolate ice cream cone with chocolate topping.

"Random Lite Check," Kameron continued to frisk his little sister.

"And you chose your sister?" Alex laughed before licking her ice cream as if she was watching a show. "How are you liking that one?"

"Random is random," Kameron lectured. "The Sentinel Guard doesn't play favorites." He turned his attention back to his sister. "I need to check your pockets."

Michelle started to get nervous. "Really, do you have to?"

"Yep, come on." Kameron could feel Grossman watching him.

Michelle whispered quietly in fear. "Kameron, I have female things in my pocket."

"What's keeping you, Dutcher." Grossman was getting itchy. "I just finished this one, he's clean."

"I have to check, Michelle." Kameron could tell she was getting nervous. Kameron emptied out her pockets. There were female products dropping on the ground, along with some money, and a folded piece of paper. Kameron picked up the piece of paper with a phone number on it. "What's this?"

Grossman grabbed the paperwork from Kameron's hands. "A phone number. You don't want it in your phone for some reason? Hiding it from the Eye?"

Alex rolled her eyes when she saw that paper. "Did you really get the number from that guy while you were on a date with another boy?" Michelle turned to Alex. "That's pretty ballsy, even for me." Alex calmly licked her ice cream. "Some guy was hitting on her while her boyfriend was in the bathroom."

"What are you doing here?" Grossman approached Alex, but she didn't budge as the big guy entered her personal space.

Alex held up her ice cream cone. "Why else would I be here?"

Kameron snickered. "Okay. You guys are free to go." Alex helped Michelle hide her feminine products from her boyfriend. Kameron studied Michelle's boyfriend, and he didn't seem upset as he stared at the piece of paper.

"Thanks, Alex," Michelle silently whispered to her.

Alex stood up close to Kameron. "Do you need to check me?" She lifted her arms.

Kameron stared into her big brown eyes against her pale face. "No, we fulfilled our quota. Your ice cream is melting."

Alex looked down at her ice cream. "I'm such a mess," She chuckled, then licked the ice cream off her hand. "I have to go." She took off in the opposite direction, almost floating from happiness.

Kameron watched her pick a blue flower out from a vendor as she smelled it. The vendor just told her to keep it, but Alex convinced him to let her pay. Then she just disappeared into the market crowd.

"Can we go?" Michelle's boyfriend was getting particularly anxious.

"Go," Kameron continued to search to see where Alex had vanished.

Michelle and her boyfriend took off as she left, talking to her boyfriend about that number.

"She's trouble," Grossman told Kameron as he continued to face Alex's direction.

"Michelle is just young," Kameron signed the pad to finalize the Lite check.

"I'm not talking about Michelle," Grossman commented. "Megan's got Power, don't give that up."

Kameron stared down the street where Alex disappeared. "Yeah, she's got it alright."

Chapter Eight

Alex and Komptin were hunting in the former quarantine area, where she stopped in front of a small garden center. They were having a sale on "Forget Me Not" flowers. The window display was a vast array of blue wonderment, and she couldn't help but stare. Seeing the quarantined area open was nice, but it was obvious to her it came at a cost. Just overnight, the United Won had left; there was hardly anyone promoting justice for Darius King, and no one really seemed to notice. From an outsider looking in, it was as if Roger was a miracle worker. Alex knew the truth, though; the Dark manipulated this town.

There was no doubt Roger's goal was to set up an F.O.R.-controlled city for the Dark. "I don't like this," Alex knelt down to Komptin. He returned the agreement as he flashed his eyes. Komptin must have caught a sense of the Dark because he led Alex into a city bus depot. It wasn't operational, but there was evidence it was starting to try to get back running.

There was only one bus in the massive warehouse. It was a basic school bus: yellow; Alex didn't miss the irony of the number four as the bus identification. A quick peek underneath the bus to verify there was nothing she needed to worry about. It was clear, but something wasn't right. The door was open to the inside of the yellow mobile metal tube. "Stay here," Alex motioned to Komptin. The loyal dog sat in the overwatch position. Alex got onto the bus, where the inside was painted in F.O.R. maroon colors. The back of the seats had the general orders of the F.O.R. imprinted onto them.

"That son of bitch is going to implement F.O.R. into the school system." Alex turned around when Komptin started furiously barking. Alex looked out the window to see three Infiltrators on all fours as if they were going to attack. Alex flashed her eyes as she whistled for Komptin to attack.

The massive dog morphed into his gargoyle state. He bravely started running toward the group. Alex ran out of the bus, and Lite Beamed the Infiltrator on the left. Komptin tackled the one in the middle, grabbed the head of the Infiltrator, and threw the beast into the last Infiltrator still standing. The two black beasts collided with each other. Alex ran at them, landing a flying kick as they got up on their feet. Komptin went to take care of the single Infiltrator. Alex dropped her knee into the Infiltrator as she Lite Beamed the one closer to her. It pushed the Infiltrator enough to skid across the floor into a workbench.

Alex got flipped over onto the floor by the Infiltrator she was fighting. Upon getting on her feet, it swung at her, connecting a hit that sent Alex twisting in the air. After landing abruptly on the concrete floor, she checked her jaw, but there was no time before getting kicked, sending her flying again. Now it was her turn to crash into the wall. The Infiltrator ran at full force at Alex. She got out of the way as the Infiltrator lunged at her. His head went through the wall. Alex immediately jumped in the air and landed on the back of her attacker, weakening the Infiltrator enough to dispose of it.

The second Infiltrator she was fighting attacked her and pinned her against the pillar of the wall. She kneed the Infiltrator underneath the chin just before it bit her. She grabbed the beast around the waist and sent it to the hardened floor, causing a small indentation. When the beast went to get up, Alex punched it again, causing it to go down again. Alex assumed it was weak enough to dispose of. She was correct. Alex took a minute to regain her strength. She watched Komptin dispose of his Infiltrator. He, too, took a minute to rest before joining Alex.

The two of them sat down on the floor, checking each other's wounds. "We got Roger by the balls now with this bus." Then an explosion occurred destroying the bus. Alex just stared at the bus with no expression. "Of course." A Demon running out the door caught their attention. The two hunters for the Lite just sighed as they got off the cement floor.

Alex and Komptin ran out of the door when she bumped into Tristan. "What are you doing here?"

"I picked up the sense of the Dark. What about you?" Tristan was scouting the area.

"Just disposed of three infiltrators," Alex wanted to get moving to find that Demon. "I think Roger is going to implement the F.O.R. into the public-school systems."

Tristan was confused. "That's an accusation out of nowhere. What makes you think that?"

"Just a hunch," Alex pointed to the window with the burning school bus inside. "Come on, let's go find your Demon."

Alex let Tristan take the lead in hunting for the Demon deep into the downtown ex-quarantined area. More and more people seemed to be out and about as they continued to head into downtown. A beautiful girl approached Tristan. "Hi, I'm Nancy."

"Tristan," he shyly smiled. "This is…"

"His sister, Alex," she quickly became a wingman for him.

The young lady smiled at Tristan. "You going to the concert?"

"What concert?" Alex was still secretly scouting for that Demon.

"The one put on by the F.O.R., silly." She gave Tristan a flyer. "Starts in a little bit. Hope to see you there." She took off down the street, handing out flyers to people.

Alex watched Tristan's reaction. "She was cute."

"She's probably F.O.R.," Tristan stated the obvious.

"So? She got in willingly; she can get out willingly. Maybe she just needs you to help her." Alex bumped his arm with her elbow. "Go get her, stud."

"No, she's way above my league," he watched the young lady hand out papers to passing pedestrians. "Should we check it out?" He held up the flyer.

"Sure. Your loss. She had eyes on you." Alex shook her head as she headed to the park. On the way, Alex saw two familiar faces. Both Devine and Dinah were approaching the two Lite Sentries. "Hey, what are two doing here?"

"We tracked the Dark to this location but lost him in the crowd," Devine let Alex know out of frustration. "This hunting is a waste of time; waiting for them to come is much easier."

Alex smiled to hear Devine was much happier when she was defending the Conduit of Lite. "Well, we were going to check out the concert; wanna come?"

"These Primates are a strange bunch, just gathering around to listen to others make music." Dinah was confused with the gathering.

"What do you do with music?" Tristan asked the neon-orange haired angel.

She snapped her head towards the rookie Lite Sentry. "We create music as one entity, and it binds us as one family; we all participate...equally."

"So, do you want to check it out?" Alex asked the feisty angel.

"If we must," Dinah did not look enthused with the idea. "Do I have to dance?"

Alex raised her eyebrows. "No, normally people don't dance at concerts." The four of them went to the park where the concert was being held. The band was singing a song as the crowd was cheering them on.

"Surprised there aren't more Demons around, since the concert is put on by F.O.R.," Tristan scouted the area. "The Dark isn't as strong sensing as I thought it would be."

Alex felt bad as she still couldn't help with the sensing. "You're telling me there is no Dark here?"

The two angels shook their heads. Tristan confirmed it. "I hardly sense anything, just the basic Dark sense of CopperTop."

Alex got a phone call from Robbie out in Minnesota. "I have to take this." The music from the band was making it hard to hear him. "Okay, she's out here? What? Let me call you back, I can't hear a damn thing with this band playing." Alex hung up the phone to see Devine and Dinah listening to the music. Tristan was telling Dinah about what music meant to him. "Hey."

Tristan stopped his discussion with Dinah. "What's up?"

"I have to go," Alex motioned with her thumb.

"I'll come with," Tristan stepped up, ready to face any danger.

"No, enjoy the night off," Alex smiled at him. "Let's go, Komptin." As Alex was leaving, a new singer jumped on stage. The music started with a heavy drum, and a choir over the speaker over the speaker system. The beat was one that Alex could only call a heavy metal power ballad. The man, who wore a black leather jacket, began his words:

> *Since the first revolve*
> *Man had the opportunity.*
> *To no problem to solve*
> *The power of the One*
> *With only major fault*
> *Is the faith of the those below*
> *Now, without warning,*

No knock on the door
Come the news of four

The Darkness overcome
Of seeing all that you have done
When the emptiness becomes
There is no threat, we are sure to run

Arrival with nature's power
The Earth he must shower
A leader who is noble and true
The last hope for the people's due
The man's heart of pure desire
The deletion before the fire
But the warmest cold of them all
Is the one who is most tall
He will bring peace to this land overall

The Darkness overcome
Of seeing all that you have done
When the emptiness becomes
There is no threat, we are sure to run

Alex just watched the singer work the crowd, almost in hostility, as he was dressed like a refugee from the eighties. Though, he did have an interesting voice. She listened to the chorus one more time before she realized she had to get back to the church to call Robbie back. "I need to go." Alex was leaving when she saw something that Devine had never shown before–shock.

***

The room was musty and cold, and he could hardly see anything, but Scotty didn't know if it was from the loss of blood or the evil that infested his surroundings. All he knew was for the first time, he just wanted to die, to end the pain. Was that too much to ask? Just to die. He was tied to the wall, and the only movement he was allowed was his head. The woman before him controlled his fate. She was tall and wore a dark maroon dress with a small upside four on the left side. There was an evil gentleness to her just before she unleashed the lavish pain.

"I'm not going to let you die," she ran her fingers through his hair. Her breath had a minty strawberry to it as she softly whispered. The demon-infested woman made sure to graze her lips on his ear.

Scotty could barely speak. "It needs to end sooner or later."

"Why do you fight? It's not for Him?" The woman pulled up to face him. Her hand caressed the side of his cheek. "You think I like doing this? Just tell me what I want to know." She turned her ear close to his mouth. "Tell me."

"It's going to be a long night for you," Scotty muttered. "You, disease-ridden, F.O.R. skank."

She stepped back in annoyance before flicking the switch on the wall that sent electricity through Scotty as a member of F.O.R. punched him across the face with rubber gloves. She just sat back in the back room and smiled as the sounds of his screams were left unheard.

***

Alex debated if she would talk to Father Richard about her phone call last night, but she was on thin ice as it was with him. She just sat in her office, waiting for him to come in. Anne had come in late morning, which was odd for her. She didn't really say anything. She just got her coffee and said she had to do some research. Alex cautiously made it from downstairs to see Megan putting makeup on at her desk.

"Late night?" Alex was curious why she was doing that at her desk.

"You could say that." Megan wiped some lipstick off the side of her mouth.

Alex felt a bit guilty as she might have put Megan into some real danger. "Look, Megan, I know we don't really see eye to eye."

Megan stopped what she was doing to pay attention to what Alex was about to say. "Okay," she replied with a bit of caution.

"But me asking you to put yourself in danger with Roger; I'm sorry to put you in that situation. As a friend, I shouldn't have done that." Alex admitted her mistake to her coworker.

"As a friend? You and me?" Megan almost laughed out of pure unbelievable shock that she said that. "Let me ask you something, Alexandria Johnson. What's my last name?" Megan stared at her. She could tell Alex was backed against a wall. "You know what your problem is; you walk around this church like you are above everyone else.

207

Everyone must look out for Alex; she's got a lot going on. You ever think Kameron left like he did to get away from you. You drove him away."

Alex fought back the tears. "You know, Megan. You don't know what you are talking about."

"I don't? I bet he took that secret assignment you said he's on as an excuse to leave you. He probably promised he loved you forever just so you don't go crazy or anything." Megan stood up from her desk. "Alex, you are not a good person."

Komptin came into the room and barked at Megan as she scolded Alex. "Komptin." Alex tried to get out clearly, but you could hear the mixture of tears in her voice. She saw Megan staring her down with a conviction of hate in her eyes.

"Go," Megan commanded. "Go and cry into the arms of Father Richard. Go run to Anne to tell her what an evil person I am. If they would even listen to you or believe anything you have to say. They just entertain you, so you don't go nuts, you manipulative little harlot."

That seemed to irritate Komptin as he was fiercely barking at Megan. Alex grabbed his collar to prevent him from lunging at her. Alex just stared at Megan. Dumbfounded, not knowing what to say.

"Go on, tell him, go. Run." Megan stood proudly as she knew she had just defeated Alex.

There was such a mixture of emotions swirling. With little grace she had left, she retreated upstairs to her office. Now, to top it off, she was out of Apollo. She just closed her eyes as she shut the lid to the cooler. All she could do was sit on top of the cooler to hide her face with her hands.

"Am I a good person, Komptin?" The massive German shepherd transformed into his gargoyle state. He put his massive head on the shoulder of the Lite Sentry, nuzzling up to her, as if protecting her from all the horror of the world. She wrapped her arms around him, burying her face into his body.

***

Devine was flying out the church window, watching the Sentry cry into Komptin's body. The angel couldn't watch the Sentry in so much pain. The angel flew to the top of the church steeple. Devine stared over the town that was being rebuilt with hidden darkness. It truly was a beautiful area once, before the primates started accepting the Dark. The Balance was starting to shift more to the Dark. It was more evident than ever from what Devine witnessed last night. Luckily, Dinah did not know the view of the East. Devine just wished there was something she could do. There was so much evil to dispose of in this area.

The angel flew off to the town and landed in the park. There were a bunch of children playing on the toy structures. Devine found herself feeling warmth at their innocent laughter.

"Which one is yours?" A woman with a stroller asked Devine. "Timothy Jordan Smith, quit pushing your sister off of the slide." The woman rolled her eyes at Devine. "Kids, right?" Then, the woman turned to the baby in the stroller.

"Mine are not here. You have a lovely child." The angel watched the mother as she wiped the mouth of her baby. Devine couldn't help but notice the F.O.R. towel she was using to wipe her child.

"Thank you." The mother watched her baby sleep. "Timothy, knock it off." The mother went to put a pacifier in the baby's mouth. "I swear that kid is the devil." The mom went over to her son to scold him for trying to push his sister down the slide.

The feeling of understanding started to engulf her. There was no hope for these people. This angel needed to do something to help them.

***

Father Carl was standing in the center of the circle of his captured parishioners. All the people's hope for physical and spiritual salvation rested on his shoulders. "Listen, they need us alive for some reason. They are not hurting us; they are generally keeping us healthy."

"But for what?" One asked from the outside of the circle. The whispers of fear were building within the group.

"We're so dead," another young guy added, not helping with the situation.

"Look, even if our bodies were to die, our souls will be safe in the Kingdom of Heaven. Just maintain your faith. They may take our bodies," Father Carl pointed to his heart. "But they can never take this, and that is all that matters in the long run."

The crowd whispered in agreement. "But what do we do in the meantime?"

Father Carl confidentially answered, "We stick with each other; we help each other. We will be each other's support to lean on. A pillar alone is easy to topple, but if you lean a bunch of them together, it becomes impossible to topple. Let us pray." Father Carl bent down to start praying but was interrupted by the door opening.

The crowd turned to the door as the guards threw Scotty onto the floor. The group immediately helped him up to the medical cot they designated. Kaylee quickly grabbed a bowl with some water.

"Get the clothes off him," Father Carl calmly stated. "We need to see the extent of his wounds."

Kaylee and Rachael helped remove his clothing. There were electrical burns throughout his body. The bruises on his face were swelling. "Why are they only doing this to him?" Kaylee had concern on her face.

"I don't know," Father Carl examined him. "But we can only hope we get answers soon." Father Carl watched as Scotty passed out on the cot. The priest closed his eyes and started praying for the protection of the man in front of him before he started his field medical treatment.

Scotty tried to open his eyes. "I hurt."

Father Carl smirked, "I'm sure you do, son. He grabbed the washcloth from Kaylee. Father Carl wiped the face of the man before him. "Can you tell me anything?"

"I hate God," Scotty muttered. "I bet You're up there laughing at me right now, saying, 'There you go, you son of bitch'. He won't give me the satisfaction of dying."

Father Carl was really confused now. Why would the F.O.R. torture a man of this much hate for his Lord? He was starting to formulate a theory about the group, but the man lying in front of him just became an outlier. "My son, He doesn't take satisfaction in your suffering."

"I doubt He's hating it; He sure as shit isn't doing anything about the situation, we're in," Scotty winced in pain before passing out.

"Is he dead?" Kaylee was afraid as she watched Scotty not move.

"No," Father Carl answered her before turning to Rachel. "Monitor his condition. Let me know if there is anything. I wouldn't be surprised if a fever starts. Keep him dry and covered. His body might be going into shock." Father Carl got up to talk to the people in the room. He needed to keep them calm and their faith strong if they were to get through this.

***

Alex hesitated before knocking on the door to Father Richard's office. She stood outside the door after just a couple of knocks. It seemed like she was waiting awhile. There was no answer. Was he that mad at her? The door was half open, so she knew he was in. He never kept his door unlocked. He really was mad at her, maybe even hated her. Alex decided to forget it and she'll do it herself. As she turned to leave, she literally ran into Father Richard.

"Oh, I'm sorry, Alex. Did you want to talk to me?" He seemed like he was in a relatively good mood, considering.

Alex didn't know how to take this. Was she nothing to him? "Father Richard..."

He laughed, "Really? Father Richard?"

She didn't know how to act. She didn't know what to say.

"Okay, Alex. Come into my office." She followed him into his office, and he shut the door. "Please sit down."

Alex sat down on the small chair in his office. Father Richard didn't sit behind his desk but pulled up a chair to sit next to her. "Look, I shouldn't have yelled at you like I did."

"I deserved it," Alex couldn't look at him in the eye.

"Maybe, but it doesn't mean I should have." Father Richard explained. "Even priests can get carried away with their emotions. We do make mistakes from time to time. Just promise me, the next time, if you think you need to do something like that again, let me know."

"I'm not going to do that shit again," Alex agreed to the kind man. "Though, there is something I need to tell you. A high school classmate of mine called me last night. His sister was working for Roger as his secretary."

"Does he want us to rescue her from the F.O.R.?" Father Richard got up to grab a water. He handed Alex an Apollo from a small cooler. "I'll need clearance from the Council for that. The

Council is still researching deconstruction of F.O.R. members."

"No, she's a die-hard Catholic. He's afraid something happened to her. Robbie is pretty paranoid since the night his dad died by a…wild animal." Alex finger quoted.

"An Infiltrator got him?" Father Richard took a drink of water.

"It was my Virgin Hunt." Alex gave him the details. "I was too late." Father Richard got up to get his coat. "What are you doing?"

"Grabbing my coat; it's cold out there." He put the coat on. "You coming?"

"Where are we going?" Alex started to follow him like a confused puppy.

"To go see the mayor. As a future citizen of this town, I have a constituent concern." Father Richard left out the door. A very confused Alex followed the bald priest to his car.

They both entered the coldness of city hall. Alex got done showing the guard the service papers for Komptin as they were going through security. "This is nuts."

"What? It's not like he's going to kill us in the middle of town in front of all these people." Father Richard went to the directory to find the mayor's office. They went to the elevator to go up to the floor.

Alex just stared forward. "What are you hoping to accomplish?"

"Just a power play." He opened the door to the mayor's office. There was an older lady at the desk. "I take it that's not her."

214

"No," Alex looked down at Komptin, who was deathly staring at the secretary. By his stance, Alex knew this secretary was a Demon. "You know who I am." Alex stared directly at the secretary.

"In trouble," the secretary gave back in equal stare.

She went to pick up phone, but Father Richard hung the phone up on her. "Really, that isn't necessary. We both know it would be a bad idea to escalate this." The secretary flashed her Demon red eyes at the priest. Father Richard didn't flinch. She gently hung up the phone. "That's a good girl."

The door opened to Roger coming out with a reporter and the Chief of Police. "Alex." He was genuinely shocked to see her. "Wow, I can honestly say, I didn't see this coming."

Another person came in from the outside entryway. He was holding a CopperTop Department of Education folder in his hand. Komptin confirmed to Alex this person wasn't a Demon.

"Mr. Somberson," Father Richard eyed him. Alex was impressed that he wasn't backing down, staring at the powerful Demon mayor.

"That's Mayor Somberson; would you like to come in and talk before my next meeting?" Roger showed him the door. "I have some time."

Alex was actually getting ready to leave, until Father Richard said. "Yes, I do, actually." He marched directly into Mayor Somberson's office. It even caught Roger by surprise. He glanced over to Alex in shock. All Alex did was shrug her shoulders in return.

Roger turned to the woman from the Department of Education. "I'll be right with you. Bea, get her some coffee or something to drink." Roger closed the door and grew his teeth while his eyes were glowing. He sat down with the continuous glow of the Dark.

"You want to play that game," Alex stood up with eyes glowing blue and fist lit.

"I think we can both agree that it wouldn't work out on both ends if we were to do this right now," Father Richard remained calm.

Roger thought about it. "Her first."

Father Richard turned to his Lite Sentry. "Alex." She succumbed and returned back to normal before sitting down.

"What a good little Sentry," Roger sarcastically said as he himself subdued his power. "What's on your mind?"

"Where's her body?" Alex flat-out asked.

"You need to be more specific," Roger leaned back in his chair.

"Jennifer Rodriguez," Father Richard maintained his unfearful stance.

"Oh, my old secretary. Yah, she got devoured by a bunch of Infiltrators. Really was something to witness. Especially when she cried out to her God that didn't show...shocker." Roger laughed.

"You were always a sick little boy, Roger," Alex made sure to emphasize his Primate name. It didn't go unnoticed.

"Really, you want to know sick. Like I didn't know you sent that little hooker to come spy on me. Didn't know you had that in you." Roger was

216

having fun playing off the hidden identity of the Dark Harridan. "Lucky, I didn't kill her."

"Why didn't you?" Father Richard really was curious about why Megan was still alive.

"Didn't feel like dealing with the consequence of her dying." Roger looked over at the wardrobe but quickly returned eye contact with Father Richard.

"What are you up to, Roger?" Alex's voice was strong with confidence.

Roger laughed, "Oh, Alex, you're cute. I think our meeting is done." Roger pushed a button and the secretary opened the door for them to leave.

Father Richard got up, "Let's go, Alex."

"Shoo, shoo, little girl." Roger mockingly flung her away with his hand.

"Roger, I'm personally going to send you to Hell," Alex got up to leave.

"Hmm, why? Is Kameron lonely?" Roger's arrogant attitude was infuriating.

Alex immediately went to charge at him, but Father Richard grabbed her before she did anything foolish. "Not now, Alex." She straightened her body and fixed her clothes before calmly bumping shoulders with the Demon secretary out of the office.

She waited until the elevator doors shut. "Sorry about that," Alex apologized.

"No big, we got some very interesting information," Father Richard seemed quite happy with the situation.

"We know what happened to Jennifer," Alex confirmed.

"That, and there is definitely something in that office." Father Richard nodded to Alex, silently telling her what his wishes were.

***

Gron was in the limo with Megan and the twins. They just sat still in a complete deadpan stare. Not at Gron, but just in general. Gron waved his hands in front of them to see if they would change their reaction. All they did was move their eyes towards him, and then back forward.

"They are such good kids," Megan said, stroking the little girl's hair.

"If you say so, hopefully, they will have some use to them," Gron sat back in the limo with a drink in his hand. He put his hand over his head as he leaned back. "I hope this works. I want to get the hell out of this town."

"We still have a lot of work to do," Megan moved the black hair out of the little boy's eyes.

"The Sentinel program will be implemented soon. Then, we'll slowly employ the F.O.R. ideals in the schools. We'll make this town the F.O.R. centerpiece of the state." Gron finished his drink. "If we can get that portal open, it can speed up the permanent shift. Then our Master will ensure the Dark overtakes the Primates and bring forth the Fallen."

The limo stopped in front of the museum where Azrael was with a multitude of fallen Angels. "Leader Gron."

"You've been busy," Gron looked over the mixture of Angels, both male and female.

"Two more sentries have been eliminated," Azrael stood proud.

"Good," The group of them made their way into the museum to the artifact. The group parted way for the twins. They reached the massive stone and metal structure. They tilted their heads as if the structure was talking to them. The anticipation in the room elevated as they stopped in front of it. There was a brief moment before the twins just turned around, shrugging their shoulders.

"Useless," Gron rolled his eyes. He put his fingers on the top of the bridge of his nose. "Take them back to the compound." He turned to Azrael. "Are you sure that symbol is hybrid?"

"Could it be the birth of two Sentries: a Dark and Lite love child?" Megan studied the relic. "There's a sun here behind some clouds." She rubbed her hands on the item.

"Perhaps," Gron was in deep thought. "Vandor was obsessed with Alex and me producing a child. Unfortunately, the other Dark Sentry is no longer with us."

Azrael and Gron both tried to answer the puzzle of the relic. "We need someone who knows both Lite and Dark texts," Azrael observed.

"Anne might be able to do it," Megan offered up the Council Historian.

"She'll die before she helps us," Gron was starting to get a headache. "We've kidnapped her before." Gron tapped his chin in deep thought as he studied the relic. "Maybe it's time you do some girls' time."

***

Kameron came home to his parent's house late at night. Megan said she needed to study up on some notes in her apartment for an upcoming meeting. Kameron secretly was a bit relieved. He pulled into the driveway to notice Alex was sitting on top of her roof from across the street. She waived to him, and he generously followed in kind. Even though the yawn he gave was a sign he was tired, he was genuinely curious on what she was doing. He felt a little awkward walking across the street as she watched him approach her house. "Are you stuck?" He asked.

Alex laughed, "No, just star gazing."

Kameron looked to the stars on this clear night. "They truly are wonderful."

She gazed back up at them. "A true representation." Then she caught herself studying Kameron as he was staring at the sky. "Working late?"

"It was a rough day." Kameron took in a deep breath. "Ended up sending someone to Rejuvenation near the end of my shift."

Alex's demeanor got a little stiff. "Wanna talk about it?"

"Not particularly." Kameron veered in the direction of town.

Alex made a playful, pouty face. "Might make you feel better. Things might be a little clearer from

220

a different perspective." She moved over, insinuating to come on up to the roof. "I have drinks." She lifted a cooler.

"Well, in that case," Kameron joked.

"Come on up, Kameron." Alex gave a final push with a smile.

At first, Kameron was just joking, but it looked as if she took him seriously. It felt like a crossroads for choices. Maybe it would make him feel a little better. Plus, he didn't want to be rude to her, so he thought he would join her for a little bit. He scanned the area for a ladder or something. "How did you get up there?"

"There's a shed in the back you can use," Alex pointed to the backyard. "Careful, there's a spot where it's pretty slick on the roof."

Kameron made use of the shed and joined his neighbor on the roof. "Nice night."

Alex handed him the cooler. "As promised." She patted on top of the blanket next to her.

He complied as she opened the cooler to a bunch of chocolate cream-filled cakes you get at a gas station. "Health food." He pulled out a green soda. "No alcohol?"

"I can't drink; it makes me sick." Alex grabbed one of the sodas.

Kameron opened one, and they bumped cans together. They both took sips from their respective containers. "It does look different up here. Almost like there are no troubles down there at all."

"Just a different outlook on what the world offers. Makes you think the higher you go, the better it may be." Alex played with her can.

Kameron didn't really say anything, but Alex could tell something was bothering him. "So, what happened today?"

"I separated a family today. The parents had Lite paraphernalia on them." Kameron took in another deep breath.

Alex turned her face away from Kameron. "Results from spreading the Lite, someone is bound to get caught." Then, she took a deep breath before going back to the conversation. "You don't seem happy about it."

"It's just that...I know the Trinity of the Fallen is established as what is best for us, but..." he just whispered. "...ripping apart families like that, just isn't easy."

"It never is." Alex was quiet. "You know, the best part of sitting up here is that nothing else can distract you from your thoughts. Nothing in the world can get you up here."

"But I'm up here with you," Kameron teased her.

"A welcome distraction," Alex locked eyes with him. It was a moment that lasted forever. Alex was the first to break the connection. "So, you and Megan, how's that going?"

Kameron stared forward. "It's okay. Her power is growing in society. She is definitely going places."

Alex bluntly asked, "Are you happy?"

Kameron laughed. "Boy, you just go straight for the gusto."

"Sorry, don't mean anything by it. It's just...you always seem to be on edge. This is the first time I've ever seen you…relax." Alex took a sip of her drink.

Kameron twirled his can. "Sometimes I feel I can never make her happy. I'm always doing something wrong."

Alex just nodded. The two of them just stared at the sky as they continued to have small talk.

"It's getting late," Kameron happened to see the time.

"It is." Alex smiled at him. They both got up from the blanket. Kameron folded it for her as Alex grabbed the cooler. The two of them carefully shuffled their feet down the roof. Kameron was the first to get down as Alex threw him the cooler. As she tossed it, she lost her footing. She slid off the roof and landed in Kameron's arms. "Sorry." She laughed and then stopped when she saw how close she was to her savior's face.

"You okay?" he gazed at her.

"Nothing is hurting," she shyly turned her face away from him as he put her down. She silently mouthed, "Wow," as she fanned her face.

Kameron picked up the cooler and blanket. "I guess…I should get going." He handed her belongings.

"Yah, I think that's a good idea." Alex opened the French doors to the back of the house. "Have a good night, Kameron."

Kameron watched her go into the house. She gave a quick wave before retiring for the night.

Chapter Nine

Alex had to grab the wall to steady herself in the hallway of the church. "Whoa, vertigo." Her eyes got big as she tried to focus.

"You, okay?" Tristan cautiously held onto her arm to try to steady the wavery Sentry.

Alex tried clearing her head. "I think so. That was weird. For a second there, I felt like I was falling." Alex pulled her arm away. "I'm good, really." The two of them continued down the hall. She was a bit dizzy, but it went away after a quick hot flash.

"I want to come with," Tristan was becoming persistent.

"I don't know." Alex secretly liked he was gaining confidence in himself. "It's just a recon mission."

"Yes, inside the office of the most powerful Demon in town." Tristan broke it down to the simplest form. "Look, no offense, but you can't sense the Dark. I can be there as a lookout or something."

"I have Komptin," She smiled at her dog, who barked up at her and wagged his tail.

"Come on," Tristan pleaded like a teenager asking his parents if he could go out with his friends. "Don't make me beg. I'm not going to get hurt. I'll just be on the perimeter."

Alex thought about it. More so, how not get him to go. "I don't know. The fewer people, the better on this one."

"Alex, I guess when the Dark overtakes me, it will be because of this one night of no training. This one training night could have been the one to save my life." Tristan playfully started to walk down the hall. "I guess I'll just spend the night picking out my spot in the sky."

"Fine, drama queen." Alex halfway reluctantly gave in. She couldn't help but laugh a little. "We will leave at ten tonight."

"Cool, thanks. You won't regret it." Tristan went strutting down the hallway whistling.

Alex stopped at Anne's office door, but she didn't answer. Her door was partially opened, and she slowly opened the door to see her deep into her books. "What are you doing?" Anne just kept on studying. "Anne." Alex was a little louder, but still, there was no answer. "Anne!"

Anne jumped. "Sorry."

"Whatchya doin'?" Alex teased her friend.

"Oh, just falling into the subterranean depths of studying." Anne had something on her desk that was the shape of a kite. It had a seal on it that Alex didn't recognize. Alex sat down on the chair on the wall next to Anne's desk. She went to pick up the item on Anne's desk, but Anne playfully slapped Alex's hand. "No touchy."

"Ow," Alex was shaking her hand. "Aren't we just a little testy."

Anne got up to put some papers in the safe. "I'm just trying to figure out some stuff."

"Gotcha. So, I have some news. I'm going to break into the mayor's office tonight." Alex was petting Komptin as his head was resting on her lap.

He closed his eyes as he was enjoying the scratching of his ears as he started snoring.

"What are you looking for?" Anne sat back in the chair.

Alex just watched Komptin sleep. "I swear this dog can sleep anywhere. I don't know, but Father Richard told me to go straight to the wardrobe in the corner. I guess he wants a new coat." Alex was verifying the time on her watch. "I hate this part, knowing the mission and waiting for the time to go."

"It'll be here before you know it." Anne peeked her head over Alex's shoulder. "Father."

Alex turned around to see Father Richard. She was halfway hoping it was Father Carl. No one has heard from him for quite some time. "What's going on?"

"I just got off the phone with the Council. Apparently, a Dark Sentry was recently killed. The Sentry who dispatched him hasn't been seen, and she's presumed dead."

"There was another Dark Sentry?" Alex was in shock. "Another Sentry killed him. Who was it?"

"Her name was Sherri Proper. If you hear anything, let me know." Father Richard started to get up before Alex stopped him.

"That name sounds familiar. Why do I know that name?" Alex was off looking in the distance. "What was her last sighting?"

"Of all things, she caused a semi to crash. Scavenged the back of the truck and took off before the authorities arrived." Father Richard was getting ready to retire for the night.

"Where was the truck headed?" Anne asked.

"University of Arizona." Father Richard was starting to get some heavy bags underneath his eyes.

"What the hell was in Arizona?" Alex turned to Anne, but she just shrugged her shoulders.

They both heard Father Richard greet Megan in the hallway. They knew he did it as a warning not to talk about Council matters. Both Alex and Anne watched the doorway as Megan came into the room. They both stared at her.

"Okay," Megan just stared at the two in the room for a moment before speaking. "Anne, I was wondering if I could take you up on that help with my book?"

"Of course," Anne told her. "You can bring it by anytime."

"Actually, it's more of a field trip, subject matter expert." Megan showed her the keys to her car.

"Sure, I can do that." Anne agreed. "When?"

"I'm free now," Megan gave her a look of hope.

Alex got up in front of Anne. She put her hands on her desk to lean into her. "You have fun with that." Alex turned around to leave. She whistled for Komptin to follow her out of the office. Alex stopped for a split second, about to say something, but all she did was shake her head before leaving.

"She's got some serious attitude issues," Megan watched her leaving, wishing she could just kill her.

Anne grabbed her jacket. "She's got a lot on her plate."

Anne was confused on why they ended up at the museum. It didn't make any sense why she would come here for a "how-to" book. Maybe it had to do with some symbolism or something. The museum used to be the old City Hall building before CopperTop turned it into a historical building. It was stone, with beautiful carvings on the pillars. The ceiling was painted with a multitude of different angelic scenes.

"I hope Roger doesn't get to paint over these," Anne admired the ceiling. "There's so much beauty and history here."

"He probably tried but got blocked by the Historical Society." Megan had to be careful and not overplay her hand. She stopped in front of an old spinning wheel. "This is what I was thinking of putting into my book."

"A spinning wheel?" Anne was confused. "Maybe if you let me read the book, I can see how it would fit."

"Not til it's done," Megan teased. "I was just thinking of using the story of Rumpelstiltskin. Taking advantage of every possible route can turn into gold."

"Actually, she basically made a deal with the devil; she took the easy route for fortune and power. Almost cost her the child she bared." Anne read over the history of the display.

Megan had to control her anger. Anne had a holier-than-thou attitude that was infuriating. She wouldn't know true power if it smacked her across the face. "Well, I guess we should look around to see if there's anything that fits."

"Sure." Anne took off her jacket as she was getting warm. The two of them sauntered around without basically saying anything. "Have you ever thought about getting along with Alex?" She came out of nowhere with that question.

"I tried, but she kept on insulting me, being passive-aggressive at every little chance she gets." Megan acted like she was trying to find something for her book but was secretly getting closer to the doorway to the massive artifact. "My sister was like that. Everything was about her. The whole family put everything into her singing career."

"She's a singer? Anything I know?" Anne stopped to study an old kite hanging on the wall. In the center of the fabric was a cross holding it together. She continued studying for a bit before Megan interrupted her train of thought.

"Here she is," Megan showed her a picture on her phone of a singer of a Christian rock band.

"I might have heard of her album." Anne mentally locked away the name of the band.

"She's a hypocritical bitch, and the rest of the family could care less about me." Megan forcefully put her phone into her pocket.

"Have you ever thought of reaching out to them?" Anne leaned on the barrier as she was waiting for Megan's answer.

Megan, in turn, met Anne's gaze. "It's too late. My parents hate me. The whole family pretty much shut me out."

"What happened?" Anne could tell her guard was down.

"I could never forget what they did to Madison."

Anne realized, for the first time, that it came down to pure, authentic emotion from Megan. Anne went into her purse to grab a tissue for Megan to hide the tears that were forming. "Once you're open to forgiveness, it exposes the door to peace. All you have to do is walk through it." Anne gave her a comforting smile. Anne moved over to the next exhibit to give Megan a second to herself to pull herself together.

As Anne gave her a moment to pull it together, it took all Megan's strength not to fall to the ground. The pain in her stomach came as a dull, nauseous feeling. She had to concentrate not to vomit all over the floor of this building. Her eyes turned pure black with a hint of red in the center. She then calmed herself down by the time Anne turned around.

"You, okay?" Anne asked.

"I'm fine. Clarity, gotta love it." Misluna focused on the follower of Lite before her.

Anne was getting a bit impatient. "We really should get going. The museum will be closing soon."

"Perhaps you're right." Misluna grabbed her purse. Then she turned to some stairs in the corner of the room. "Hey, where do these go?

Anne saw the doorway where she was pointing. "I don't know. You think there is more downstairs?"

"Come on, let's go look. It won't take long."
Misluna led the way downstairs.

Anne put her coat on since it wouldn't take
long before they had to leave. The spiral staircase
down was metal and echoed to the room downstairs.
Anne noticed the elevator to the right of them,
verifying that it was handicapped accessible to the
exhibit. It was such a high ceiling for being in the
basement. "What is that?"

Misluna stopped as she watched Anne approach
the structure. She had to play it off of not being that
excited. "I really don't know."

Anne stopped in front of the stone and metal
structure with carvings on the side. Her hand
touched the carvings delicately. She stopped when
she came across the circle with carvings inside.

"What is it?" Megan held her breath with
anticipation. "Do you know what that is?"

"I've seen this symbol before," Anne
whispered. It was almost as if she was talking to
herself and not Megan. The Church Historian
continued to study the carvings. "This symbol
could mean 'gate of out.' Doesn't make any sense,
considering this one over here almost represents
transference, but not from one place to another."
Anne turned to Megan. "But this one here…can't
be possible." She pointed to the symbol of the cloud
covering the sun.

Megan walked up to it. "What do you mean?
Just looks like the sun behind the clouds."

"Not that one, this one." She pointed to the one
below it.

"The deer, what about it?"

"So, check this out. The clouds covering the sun; represents the Dark overtaking the Lite. That could mean anything, just a symbol of the fight for the Balance. But, having that above this deer without a separator." Anne pointed to other symbols with a faint line in between the pictures. "This means it's one scene. See how the deer is half chiseled out."

"Yah, okay," Misluna could feel the eagerness start to overtake her.

"This doesn't represent deer, it represents a 'Hart,' you know, the animal, but at that time, man didn't have a symbol for the human heart. The common heart symbol didn't come about until the mid 1200s; this is much older as represented by this symbol." Anne was putting it all together.

"What are you telling me?" Misluna was eyeing the symbol.

"The half-chiseled deer represents the hybrid of a Pure of Heart within the Dark," Anne told her.

"How can someone Pure of Heart be infested with the Dark?" Megan was confused.

Anne was studying the structure, but Megan caught her attention. "You know about the Dark?"

Megan had to cover her tracks quickly. "Evil, right? Aren't you just being dramatic by calling it dark?"

"Yah, I was." Anne was worried she let out too much before she was indoctrinated into the Council. "According to Christian Folklore that I once read; I'm just saying, this is a hybrid of a Pure of Heart infested," then Anne stopped herself. "Not infiltrated but infested. How would someone get

the Dark into them without infiltration?" Anne murmured to herself.

"What would this hybrid do?" Misluna was edging her on.

"They are used to refill the key, by this symbol here. A key to open a…" Anne stopped herself. She looked at the top of the structure, where there was a placeholder of a horizontal line over a vertical one with an arrow on the bottom. Anne stepped back in terror. "Holy shit!" Anne quickly turned to Megan. "This is a man-made Conduit of the Dark."

"And the key?" Misluna was inching forward.

Anne stopped and thought of the kite on the wall. "I have to get back to the church."

Misluna watched Anne run up the stairs. "So close."

**

Alex was lying on the floor next to Komptin as he put his head on the bed Kameron made. It was a calming solace as she scratched his ears as he gently slept. The memory of Kameron sacrificing himself was running through her mind. She truly lost him forever. The clock ahead of her was clicking. The hour was approaching for her to go on the council-sanctioned operation to literally break the law. A quick prayer that she didn't get arrested wouldn't hurt.

The big hand on the clock told her it was time for the pale-skinned Sentry to change into her hunting clothes. The outfit of choice was her black pants and a long dark blue exercise shirt. She stared at herself in the mirror after she put on her makeup. The leather collar covered her scar from her first fight with a Demon. Inside her closet, she grabbed her leather vest. After she zipped it up, she tied her hair with a dark blue tie. The boots she wore were specially made for Secret Service agents. They were soft, durable, and very comfortable. Most important, they were quiet. Kameron had gotten her a pair. There was no reason at all. He had just gotten them for her. He always thought of her, and she returned the sentiment. She picked up a picture of Kameron and her at Christmas that she had reprinted. It was the happiest she had ever been. A knock on the door interrupted her trip down memory lane. "Come on in." Normally, she would put the picture down, but tonight, she didn't want to let it go.

Tristan came into the office. "It's almost time to go."

She just nodded, still holding the picture.

"You don't look good?" Tristan studied his mentor.

"I've been better," Alex turned to Komptin, still sleeping in his Gargoyle state.

Tristan put his jacket on that he was carrying. "I'll meet you outside the church."

"You don't have to go," Alex reiterated. "It's just a simple recon mission."

"What's the worst that could happen?" Tristan gave a false confident smile. "I'll be outside."

Alex got a sudden shot of nervous energy as a precursor of tonight's events. A kiss from Alex awoke Komptin. He slowly opened one eye to see her. "We got a couple more minutes. There's some stuff I have to do, then we'll go." She gently scratched behind his ears before getting up to go give a quick prayer at the altar. She walked downstairs to see Anne with her white coat on. "What are you still doing here?"

Anne yawned. "Oh, excuse me. I got swept up in a project. Good luck and be safe tonight."

"Will do. Bail me out of jail tonight?" Alex joked. Anne hugged her before leaving for the night. The Lite Sentry took advantage of the couple minutes she had to venture in front of the congregation. She closed her eyes, with small hopes of a sense of a connection.

"Don't worry, I got this." She winked at the crucifix before leaving. The Sentry whistled for Komptin as she left out of the church. Her hunting partner slowly came down the stairs in his German Shepherd form to join Alex.

Celestial came out from the small candle room with her guardians. She seemed to float through the aisle to watch the party leave for their mission. The Conduit of the Lite just stared at them as she said, "Call for the gathering. We do not have much time." Devine and Dinah were in the hallway entryway in the corner from the Sentry before they came out to the massive hall. They locked eyes with Celestial as she slowly nodded her wishes. They both confidently walked out of the church to take to the skies.

Alex was surveying City Hall from the building across the street within the shadows of the building. She had sent Tristan scouting on the other end of the building.   There were guards on the front door. Alex tapped the side of the wall with her finger. She smiled down at Komptin, who was scouting the area.   His ears were perked and on alert.   "I know you'd rather be out in the woods."   She scratched his ears.

He licked her hand as his eyes flashed.   Then his attention turned to behind him.   Alex knew he was alerted to something.   Her eyes started to glow as she turned out to the darkness.   From the glow of her hands came the outline of two angels.   She dissipated the glow of her hands.   "Devine, Dinah, what are you doing here?"

"We followed the Dark to this location." Devine looked over the building.   "What is your plan?"

"Well, I can't break in without sounding an alarm of some sort."   Alex turned to look at the building.   "I was actually thinking of going in through the roof," she pointed out.

Devine studied her proposed route.   "I can carry you."

"Thanks, but if you can, carry Komptin.   Dinah, can you watch Tristan's back?"   Alex asked the orange-haired angel.

"Why do I get stuck with the menial tasking?" Dinah shook her head before she took off to find the new Sentry.

"She really doesn't like people, does she?" Alex watched her take off.

Devine gazed in the direction she was heading. "She has always been bold, tough, but she speaks her thoughts.   That is why she is being punished."

Alex knelt down to pet Komptin. "What do you mean?"

"She speaks her thoughts. It scares her that Azrael's influence almost took her heart." Devine picked up Komptin.

"So, now He banished her to Earth?" Alex was confused.

"She needs to clean her heart; it is too dangerous to send an angel to Heaven with the potential to turn. It could open the gates just as when Azrael turned to Dark. Plus, she disrespected the Father." Devine smirked.

"How does she cleanse her heart?" Alex watched Dinah disappear to find Tristan.

"Only she knows. It is different per individual," Devine pointed to the spot on the roof to meet up.

Alex grabbed her phone to text Tristan that she would go in through the roof, and Dinah was on her way. "Well, let's go see what's in the office?" Alex knew that Devine could get to the roof faster, but they wouldn't be able to see anything written for the Dark that might be in the office. The Dark was blind to the Lite Texts, just as the Lite is unable to interpret the Dark. Alex almost thought that is why He created the Lite Sentries. Humans have the choice to follow either the Dark or Lite; giving them the choice to see the Dark writings or understandings.

The angel and the protector made their way to the roof. They would provide overlook for Alex as she made her way up. She cracked her neck as she ran behind the building. There was a dumpster underneath the window to the first window. There was no doubt that it was alarmed, so she couldn't go in through that way. She ran to the dumpster to close it gently. The fire escape was pretty high, so Alex jumped towards the side of the building and pushed herself off to grab the ladder. She climbed up it to the roof where Devine was knelt on the ground, scratching Komptin behind the ears.

"What took you so long?" Devine continued to give Komptin some rubbing behind the ears.

"Cute," Alex motioned with her head over to the entrance door. A motion caught her attention as Dinah lifted Tristan up from the street onto the roof. "What are you guys doing here?"

Dinah threw Tristan onto the roof before landing. He barely caught himself from falling before straightening his clothes. "The primate believed he needed to go into the room with you."

"No, I'll be fine," Alex turned around, almost angrily. There were too many people for a stealth break-in.

"Come on, Alex," Tristan was unhappy being on lookout. "How am I to learn if I'm out on the perimeter?"

"I don't know what's in that office," Alex pointed to the door. "They could be doing Infiltration right below us, and I wouldn't know."

"But I would," Tristan pointed to himself.

Alex's face turned red with irritation. "Whatever, it's your funeral."

"If you do find something down there. It would be better if one of us carried it, the other for security," Tristan marched through the door.

Dinah yelled to Alex, "Are you going or are you not? We do not have much time."

Alex looked at her watch, "What's the rush?"

Both Dinah and Devine glanced at each other as the two Sentries went to the roof access with Komptin.

The stairwell down was black, with only the emergency lights on. Alex never understood why she just couldn't have a well-lit place to do her hunt. They reached the floor where the mayor's office was located. Alex motioned to Tristan if he sensed anything. With a quiet negative reply, the two of them opened the doorway to the empty hallway.

They reached the lobby office door, where Alex just had a feeling that the secretary was around here somewhere. To Alex's shock, the door was open. That meant the old woman was around here somewhere, but she had no idea where she was. Alex was going to feel halfway guilty if she had to kill an old woman like that, even if she was a Demon.

"It's open?" Tristan said out of shock. "Is this good, or really bad?"

Alex had to swallow her pride a bit. "Sense anything?"

"Just normal Darkness." The two of them snuck into the lobby where the secretary sat. The two of them slowly opened the door to the mayor's office. "Alright, we're lucky."

"Weird. I wonder why this is unlocked with no one here." Alex looked down at Komptin to give him a reassuring smile. "With our luck, I don't think this night is going to be that easy." The two Sentries snuck into the office.

It was empty and scary. The only light coming in was from the streetlights outside. Alex went straight for the wardrobe. "Go look around our wonderful mayor's desk for anything suspicious."

Tristan went to do what he was told. Alex took a deep breath to open the wardrobe, but she couldn't get it open. It was as if a Dark force was preventing her from opening it. She turned around to Komptin. "Come here, boy."

Komptin morphed into his gargoyle state. He bit on the doorknob as Alex took the other. They both pulled on the doors, and it budged about half an inch before they both lost grip. They both tumbled onto the floor with Alex and Komptin tangled into each other. Alex couldn't help but laugh as Komptin started licking her. She grabbed him by the cheeks and kissed his gargoyle nose. "Come on. Maybe Anne knows something about this. Hopefully, there's something in the desk."

Alex joined Tristan to rummage through the desk but couldn't find anything. She found a notepad on the desk. Alex leaned back in the chair and put her feet up on the desk as she started reading it as Tristan went to the secretary's desk to see if he could find anything. The notepad was in a female's handwriting about setting up a meeting with the governor once the Sentinel program showed results. Then, something about the curriculum in the schools.

Komptin turned his head towards Alex and flashed his eyes. Tristan came running into the office, "There's someone coming, Dark."

"Shit," Alex knew they were going to have to battle their way through this. More than likely, they all were going to be Demons. Alex silently told Tristan to close the door. Alex went to the side of the door next to the wardrobe, and Tristan went to the other. "Komptin," Alex whispered. Her hunting partner was just standing in front of the door. "Komptin," Alex whispered a little bit louder. The gargoyle turned and slowly walked towards Alex to join her on the side of the room. Alex rubbed his head as he sat by her. She looked at the ceiling to see if there was a leak, as he was dripping wet.

There was whispering of two individuals. Tristan pointed to his teeth and eyes to tell Alex they were Demons. There was no doubt about it now: Tristan was about to fight his first Demon. Alex flashed her eyes in preparation for the upcoming battle.

"This assignment is beneath me," the man was talking.

"If the Leader Gron heard you say that, you'd be dead," the voice was that of the secretary. They could be heard from behind the door.

"It's in the main office," the old lady started to open the door.

Alex could feel her anticipation. Whoever entered first would see Tristan. The old woman turned when she felt the Lite of Tristan, who hesitated at the sight of the Demon. The old lady attacked Tristan with a mixture of growling and hissing. She punched Tristan across the face, sending him into the wall. She followed suit by grabbing him to throw him across the room.

The male rushed into the room to see what was going on. His teeth grew as he flashed his red eyes. He went to attack, but the old lady stopped him. "Go! Get the Dark Harridan out of here."

Alex flashed a bright blue all over her body as she heard the Dark Harridan was close by. The Demon took off out of the office as the old lady turned to fight Alex to bide time for the other Demon. Alex fought her, quite easily took her head, smashed it against the wall that turned the light on, and then tossed her to the side for Tristan to deal with.

"Come on, Komptin, we got a chance to find out who she is." Alex turned to Komptin, who was now a grayish purple, with very little Lite in his eyes. Alex hesitated as her heart sank. "Komptin," she said very softly. Then, the massive gargoyle just dropped to the side. "KOMPTIN!" Alex screamed. "DEVINE HELP!!"

The windows came smashing in as the two angels came into the room, ready for battle. The old woman faced the Angels with a growl while her eyes growled. Without hesitation, Dinah formed two small swords and decapitated the old woman. She wasn't even finished melting into the ground by the time the angels reached Komptin and Alex.

"We do not have much time," Devine told Dinah.

Dinah helped Devine get Komptin. "We can save time by going through a doorway." An opening appeared where Celestial with Guardians came out.

"Bring him; we must attend the Gathering," Celestial showed Devine the way to bring him to the doorway, but Dinah stopped before entering the doorway.

She put Komptin's legs down. "I cannot go home."

Arome and Omelia grabbed Komptin from Devine to carry him into the doorway, where Celestial nodded to Alex before entering the Conduit. Alex started to run after Komptin, but Devine grabbed her. "Sister, you cannot follow him."

"But," Alex was streaked in tears. "Komptin!"

Tristan came up to the girls, holding his lip. "What's going on?"

"We must go," Devine grabbed Alex and jumped out the window.

"Where are they going?" Tristan asked Dinah.

"Come on," Dinah said out of annoyance. She grabbed Tristan as he put his arm around her neck. She, too, jumped out the window carrying a Sentry.

***

Father Carl was praying for the protection of the beaten man before him. Not just for his physical body but for his soul as well. The man had evidence of fighting his inner Demons.

"It's useless to pray for me," Scotty tried to sit up on the bed.

"You're not as hurt as I thought, but then again, I'm not a doctor." Father Carl motioned for Rachel to bring him some water.

"He only healed me faster so I can get tortured more," he chuckled lightly. "Ow." He held his side.

"I don't think He likes his children to suffer," Father Carl grabbed a washcloth that Kaylee had brought him.

"He may not like it, but He still allows it." Scotty put his hand on the washcloth to apply pressure on his head.

"It's the sin of man; the freewill He had given us. We pervert all He has given to us for our own guilty pleasure." Father Carl continued to check over his wounds.

"Do you sin?" He looked over at the priest.

"Every day," the gray-haired priest admitted.

"What, forget a blessing when eating a fast-food bacon cheeseburger?" Scotty flinched when Rachel and Kaylee were checking his bruises.

Kaylee smiled at him. "Sorry."

"Pride. Wrath. I take out my anger on an individual that I shouldn't. My pride won't let me understand the situation they are in or appreciate what she does for us." Father Carl opened himself up.

"I guess you're not perfect. I'm a fan of lust myself." Scotty joked.

"Most are," Father Carl started picking some dirt out of his cuts.

Scotty seemed to let his guard down a bit. "But God will never forgive me for how much I hate Him. He won't do shit for me."

"What is it that caused you so much negativity for the Lite?" Father Carl pointed to a wound for Rachel to clean.

Scotty took a moment, but as he was about to talk, the door opened to the girl who oversaw his torture. Scotty tensed up; he knew it was time for more.

"Time to talk," the confident lady-demon smirked with glowing red eyes.

Father Carl stood up in front of Scotty in protection. "No. He's had enough."

"Get out of the way, or I'll kill you." The girl annoyingly stood in front of the priest, who stood in the way of her tasking.

"No, I said he's had enough. I will go in his place. Think of the enjoyment of torturing a priest." Father Carl offered himself.

The girl took a moment to think about it. "Tempting, but I have my orders." She grabbed the priest and easily threw him into the stone wall. "You get in my way again, and I won't kill you; I'll make you watch as I rip that baby right out of that mother's womb." One of the male Demons grabbed Kaylee and put their sharpened claws on her stomach.

"It's okay, I'll go, I'll go." Scotty stood up and straightened his clothes. He started to limp towards the doorway. "I'm actually starting to enjoy it."

"Isn't he such a hero?" one of the male Demons said just before he tripped him as he fell to the ground. "You're not getting your Martyr moment." The Demon picked him up with ease, shoving him into the wall.

The female turned to the group with anger. "The Lite abandoned all of you. Your deaths are only here to fill my master's life upon his return. Get used to it; you're all just cattle."

Kaylee and some of the other prisoners ran to Father Carl's side to help him up. Father Carl let them know he was okay. "Now is the time we must keep our faith; it is more important now than ever."

***

Alex refused to leave Komptin. His body was now a dull mixture of gray and purple. The Sentry wiped a little bit of blood dripping from his nose, and she reached over to grab a cloth soaking in water. Father Richard was in the back of the room with a weeping Anne. Devine was on the other side of the room, trying to maintain strength over the hard-to-watch scene. Celestial was on the ground next to Komptin, her ear to his chest. Her guardians behind her were awaiting her orders.

"What happened to him?" Alex asked in between the wiping of her tears.

"Sana's blade, we were never able to heal it," Celestial informed her.

"Why didn't he just stay in Heaven?" Alex continued to rub his head.

Celestial lifted her head to meet with her Sentry's crying eyes. "His promise to Osiah, but most important of all, his love for you."

"Can't you take him now? You can't die in Heaven." Alex pleaded.

"I am sorry, Alexandria, it is too late." Celestial was now playing the strong mother figure Alexandria needed right now.

Father Richard put his hand on Anne, motioning that it was time to leave the room. Anne left the room crying as Father Richard tried to comfort her. Alex wiped more of the blood dripping from Komptin's nose. Komptin tried to lift his head to look at Alex.

"This is not the way for him to go," Alex combed her hand through her hair, refusing to wipe the dropping tears.

"Alexandria, this is exactly how he wanted it," Celestial cleansed the tears off her Sentry.

Alex put her hand on his head to prevent him from struggling to lift it. "Don't die. I need you." Her attention was on Celestial. "You knew, and you didn't tell me?" Alex started to cry harder as she hugged her hunting partner for the last seven years.

"I could not," Celestial told her. She turned to face her guardians, silently letting them know it was time. "Alexandria, we must attend the Gathering."

"The what?" Alex lifted her head. "What about Komptin? I'm not leaving him."

Celestial gently placed her hand on Alex's head. "You will not; he will be the focus of all in the room."

"My lady, he does not possess the strength to make it down the stairs," Arome softly observed.

Omelia concluded, "We shall carry him."

Celestial nodded as she helped Alex off the ground. Alex turned to her, hugging her godmother. "I can't lose him." Alex lost the control to hold in her crying. The only comfort she had was holding onto Celestial as tightly as she could.

"Come, my child. It is time," Celestial motioned to escort Alex downstairs. "Be strong."

Arome and Omelia struggled to pick up the dying gargoyle. As gently as they could, they carried him down the stairs. Devine walked backwards down the stairs as the new Guardians of the Conduit carried Komptin. She was focused to make sure if they dropped him, she would be there to catch him. They made it just outside the main congregation hall. Alex was in complete shock. The assembly was packed with Angels of the Lite. The faint harmonic sound of a choir of humming angels came from the room.

Alex jumped in front of the guardians before they entered the room. "Stop, please. Let him walk; let him go with head held high." Alex pleaded to Celestial.

The blonde angel nodded as she motioned for Arome and Omelia to let him down in front just before entering the congregation hall. Celestial made sure Alex paid attention, "Be sure to be strong for him." Celestial gracefully began to head towards the front of the room. All who were attending turned their heads to watch.

Alex closed her eyes as she began walking beside Komptin, who was struggling to make it towards the altar. She had never seen him so weak, when normally he was so full of life. Arome and Omelia broke off to the sides to head towards the altar to stand behind Celestial as she put herself at the head of the room.

It was difficult for Alex to hold her head high without silent tears dropping onto the church floor. The harmonizing singing of the angels was truly emotional. The Lite Sentry saw Anne and Father Richard were in the front pews. It was evident Anne was in tears. Tristan was in the second pew with Dinah next to him. Alex could see the room was packed with other angels to give Komptin the honor he deserved.

They were about halfway down the aisle when Komptin dropped to the ground. Celestial was already at the altar with golden tears in her eyes. Alex had to be strong for Komptin as she knelt before him. Gently, she picked up his head, and locked eyes with his fading glowing eyes. "You can do this. Do you hear me?" She told him, holding back from crying. "It's just a little further, then you will be honored for all time in the sky above." Alex swallowed hard. "You can do this; look at me, you can do this." It took all her might to show the strength he needed to walk the short distance.

With much pain, and losing life, Komptin got up to walk beside Alex to the front of the church. All the angels showed sympathy for Komptin, the Protector. Even Dinah was crying as Tristan offered her a tissue. Once Komptin and Alex got to the front of the church, Celestial silently told Alex to sit down so Komptin could rest his head on her lap. Devine stepped off to the side to join her brothers and sisters in the congregation.

The choir continued to sing as Celestial placed her hands on Komptin. Alex thought the Conduit of Lite would start speaking to the room, but all she said was, "His loving care for you is the only reason this will work. You need to know that."

Alex didn't really pay attention as she watched Komptin fighting to breathe. Then, a tunnel of sunlight appeared with a gentle beam of white light aimed at Komptin. A gentle wave of blue mist entered the beam. Alex watched Komptin's life force of be taken to the stars to be remembered forever.

Then, a second beam came from the Lite tunnel, hitting Celestial. She slowly moved her hand and placed it on top of Alex's head. Komptin's body gave one last breath before turning completely gray. Then Alex's body began to shiver as a sudden burst of warmth ran through her body. It felt as if the Lite was pushing out the Dark that was blocking her connection to the Lite. This caused Alex to widen her eyes as she tried to catch her breath.

The choir of Angels began to sing louder and stopped just as she felt the sensation end. Alex turned to Celestial as she closed her eyes to take in a deep breath. She opened her gentle glowing eyes of gold before they turned back to normal. She smiled at Alex, with tears of mixture of sadness and happiness. She confirmed what Alex was feeling. "It was his last act of protection. He did it for you."

Alex didn't know what to do as she watched the tunnel of Lite gently close. The warm, powerful sense of the Lite was a feeling she just could not explain. The warmth of the church, the angels around her–it was something she could not explain.

The only thing Alex couldn't feel was the Lite from Komptin.

Komptin was now completely gray, his body stone, before crumbling to sand. The angels began to leave for their respective positions, leaving Alex's friends and family behind.

Devine had a very small vial in her hand as she approached Alex. "Alexandria, I will take care of the remains. This is something you should not do."

Anne approached Alex, "Come on, sweetie."

Alex closed her eyes as she continued to feel the warmth of the church. The gift Komptin had given her was something she would forever keep close to her heart.

***

Kameron busted down the door to an apartment. Grossman was behind him, as were the rest of the Sentinels to provide cover. Inside the living room of the small apartment was a small group of people giving their kids a Lite baptism.

"Secure the kid," Grossman ordered one of the Sentinels. "Stay down, dad." Grossman held his weapon at the father of the child.

The mom started crying and screaming as she held her baby to prevent the Sentinels from taking him. The father approached the enforcement officers. "You're not taking my son."

Grossman didn't even hesitate as he took his stick to beat the man. He instantly fell to the ground, screaming in pain. "Get him out of here. Drag his ass down the stairs, make sure he feels every step." He turned to the mom, pausing. "Give us the baby, now."

The woman screamed as she turned her body away from the Sentinel–the Soldier of the Fallen. With the help of another, he yanked the baby from her arms. Trying to save her baby, she swung at one of the soldiers, scratching his face. Grossman pulled out his side arm and shot the mother. Her lifeless body dropped to the ground, tipping over the baptism water. Kameron watched the blood and water mix spread all over the floor.

"This is going to be so much paperwork," Grossman holstered his weapon. "Damn these Lite followers for causing me so much work." He spit on them as he turned away.

"I can't believe we have to rip another family apart." Kameron just stared at the body in front of him.

"Keep the scene secure while I go call clean-up." Grossman left Kameron alone with the body.

It was late before Kameron pulled into the parking lot of Megan's apartment complex. He didn't know how long he stayed in the car. All he could think of was the parent's pain and fear when they busted into the apartment. That baby being yanked from his mother's arms will be ingrained in his memory. The father being beaten, the lifeless body of the mother from being shot; Kameron should be tougher than this. He was a Sentinel. Though, it just was a bad situation.

Kameron finally got the strength to go upstairs. All he wanted to do was grab a drink and go to bed. Hopefully, Megan was in a good mood. He was cold and wanted some warmth. After he unlocked the door to the apartment, he heard a sound from down the hall that caught his attention. It almost sounded like Megan was being muffled by someone. The only thing Kameron could think of was the Lite was retaliating for what happened today. Kameron put his hand on his weapon, and he opened the door to the bedroom to see Megan and Roger Somberson in bed together.

"Kameron," Megan covered herself. "Get out of here."

Roger turned around and sat up in the bed. His smug face almost caused Kameron to shoot him when he said, "I can see why you're with her."

"Kameron," Megan got out of the bed, completely naked. She put her bathrobe on and she grabbed him by the arm, escorting him out. "How could you embarrass me like this?"

"Wait, what?" Kameron was dumbfounded.

"Roger wanted to share his power with me, but you're ruining this for me." Megan forcefully grabbed his arm to escort him to the kitchen.

Kameron was in an utter state of confusion. "What?"

Megan guided his hand to holster his weapon. "Look, I'm still dating you. You should feel honored that Roger Somberson is also connecting with your girlfriend."

Kameron was still in complete shock, "What?"

Roger yelled from the bedroom. "We need to hurry if we are going to make that meeting tomorrow morning."

Kameron was about to go into that bedroom and beat Roger to death. Megan put her hands on Kameron's chest. "Don't embarrass me."

"Whatever," Kameron waved her off. "I need to go. I can't deal with this right now." He grabbed his keys and decided to go for a drive. He ended up at the lake, in hopes the calm water would help deal with Megan's betrayal. He decided to call Kale about what happened. "And then I open the door and see Roger on top of Megan."

"Dude, that sucks," Kale told him. "But Roger Somberson, that's pretty awesome that the Leader wants to schtick your girl."

"Really? How would you feel if he did that to Anne?" Kameron continued to talk on the phone.

"Won't happen," Kale told him with confidence. "But if she were to give herself to someone, I could think of worse people than Roger Somberson."

"I guess," Kameron noticed a fire in the woods in the distance. "Look, I gotta go." He gladly hung up the phone. He went to the back of his trunk to grab a fire extinguisher. The last thing this town needed was to be up in flames. He approached the fire to see Alex on her knees.

The fire reflected off her pale skin face. "Hey, Kameron," she gently put her hand in her pocket. She must have been putting away her lighter to start the fire. Alex wiped the tears from her face.

"What's wrong?" Kameron put the fire extinguisher down.

"I lost a good friend today." Alex wiped the tears.

"I'm sorry," Kameron approached her. "Wanna talk about it?" He sat down on a log. "Trust me, I would love to hear that someone else is having troubles besides what's going on in my life." He adjusted his utility belt.

"Don't really want to talk about it." Alex smiled at him as she joined him on the log. "But I appreciate it." She wiped her eyes. "So, bad day, huh?"

"Really crappy," Kameron picked up a stick to play in the sand. "Really bad day at work. On top of that, I come home to see Roger Somberson nailing my girlfriend."

"Yah, that is a bad day," Alex laughed. "So, I'm assuming you guys are done."

"I don't know," Kameron admitted.

"How are you not done?"

"She said I was embarrassing her, and at the same time, she said we were still together." Kameron flicked a rock with the stick into some shrubbery. "She is so...so...."

"Manipulating," Alex just blurted out. Then she realized she said it. "Sorry, I shouldn't have..."

"It's okay. Sometimes, I would have to agree with you." Kameron just sat there.

Alex was quiet, then asked, "What is it you want in a relationship?"

"Well, I know the textbook answer is absolute power in order to command at will in honor of the Fallen." Kameron continued to play in the sand.

"But..." Alex egged him on.

"Sometimes, I just want a partner. Someone I can hold when she's sad, laugh with at those moments in life, and recognizes the needs I have. I'm not talking because of the power I would have over her, but because she wants to." Kameron explained.

"Sounds like you want equal partner," Alex zipped up her coat and buttoned her pockets.

"I think it makes relationships stronger," Kameron continued to doodle in the sand. "Better be careful. People might think we're talking like Lite followers."

Alex raised her eyebrows. "Yep, time to handcuff you and take you away." She playfully nudged him.

Kameron turned to her as they locked eyes. Her big brown eyes were so gentle. The glow of the fire against her very white skin only emphasized her memorizing features. No words were said, but a conversation was taking place. They leaned into each other to close the night with a kiss.

Chapter Ten

Alex stared out the window at the sun coming out over the town. A small amount of guilt washed over her as she should be mourning her friend...but the gift he gave her; she just couldn't explain. The Sentry closed her eyes to feel the warm connection to the Lite. She couldn't help but smirk as she felt the presence of Celestial in the room. Alex would have turned around but didn't. She just stared out the window as she approached.

"All your connection has been restored?" Celestial was asking like a doctor verifying with a patient. The Conduit of Lite gently placed her hand on her shoulder.

"I haven't stepped off the property yet," Alex continued to stare forward. "I'm afraid I won't feel it again."

Celestial joined Alex to take in the beauty of the sun rising. "You have nothing to fear."

Alex just nodded in acceptance. "How long did you know?"

"Right after the time of the stabbing. We were not able to heal the wound, just prolong the inevitable." Celestial saw a pair of doves fly off from the church ledge.

Alex touched her side where Sana had stabbed. The heat still radiated off her charred skin. "Just as my side isn't healed."

"Yes, the only reason Komptin survived as long as he did was his strength and dedication to you."

She put her hand over Alex's still on her wound. "You need not worry; your wound is not fatal."

"Tell you the truth, it wasn't really on my mind. I should have connected it. Maybe he'd still be alive." Alex turned to Komptin's bed that Kameron made for him after their first date.

"You love them both," Celestial stated the obvious.

"I do; so much loss." Alex rubbed her hand over the wood Kameron had used to create Komptin's bed.

"They both sacrificed themselves for you; love will keep you connected to them." Celestial approached Arome and Omelia. "We have to go." She placed her hand on Arome's shoulder.

"He deserved to become a star for all to see." Alex moved her eyes to the sky.

"Just because he is not a star does not mean he will not be remembered." Celestial saw Komptin's service animal harness hanging on the wall. "You must resume your hunts; the Dark shifted the Balance, and we have not been able to counteract it."

"I'll go tonight," Alex assured. "It will be weird not having him with me."

"The Dark will fear when they see you coming," Celestial smiled at her.

"Doubt it," Alex forced one in return. "But I appreciate it." After Celestial entered the doorway, Alex went to Komptin's harness. She felt Devine as she came into the room. "He hated this harness."

"Do you blame him?" Devine studied the Sentry.

Alex laughed, "No." She took the harness off the wall. "It feels weird to get rid of it."

"I know what it is like to lose a partner who risks their life to protect you, and you do the same for them." Devine gently grabbed the harness. "Do you wish me to take care of this?"

Alex nodded. "But not the bed. I don't want to get rid of that."

"Understood." Devine's body language was that she had something else to say.

"What is it?" Alex asked her surrogate sister.

Devine went into her satchel. "When Ariel joined her brothers and sisters in the stars, the biggest regret I had was not having something of hers that was just for me. I feel like that is selfish."

"No, not all. You two spent almost an eternity together, relied on each other." Alex continued to stare at the harness on the wall. "It's okay to think that."

Devine handed her a small vile. "This is a piece of Komptin. I believe he would want this."

Alex dropped tears. "Thank you." Alex took off her necklace. She unclasped it and put the vile on the necklace. The angel Kameron got her was positioned as if she was always meant to hold it. Alex put it back around her neck, noticing Devine had something else on her mind

The angel was about to speak before she stopped herself. "You need to hunt tonight, alone." Devine managed to get out.

Alex nodded in agreement. Devine jumped out the window to do whatever she did during the day. Alex didn't really know. She hesitantly decided to go downstairs to the floor of the congregation room. The massive room was where Komptin passed away. She sat on the front pew, staring at the stained-glass window.

She closed her eyes as she enjoyed the warmth of the Lite. Sooner or later, she would have to step off the property. There was no time like the present. Outside on the edge of the property, she was genuinely scared to take that next step. She stared at the invisible line of property. The fear of permanently losing her connection to the Lite again was something she couldn't handle.

"Come on, Alex," she said aloud to herself. She lifted her foot and closed her eyes, then just took that step. The sudden blast of sensation of the Dark didn't knock her down, but it was present. The stale air, the lack of Lite, it was a familiar feeling.

"What are you doing?" Megan's voice could be heard.

Alex opened one eye to see her coworker who was standing in front of her. "Just taking it all in."

"Is Anne here?" Megan searched for her car but didn't see it. "There's something I need to ask her."

"It was a late night for her and Father Richard. They probably won't be in today. Have you heard from Father Carl?" Alex faced the church. She took a deep breath, staring at the property line.

"No," Megan studied Alex. "There's something different about you."

Alex considered what would happen if this didn't work. Then, with a leap of faith, she jumped back onto church property. The warmth of the Lite caused her to start to giggle uncontrollably. She started to jump back and forth off church property, laughing like a small child. Going from the staleness of the Dark to the warmth of the Lite. Alex's tittering was genuine as it was coming out.

It was so contagious that even Megan chuckled a little. "What are you all happy about?" Alex just laughed as she needed to hug someone, anyone. So, she hugged Megan. Megan stood frozen with fear. She didn't know what to do. "Tell me what's going on?"

"My best friend just gave me a gift, a gift that I could never repay him for, and I haven't felt this good for a long time." Alex let go of Megan as she wiped a tear. Alex was still somewhat laughing. "Tristan is in the church, but that's it. Anne and Father Richard will be off today. I'll be at my parents' house." Alex went off into town on foot, a spring in her step.

***

Gron did an inventory of his office to see what the Sentry discovered. The first thing he did was check to see if the Dark Texts were still in the wardrobe. The wardrobe still had the book inside, along with all of its extra files. Most important of all, the pages were still intact. "What were you looking for Sentry?" he growled under his voice.

His security guard, Volen, came in with wounds on his face. "What happened?"

He took out his pencil from the back of his pocket and pulled out his old school notepad. "I did a complete inventory. Nothing was taken. When I came in, the male Sentry was here," he pointed to the corner. "The female and her mutt were right where you are standing."

"Nothing taken?" Gron performed a visual inventory of the room.

"No, my Leader," The woman commented.

"She killed my secretary. Why didn't you stay and finish them?" Gron slowly closed up the wardrobe.

"Misluna was downstairs. If one of them broke free, her cover would have been blown." Volen stood by his decision.

Gron respected his stance. Even though he wanted to kill him, or anybody, for losing his secretary, he made the right choice. "Whatever, find me a new secretary." He went to his desk as Volen left. Gron went back into his school implementation program when he was interrupted by a knock on the door. "What?"

The police chief came in. "Sorry, Mayor Somberson, your secretary wasn't at her desk."

"I'm transitioning the position," Gron continued his reading. "Have a seat."

The Police Chief sat down with this Lieutenant. "We are all set to implement the Sentinel Program. Space and desks are all set up in a special division of the building. I made it clear that they will report directly to you." He handed Gron a folder with pictures of the desks. "I just need a list of names of the Sentinels for access to the building."

Gron reached into his desk drawer. "Here you go. They were all handpicked personally by me."

The police chief reviewed the names. "Sir, with all due respect, I'm getting calls from some of the residents and even some of my officers regarding the legality of this program."

"Let me worry about that. That's why I was elected." Gron confidently told the chief. "The Sentinels' first task is to promote the positivity of freedom for public display. Once that is done, they will be tasked to remove all artifacts from the view of the people of this town. After that, it's just simple: they will fine, arrest, and properly handle anyone disobeying those rules."

"And that is supposed to maintain order in the town?" the Lieutenant asked.

Gron shot him a dirty look. "What's your name?"

"Lieutenant Collins; Ralph Collins."

"Well, Ralph," Gron made it a point to call him by his first name. "As mayor, as I should be addressed, it lays down the framework of how this city's policing will be run. It will trickle down to the citizens of this town. People will welcome the realization behind the true meaning of absolute power."

***

"Every time we do this, it's the same routine, time and time again," the female Demon, Shantaree, was getting agitated. Scotty had been strapped with arms above his shoulders, going through her tests of human endurance for quite some time. "Look up at me, go on, look at me," she said with a soft, gentle tone.

Scotty could barely lift his head up. Sweat and blood dripped from his face. "Just kill me."

"Oh, I will, maybe, perhaps," the possessed girl approached him to put her arms around his neck with a gentle hug. "Just tell me why you hate Him so much."

"Right now, you're coming in a close second, you bi–" He started to scream as he was being electrocuted. He screamed so loud the female Demon covered her ears with an evil grin.

"Just tell me, and I'll end your pain. I promise." Shantaree turned to the male Demon, who was controlling the electrocution. "Go on, leave us." The male annoyingly came up to Scotty to punch him across the face. "Well, that was a little unnecessary." She locked the door. Then she motioned for him to be quiet as she unveiled a camera in the power outlet. "He likes to watch." She took off her suit coat as now she was in a skirt and tank top. "It's hot in here."

"I don't know what your game is," Scotty muttered.

"I just want some privacy." She put her fingers through his sweaty hair. "I just want to talk." She started to nibble on his neck. The sweet nectar of his blood tasted so good. "Just tell me why you hate Him."

Scotty closed his eyes as the small bites of his neck were a welcoming sensation over voltage running through his body. "I can't."

"Okay," she went over to the machine controlling the power. A quick turn of the switch sent Scotty into a state of screaming. "I don't enjoy this."

"I don't either." Scotty could barely get out as he screamed. "Just end it, please."

"See, we have more in common than you realize." She went back up to him. "You know, it's just one little story, and I'll end your pain." She gently kissed him on the mouth. "Just tell me."

Scotty didn't sleep the night before. If he knew what kind of day he was going to have, he would have tried to get some sleep. The sound of his mom trying to hide her crying in the living room was echoing through the house. Downstairs in the living room was his mother, crying in the arms of Reverend Shlep. A police officer stood in the doorway. Scotty rubbed his eyes to try to wake up. His mom hugged him hard as she told him about his dad getting killed in a car accident.

Scotty returned the hug, full-out crying. That day, at St. Phillips, the Christian school for boys, a lot of the teachers and kids were being overly nice to him. Which, for some reason, irritated him more. Counselors asked if he wanted to talk, and more teachers than he knew were there to check on him.

At lunch, he overheard one of the kids telling his friends his dad was the sheriff, and he heard him say that Scotty's dad was suffering from PTSD from the war. He intentionally ran into the side of the building. Scotty lost all his anger and started attacking the kid. The fight resulted in Scotty getting severely beaten.

Reverend Schlep picked him up from the Dean's Office because his mom was dealing with the death of his father. He had told him to put his faith in God…because even through bad times, He wants us to be there for each other. A couple of days after the funeral, they found out his dad had spent all their money on illegal drugs. They were broke.

There was no money coming in, and Scotty's mom had gotten a second job as a bartender at a local bar outside of town. She would work late, but the money hadn't become an issue anymore. She always had cash on her. One day, one of his mom's coworkers came home with his mom. She was attractive in her late twenties. Scotty was turning sixteen that night, and this was the first time his mom brought someone she worked with home with her.

Scotty's mom told him that she had to go meet someone. She left while he stayed with his mom's coworker. The two of them sat on the couch as they watched television. The woman told him his mom regretted working on his birthday. She wanted him to have a special birthday. So, the beautiful woman brought Scotty up to his bedroom for a present he would never forget.

Later on, St. Phillips found out what his mom was doing for extra money, which got him barred from the school. The school filed a junction against his mom, where he got thrown into a foster family. They were strict and preached the Bible every night. They made Scotty repent for giving into his lust with a prostitute. His senior year of school, his mom was released from prison and tried to make penance for what she did.

His mom had found religion while in lockup. She was born again and decided to attend church where Reverend Shlep preached. He spent the entire sermon passive-aggressively ridiculing his mother for her past and exclaiming the shame she put on the community. His mom had lost her new job she got while on parole. This sent her into a falling state of depression that eventually overtook her. When Reverend Schlep approached him, Scotty asked if God sent people who commit suicide to Hell. His response was, "murder of the body is a sin regardless of whose, and she had no time to ask for forgiveness."

"Thank you," Shantaree continued to hug him as she kissed his cheek. "Thank you," she softly whispered in his ear again. She kissed him on the side of the face. "And now, I shall end your pain."

***

Watching her parents supervise the movers as they packed up the house wasn't something she really enjoyed doing. Even though she was happy they were getting out of the CopperTop, it was still hard to watch. It was a weird feeling; they wouldn't be here in a couple of days.

"Do you want this lamp?" Her mom held a seashell lamp they bought in Hawaii.

"No, mom, I've seen some horrible things in the past, but that lamp takes it to a whole other level." Alex continued to watch her mom get more emotional over the stuff.

"Really?" Her mom studied the lamp. "I thought it was nice." Her mom placed it in the garage sale box.

Her dad came up behind her, leaning on her car. "How are you doing with this?"

"I'm fine," Alex let him know. "Really, I'm good."

Michael put his arm around his baby girl. "You've had a rough year, first Kameron, now Komptin. Are you going to get another dog?"

Alex shook her head. "No, I don't think so."

"What about your PTSD?" Michael was reviewing the checklist with the driver. "That sheet is good. Thanks."

"I think I'll be okay." Alex stated confidently. "He helped me when I needed it. Though, I'm going to miss him."

"Can I ask you something?" Michael was watching his wife go through the garage pile to make sure nothing was in there that wasn't supposed to be.

"What's that?"

"Tell me the truth about what happened with Kameron?" Michael saw that Alex's mother went into the house frantically telling the movers what shouldn't be packed.

"What makes you think we didn't break up?" Alex stared forward. She then got a feeling, a feeling she hadn't had for some time. She started to pay attention to the trees around her and then to the sky. It only emphasized she needed to hunt tonight.

"You, okay?" Michael didn't miss his daughter's reaction.

Alex shook the cobwebs out of her head. "Just trying to figure out the words." Alex took a couple more moments. Her mom came up with three cups of coffee. Alex graciously took one of them. "This is the official report from his work; while on a mission to deter a national threat, Special Agent Kameron Dutcher is pronounced missing in action. No confirmation of his death, whereabouts, or status is available."

Michael and his wife were shocked. Alex's mom was the first to hug her daughter. "Oh, Alex."

Alex returned the hug. "It's okay, mom. I'm going to get him back. I don't know how, but it's going to happen. There is something else I need to tell you, something I regret not letting you know."

"What's that?" Michael nodded to the movers as they were motioning, they were going on a lunch break.

"He asked me to marry him before he left, and I accepted." Alex just stared out at the forest.

Michael and his wife just stared at Alex in shock. They didn't know what to say. Her mom had tears dropping as her dad thought about it before saying. "Well, you keep this strong." He pointed to her heart. "You listen to that; it will tell you if he is going to come back to you or not."

Later that evening, it was weird entering the woods without her hunting companion at her side. However, it did feel good to be by herself. The woods were quiet, with just the sound of animals. It never failed. Whenever she wanted to fight, there was never an Infiltrator or Demon to be found. She almost felt like she was back on her virgin hunt.

There was sure to be something near the F.O.R. Compound. For sure, she would be able to find something to deliver into the ground. Alex continued forth where she ended up in the field where she saw her first ceremonial Infiltration. She was sneaking around the perimeter, trying to catch a glimpse of anything Dark. The sense was definitely strong; there was something about. She ended up in the center of the small ceremonial field. "Where the hell are you guys?" she yelled from the middle of the grass circle.

"Well, that took the fun out of it," a Demon came out from the forest.

Alex watched the man approach from the direction of the F.O.R. Compound. "What's your name?"

"Death," he answered sarcastically.

Alex rolled her eyes. "You're an idiot."

The Demon went immediately into a fighting stance, but then stood up. "You know, as fun as it would be to kill you right away. I think I want to record this." He took out his phone to show her, then he placed it on a stump. He steadied the phone before gently stepping backward. "You think that will be a good shot?"

Alex immediately punched him as he turned around. The Demon went spinning as he hit the ground. "Yep, good shot." Alex immediately turned around to see multiple Infiltrators appear from a mist. "Uh oh," was all she could say. The Sentry adjusted her stance as she was prepared for

the fight of her life, which, according to these numbers, wouldn't last long. Alex lit her fists as the wave of Infiltrators started to attack. The first one lunged at her, and she easily smashed it into the ground. Then she grabbed another and swung it into three more. She punched one across the face and sent it into another group.

The Demon recording this event, shook the cobwebs out and then saw how Alex was manhandling the Infiltrators. "This is not possible."

Alex shot a Lite Bean into one of Infiltrators, causing it to forcefully crash into others. The ground shot up in the air from the indentation of the impact. Alex got punched across the face from one, but it didn't stop the onslaught of her attacks. She formed a knife and started to dispose of the black beasts with a single slice from her Lite. The grounds started to get infested with the melting bodies of the Infiltrators.

Alex surveyed her recent massacre. She was breathing a little heavier than usual, but it was more out of shock. "Holy shit!" She had no idea how she survived the attack. Though, she really wasn't complaining.

The Demon made sure the phone wasn't disturbed to still record the event. "If you want something done right…"

Alex put her finger up. "Hold on one minute." She wasn't tired; she wasn't hurt. "I really need to figure out what's happening."

"What's happening is your demise!" He roared as he flashed his eyes.

The Demon attacked Alex, but the Sentry let him hit her. It was able to knock her down, and it hurt, but not like it used to. She regained her position with her fists lit. She motioned for the Demon to attack her. It swung at her, but she ducked out of the way, punching it in the stomach. It bent over from the pain; this gave Alex a clear shot to the side. Alex could feel the Demon start to weaken, but not enough to dispose of yet. There was a rock just below her feet. She grabbed the Demon's head, jumped in the air, and slammed it against the ground. The Demon stood up, barely able to move.

"Who is the Dark Harridan?" Alex asked him.

"I'll never tell you Misluna's name," The Demon could barely say.

Alex rolled her eyes at the ridiculousness. "Well, that's more than I had. Thanks." Alex grabbed the Demon's throat and tossed him in the air. Then she immediately slammed it against the ground. The Lite Sentry formed a knife and jabbed it into the center of the Demon's chest. She stood up and cleaned herself from the fight, brushing dirt off her shoulder. Along with her adjustments, she had to wipe some dirt off her pants as she approached the phone. She had a sense of confidence to her as she approached the phone, until she tripped on a log and fell to the ground face-first. She bled from hitting the ground, and instantly got up to make sure no one saw that. Then she remembered that Demon was recording the fight. The phone was on a live feed. "Gron, Misluna, enjoy your night; you don't have many left." Then, she cut the video stream.

***

Kameron was helping in his father's shop in the backyard. It needed a good cleaning before winter hit. Kameron was organizing the tool bench while his dad was servicing the snowblower.

"Damn it, I keep on forgetting this thing is metric. Can you hand me the metric sockets?" Kameron handed his dad the correct blue case.

Kameron switched it with a red one. "Here you go." He put the other one away, along with some other tools.

"If I had the massive absolute power, I'd get rid of the systems and make everything standard." His dad found the correct socket to remove the blade of the snowblower.

"Dad, can I ask you something?" Kameron grabbed a beer from the refrigerator. He also grabbed one for his dad.

His dad nodded as he took the bottle. "Must be serious, beer talk in the shop."

"I caught Megan in bed with Roger Somberson," Kameron admitted.

His dad stood up from the snowblower to look at his son. "He's got great Power, son. She should be thrilled that he chose her like that. And the fact that you're with a girl who Roger decided to bed, is quite an honor."

"Generally speaking, I'm confused. I'm angry about it, but also a little relieved." Kameron told him. "Would it be a mistake to end it with Megan?"

"What are you nuts?" His dad joined him to lean on a bench. "Megan is going to go places. With Roger's guidance, she will only increase her Power. All you need to do is go along for the ride."

"I guess. What if you actually found someone who you have feelings for? Like you had with mom." Kameron stared at his bottle.

"Your mom succumbed to my Power in the relationship. It's how relationships are supposed to work, one over the other. One in charge, one to follow. The follower will eventually accept that because of the feelings for the other. It's how life works." His dad explained. "Is there someone else in your life?"

"Just a racing mind," Kameron was peeling the label off the bottle. "I need to get going. I have to pick up Megan at work. We have social at the mayor's house."

"See, you're already taking advantage of the Power." His dad finished his beer.

"Thanks, dad." Kameron handed him the rest of his beer so his dad could finish it. He got to his car, parked in front of dad's house. He noticed Alex in a coat on the bench in front of her house. Her pale skin could be seen in the shadows under the porch. Kameron could barely make out the green drink with ice she was drinking. He took a deep breath, then waved.

She returned the wave. The two stared at each other until Alex got up from the bench to come towards him. Kameron shut the car door and approached her. "We should really talk," she suggested.

"Yep," He kept his hands in his pockets. The two just stared at each other, not knowing what the other was going to say. "I don't want to apologize for what happened."

"Good," she shyly smiled. "But now we have this thing out there."

"I'm with Megan," Kameron reminded her, or was it to remind himself?

"Does she make you happy?" Alex tried to stare at Kameron, but he couldn't look her in the eye. "Asked and answered."

"She's got potential of some real Power." Kameron explained to Alex. "Plus, we've been together since college."

"And I'm a dropout who works at Purch-Mart." Alex got a little irritated.

"Well, it would be a mistake to pursue this, would you if you were me?" Kameron felt he was falling into this conversation. There was no way of stopping it. "It's not what I should do."

Alex got a little forceful. "Kameron, I don't give a shit about what you think you should do. What I care about is what this wants." She pushed her finger directly into his chest. "Because I know damn well, what mine wants."

Kameron just stood there in shock. He had never seen a girl with such passion pan over him as Alex. The mere fact of the situation—he wanted her just as bad, but he was with Megan. Megan, who was sleeping with Roger on the side.

"Alex, … I …" Kameron struggled with his words.

Alex closed her eyes to prevent herself from crying. "Okay, I won't make this hard for you." She turned around to leave, but Kameron grabbed her hand. He twisted her into him. She placed her hands on his chest as she looked into his eyes. The two kissed in the middle of the street underneath the lights within the darkness of the streets.

Chapter Eleven

Alex giggled a bit as she touched her lips. Both Father Richard and Megan turned to Alex, who had a strange smile on her face. There was even a little red coloring to her embarrassed pastel face. "What?"

"What's so funny?" Father Richard stopped his study of when the first church service would be held.

Alex just chuckled. "I really don't know. Just a flashback to a feeling, I guess."

Megan continued taking notes but paid more attention to what was lacking around the room. "Where's Anne?"

"Working on something downstairs." Father Richard continued to write down some potential dates. "Besides, we just need to work on opening this church. Services need to start before the Pure Freedom Act officially kicks in and the Sentinel program begins their totalitarian purge."

"I think it's a mistake to open the church." Megan put her two cents into the pot. "We haven't even finished remodeling."

"Well, it's a good thing you're not in charge then," Alex's face got serious. "I think it's a good thing. Who gives a crap what it looks like? This town needs all the church openings it can get."

"Agreed. I had a meeting with the other churches in town. Attendance seems to be increasing a bit." Father Richard was writing. "It's been so long since I wrote a sermon. I hope I still remember how." The overweight bald priest chuckled to himself.

"We do have an issue, though," Alex brought up.

"What's that?" Father Richard scratched out a word in his notebook.

"Advertising we're open. Our P.O.S. mayor will implement that stupid ass law very soon that we can't promote without being taxed. Internet, flyers, ads, hell, we can't even put a sign in the churchyard." Alex turned as she could feel Megan stare at her.

"Yes, I was thinking of that." Father Richard tapped his pen on his desk. "Means everything will have to be word of mouth."

Alex got fed up. "What I wouldn't do for one chance with him, one on one, no way out?"

Megan turned to her. "Why, what would you do?"

"Alright, ladies, meeting's adjourned." Father Richard got up. "Has anyone heard from Carl?"

Both Alex and Megan shook their heads. Megan was the first to speak. "I know if I had an emergency, the last thing I would want is to be bothered."

"I'm going to go take off. There's something I need to get done," Alex took her lunch a little early to head to the mall. After getting her mandatory vanilla and Apollo shake, she passed some F.O.R. members trying to recruit. The group of misled older teenagers were nonchalantly pushing pamphlets while talking up the F.O.R. There was a small urge to mess with them, but then a larger woman came up to them demanding to know what happened to her son. From what Alex could hear, she hadn't heard from him for quite some time. Alex was about to intervene until security escorted the frantic mother away. Alex felt sorry for the mother as she thought about all those kids in the F.O.R. compound. Her thoughts stayed with her as she entered a jewelry store where the displays seemed to sparkle brightly. The engagement rings were catching her eyes, glistening so beautifully.

"Can I help you, miss?" The older gentleman approached.

Alex put her hands to the back of her neck to take off her necklace. "Yes. Can you fuse this vile onto the angel's hands?"

The man's hands shook a bit as he studied the necklace. "We can do that. Such a beautiful piece." He put a looking device onto his eye. "The craftsmanship on this was made with much love."

Alex couldn't help but think of Kameron and Komptin. "When can I pick it up?"

"I can have it ready for you tomorrow." the man was still studying the piece.

Alex took a deep breath in. "That's fine. I'm going to feel a little naked without it."

The old man winked at her. "Let me see what I can. Can you come back in an hour?"

"Thank you." Alex signed some paperwork before leaving the store with one more glance at the engagement rings. There was public seating in the middle of the mall where she could finish mixing in her Apollo Energy Drink and ice cream. It was calming watching the people in the mall. It was disturbing, though, watching the card store take down the angel statues as they were fear of being taxed. The couch sank in a little as a man sat next to her. She just moved her eyes to see what he wanted.

"I'm not going to hurt you." He was tall and muscular, with shiny, short corn-rolled hair and a goatee.

"Wasn't too worried about it," Alex started to pay attention to her phone.

"I have a meeting in town and wanted to come look at the happenings." The man was wearing black leather pants with a white leather biker jacket. The dark-skinned man watched some kids with F.O.R. jackets pass by. "I heard of them."

"If I were you, I'd stay away from anyone associated with them." Alex gave some friendly advice.

The man gazed down at his watch. "No, I'm not looking to get into it."

Alex adjusted her body to the man. "FYI, a person doesn't actively seek to get involved with a cult; especially one as dangerous as that one."

"Sounds like you have some knowledge about them." The man took his phone out of his pocket.

"More than I wish to have." Alex got a message that lit up her phone with a picture of Kameron and Komptin together. "I'm Alex."

"North." The two of them shook hands.

"North? Last name?" Alex adjusted in her seat.

"Sure, we'll go with that." The gentle man snickered.

Alex got a message from Anne about bringing her lunch. "You must have been military; they always identify just using last names."

"Not military, but I do serve." North watched the F.O.R. members push more of their agenda on the people in passing.

"Ah, government employee; makes sense. My fiancé did government work." She showed a picture on her phone of him and Komptin.

"He's a good-looking fellow." The man commented. "Looks prestigious."

Alex rubbed her finger on the picture with sadness in her eyes. "I lost them both. The two of them were the same, so strong and kind. This is my favorite picture with Kameron," she opened up the picture of the two of them at Christmas after he gave her that necklace. "This is right after he gave me a necklace that I'm having fixed right over there."

"He has a certain kindness to his eyes," the man observed. "You two look opposite but complement each other."

"He's got one of the purest hearts I know of," Alex studied the picture, wishing she could go back to that time. "Do you have anyone special?"

"I'm married to my work," the man let her know. "But, as corny as it sounds, I get to live vicariously through seeing others happy."

"Well, stay out of this town then," Alex warned him. "It's getting Dark here."

"Why are you here? You seem like a pleasant young lady."

Alex noticed it was almost time to pick her necklace up. "I'm here to help give this town hope, even though they don't know it." She got up with her ticket in her hand for her necklace. "It was really nice talking to you."

"You too, I learned a lot." The man waved to her as she got up to leave. "Know anywhere good to eat?"

"Go to Marty's. Can't go wrong with the double cheeseburger." She winked at him.

"Sounds good." He laughed. She took a couple of steps before he called for her. "Hey, Alexandria."

"Yah," She faced him. She couldn't help but notice his peaceful smile.

"If you had a chance; would you break down the gates of the Hell to get to him?" The man studied her.

"Well, that's a situation I will never have to face," Alex admitted the truth to herself.

***

Anne was deep into her research, but there was nothing on this symbol that bound the metal strings. The cloth was something she never felt before. She felt bad that this Sentry would never get the recognition by the Council she deserved. It was confusing why Celestial didn't want the Council to know about this. Also, what about Sherri? Was she rogue? Anne got up to lock the door to her office to make sure no one came in. The safe in the corner of her office held the mysterious artifact that Sherri had given her.

She held the wrapped piece in her hand as she sat down. Whatever was inside was metal. The seal was something she had never seen before. It wasn't wax. It was almost a mixture of metal and cement, just like the structure in the museum. The string holding the wrapping consisted of a material she had never felt before. Anne didn't understand why it was so secured with this when a person could just break open the cloth with a pair of scissors. The cloth itself was rough, very dirty, and held marks of being burned.

Anne debated on whether she should try to open it or not. She put it back in the safe and turned to her translations of these new texts she received. These texts had a hint of ancient Dark, but the grammar was written in modern language. There were just a couple of words she didn't know, but they were because of the moderation of the sentence structure.

What she got out of it was that the artifact in her possession was the key. Now, it didn't take a genius to realize that the museum piece and this key coming together in CopperTop wasn't by accident. She hadn't told anyone of possessing it. If this was a key to open the man-made conduit to the Dark, it would be far more dangerous to tell anyone. Plus, would Alex be that reckless to try to get Kameron back, unleashing the Dark onto this world?

It was quiet when a knock scared Anne, making her jump. "Yes."

"Door's locked," Megan said from the other side. "Oh, yes. Sorry."

Anne locked the artifact in her office before answering the door. "Hey, sorry, I was working on something."

"Father Richard wanted me to tell you to start the VC-153 for me. Whatever that is." Megan laughed.

Anne smiled as she knew it was the beginning to get her into the Counsel. "I'll start it." Anne sat back around her desk. Megan was about to leave when Anne called her back.

"What's up." Megan sat down in her office.

Anne watched her study the office surroundings. "There's a lot of history on those walls."

"Ever wonder what the stories behind some of the artifacts are?" Megan stared at a picture of a man exorcising a Demon out of a man.

"All the time," Anne tapped her finger on her coffee. "Let me ask you something."

"What do you have, Anne?" Megan's curiosity was peaked.

"If you had information, information that could be helpful or harmful, depending on how the person reactions, would you tell said person?" Anne just had a distant stare to her.

"Sure, why not?" Megan was hoping this had to do with the conduit. "You could tell me, and I could give advice on the danger level to see if you should tell that person or not."

Anne had a serious facial expression as she didn't know what to do. "No, this is something I need to think about myself. Thanks."

"No problem.   I'm going to head home. Night." Megan got up and left her office.

Anne pulled the artifact out.   She needed to know what was inside to make a logical decision. She tried pulling the strings off, but they didn't break.   She tried to use scissors, but the handles broke when she squeezed them.   A pair of wire cutters in the hall closet she grabbed; she was sure would work. But it was futile. Her last-ditch effort was to grab a knife from the kitchen to cut the cloth. There was no hope; the blade only left a tiny mark. "Ugh."   Anne wiped the agitation off her face. "This is God telling me to give up."   She put the artifact back in the safe.

Anne ensured her office was locked before heading up to the congregation hall. As she was walking in the back hallway, she noticed Megan's car leaving the parking lot.   Tristan was coming down the hall with his coat on. "Heading out?"

"Going for a walk," he coded to her. "I texted Alex the location I'll be heading."

"Be safe." Anne made it to the congregation room, where she sat down and closed her eyes for guidance.

Father Richard noticed Anne alone in the massive space as she stared at the stained-glass window. "Hey, are you okay?"

"I'm stuck, and I don't know what to do," Anne admitted to the priest.   "The church is locked up right?"

"Yah, I think everyone is gone. I was just on my way to check on Father Carl's apartment to see if he's okay." Father Richard sat down next to Anne.

"I need to tell you something as a priest, not a member of the Council." Anne needed to get this off her chest.

"Of course, strictly confidential," he confirmed for Anne's sake.

Anne took a deep breath. "I think I found a way to bring Kameron back, but it's really, really, dangerous."

"Dangerous for who?" Father Richard was not expecting this. He could feel his heart start to palpitate.

"The world." Anne started shaking her leg from nerves.

"And you don't know if you should tell Alex or not. Not sure what she would do with the information." Father Richard sat back. "That's tough. You're afraid it will ruin your friendship."

Anne nodded. "Should I gamble and keep this secret, or should I tell her, and let her make a decision?"

"What did you find out, Anne?" Father Richard leaned forward to listen to what his historian had to say.

"I believe the museum has a man-made Dark Conduit, and I have the key to opening it." Anne flat-out told him.

Father Richard's eyes got big. "Something like that shouldn't exist. How did it get here?"

"I don't know." Anne took in a deep breath. "If we try destroying it or the key, Kameron will have no chance to get back home. An innocent man will remain in Hell forever."

***

When Kameron opened the door to Megan's apartment, he sarcastically yelled, "I'm here. Just in case you're doing something I don't want to see." But then Kameron thought to himself. "Why does it matter? He's moving all his stuff out today. He's ending it with Megan."

He had a small suitcase with him to pack all his clothing from his drawer. In the closet were his dress uniforms he kept on the hangers. Luckily, there wasn't a lot of his stuff here. He returned from the car to leave her key when he saw Megan giggling on the phone. There was no doubt she was talking to Roger. She lifted her finger as if she would be right with him. It was so clear to Kameron now who she actually was.

"Okay, see you tonight at the town meeting." She now acknowledged Kameron in the room. "Where were you?"

"Packing."

"Going to training or something?" She went to the refrigerator and pulled out something to eat for herself.

"Megan, why are we together?" Kameron flat-out asked her.

"Well, obviously, you're the one mainly benefiting from it," Megan sat back on the counter. "Are you trying to break us up? Why would you do that to us?"

"Hmmm, that's a tough question. Could it be, you shticking the Leader a couple of nights ago?" Kameron couldn't believe the conversation he was having.

"Oh, please, that was career thing, though it was enjoyable," she snickered.

Kameron just shook his head out of disbelief. "I just don't think we're right for each other," he was finding it quite easy to do this.

"Look, if you just want to nail that irritating little goth chick from across the street of your parents, just do it and get it over with. I don't care." Megan continued to eat her salad. "But if we break up, it will look bad in front of everyone."

"No, I want more out of a relationship." Kameron grabbed his keys from his pocket to take off the apartment key. "I want someone who gets me...to connect with."

"Almost sounds like a partnership. That's borderline Lite thinking. You better be careful." Megan warned. "Not having power over another in a relationship is not healthy."

"Find your power over someone else. I'm done with you." Kameron placed the key on the cabinet in front of her.

"You can't break up with me, Kameron Dutcher. I'm the one with the Power." She got up to his face. "You can't break up with me."

"I'm sorry, Megan. I'm done with this." He turned around to leave as she screamed on what a pathetic loser he was; no one would ever make him truly happy.

It was three months since Kameron broke up with Megan. He had seen her at church, close to her Roger's side. It was no secret they were seeing each other, but truthfully, it really wasn't bothering him. His relationship with Alex had been blossoming. He never felt anything like this before.

They laughed together; she was supportive, and even after the first time they got mad at each other, it felt like it was going to manage through anything. Even work was going rather smoothly. The Lite notifications were decreasing. He just got through finishing a random Lite check. There was nothing, thank the Fallen, because he had a date with Alex tonight.

He patrolled with Grossman down the street, where he saw Anne and Alex coming out of a restaurant. "Hey." He couldn't help but smile at the sight of his girlfriend.

Alex smiled back. "Anne and I just grabbed some lunch."

"You two have been hanging out a lot," Kameron saw Anne and Alex giggle over some little secret they had.

"She's good people," Anne rubbed Alex's back.

Kameron got a phone call from his mother, who was frantic over the phone. "Okay, mom. I'll be right there." He turned to Grossman. "There's an emergency at my parent's house."

"We'll take the patrol car. Come on." Grossman and Kameron took off down the street with their car, lights flashing and sirens blaring.

Kameron pulled up to the house to see other Sentinel patrol vehicles already there. Alex and

Anne weren't far behind. "Mom!" Kameron rushed into the house. He came into the living room where his dad was holding his mother as his sister, Michelle, was in handcuffs, tears coming down her face. The sergeant on the scene came up to Kameron. "Look, Kam. It's pretty serious."

"What's going on?" Kameron was afraid of his original suspicions.

He turned around as both Anne and Alex tried to get into the living room. A Sentinel was going to stop them, but Kameron told him it was okay. Alex was stunned as she saw Michelle in handcuffs, sitting on a living room chair. "What happened?"

The sergeant read over his notes. "Her parents were coming home because they forgot their wallet. They happened to hear Lite music coming from their daughter's room. Upon searching the room, they found a bunch of Lite contraband." The sergeant turned around to grab an evidence bag. Inside the bag was a crucifix, a Bible, a bunch of rosaries, and a big stack of pamphlets for the Lite. "Those pamphlets are obviously for distribution."

"This is bad." Kameron wiped his face.

Alex made her way to Michelle. She moved Michelle's hair away from her face. "What's going to happen to her?"

"Well, pending the prosecutor, if she cooperates and tells us who and where the rest of the Lite Followers are, we can maybe reduce her sentence. Regardless of the fact, she's going to Rejunivation."

Kameron's mom screamed aloud as she cried into her husband's chest. Harold looked to Michelle with fear over his daughter. "Tell them who they are, Michelle. It's not a hard choice."

Michelle turned to Alex, who gave her a look of hope. Alex softly spoke. "You can do this."

"Michelle," Kameron called to his sister. "Who are they?"

Michelle closed her eyes. She took in a deep breath. "Be strong and courageous. Do not be afraid or terrified because of them, for the Lord your God goes with you; He will never leave you nor forsake you."

The sergeant was irritated at Michelle. "Take her out of here."

The Sentinels picked her up and forcefully got her out of the chair. The sergeant pushed her on the back of the head as she was being escorted to the car.

"Hey!" Alex got up. "That wasn't necessary."

"Quiet, or you'll go with her for interference of a Sentinel investigation." The sergeant on the scene told her.

"Alex," Kameron grabbed her hand to pull her towards him, in almost a protection mode.

Harold let go of his wife. "Will we be able to see her?"

"She'll be tried tonight by the magistrate. Then sent to Rejunivation." Kameron explained the process.

Grossman motioned to the parents. "Come on, there's a spot in the process where I'll get you to see her before she leaves."

Kameron turned to Grossman. "Thanks."

The next day, Kameron didn't really sleep. Both his parents took a hefty amount of sleeping pills to make sure they got some rest. It was going to be close to noon by the time they got out of bed. Kameron went into the shop and started to tinker with the snowblower.

"Hey," Alex's voice said from behind him.

"Hey," He continued to work on the snowblower. "Pick up a wrench."

Alex sat on the floor with him and picked up a tool. "Don't know the first thing about engines."

Kameron wiped his hands on a rag before giving her a kiss. Then his attention was back on the machine. "I can't believe she got sent to Rejunivation."

"She's a tough girl. She'll make it through, okay." Alex ensured him.

"I'm a Sentinel. How can I not see a Lite Follower who is my own sibling?" Kameron just shook his head. "Some soldier for the Fallen I turned out to be."

"You never know what someone is going to do." She inched her way a little closer to him.

"I don't know what's worse; not knowing my sister was a Lite Follower or her not telling me." Kameron got up to grab a socket.

Alex stood up. She grabbed his hand to gain his full attention. "Kameron, the people she was protecting." Alex started to say.

"What about them?" Kameron got lost in her brown eyes.

Alex grabbed the tool in his hand to put it on the work bench. "Kameron, I have never felt anything like I have since we've been together."

Kameron smiled down at her. "Being with you is something I never felt before either."

"So, what I'm about to tell you; it means a lot that you know." Alex squeezed his hand.

"You can tell me anything." Kameron was now fully engulfed in her.

Alex took a deep breath. "Kameron, I'm the Natural Leader to the Lite Followers in this area."

Kameron took a step back. "You got Michelle into this?"

"No, no, she contacted us to start a chapter here. That's why I moved here with my sister."

"Your sister is a Natural Leader as well?" He was completely flabbergasted.

"No, she's a Community Outreach Leader." Alex slowly approached her boyfriend. "But what I need to know, what's going to happen now?"

Kameron sat there to think about it. "I could get in a lot of trouble on knowing about this and not reporting it."

"What are you going to do?" Alex didn't know the outcome of the conversation.

Kameron took a minute to think about it. "Alex, there is something about you that is so special. I'm not going to say a word. I can't risk losing you."

Alex approached him to give him a kiss. The two embraced but were interrupted by Anne knocking on the door. Alex wiped her mouth. "Sorry, Anne."

"Alex," she replied, almost cold.

Alex went to leave. "Meet up for lunch later?"

"Perhaps," Anne turned her attention back to Kameron after she left.

"How much of that have you heard?" Kameron could tell from her demeanor that he already knew the answer.

"Enough to hang you both." Anne crossed her arms.

Kameron tilted his head back. "What should I do?"

"Look, Kameron. I like Alex. I like her a lot. You are playing with fire, though." Anne warned him.

"What are you saying?" He could feel the beads of nervous sweat start to form. "You're not going to say anything?"

"No, but sooner or later, you're going to have to make a choice," Anne warned him as she left. She herself was debating in her head if she was going to end her friendship with her newly found companion.

Chapter Twelve

Alex, for some reason, began getting nervous as she approached the church from the back parking lot. Then, the feeling of warmth from the Lite overtook any anxiety. That sensation of warmth was never going to get old. Alex wanted to check on Anne to see if she wanted to get something to eat, but her office was locked. It was late enough not to raise concern that she wasn't there. Alex was actually glad since Anne had been working so hard lately. She decided to head upstairs to the congregation room before going out for a hunt.

She saw that Anne and Father Richard were in the massive room, obviously engaged in conversation. "What's going on?"

"Where were you?" Father Richard got up as he patted Anne on the arm.

"Just getting something taken care of." Alex sat down. She instinctively went to pet Komptin at her feet, but then quickly realized he wasn't there. After a quick intake of breath, she asked, "Why, what's up?"

"I was going to go check on Father Carl, wanna come?" Father Richard shook his keys at her.

"That sounds like fun," Alex was trying to think of a reason not to go. "Would love to see what makes that man tick." She took in a breath and was about to whistle but stopped herself. He wasn't going to be coming.

Anne didn't miss Alex's attempt to whistle for Komptin. Her friend got up from the pew. "You know, I would love to go as well."

Father Richard silently understood why she was coming along.

The three of them got to the door of the small duplex house. Alex noticed the curtains had a small opening to them. "Not really what I expected." There were some decorative lawn pots she had to bypass to peek in the living room window. "Everything is so...organized and straight." She turned to her friends. "I don't think he's home."

"Does anyone have a key?" Anne was squeezing her coat tighter.

"I do," Alex flashed her eyes. She was getting ready to kick in the door when she felt a tap on her shoulder.

"So do I." Father Richard lifted up a housekey.

"Oh," disappointed, Alex stepped aside to motion for him to open the door.

Father Richard knocked on the door and rang the doorbell.

"I guess we should have done that first," Alex laughed. They stood outside the door, waiting for him to answer. "Anybody wanna grab something to eat after this?"

"I could go for Thai?" Anne suggested.

"Sounds good to me, father?" Alex's stomach was rumbling.

"I could eat." He slowly opened the door. "Carl?" They all entered Father Carl's living quarters. It was a neatly put-together apartment where everything had its place.

Alex was the first to enter. "There's no Dark here. Cuz, you know, I can sense it now." She seemed to prance into the house. Both Father Richard and Anne looked at each other with a smirk. Alex scanned the area where her attention focused on a framed Purple Heart citation on the wall. It read how he got shot in the line of duty. "Damn."

"You never know what someone's past actually consists of," Father Richard tapped Alex on the shoulder before going to search the rest of the house. Alex ventured to check the garage. She opened the door to see that Father Carl's vehicle wasn't in there. "His car isn't here."

"But none of his personal stuff is gone. Nothing is packed. Everything is so neat, like everything has its place. There are no missing spots." Anne came out of a bedroom. "Not even any underwear."

Alex tilted her head towards Anne. "What kind of underwear do priests wear?"

Father Richard eyed her with annoyance. "Holy underwear, Alex. Holy."

Alex smirked, but then it stopped as a thought hit her. "Where's his bedroom?"

"Last door on the right." Father Richard pointed down the hall. "Why?"

"When Kameron takes off with very short notice, he always has a bug-out bag packed and ready to go." Alex started down the hallway.

"It's how I knew Kameron was in trouble in D.C." Alex went into the closet. "There's nothing in here. He must have taken off."

All three of them looked at each other, convinced he must have taken off. "Makes sense. Okay, let's go get something to eat." Alex did a final scour of the dwelling. "But he always told me he was leaving," she said under her breath.

They all stopped off to get some ice cream after having some Thai food before heading back to the church. They headed into the church, where Dinah was arguing with Tristan over something. "What's going on?"

Tristan was annoyed. "I was in battle with an Infiltrator. She came up from the top to kill it."

"He was going to kill you," Dinah argued, pointing in the direction of the forest.

"He was not!" Tristan was yelling his point to Alex. "I had him dead to rights."

Alex just licked her ice cream, watching the fight. "You guys done?" Alex waited for the silent answer. "Good. Tristan, you should never deny someone helping you in a fight. When you are risking your life, you should appreciate any help."

Tristan kept his mouth shut, but as he was about to leave. Father Richard stopped him. "Hang on a minute. Alex, you got a minute."

"Sure," Alex stopped. "What's going on?"

Anne suddenly got nervous. "There's something I need to talk to you about. Let's go into my office." The five of them went into the office, where Anne made sure everyone was in before they closed the door. With a simple click, Anne went over to her desk and sat down. No one was saying anything.

"Why did you bring us down here?" Dinah asked as she leaned against the wall. The angel still stared at Tristan, annoyed.

"Alex," Anne began to say, but she stopped herself. "Alex, I found a way, possibly, to open a Dark Conduit."

That caught everyone's attention. Alex froze in place. "What do you mean?"

"How are you able to do this?" Dinah was fully attentive on Anne.

Anne got up and opened the safe, showing the texts. Dinah halfway forcefully snatched the papers. "I do not get it. There is nothing on the pages."

"They are written in Dark Texts; you won't be able to read them." Anne pointed out.

Dinah immediately held them with two fingers to hand them over to Anne. "Eww. If what you are saying is true, what you have is truly dangerous."

Alex was getting anxious. "What do they say, Anne?"

Anne read the text. "It's basically stating there is a man-made Dark Conduit. But nothing really how to open it."

"Why hasn't the Dark opened it?" Tristan was peeking at the gibberish of the papers.

"They do not know how," Dinah stared at the blank papers on Anne's desk. "Though, I am sure they have attempted." Dinah reiterated, "That is bad."

"Why is that bad?" Tristan was confused about the situation. "If we can get Kameron back?"

Alex was surprisingly quiet, and she just sat there, leaning in the dark corner. "Because if the Dark finds out how to open it; we're in some really deep shit," Alex finally spoke with a bit of a cold tone. "Kameron's torture isn't worth the chance of letting Vandor free." Alex wiped a tear from her face.

"Where is this conduit?" Tristan was kicking himself for asking such a stupid question. Of course it wasn't worth the risk.

"The museum," Anne almost had a bit of hesitation in her voice. "I've seen it."

"How did it get there?" Dinah was confused.

"Don't know," Anne shrugged her shoulders.

Father Richard felt he had to ask the obvious question. "How do you open it?"

"The key, I am assuming." Anne got an object wrapped in cloth from the safe. "I just don't know how to unwrap it."

Dinah tilted her head when she saw the item sitting on Anne's desk.

Tristan noticed her reaction. "Do you recognize it?" He whispered to her.

"No, but I think I know who would. Do not do anything until I return." Dinah got up to leave the room.

The group watched her leave. Alex stared at the object wrapped in a cloth sitting on Anne's desk. Anne did not miss Alex's face as she stared at the object on the desk. "You okay, sweetie?"

"What is it?" Alex continued to stare at the object.

"I don't know, my guess, it's a cross." Anne put her hand on it. "But the seal, string, and this cloth cannot be broken."

"Does the Council know?" Alex just blankly stared at the key.

Father Richard shook his head. "Not yet."

Alex had no expression, no movement, and was completely monotone when she spoke. "They should."

***

The room was full of blackness, minus the small red light above that provided some illumination to the room. Father Carl just finished a small sermon to the group. It wasn't the feeling of preaching to a full room in the church, but it felt just as genuine. It almost made him feel warm in this cold dungeon.

"Father," a man came up to him.

"Yes." He put his rosary in his pocket.

The man sat down on the bed. "We are going to die, aren't we?"

Father Carl sat next to him. "It's a possibility."

"I was listening to what you were saying, about the Kingdom of Heaven, if we repent for our sins." The man wiped his nose.

"Yes, asking for forgiveness and meaning it, is the key." Father Carl could tell something was on this man's mind. "It's not a get-out-jail-free card." He teased the man.

He forced a smile. "I'm not a good man, and I don't think I'm going to make it into Heaven." He finally admitted.

"Why do you say that?" The priest put his hand on the man's shoulders. "It stays with me."

The man made sure no one was listening. "I have a son; I haven't talked to him in over a year. He caught me cheating on his mom. It's what led to our divorce. I've stolen money from my ex-wife; she doesn't even know it." The man wiped a tear. "Prostitutes know me by name."

"Flesh of the man is not an easy obstacle to conquer." Father Carl explained. "But I will say this one thing: the key for another person to forgive you, is for you to forgive yourself."

"I've tried," the man seemed hopeless. "I don't know how."

"First, confess your sins to God, then ask Him to help you forgive yourself." Father Carl wrapped his rosary around his hand.

"Through confession?" The man was feeling a bit uncomfortable.

Father Carl nodded. "Yes, you basically confessed your sins to me already."

"I'm not Catholic." The man let him know with worry on his face.

Father Carl chuckled. "You know, it's not the first time I've had someone tell me that."

Some extra light came in when the door opened. A woman was thrown into the room by a Dark Angel with a bird-like creature on his shoulder. Father Carl ran over to her with some others to help her up. A woman who took Scotty earlier came out from behind the big angel.

"Your entre tonight will be rice with a side of broccoli, and each of you has the honor of having one cot for every three of you. So, enjoy." She turned to leave.

"Where's Scotty?" Father Carl called out to her.

She stopped as if she was annoyed. "He will not be joining you as his life is now over." She flashed her eyes and grinned her teeth. "Have a good dinner." The door slammed shut, causing shivering fear.

***

Alex waited in her office with Anne for Father Richard. No one was really saying anything. Anne seemed to be on edge around Alex. It didn't help she wasn't saying a word. The sounds of footsteps coming up the stairs only meant Father Richard had just gotten off the phone with the Council. He opened the door to sit down. It looked like it wasn't a good conversation.

"Not a good talk?" Alex finally spoke. Her arms crossed with her pinky finger rapidly bouncing.

"No," he answered. "They want to know where you got those texts and the artifact." That was directed towards Anne.

"They just appeared at my door." In Anne's mind, she told the truth without indulging what Celestial wished of her.

"Did the Dark drop them off?" Father Richard was trying to get a hold of the situation. "Maybe they couldn't figure it out, I mean, you translated those texts in D.C."

"No, I don't think so," Anne was hoping this conversation would veer off in another direction.

"Regardless of where they came from, we have them. The problem now is securing them." Father Richard was obviously stressed to capacity. "We keep them here until we hear from the Vatican Council."

There was a knock on the door, and Tristan slowly opened the door. "Dinah has returned."

The three of them got up to head downstairs. Father Richard peeked into the lobby where Megan was sitting at her desk. "Megan, I'm waiting for an important phone call from the Vatican. Can you come get me in Anne's office when it comes?"

"Yes, father," Megan watched the group head downstairs to Anne's office.

They passed the congregation hall where Dinah was in the room with Devine and another angel Alex had never seen before. All three of them were praying before turning around to see the group.

"Who is that?" Anne whispered to the orange-haired angel.

Dinah shook her head with confusion. "Devine, former Guardian to the Conduit of Lite."

Tristan gave a small chuckle.

Alex was annoyed, "No shit, the other one?"

Devine spoke up before something escalated. "This is Juriel. The Lite Chronicler."

The angel had short brown hair with a bit of sparkle to it. "Alexandria Johnson, I am sorry about the loss of The Protector. He was a fierce opponent of the Dark."

Alex forced a smile. "Thanks, what are you doing here?"

Dinah answered for him, "He is the recorder of the Lite actions. He may know the item."

All of them ended up in the gathering room outside the kitchen area. Anne asked for one of the angels to escort her as she carried the artifact and texts. Devine agreed to escort the Church Historian to her office to grab the artifacts. Anne felt safe having Devine watch over her as she accessed the safe.

Devine stood outside the door, keeping guard. "How is the Sentry?"

"She's doing okay. She's happy she's got her connection back, but I think she would rather not have given up Komptin." Anne was spinning the lock.

"There is so much suffering." Devine was in a blank stare. "So much evil walks this living rock. It should have never gotten this far."

"Yes, now this potential to bring Kameron back isn't helping matters." Anne grabbed the texts and cloth.

Devine was in deep thought. "The Dark does a lot of damage. Some of their attacks are never truly healed. There are always constant reminders."

"Is anyone coming?"

"I will keep vigilance." Devine stared down the hallway.

Anne put the artifact and text in a satchel as Devine watched down the hallway. She closed the safe and locked it. There were other items in the safe that needed security. Devine escorted Anne into the gathering room. Dinah stayed by the door to make sure no one was coming. She shut the door but maintained her position at the entryway.

"What is that you have?" Juriel was curious why he got called down to the planet. He never really comes down that often.

Anne pulled out the artifact. Devine got a stone-cold expression on her face. "Where did you get that?"

Juriel was equally shocked. "I did not see this coming."

"Do you know what it is?" Alex's stomach got a little nervous.

"No, not at all," Juriel admitted with a bit of humility. "But it is wrapped with cloth made of angelic garment. See this strap; this is made with the same substance to hold their battle harnesses."

"What about the seal?" Anne tapped on the medal medallion.

"Well, it is a Courier seal created by the NEWS. They are the reporter to God. You see the top one here, that is North. One who directly authorizes the Message. The two on the side. This one is the East. The other one is the West. They are supporters of the Message."

"What about the one coming from the bottom?" Anne pointed to the symbol of a black wavy triangle. "I'm assuming that is South."

"Correct. The one who delivers the Message."

"What's the Message?" Father Richard stepped up to the symbol. "I'm assuming they send a message to God."

"Only the four of them know." Juriel continued his lesson. "It could be anything."

"I doubt it's the weather report." Alex stared at the symbol.

Dinah was a bit confused. "Why would they report the weather? God knows what the weather is; He created it."

Alex didn't even bother to explain her comment. "But why are they sealing whatever is inside?" Alex was trying to control her impatience. "What's in there?"

"I think it's a cross," Anne held it up.

Devine turned to Anne as she said that.

"How do we open it?" Alex continued not to move. She was so cold in her tone.

Juriel put the artifact down. "Only the Couriers know."

"Where are they?" Tristan asked in the background, standing guard with Dinah.

Alex chimed in, still with her arms crossed. "I think the better question is, what are their intentions and who are they?"

Juriel answered, "They are four brothers who directly report the Message back to God, but what they report is unknown. All I know, is that they convey randomly; other than that, they are separated."

A knock on the door interrupted the eerie quiet that engulfed the room. Tristan only opened the door slightly. "Hey."

"I have a phone call for Father Richard." Megan waved the phone.

"Come on in, Megan." Father Richard told her. Alex looked at him like he was crazy. He received the phone from Megan. "She's on her way to be part of the Council anyways." He put the phone to his ear. "Father Richard." He listened for a while and then hung up the phone.

"Well," Alex was waiting for the official word. The air was tense while waiting for the final decision.

"It's a negative. They want the artifact brought to the Vatican." Father Richard told the group.

Everyone was expecting Alex to blow up, but all she did was slowly close her eyes as she wiped a tear. "If that's what they said. Excuse me." Alex got up to leave with the group watching her. Anne grabbed the artifact and text to secure them back in the safe.

"She did not look happy," Devine quickly moved to ensure Anne got the artifact back to the safe.

"You think we need to watch her?" Tristan asked, a bit of caution in his voice.

"She knew the right thing to do before I even called the Council. She just needed them to say it, so she didn't have to." Father Richard watched the conflicted Lite Sentry disappear around the corner.

Megan just moved her eyes around the room. "What's going on?"

***

Devine watched the Pure of Heart chase after the Lite Sentry after taking the Cross of Darkness to the metal box. The angel of the Lite slowly strolled into the congregation hall. Everyone else stayed downstairs. The massive stained-glass window seemed to stare down at her with disappointment. There was stealth in every step she took. It was almost as if she was trying to hide her thoughts. This was the first time her nerves seemed to be taking over her body. She was anxious before, but nothing like this.

Devine didn't stay long in the worship hall before going down the staircase, which led her straight to the Pure of Heart's office door. Devine liked Anne; there was a tremendous amount of guilt about what she was about to do, what she had to do. The angel did not like having to second-guess her actions. With minimal effort, she busted into the office door.

The metal container across the room holding the cross was her target. Devine stared at the container, for there was no turning back now. She grabbed the handle as she held her breath. Once she did this, it would bring hope to the world. The angel had a determined look on her face just before she yanked the safe open. The artifact wrapped in the Courier's cloth container was now in her hands.

There was a cutting tool on the desk within her reach. She opened the contraption to expose the edge. She sliced the palm of her hand to have her neon blue blood start to ooze out. The blood dripped onto the center of the seal. The building shook as the seal broke with ease. The angelic straps loosened to allow Devine to unravel the artifact.

The Pure of Heart was halfway correct; it was a cross, but one made of pure evil. Devine flipped the cross so it appeared to be upside down. The arrow was facing the ground. In the center of the intersection was a clear ball with pure black liquid. There was only one way ahead.

***

"I don't want to!" Lilly threw her pencil on the table.

"Lilly, do your predestination homework!" Her mom screamed so loud at little Lilly that she had to cover her ears. The seven-year-old girl almost spilled her drink all over the table. The cigarette ash she held fell onto Lilly's *Child's Guide to Power* book. "Look what you made me do!"

"I don't want to do this!" The little blonde-haired girl started to cry. "I want to go back to school with my friends!" One of the cats jumped onto the table from the dog chasing it around the house. Lilly rubbed her eyes from the cigarette smoke that filled the room.

"Your father is going to be home from his F.O.R. meeting. This needs to be done by the time he gets home, so get it done!" She slammed her fist on the table, then went into the fridge to get another beer.

"I'm hungry!" Lilly started to pout.

"I'll put the frozen dinner in the microwave after you finish your homework. That book is the priority. Read the book, get the food." She went into the living room to sit on the floral-patterned couch. Lilly's mom picked up the ashtray from the end table and continued watching the television, playing an F.O.R. Self-Help video.

The dogs started barking as the sound of her dad's broken muffler truck came home. "Shut up, you stupid-ass dogs." The rusty truck door shut. He came into the entryway to the house, stomping his feet. He threw his greasy coat on a table next to the door that was full of endless supplies of used car parts. "I'm home."

"Your daughter is refusing to do her homework." Her mom put the beer bottle to her mouth.

"So, make her do it!" He put his lunch box on the floor, and the dogs started to sniff around the lunchbox for scraps.

"Oh, like I never thought of that." Her mom flicked the ashes off her cigarette.

"Lilly, get it done." He angrily pointed his finger at her. "You are seven years old. When you get older, you will be doing the work of the F.O.R. Do you want to be behind everyone else on the Roadmap to Absolute Power?" He then opened the refrigerator to grab a beer.

"There's a Salisbury steak dinner in the freezer, behind the pot pies." Lilly's mom turned the volume up on the television.

"Me and the boys ate at the bar after the meeting," He turned to Lilly. "Get your work done, now."

"I want to go back to school." Lilly continued to mope.

Her dad slapped her across the face. "Do what you're told!" The house seemed to shake for a split second. Her dad just froze, as he didn't know what happened. "Was that an earthquake?"

Her mom got up, "Felt like it." The two of them didn't move, then shrugged it off. "I have my Lady F.O.R. meeting tomorrow, so you have to be home with Lilly."

"Maybe you could clean this house before you go." He threw his beer cap toward the garbage but missed it. He just left it on the floor as he went over to Lilly. "Get your homework done." Her dad walked over to her mom to grab one of her cigarettes. "What happened to that five hundred dollars we had left on the credit card?"

"I used it to buy these videos from the F.O.R. Seminar." Her mom pointed to the show she was watching.

"Why the hell did you do that? I needed that to purchase my next stop on my Roadmap to Power!" He started to yell. "This isn't even on the Map!"

"I needed them for my Journey. It will get me there faster than you are taking on yours." Her mom took another drink out of her bottle.

"Look, my Power is more important. The higher I get, the better off we'll be. You really screwed me over!" Lilly's dad was the anger that scared Lilly.

Her mom started to match his volume. "Why is it always your Power, where mine is just as important as yours."

The dogs started barking at the noise, which caused her parents to start yelling louder. Lilly put her pencil down in her book. She ran outside the back door down the rundown deck. Her only safe place was her hiding spot by the corner of the broken fence in the backyard. She had tears running down her cheeks. The only peace she had was at school with her friends. She ran outside to hide when something caught her attention.

A tall, black figure stood completely still near the fence at the end of the yard. He was next to one of her dad's old cars and a stack of old tires. He wasn't moving, just standing still. Lilly carefully approached the figure. "Hello." The figure slowly turned as he was wearing a very dark black robe with hood draped over his head. Lily couldn't see the person's face inside the black hood. There was no cloth covering the face, just blackness.

The dark man lifted his hand to Lilly's face, where her dad slapped her. The black gloves he was wearing were soft to the touch as he gently rubbed the cheek of the young girl in a caring fashion. He tilted his head as he gently continued to try to make Lilly feel better. The child tried to see the lengthy figure's face, but still was nothing but empty darkness. The pain in her face was obvious, as was how sad she was. The figure lifted his other hand in front of where his face would be and lifted his finger. It was as if telling her to be quiet. Lilly had a rush of warmth run through her as she smiled with peaceful calmness. "Yes."

The dark figure removed his hand from her cheek to take his glove off. The dark gray skeleton hand was gently placed on top of her head. With a slow generation of a dark green light from the bony hand, Lilly's body dropped to the ground.

The parental male saw the dark figure through the window. The dark figure seemed to step in front of the disappearing little girl's body, almost in a protector mode. "Who the hell are you?" The male came running at him. "Get off my property."

The female half of the parental unit came out, "Where's Lilly?"

The dark figure put the glove back on and then generated a scythe from the same dark green light. He slammed it on the ground with a spark on impact as he approached the two adults.

***

Anne had chased Alex up to her office. She was such in such a rush to check on her friend that she had to think if she actually locked up her safe. Alex was already in the cooler, grabbing an Apollo by the time she got up there. She made her way to the window, leaning on the wall. She was staring out from the side, going back and forth to Komptin's bed.

"You okay, sweetie?" Anne peeked her head into the office.

"You can come in," Alex just took a sip of her drink. "I'm fine, Anne."

"Are you?" Anne was a bit nervous as she moved to the other side of the window. "I wish the Council would have given you permission to try to get Kameron back."

Alex just stared out the window. It was quiet before she actually answered Anne. "They made the right call." There was something calming about her statement. It wasn't acceptance; for the first time, Alex truly sounded defeated.

Anne didn't say anything. She just stared out the window when they both felt a small tremor. "What was that?"

"Knowing my luck, the apocalypse." Alex didn't take her eyes off staring out the vastness of CopperTop Mountain.

"Well, I'm going to go home, make myself dinner, and for a treat, I'm going to have a strawberry milkshake." Anne was halfway hoping to have Alex join her. "You wanna come over."

"No, I'm good." Alex strolled, unemotively, to her closet to pull out her hunting clothes.

Guilt started to overcome Anne as she felt she should have told Alex. There was too much at risk; when it came to Kameron, Alex might not look at the big picture. Anne made it downstairs, where she came across Megan, who was getting her jacket on. "Heading out?"

"I have a date," Megan smiled.

"Anyone special?" Anne was hoping it wasn't Roger.

"We'll see," Megan headed out with Anne.

Anne put her hand on her back. "I truly hope you find happiness."

Megan rolled her eyes behind Anne's back. The church historian stopped in her tracks by her office door. "Your door looks like it was broken into."

Anne's heart just dropped. She slowly opened the door to see her worst nightmare. The safe was open. She ran up to it to see the artifact was missing. The only thing left was the casing it was wrapped in.

***

Kameron sat in his patrol car, tapping his pen on his leg. He couldn't help but think of how much trouble the two of them were going to be in when she got caught following the Lite. Would she give him up? Would Kameron fall on the sword with her? It's a scenario he hoped never to get into, but for some reason, he felt as if it was going to happen. It was just a matter of time.

Grossman just got off the phone with his wife. "Don't ever get married."

Kameron chuckled. "Not in the immediate future."

"Right," Grossman laughed. "That's what I said. It's no doubt, you have your Power over this woman you've been seeing."

"I don't know if it's Power. I feel power when I make her happy–by the look on her face, she gets the same when she does the same for me." Kameron could only think of Alex's genuine smile.

Grossman moved his eyes to his young protégé. "Careful, that's borderline Lite talk."

Kameron immediately clammed up. "Sorry. It's just, we fit together."

The two got out of their car to conduct a Lite Check on some random pedestrians as they were minding their own business. Grossman glanced down at his watch. "Let's hurry this up. I want to get home. Pick someone we know that isn't going to be a Lite Follower."

Kameron couldn't help but think of Michelle. He knew his sister, but she followed the Lite. His girlfriend...she followed the Lite. There was no way of knowing who was truly in the order of the Fallen Trinity. Then, as they turned the corner, they saw Megan and Roger Somberson coming out of City Hall. Kameron immediately got a sour stomach as the air got thick.

"Perfect. Get your ex-girlfriend." Grossman saw the opportunity.

"Let's grab someone else," Kameron got a sour feeling in his stomach.

"We know for a fact she won't be a Lite Follower," Grossman led the way to Roger and Megan, who were going over some plans. "Excuse me, I'm Sentinel Supervisor Grossman, just conducting a random Lite Check."

"Really?" Megan gave an annoyed look to Kameron. "Trying to humiliate me some more?"

Kameron softly admitted. "Would you believe any answer I give?"

"Let's get this over with," Megan handed over her purse.

Grossman went through the purse for her items. "There's nothing here."

"Shocker," Roger annoyingly stated. "Look, there are true Lite Followers growing in this town, and you are checking the secretary to the Leader of the Fallen? What right do you have..."

"Random is random," Kameron reiterated.

Both Megan and Roger snapped their necks over to Kameron with contempt. Then something else caught their attention. Alex came walking down the stairs with another two people. Alex was shocked to see them, almost not knowing what to do. Alex tried to act nonchalant as she approached the group.

"Hey, what are you doing here?" Kameron secretly squeezed her hand.

"Ah, we put in a request for Michelle's status. But it's looking like they won't give us any update." Alex stared at city hall. "I truly hope she is okay."

"I can't either, even as a relative. I'm told I shouldn't even be asking because it could bring an investigation onto my family." Kameron tried to give a coded warning.

Alex acknowledged by putting her hand on top of Kameron's in a loving fashion. "She'll make it through alright." Alex smiled at him.

The obvious connection between the two of them had sent Megan into a fit of rage. It was obvious her ex-boyfriend had a certain glow to him when he was with her. "Hey, Kameron, don't you have to conduct your random check?"

Kameron got all tense. He turned to Grossman for clarification, almost begging. His boss commented, "Just do it quickly so we can go home."

Alex's eyes got big as she now knew she was going to get caught. The two other people started to argue. "Check us." Alex turned to them and shook her head.

"Is there a reason you don't want her checked?" Roger Somberson's attention was now piqued. "Why would you volunteer for something like that?" Then he put it all together. "Check her now!"

Grossman moved behind Alex to prevent her from moving. "Get her purse, Kameron."

Alex veered up with him, almost with a confident annoyance.

Kameron hesitantly let go of her hand. "This will be awkward. We're dating."

Roger stepped up to him. "You show your Power the Fallen has given you. The dedication shown to the Fallen Trinity is represented directly by your choices. Check her, or you will be charged with conspiracy of religious radicalism." Roger pointed directly at his chest. "Check her."

Kameron didn't know what to do. Roger definitely had the power in the community, but no legal right to order him around. Then he looked at Alex; his love for her gave him the strength. "No. You have no right to command a member of the Sentinel Guard."

It was as if Roger's eyes turned red with anger. "You just signed your own death certificate…"

Alex stepped up, almost as if Roger had no effect on her whatsoever. "It's okay, Kameron. Let's just get this over with." Alex showed him her purse.

Kameron stared at her brown, sad eyes. "I don't want to."

Grossman chimed in. "Kameron, as your supervisor, I do have the right. Get this check done so I can go home."

Roger appeared over his shoulder with Megan behind him. "It's not a matter of wanting to; it's a matter of having to. Now do it."

Kameron searched her purse, but there was nothing in it. Kameron's heart actually skipped a couple beats as he went through her purse. "Nothing."

"Really?" Roger couldn't believe there was nothing in there. He turned to Megan. "There's Lite radiating from her. I just know it."

"I was overwatching, and there was nothing in there," Grossman confirmed. "Now, can we go home?"

Then Megan saw a flash of gold from the sun reflecting on Alex's neck. "Check her necklace." She pointed to Alex's neck.

"We conducted our check, we're done." Kameron handed back the purse.

"Check her necklace!" Megan ordered him.

"I said we're done." Kameron put his foot down. "Alex, you're free to go."

Roger Somberson got angry as well. "Just check her damn necklace. As Leader of the Fallen, I order you to check her necklace."

"You have no legal authority over me. You can't order me to do that." Kameron stood up to him, which sent Megan into a higher state of anger. She rushed Alex, ripping the necklace off her. The necklace dropped to the ground as a Lite Angel pendant bounced on the sidewalk.

Kameron closed his eyes in disbelief that this was actually happening. Roger Somberson picked up the necklace pendant with a red handkerchief from his pocket. He studied it intensely. "This is the Conduit of Lite."

Alex stared directly at the red-headed leader of the Fallen. "And her replacement will announce the starting of bringing Lite to the world."

Grossman didn't even hesitate. He threw her on the ground, having her face slam into the hot pavement. The other two members started to attack Grossman, so Kameron had to step in to defend his partner. He took out his baton and smashed the knee of the girl. She went down screaming in pain. The man continued to assault Grossman, trying to set Alex free. Kameron threw him onto the ground to cuff him. Kameron had his knee on the back of his head as the girl was crying over her broken kneecap.

Alex stared at her friends. "What's going to happen to them?"

Grossman picked her up once he put the cuffs on her. Roger approached her, and gave her a hateful look. "They risked everything to protect you. You must be something pretty special." He eyed her up and down, then licked his lips in a sexual manner. "You should be more worried about what is going to happen to you."

Alex stared into his eyes, and without hesitation–she spit right in his face. "No matter what you do to me, I know the Lite will be my pillar of strength, you son of bitch."

Grossman started to take her away. Kameron watched as someone he truly cared for was being hauled away. Roger approached Kameron while wiping his face, kicking the girl's knee as he approached the troubled Sentinel. "Megan is the only reason I don't report your ass right now. Now, thank her."

She had an evil smirk on his face. "Yes, Kameron. Thank me."

Kameron just stared at her with contempt. "Thank you, Megan."

Chapter Thirteen

Alex got a sick feeling in her stomach from a sudden shot of nerves, but then it quickly vanished. Everyone was in the office of the Church Historian. It reminded Alex of their own private Council meeting. Anne sat in shock as she sat behind her desk. Alex had seen her like this only once before...at Kale's funeral. She had a weird look on her face, as if she was in a state of confusion while trying to figure out what was going on. Alex was leaning on the bookcase behind her, trying to make her feel better. Dinah and Tristan were standing by the doorway on point. They were worried about whatever Dark stole the artifact would return. Father Richard was next to Megan, who was trying to act as if she didn't know what was going on. In her defense, she really didn't know.

"I can't believe someone came in and stole that, right underneath my eyes." Anne just shook her head in disbelief.

"Who would do such a thing?" Megan was actually curious about this. "Who would break into a church and steal?"

"The Dark," both Tristan and Dinah said simultaneously.

"No way," Alex contradicted them. "That is impossible. Both Tristan and me, you, would have known. It must have been a person."

"Unless the Dark has a new way to hide their sense, just like how that Harridan blocked your senses." Anne rubbed her eyes.

"If that bitch found a way to do that..." Alex clenched her fists.

Megan deceitfully played it off. "What's a Harridan? And this talk about the Dark?" She whispered to Father Richard.

He only replied, "Later." Father Richard calculated what time it was in the Vatican after seeing what time it was. "We need to inform the Council." Father Richard wiped the sweat off his bald head.

"I don't even know what to tell them. They don't even know where I got it?" Anne admitted.

Megan was careful not to sound too intrigued. "Where did you get whatever it is?"

Anne refused to say. "I just came in possession of it."

"We have to find it, but where do we even look? I'm telling you, there is no way the Dark came in here without us knowing." Alex was stern in her conviction.

"They must have sent a regular person like Alex suggested," Tristan suggested. "That's the only explanation. Someone we couldn't sense."

"There is no way," Dinah argued with him. "Look at that safe. It was yanked open."

"No human could pull that open that fast. That safe has a one-hour break in time." Anne told the group. "It would have to be someone supernatural and doesn't give off Dark."

The group all looked at each other. Alex stood up in fear. "Did Azrael get to someone?"

Everyone looked at Dinah. "What?" She asked. "You think Azrael turned me?"

"It's not personal. We just need to make sure." Tristan let her know. "Eliminate all seeds of doubt."

"How do we know?" Father Richard realized they were indulging too much with Megan around. "Hey Megan, do you mind going up to the office and getting a hold of the Council?"

"Yes, Father." Megan left the room.

Tristan shut the door when she left. "How are we going to make sure?"

Alex turned to the two angels in the room, "We have no strength on church property."

"So that leaves the two of us," Dinah turned in disbelief that her loyalty was being questioned.

"You have disobeyed Him before," Juriel reminded her.

Dinah shot him a dirty look. "I questioned Him. There is a difference."

Tristan immediately stood in between them. "How are we going to prove both of them are telling the truth?"

Alex just shrugged her shoulders for a last hope. "Just show us your wings and halos. The Dark angels are black with makeshift horns."

"Sounds good to me," Juriel showed his wings and halo. "Happy?"

"I'm good," Alex turned her attention to Dinah. "Your turn."

"I am telling you; I am not working for the Dark." Dinah was insulted by the actions of the group. "I said no when he tempted me before."

"Dinah, please," Tristan gently touched her arm. "I believe you; we all believe you. But we humans live in constant doubt and fear. This would just eradicate that."

Dinah looked at him in the eyes and softly nodded. "Okay." She generated her halo and wings in the room. "I told you I was not working for the Dark."

"No offense, Dinah. I kind of wish one of you were," Alex wiped her face with her hands. "Then we would have answers."

"We're back where we started," Father Richard sat down in a chair by the window.

Dinah's face was nothing but panic. "Has anyone seen Devine? When was the last time you saw her use her wings?"

***

Gron strolled the halls of the F.O.R. Compound on his way to see the Pure of Hearts. There was a young lady with dark makeup and black hair walking past him with her Roadmap to Absolute Power. She nervously smiled shyly at him as she stepped aside to let him by. He made it downstairs to see two guards keeping the Pure of Hearts secured. "Open the door," he commanded. The guards opened the door to the room, where the outline of the bodies seemed to huddle around each other. Gron loved the power of fear in people.

The priest stood in front of his flock. "I'm Father Carl Gray. Identify yourself Demon."

"You are a brave one," Gron said, surprised at his conviction. "You'll die, just like the others at the hand of my Master. My only worry is, are you fed first for the others to watch, or would it be more fun for you to watch them die one by one? What do you think. shepherd?"

"He may take our bodies, but he won't take our souls. They belong to Him." The priest held his rosary tight.

"Let me ask you this, if He loves you so, will He send someone to save your sorry asses?" He laughed. Gron waited, moving his eyes around the group. "Didn't think so. You're all going to die a horrible death upon Vandor's return."

Father Carl stepped forward. "He will send someone, the Lite Sentry."

Gron lost his confident facial expression. He turned away without saying anything. Why can't he get away from that woman?! Everything is connected to her. Mole was her brother, the Pure of Heart dedicated to Vandor's feast was her surrogate sister, they lived in the same town, and they went to the same school. Gron slammed the door to the prisoners, locking them away. As he returned to his office, the memories of Gron's past returned to him.

Roger's father was returning from work as manager of a fast-food taco joint in town. His mother was still working the swing shift at the convenience store just down the street. The house they lived in was rundown, small, and could barely fit them, let alone his pregnant younger sister. Roger was in his room listening to music while painting his demonic figurines for a game he was into. He could barely hear the knock on the door.

"What?" He snapped.

"Hey there, champ, just wanted to let you know I was home." His father peeked his head into Roger's confined space for a room.

"Stop calling me champ. I hate that," he continued to work on his figurine.

His dad picked up the remote to his stereo to shut it off. "You are my champ."

"Whatever," he continued to paint the red eyes on the demon figure. He watched as his dad picked one of them up.

"This one is pretty neat. What does he do?" His dad studied the metal figurine.

"He's nothing. All he does is document the actions of others. He's pretty worthless. This one, this one is the general of his army. He is feared among the peons he comes across." He showed the figure he was holding.

"Any plans tonight there, stud?" He started to playfully headlock him. "Any girls you got your eye on?"

"Dad, stop it. You're going to make me spill my paint." Roger was getting agitated.

"Okay, okay," His dad stopped. "Why don't you go out tonight? Isn't there a party or something you can go to with your friends? It's the last summer before your senior year."

"No," Roger sat here with a scowl on his face.

His dad reached into his wallet. "Here's ten dollars. Go out, have fun tonight, enjoy your summer."

Roger took the money. "What am I supposed to do with this? Get a meal at Marty's?"

His dad had hurt written on his face. "I wish I could give you more, champ. You just seemed so miserable lately."

Roger got up and grabbed his leather trench coat. "Look at my life, dad. What pleasure is this? This place smells like fast-food tacos all the time. My sister is knocked up by some dude, she doesn't even know who, and mom works at a gas station. Tell me what future do I have?"

"You have whatever future you set forth. One step at a time?"

Roger got mad. "Really, how did that work out for you, dad?" He left out the door to see Marcus across the street, leaving his house in anger. "Your old man again?"

"He's an asshole," he rubbed his eye.

Roger saw the mark under his eye where he was hit. "You wanna kill him?"

Marcus laughed, but then he stopped. "You're serious."

"Yah, come on, it'll be fun." Roger thought about how to go about it. "We'll sacrifice him to the devil or something. Really freak him out before we shove a knife into his chest."

There was a brief moment of fear in Marcus's eyes. "Dude, you had me."

Roger laughed. "Come on, there's a party at Cindy's house. You wanna go?"

"Dude, really? Why?" Marcus checked for his lighter.

"See how lame it is?" Roger started heading towards town. "Come on, I know where she lives."

329

Roger just entered the door of Cindy's house, which was packed with people. The music was loud, and red solo cups were in abundant supply. Roger saw Alex, the small little goth chick who was easier than a kindergarten math test across the room. She was talking to Sara, who had her eye on the guy across the room.

"What are you doing here?" Shawn came over with a girl around his arm.

"Oh, it's a party Shawn, the more the merrier," she was obviously drunk. She whispered something in his ear before licking as she pulled away.

"Go on upstairs. I'll be up in a minute." Shawn watched her stumble upstairs a bit.

He turned to another girl as he smiled at her. Roger was actually finding himself a bit jealous of him. "I'm going to get a drink."

"Look, maybe I'm in a good mood or something. Or the fact that I know I'm about to get a little something." He pointed over at Alex, who was going to the next room by herself.

"What about her?" Roger eyed her up. He couldn't help but check out her figure as she disappeared behind the door.

"Mole just got sent to juvey, so she is feeling a little lonely, probably a little vulnerable. Why don't you go and take advantage of the situation?" Shawn motioned with his head.

"Why don't you?" Marcus jumped in.

"I already had it. Plus, I just want to see if she would." Shawn was only curious how easy Alex actually was. "I gotta go. Let me know how it goes."

Roger got an evil smile. "Thanks, I won't forget this. I'll pay you back."

Shawn rolled his eyes before heading upstairs.

"Should I?" Roger leaned over to Marcus, not taking his eyes off that room.

"You nail Alex, that would be awesome!" He laughed as he scanned around the room. He was on the hunt to score something else besides a girl. "I'm going to try to get a dime bag."

Roger opened the door to the room where Alex was sitting on the couch. Her somber state while sitting on the couch was obvious. She held a drink in her hand and poured her Apollo into it. Roger sat next to her, close to her.

She scooted over a bit away from him. When he put his arm up on the couch, she grabbed it to give it back to him. "Really, Roger?"

Roger quickly recovered, worried he had blown his chance to get with her. "What's with you?"

"I'm having a bad day," Alex saw one of Cindy's dogs walk by. "Come here, boy." The dog just continued going. "I swear, I will never have a dog. Loyal, my ass."

"What are you so bummed about?" Roger leaned in a little closer. He noticed she didn't back away.

"My dad. He's such an ass." Alex started breaking down her wall. A tear was forming on her face. He wiped it off of her. She smiled. "Thanks."

"I can relate," Roger tried to make a connection. "Have you talked to your boyfriend Mole about it?"

Alex closed her eyes. "We're not dating, and he went away for the summer."

"So, you have no one, you're all alone." Roger inched closer to her. "I could be there for you."

Alex turned to him. "Roger, I'm not good for you. I'm not good for anyone."

Out of pure impulse, Roger put his hand on her face and kissed her. "I think you are perfect for me." He couldn't believe it as she kissed him back. He didn't know how long he was kissing her for, but he thought he would go for broke. He started to move his hand up her shirt as he whispered. "Let's go upstairs." To Roger's surprise, she didn't say no.

"ALEX!" Sara came into the room. "It's time to go."

"No, she's good," Roger kept on trying to kiss her.

"No, I'm done." Alex got up to leave. She wiped her mouth as she got off the couch.

Marcus watched Alex being comforted by Sara. "Did you get any?"

Roger leered at Alex as she left the party. "I would sell my soul to have another chance to hit that."

Gron opened the door from the basement in a fit of rage. He angrily marched down the hall of the F.O.R. Compound. He saw that brunette with dark makeup from earlier as she stepped aside again. He made it a couple of steps past her before he stopped. Then backed up to her. "How would you like to see my office?"

She nervously nodded as she gave her hand to him. They made it to his office couch, where he didn't waste any time in letting her know his intentions. He was kissing her with force when she started fighting back. "Ow, please, stop. You're hurting me."

"No, you want it. You like this." Gron explained to her.

"Stop, my leader, STOP!" She slapped him across the face.

Anger engulfed Gron as his eyes turned red and his teeth grew. He tore into the girl's body. She didn't have a chance to scream. The mess of her body was all that was left as Gron was huffing and puffing over what was left of her. Azrael flew in through the window. "Something has happened."

"What?" Gron continued to stare at the body.

"I don't know, I can't explain it, but there is something off out there." Azrael came up to Gron to stare at the body. "Who was she?"

"Don't even know her name." Gron wiped his mouth. "What's going on out there?" He turned to motion to the Infiltrators to get rid of the body.

"There's a feeling in the air. I can't explain it." Azrael watched as Infiltrators came in to clean up the rest of the body up.

The phone rang. Gron answered his phone with annoyance. Misluna on the other end. "What's going on?"

***

"There's no way Devine turned to the Dark. I won't accept it." Alex protested to the group.

"It makes sense, Lite Sentry," Juriel pointed out. "Perhaps the rape did more to her than we understood."

Alex got infuriated. "That's low. How could you bring that up?"

"Sweetie," Anne put her hand on Alex. "That trauma could have done more to her than anyone can see."

Alex tightened her lips. "I refuse to go down that road. She is not Dark."

"Perhaps not, then why else would she take the artifact?" Dinah called out Alex's theory.

"We don't know that she did!" Alex pointed to the safe. "Why the hell would she take it? That being the case, how the hell did she know how to open the casing?"

Father Richard wiped the sweat off his head. "I think the more important question is what she plans to do with it, whatever it is?"

"We don't know she took it!" Alex got a phone call from a strange number but denied it. "Not in the mood for some spam call." She put the phone down on Anne's desk. "Why don't we just ask Celestial?" The phone rang again from the same number. "Ugh!" she hung up the phone.

"She will not know where she is. Remember, we could not find her after her..." Dinah was careful with her words. "...trauma."

Alex's phone rang again. "I swear these damn telemarketers." Alex picked up the phone. "No, I don't care that my computer virus program expired." Alex stopped and listened. "Hang on.

Let me put you on speaker." Alex put her phone down on Anne's desk. "Go ahead."

"Hey, it's Weston. I'm here with Midnight, who is barely out of her coma."

Father Richard gave the sign of the cross. "Oh, thank God."

Weston continued, "She said something that doesn't make any sense to me."

"What's that?" Alex was glad there was some good news on this night.

Weston could be heard grabbing a piece of paper. "Bear with me on this, but this is all I could get before she went back to sleep."

Anne picked up a piece of paper and a pen. "Go ahead, Weston."

"Me, gun, is my be hair done?" Weston said slowly. "Any ideas?"

Alex studied it. "No, but who knows what you dream when you are in a coma."

"How is she doing, Weston?" Anne was studying the words that Alex had written down.

"Doc says it might take a while, but she'll live," Weston answered. "She's in for some painful therapy sessions."

"Okay, keep us informed," Father Richard, in turn, studied the words. "Blessings."

"Take care," Weston sounded stressed. "Out."

"Well, thank God for small favors," Alex grabbed an Apollo from Anne's cooler.

There was a moment of silence in the room as no one knew what to say. Tristan was the first to speak. "So, what do we do now?"

The group all looked at each other. "I don't know." Alex had to admit to herself.

Father Richard saw what time it was on his watch. "Still no word from the Council, that's odd." The big bald priest got up. "I guess I should go see what's taking so long." Tristan and Dinah got out of the way to let Father Richard through.

"Well, I guess we could go search for her." Dinah grasped for straws.

"The only thing I could think of that fitting is that artificial Conduit, but why would she do that?" Anne threw out the group. "I wish Megan and I never saw that thing."

Alex's eye caught the message from Midnight written on her desk. "Megan." Alex studied the message. "My, gun," she softly whispered. "is my hair done," Alex repeated. "My hair done."

"Alex, what are you talking about," Tristan could tell Alex was in deep thought.

"My gun, my be, hair is done," Alex said a little faster. "My gun my be hair is done." Then she said it faster. "My gun maybe hairisdone." Alex mind was racing, all her thoughts were just putting it all together. Then it was like a light bulb as her it just came clear to her.

Anne's eyes got big as she knew where Alex was going. "No. Do you think?"

Alex's eyes flashed blue. "That conniving…," Alex stormed out of the office, a glow of blue could be seen from down the hallway. The rest of the group all looked at each other and headed out the doorway.

Misluna quickly got off the phone with Gron about the artifact missing when Father Richard came into the room. "Did you get a hold of the Council?"

"Couldn't get through," Megan showed him the phone.

Father Richard picked up the phone to dial the Council himself. "Si, Padre Partinello, per favore. Mi chamo Padre Richard. Grazi." Father Richard was on hold as he turned to Megan. "Ever get that feeling that it's going to be a bad night?"

"Nope, I control my own destiny," Misluna continued to text Gron details of the break-in.

Father Richard was still on hold. "Have you heard from Father Carl at all?" Then, a blue light caught Father Richard's attention. In the doorway was Alex, covered in blue. Her eyes were covered in blue light. Her fists were clenched at her sides as she breathed heavily from emotion. Anger was portrayed as she just stared at Megan with contempt. Father Richard was in shock, and angry Alex was using her powers in her sight. Then it hit him, Alex was using her powers on church property. "Alex, how are you able…". Then he realized his Lite Sentry was full out using her powers in front of the church secretary. Father Richard stared down at Megan, who was in a calm demeanor. There was no doubt she was trying to hide her fear at the sight of this. Father Partinello got on the other end of the phone. "I'll have to call you back." He slowly hung up the phone.

"Now, Alex, you can't use your powers on church property," Megan calmly sat in her chair as she stared at Alex.

Alex's lite dissipated, but the glowing of her eyes was the last to be shut off. "I don't need powers to kick your ass."

"How do you know about her..." Father Richard started to ask.

Megan turned to look up at the balding priest. For some reason, she had darker circles under her eyes, and she gave him an evil grin. Father Richard was in shock and confused. Before anyone could react, Alex was at Megan's desk. Megan punched Alex across the face, but that didn't phase her at all. Alex punched her across the face, knocking her back down and into her chair.

"Will someone tell me what the hell is going on?" Father Richard pleaded.

"Our little Megan here is the Dark Harridan," Alex stood over her.

Megan rubbed her jaw. "My name is Misluna, thank you very much."

Now, the crowd was in the lobby watching Alex tell Father Richard about the words she put together. Alex's eyes were in full-out glow along with her fists. "Now, you tell me," Alex could barely get out from anger. "How long have you been the Harridan?"

She just stared at the Lite Sentry with arrogance. "Well, between now and sometime before this... 'shoot me, Kameron, shoot me.'" Megan started to mock her.

Alex's anger overcame her as a quick flash of blue burst from her body. In an instant, Misluna was picked up out of her chair and body slammed onto the ground. It wasn't enough to hurt her, too much. It was just enough to stun her a bit.

Dinah was in the doorway, and she gave out a quick snort of laughter while everyone else was in a stunned position.

"Alex," Father Richard grabbed her arm. "Not on church property."

Alex thought about it for a minute. "I want answers." The Lite Sentry stepped over Misluna. She bent over to grab her hair. The Lite Sentry started dragging Misluna across the floor as she kicked and screamed. The crowd outside the lobby parted like the red sea as Alex continued to drag her by her hair across the floor.

Father Richard joined the crowd as they watched Alex manhandle Misluna into the nearest bathroom. Alex kicked the door open. The group of them somehow all fit into the bathroom as Alex shoved Misluna's face in and out of the toilet. "Come on, we shouldn't be watching this."

Dinah laughed, "I am not missing this."

Juriel made up some excuse. "I have to document historical outcomes of the Lite."

Anne pointed to herself. "Council Historian."

Tristan was still in shock at what was going on. "Overwatch."

Alex was screaming in outrage. "Tell me what you did with Kameron!" Alex continued to shove her face into the toilet.

In between shoving her face in the toilet and pulling her out. "I thought you would be happy. I told him how to save the world. He chose to jump into the Dark. Bye, bye, Kameron."

Alex flashed blue again as she shoved Misluna's head deeper into the toilet.

Father Richard spoke up. "Alex, that's enough." Alex didn't listen; she just continued to hold her head into the toilet. "Alex."

Both Dinah and Tristan came to Alex. They both pulled Alex off Misluna. Dinah held Alex against the wall as Tristan pulled Misluna out of the toilet bowl. The Dark Harridan was too weak to get up. She lay on her stomach and started coughing up toilet water onto the bathroom floor.

"Control your emotions, Sentry," Dinah pinned Alex against the wall. Tristan held Misluna to the ground with his knee. Dinah made sure he had Dark Harridan secured since he had no power on church grounds. She turned back to the Sentry. "Are you in control?"

Alex nodded. "I'm good." She was let go by Dinah. Alex kicked Misluna as she stepped over her. "We're going to have to find out what she knows."

***

Kameron sat in the interrogation room waiting to begin his interview with Alex. He was ordered by Grossman, by way of Roger, to interview Alex as a way to show his loyalty to the Fallen. The echo of the door unlocking gave Kameron a quick moment to prepare to see Alex. She came in wearing a dark red jumpsuit as she had her hands bound behind her. The Sentinel Guards that brought her in were using a rope around her neck to easily control her. The bruise under her eye was starting to swell, and her cut lip seemed to trickle a bit of blood.

They undid the cuffs so they could attach them to the table. They gave her a little push on the back of the head before leaving the room. The door slammed shut as the two of them were left alone in the room. "Proving your loyalty, huh?" Alex moved her tongue in her mouth to see if a tooth was loose.

Kameron nodded. "What can you tell me?"

Alex sat back. "Nothing, I'm willing to tell you, well, nothing that I want sent back to those Fallen bastards."

"This will not end well for you, Alex." Kameron wasn't taking any notes or even looking at her.

"It was bound to happen," Alex tried to ease his guilt. "I never wanted to hurt you or put you in this situation."

"Tell me where your sister is," Kameron said a little louder, as if he was overcompensating for something.

"That's not going to happen," Alex chuckled. The leader of the Lite took a moment to study the man she had hard feelings for. "You tell me this, was it Power over me or equality of love?"

Kameron swallowed hard. "Alex…" he said softly. "I really need to know where your sister is."

Alex shook her head. "You tell me, I will answer your question if you look me straight in the eye and tell me what you feel."

Kameron got up from the table. He stared at the mirrored window at his reflection where on the other side, he was being monitored. "Alex." He turned around to look at her in the eye. He didn't say anything; he didn't have to.

"My sister is somewhere between here and over there; I have no idea where she currently is." Alex stared directly at Kameron.

Kameron halfway wished she hadn't answered him. The door opened to Roger coming into the room. "This is unorthodox. You can't come in here."

"As Leader of the Fallen, I need to interrogate this prisoner to find out the dangers she's spreading." Roger started rolling up his sleeves.

"My ass you do, she is my prisoner." Kameron stood in between him and Alex.

"Technically, she's Grossman's jail meat." Roger corrected him.

Grossman came in the door and pulled Kameron out of the room. The big man escorted Kameron to the other side of the mirrored window. "You need to watch this."

Roger started yelling as he began hitting Alex during his interrogation. There was nothing Kameron could do but watch as the woman he loved was being beaten.

Chapter Fourteen

"Alex," Father Richard put his finger to his nose.

Alex checked her nose as she could feel the blood dripping. "Damn it. Megan must have hit me harder than I thought."

"What do we do with her?" Tristan stared at Megan, who was giving him the willies. She was licking her mouth as she was staring him down.

"Never realized how cute you were." Megan continued staring at him as she moved her tongue inside her mouth. "You know, Lite Sentries don't have the greatest reputation around here when it comes to relationships...just ask this one." She motioned her head over to Alex. "Aren't you just a little curious?"

"Quiet," Dinah pushed her head from the back.

"We could kill her," Alex hopped off the table in the common area in the basement of the church. "I'll do it."

"Alex," Father Richard felt he had to hold her back, at least verbally.

Alex's threat didn't even phase the Dark witch, who was just staring Tristan down. They had no ropes to tie her with, so they improvised by wrapping her around with an orange extension cord. She seemed to be enjoying it. Alex approached her; she nonverbally let everyone know that she wasn't going to hurt her. "Tell me, what did you do with Kameron?"

"I just told him how to close the door; it's all your fault he's down there. You sacrificed your boyfriend because you were too chicken to do it yourself." Megan finally turned her attention away from Tristan for a moment, leering at Alex.

"He shot me," Alex pointed to the scar on her leg. "There's nothing I could have done."

"Did you even offer? You found a way to save yourself, and let him dive directly into the Dark," Megan started laughing. "Nice job."

Alex flashed blue and went to hit her, but Dinah caught her fist. "That is just what this witch wants."

Alex knew Dinah was correct. "Ugh," She turned away in anger.

"You would have made a good General for the Dark, Alex. You really have the mentality for it." Misluna loved she was getting under Alex's skin. "Vandor was right. You and Gron would have crafted something really amazing."

"Seriously," Alex now had her arms crossed as she stared at Megan.

"We have to do something with her," Tristan was now behind Misluna. She was about to say something, but then Dinah put a sock in her mouth, and Tristan quickly secured it with duct tape.

"Nice," Dinah admired his ingenuity.

"She wasn't doing us any good besides getting Alex mad," Tristan tossed the tape on the table.

Father Richard wiped the sweat off his head. "I'll have to inform the Council." He stopped himself before leaving. "Alex, promise me you won't kill her. We're still on church property."

Alex flashed her eyes as she punched Megan in the nose. It sent her backward on the chair. "Didn't kill her."

Father Richard took the handkerchief to wipe his forehead. "Anne," he called over for her to join him upstairs.

Dinah and Tristan picked the witch up from the floor. Tristan quietly asked Dinah, "How is she able to use her powers on church property?"

Dinah shrugged her shoulders. "Maybe it has to do with her absorbing Komptin's Lite. I have never heard of it before." They sat Megan back up. She turned to Alex, who was staring at Misluna in deep contempt from across the room. "We still need to figure out what Devine plans to do."

"We need to get to the museum," Alex continued to stare at Megan. "That is the worst-case scenario."

"Then we assemble to stop her," Dinah gave herself false conviction as she did not want to fight her sister.

"We'll go right after Father Richard gets back from talking to the Council." Alex went to the freezer to grab some ice cubes. She put some into her glass, and as she walked by Megan, she put one down her shirt. Alex was a bit amused as she started to squirm, causing her phone to drop out of her pocket.

Dinah noticed a flash from the communication device on the floor next to the Dark Harridan. "This metal box just flashed."

Tristan picked it up to read. "A message came in from Gron." Alex ripped the tape off Misluna and held her face so Tristan could unlock the phone. He said to make sure to document what she finds in the text." Tristan also read. "Just telling her to make sure she finds out what we know about the artifact."

Alex didn't put the gag back on Misluna. She took a chair to sit in front of her. "You rewrote the Dark Texts." Misluna didn't say anything. She just sat there with an arrogant quietness. "That's what's in that closet in Gron's office."

"They are going to move it once they find out we have their Harridan," Dinah pointed out. "We've got a chance to deliver a wound to the Dark, perhaps start to get the Balance back into place."

"What about the portal opening?" Tristan was getting a bit anxious in his tone, mainly out of fear.

Alex thought about it for a moment. "We've got to take care of them both tonight. If we have a chance to put the Balance back into place tonight, then what choice do we have?"

"It will not put it back into place," Dinah corrected her.

"No, but it will definitely put it on the right path," Alex countered Dinah's negativity.

"Who goes where?" Juriel, who had been sitting in the corner and keeping quiet, spoke up.

Alex jumped a bit, "I forgot you were there, sorry." Alex was mentally thinking of the teams. "Wish we had more people for this."

Tristan, for some reason, stepped up next to Dinah. "This is what we have."

Dinah nodded to his confidence, "It is all we need."

Alex agreed, "Okay. Dinah and Tristan, you two go get the book. For some reason, I couldn't open the cabinet."

"Probably too much Lite in you," Dinah squeezed her hands on Misluna's shoulders. "She will have to open it."

Alex wasn't too keen on that possibility. "She'll try to escape at every chance."

"If she tries to escape, I will simply end her existence," Dinah said, an eerie calmness about her.

Father Richard came back down the basement with Anne. "I just got off the phone with the Council. Truth be told, they didn't really know what to do with her. She's not possessed by an Infiltrator, she's not a Dark Angel; they think killing her would be murder."

"Good for them," Megan agreed with the Council's decision.

"Shut up," Alex gave her a warning. "So, what are we to do with her?"

"The Council will be taking to her an undisclosed location." Father Richard wiped his head again.

"So, we have about twelve hours before they get here. That should be enough time." Alex thought about it.

"What are you thinking of doing?" Anne had her arms across her body.

"We have to stop Devine." Alex went to get her coat. "This is our last chance to get that book. Tristan, Dinah, Juriel, and Father Richard, go get that book. Anne and I will go stop Devine."

Tristan picked up his coat. "Be careful."

347

"Don't take any unnecessary chances. If you can't get that book, get out of there." Alex warned him. "Okay, let's go to work."

**

Devine nervously hugged a tree on the outside of the F.O.R. Compound. The feeling of being dirty was felt on many levels. The memory of what they did to her, the children that were ripped from her body, and now she held an artifact that is an abomination of the initial reset for humanity. She could have sworn it had a smell to it.

She placed herself deep into a tree where she couldn't be seen by anything Dark related. She knew she couldn't be seen by any primate unless she wanted them to, but Dark influence, they could see her. What was she doing here? Every ounce of her body told her not to be here. But she had a chance to fix two problems at once. Did two wrongs make a right?

There was movement all along the compound, like ants working all day. She always knew that people who willingly gave themselves to the Dark were misled, but these primates below almost moved like the walking dead. There was no Lite here at all. It was only her.

Ariel's star could be seen from in between the pine needles. How she missed her sister. It was like a part of her was missing that couldn't be filled. Was this why she convinced herself to do this? To make herself feel something besides the feeling of not belonging, to be not viewed as a dirty being of Lite.

Devine flew through the thicket of the trees, hugging a tree every time she needed to stop from being seen. She would wait until it was clear before flying around to the other side of the compound. It was completely fenced with no access. There was a fast-moving river next to a swamp land before a thicket of the forest prevented anybody from coming in from that direction. There was a maroon light on the upper floor of the building across from her.

The angel flew outside the window to see her two children, the children she gave birth to, the children who she didn't even know their names. This was wrong, but she needed to do it. She was floating outside the window, watching them sitting in the middle of the room. The boy had jet-black hair cut short; he was tearing the heads off some of the dolls next to him. The girl had straight black hair, and she was finding amusement by trying to force a black bear into one of her stuffed animals.

Devine was about to come through the window to talk to them, but an elderly woman entered carrying a satchel. She stood proper but had a sense of strict evil to her. They put their toys away with no emotion before leaving with the elderly woman. Devine flew away as the twins turned to the window.

She was about to head to the museum, but she stopped herself. No, she needed to do this. She decided to go into the Compound. The angel landed on the ground next to a barred window. She pulled them off the window frame. With no noise, she landed on the floor inside the building. The room wasn't familiar. Almost looked like a study of some sort.

She was about to open the door but heard someone talking on the other end. The primates were speaking about some books, and he left the room. Devine saw a small pile of books on the table in the corner. They were coming in here. The back of the door provided some cover in hopes he wouldn't see her.

It wasn't her luck as the boy shut the door, exposing her to the room. There must have been just enough Dark influence in the boy as his face turned white when seeing the purple-haired angel standing by the door. Devine generated her Lite Bo and knocked the boy out on the floor before he had a chance to scream. She didn't kill him, though, in the back of her mind she probably should have since he was probably going to become a Demon. He would perish at the hand of the Lite sooner or later. Devine made the choice of it being later. Maybe, just maybe, he would turn to the Lite.

She hid the body in the corner after she dissipated her bo staff. There was no sign of anyone else outside in the hallway. Quietly, she snuck down to the opening at the end of the massive hallway. In the center of the lobby were the twins staring at her, all alone. Devine, for the first time in her life, got tunnel vision. There was nothing around her, just the focus on her children. The angel of the Lite slowly approached them, almost afraid of scaring them off. They tilted their heads in confusion as they watched her approach.

"My name is Devine." She didn't know what else to say. "What names did they give you?" The children just watched her slowly approach as her hands were shown that she wasn't a threat. She didn't know what to do. They had no emotion to them. "Do you know who I am?" She was about an adult body length away from them. Frustration was starting to get to her. She knelt to their eye level, one knee on the ground. She untied two of her leather bracelets on her wrists. "You see these. These were given to me by my sister. Your aunt Ariel." The twins just moved their heads to look at them. "Would you like to have them?" She put her hands out to offer them to her children.

The twins turned their heads to each other, then back to the angel. With no warning, they each pointed a finger at her while giving a consistent shrilling scream. Devine had to cover her ears from the sharp pain. The noise seemed to throw Devine against the wall. The screaming stopped, so Devine got to open her eyes, but it wasn't good.

Multiple Infiltrators now surrounded her. There were five Dark Angels flying above her. Demons arrived to block her exits. She couldn't help but realize it was a mistake coming here. The first to lunge were the Infiltrators. Devine quickly ignited her bo to defend herself. She knocked one of the black beasts into a group of three more. A Demon came around the corner to jump on her back, and she flipped him over on the floor. This wasn't going to be a fight to kill them. She needed an avenue of escape.

One of the Dark Angels came down with tremendous speed, but she was able to swing her bo staff into the Dark Angel. She recognized him. It was Raguel. The hit caused him to put a hole into the wall, giving her a flight to the outside. She took advantage of it as she stabbed an Infiltrator. She quickly pulled it out and threw it at a Demon close to the opening. She ran outside, pulling her bo staff out of the melting beast. Her wings opened as she took to the air.

Devine flew into the starry sky, where she was met by Azrael. He just stayed still as he floated, staring at her. "You didn't have to kill that Demon."

"It will not bother me," Devine held her bo staff in a battle-ready position in mid-air.

"We were made stronger than you, the first to protect the Conduit of Lite." Azrael still wasn't acting as if he was going to attack her.

"We lasted longer, a lot longer," Devine reminded him.

"We have such arrogance, us angels. But why, no soul likes the primates, live to only serve Him." Azrael watched as the F.O.R. members started to clean up the mess from the hole in the wall like good little drones. "Never having a choice."

"If we did not have choices, you would not be in the status you are," Devine pointed out.

Azrael gazed hard with his black eyes. "This is the side that will try to end this war. As long as those primates have a choice, the Balance will always be in a fight. There will never be a winner."

352

"The win is allowing them to choose for themselves. The war may never end, but we fight for Him, we fight for them." She pointed to the ground. "You failed to realize where true power comes from."

Azrael got angry. "And you failed to protect your sister from her death."

Devine refused to fall into his trap. "She died honorably; she did not die from her sibling's hand. Can you say the same of yours?"

"He failed to realize the Absolute Power of the Dark." Azrael flew next to Devine, still not ready for battle. "He was a means to an end, much like you were."

"You knew? You were okay with what they did to me?" Devine flew back from her brother.

"I wasn't against it." Azrael flew back a bit, not knowing what she was going to do.

"I am your sister, and you have no remorse over the violation, the humility, the hopeless feeling someone…" she couldn't even finish her statement.

"The twins were needed to open the portal," Azrael justified the trauma induced on his sister with no emotion. "They are an unusual pair, are they not?"

"They are my children," Devine dissipated her bo and stared down at the Compound.

Azrael tried to hide his smirk. "And you can be with them. They need their mother. Someone to guide them, teach them, and most of all, to protect them. Who better than you?"

Devine just stared down at the building that housed her babies. "They were created from an act of evil."

"They are still your children. You are the only parent they have left. Are you to abandon them?" Azrael held out his hand. "Come with me, sister. I will take you to your children. You can be with them."

Devine saw the open hand he offered. Her children were below, and she could be with them. She closed her eyes as she knew what was going to happen next. She raised her hand next to Azrael's and placed her hand underneath his to close his hand. "I am Devine. Former Guardian to the Conduit of Lite. You, my brother, will come to regret your decision." In the distance, she saw five more Dark Angels start to come her way. She knew fighting would be futile. One more glance at the compound before she flew off to salvage what was left of her own mission; to do something right.

***

Alex was reluctant to change into her hunting clothes. This was going to be a fight she did not want to conduct. Did Devine turn to the Dark? Was she going to have to fight her? Nothing in her closet seemed right to wear. She put on her dark green shirt. It didn't look good. It got thrown in the corner of the room. She tried on the dark blue one, but that didn't seem right either. On top of the green one, it landed.

354

"There's nothing that looks right." She caught herself talking to Komptin like he was still here. The reminder he was gone didn't help the night. She didn't really know what tonight was. There was no idea what Devine was up to. Why hasn't Celestial come to talk to her about her surrogate sister? There were so many questions with not enough answers to go around.

Alex grudgingly decided on an outfit to wear. She wasn't happy about it. It just didn't seem right. She was about to change until she saw something on Komptin's bed. It was a box with a note attached to it. Alex didn't remember it there before. She picked up the note:

Little Sister,
The Dark has taken so much from us, more so than we have them. They are without honor, without feeling, and most of all, without regret. There is Lite still in the world, but it is diminishing. The worst of it, is seeing all you sacrifice without hope for the future; well tonight, I shall give you some.
Sincerely,
Devine

Alex opened the box to see a dark purple vest with a dark blue shirt underneath. Inside was a collar that had purple and green stones. It truly was something remarkable. Devine had never really given her anything before. Alex put it on, and it fit her as if it was always meant to be. Right then and there, Alex knew Devine's allegiance wasn't to the Dark. Then what the hell was going on? Devine wouldn't have given a gift if she was Dark. Devine must have still been with the Lite; she had to be. Alex couldn't bear to think what it would be like if she lost Devine to evil.

Though, it would have almost been easier if she had turned to the Dark. If it came down to the portal opening or killing the former Guardian to the Conduit of Lite, the portal would not open. Alex picked up the necklace she got from Kameron. The pendant of the angel holding the vile of what was left of Komptin. She closed her eyes as she prayed.

She finished her prayer but kept her eyes closed. Thinking about one of the happiest moments she'd had. Alex was just coming back from the store with Anne. They spent the afternoon grocery shopping for the Super Bowl that night. Kameron was so excited that his team was in the game. The two girls spent the time prepping the meal: marinating chicken wings, organizing some snacks, and decorating the table in his team's colors.

When he walked into Anne's apartment, he was so excited. He tried to hide it, but Alex could tell by the glow of his happiness. They ate his favorite pizza from down the street and nibbled on some snacks before kickoff. The four of them ended up on the couch together. Each of the girls snuggled up to her guys as they watched the game. Komptin was curled up on the floor next to the electric fireplace in the corner, fast asleep. Kameron's team lost the game that night. But for some reason, it didn't seem to faze him. Alex had never seen him so relaxed and happy, it reflected onto her. She nestled into him, completely relaxed. Her doing something special for Kameron unknowingly provided her a calm she had never felt before. She was in love.

Alex kissed the pendant before putting it on. She made sure it was securely tucked underneath her shirt to prevent it from getting lost, then tied her hair into a ponytail in the back to ensure it didn't get in her way. She grazed her finger down over the scar where she'd had Sarah's dad jab his finger into her neck. She was a Lite Sentry; tonight, she had to protect the Balance. No matter what the cost. She put the collar on Devine had given her before heading downstairs to meet the others.

***

"You can't tell me you didn't know!" Grossman continued to belittle Kameron. They were in Supervisory Office while the Colonel of the Sentinel Guard was just sitting watching Kameron. Roger and Megan were standing close together in the back corner while Kameron's interrogation continued. Kameron was about to answer, but Grossman interrupted him. "Stop, don't say anything that will get you sent to Rejuvenation."

Kameron thought about it. "Where's Alex? Will I get to see her before she's sent to camp?"

Roger spoke up. "I don't think Rejuvenation is right for her."

The Colonel nodded. "I agree. She's far too dangerous of an insurrectionist. She needs to be made an example. I recommended to the prosecutor a no-trial execution. She already admitted to leading a Lite faction here in town. We have enough witnesses; everything would be legal. The prosecutor agreed." The tall bald man with little hair on the side of his head stood up. He came around to sit on his desk, with Roger joining his side. "If I get on the phone with the mayor, you'll lose your job and be sent to Rejuvenation immediately."

Kameron turned to Roger, who was grinning. The Leader of the Fallen Trinity decided to put his two cents in. "There may be a way out of this."

The Colonel kept his eye on Kameron. "How is that?"

"It would have to stay within the five of us. It cannot leak out of this office." Roger got off the desk to come behind Kameron. The Leader of the Fallen Trinity put his hands on the Sentinel soldier.

Grossman got excited, "Listen up, Kameron. The Leader is going to get you out of this."

Kameron was leery of anything Roger was going to offer. "I'm listening."

Roger pointed to the window at the crowd of people outside chanting to bring them the Lite Follower. "We are getting a volatile situation out there. How the hell did these people find out what is going on already?"

The Colonel went to the window. "Who knows how these things get leaked? Promise of money or power." He went back to his desk to sit down.

Roger leaned on his desk, staring at him. "If the people find out a Sentinel was dating a Lite Follower, their confidence in the program could falter."

The Colonel was on his way to getting a migraine. "What do you suggest we do?"

Roger went over to the Sentinel Guard leader after thinking about it for a bit. "We announce to the crowd that Kameron was working undercover in an operation where we suspected Alexandria Johnson as a Lite Follower. His job was to get close to her, infiltrate the group, and oust every single one of them."

Kameron recognized Megan's touch as she replaced her hands on his shoulders. They seemed cold and callous. It almost made Kameron shiver. Megan squeezed her hands. "We'll have to convince the crowd."

Roger had a smile on his face as if he had the perfect solution. "We'll have Kameron execute her in front of the crowd."

Grossman got excited over the idea. "It will show strength to the Sentinels, simultaneously clearing Kameron from any wrongdoing."

Megan came down to Kameron's ear. "As a bonus, we'll get rid of a major player in the Lite Followers." She nibbled on Kameron's ear before licking the inside of his ear.

"Kameron, look at me, son. Do you agree to this?" The Colonel's face had worry written all over it.

Megan wrapped her arms around Kameron from the back. "Take the deal. It's a lot better than Rejuvenation."

Kameron could start to hear the chanting from the outside crowd for the execution of the Lite

Followers. Kameron closed his eyes. "On one condition, let me talk to Alex alone."

"She is sitting in her cell; she isn't going anywhere." Grossman almost seemed like he stood up for Kameron.

Roger got a little perturbed. "Fine. Do it fast."

"Grossman and some other guards will escort you down." The Colonel motioned to Kameron's supervisor.

Kameron didn't like the echo of the prison door. It seemed cold, sterile, and the hint of death was in the air. He approached Alex's cell, where she was sitting down on cement floor, holding her prison outfit sleeve to her lip. There were blood stains on her clothes. The bruising on her face was starting to show. There was a cut on the side of her face where Roger took one of her own rings to scrape the side of her face while he was interrogating her. She may have been bleeding and bruised, but Kameron still thought she was beautiful.

"I'm not really looking my best right now," Alex chuckled. "I was halfway hoping your last memory of me wouldn't be me all bloodied."

Kameron halfway laughed, "For some reason, it makes you more beautiful and stronger than I took you for." He approached the cell, then got really serious. "They are going to execute you."

"Yep," Alex agreed. "They say how?"

"You really want to know that?" Kameron softly spoke.

Alex thought about it. "Yah, I actually do."

"Hanging. Right in front of the crowd that formed outside this building." Kameron felt ill as he said that.

Alex could hear the screaming of the crowd as they cheered for Roger. "Well, I guess I won't have to wait long. Because that would really suck." Alex got up to see Kameron. The only thing separating them was a jail cell. Their foreheads touched in between the bars. "What's going to happen to you?"

Kameron got hit with a massive amount of guilt. "They want me to put the rope around your neck and pull the lever."

Alex kept her head on Kameron's as she laughed. "Of course they do. And if you don't?"

"I lose my job and immediately get sent to Rejuvenation." Kameron and Alex's hands were interlocked through the bars of the jail as they kept their foreheads together. "Alex, give them your sister. Maybe you can get out of this."

Alex shook her head. "No, the Lite must be brought to the people." A tear started to drop from her face. "Kameron, I know you feel it. I only pray you accept it. It's the only way out of the Darkness you sit in."

The door started to unlock. Kameron and Alex only had a few moments left. They kissed each other as the guards came. "I love you, Kameron."

"I love you." He whispered just soft enough so she could hear.

The guards came in with Megan and Grossman behind them. "Kameron, it's time." Grossman took his cuffs out. He turned to Alex. "Put your hands through the hole in the cell door."

Alex quickly made a sign of the cross before putting her hands through the cell door. Megan was staring at her with an evil grin. "You're going to die," Megan smirked.

Alex stepped out of the cell and immediately head-butted Megan. "No shit, Sherlock," Alex told her confidently. "You're a bright one." Alex boldly walked down the hallway to the gate of the cell block.

Megan grabbed her mouth, with blood dripping from it. Her body tensed as she turned to Kameron. "You see, Kameron. She has no respect for Absolute Power. You need to execute her, show the world your allegiance to the Trinity of the Fallen." Kameron didn't say anything. He just kept his eyes locked on Alex. "Kameron!"

"Let's get this over with." Kameron watched Alex as she turned back to see him. They just kept their eyes on each other until Grossman forcefully guided Alex out the door for execution.

Chapter Fifteen

Alex locked eyes with her own reflection while staring out of the car window. The museum was just behind her mirror image of the troubled Lite Sentry. So many emotions were running through her. A feeling of unsettling nerves took over everything, as if something bad was about to happen. Only thoughts of Kameron's suffering dominated. This was going to be it. She was going to lose him forever, and she was going to allow it. In fact, she had to ensure it.

"You okay, sweetie?" Anne was dressed in her version of hunting clothes–a pair of blue jeans and a sweatshirt. There was a satchel in the back seat with her that held Dark Texts. The young historian still refused to reveal where they came from.

"You know, growing up in CopperTop, I bet I went by this building on multiple occasions. Never went into it." Alex just stared at the cement pillars at the entrance.

Anne chuckled at her friend. "We went in during high school for History 305." She grabbed the satchel to ensure the texts were secure.

Alex touched the lower section of her stomach. "That was on the day I had my hysterectomy." Alex snickered. "Funny thing, I told them I wanted it on that day, so I didn't have to go." Alex felt a bit of a cold shiver down her spine. "I never really knew how much not able to have children would affect me, until I met Kameron. He would have made such a great father."

Anne rubbed her back. "It's hard losing the men we are meant to be with. I found out Kale wanted to have children. Asked his mom if he was ready and everything. It's a natural state of being to want to produce someone out of love. Someone to share your experiences, your knowledge, someone to mold so they can experience the enjoyments and survive the fears of what life has to offer."

"Infiltrators, Demons, Dark Angels, and a general state of fighting in the world." Alex teetered on, pushing out the seriousness of this conversation.

"You think that's all life is? Constant evil? If you do, then Dark has already won. Why are you even fighting?" Anne asked her.

Alex turned her head to Anne. "I hate you. When did you get so wise?"

Anne laughed, "Sweetie, no matter how much Dark there is, there will always be a shining Lite."

Alex had to admit that for some reason, that made her feel better. "Without getting into a history lesson, what is this building?"

"It was the old courthouse. Right over there was where they performed executions back from its erection to the late 1800s." Anne pointed to the center of the building. "The basement is where the stone artifact is; that's where they held the worst of the prisoners before they, well, you know." Anne motioned execution by sliding her finger across her neck.

A car pulled up to them with Tristan behind the wheel. Dinah was next to him, while Julian and Father Richard sat in the back with Megan tied up between them. Dinah was as white as a ghost as she gripped the door handle.

"What's with her?" Alex motioned over to the angel.

Tristan tried not to laugh. "She was freaked out on how fast we were going."

Anne peeked over at Dinah. "Oh my, she's really scared. How fast were you going?"

Tristan tapped on the steering. "We topped at thirty-five."

Father Richard covered his mouth not to show that he was laughing.

"This metal carriage is an instrument of death, and you wheeled it like you do not care how fragile your life is. I was only concerned for you." Dinah carefully let go of the door, leaving an imprint from her fingers. "I was not concerned for my safety."

"Good, because we still have a way to go before we get to the mayor's office." Tristan gave a little tease.

Dinah tensed up as she held onto her seatbelt.

"I'd avoid the highway, if I were you." Alex turned her attention back to the museum.

Tristan nervously took in a breath before starting up the car. "Here we go."

"Tristan," Alex called out to him before he took off.

"Yes," he couldn't hide the cracking in his voice.

Alex felt as if she was a mother bird letting her baby fly out of the nest for the first time. "You got this, right? Stay out of your own head." He silently agreed before he took off. Dinah could be heard yelling at him that he had started off too fast.

Anne checked her satchel for the texts one more time. "We really should get going."

"Are you sure you want to do this?" Alex couldn't help but notice how tense her friend was. "I can do this myself."

"Are you able to interpret this?" Anne patted the satchel around her.

"Good point." They both exited the car and slowly made their way to the stone building. On such a clear night, there seemed to be darkness starting to overtake the sky. Alex tilted her head back to see the missing stars. "Huh, that's not a good sign."

***

Gron checked his cell phone again, but still, there was no message from Misluna. The last he heard was there was something going on at the church. Then there was silence. The leader of the F.O.R. sent her to investigate. With no word, that meant she might have been caught. This was inevitable. He watched as the Lite and Dark angels floated in the air, talking to each other. The Leader of the F.O.R. didn't understand why he just didn't kill her. That Lite Angel was such a thorn in the Dark's backside. She had killed many of the Dark in protection of the Conduit of the Lite. It was almost painful watching her being let her go.

"My Leader," A girl came in with a message. "Bring him in."

The black man in a dark navy-blue suit with a red tie entered the room. He was carrying a briefcase as the two of them sat at Gron's desk. Gron, of course, was sitting across with a position of power. "My Leader." He handed over the financial report from the city.

Gron studied the report. "Doesn't look like it's going to be that bad." He circled some parts with little notes. "We'll initiate ten counsels within the city: education, commerce, policing, fire, interior, exterior, foreign relations, public affairs, city government, and the Sentinel Program."

"You'll need the vote of the council to give you direct power over these factions." He received the notes and added some more for his actions.

"I'm not too worried about that." He got up from the desk to sit down on top of it. He stared at the man before him. "What I am worried about, is that little whore of a daughter of yours testifying before a state or federal government?"

"We are trying to find her, my Leader." He closed up his briefcase. Gron's eyes were vicious with rage as they glowed blood red. His teeth grew with the ability to tear into his body. Before he knew it, Gron had him on the floor, choking him. "Maybe if we put her daddy into the hospital, she'll come out of hiding."

He could barely speak his words. "My Leader, she hates me with all her heart. She would rather spit on my grave than be at my deathbed."

Gron took a second and then stood up calmly. "Perhaps you're right." He rotated to the window as Azrael entered the room. The Dark Angel saw the man lying on the ground, gasping for air. "He'll be fine, what'ch ya got."

"She is leaving; there was determination in her eyes. How did you know she would be coming here?" Azrael watched as the primate gathered his belongings and left the room.

"Call it a hunch. Look, I haven't heard from Misluna. Can you take a demon and a couple of Infiltrators to ensure the book is secure? If the Lite did capture her, I need that book secured by the best." Gron went to the closet to grab his coat.

"Where are you going?" Azrael watched as Gron grabbed his keys.

"There's an errand I have to run." He chugged down the last of his drink.

"Yourself?" Azrael inquired.

"No, I will take one of the Dark Angels with me. Later." Gron left out the door, leaving the Dark Angel to find a Demon and Infiltrators to ensure the Dark Texts were safe.

Azrael couldn't help but wonder why Gron would go on this secret errand while Misluna was a possible captive of the Lite, putting the Dark Texts in jeopardy. Azrael didn't really care. There was a chance to kill the Sentry as she attempted to acquire the book, plus convert one of the strongest. He walked out to the balcony to stare at the stars. All the remembrance shining in the sky of his brothers and sisters seemed to be not showing on this night. So many died in this everlasting battle. Hopefully, he could make the war stop.

***

Anne pulled on the museum door. "I don't even know why I tried; it's obviously locked."

That didn't stop Alex from forcefully opening the door with one hand. "There you go; open." Alex stopped in her tracks, almost scared.

"What is it?" Anne got nervous.

"No alarm." Alex scanned the area for the security guards. "Not only that, but there's also no power or backup to the security system. This is not going to be a good night." Alex just hung her head in disgust before taking a deep breath. Then, she just boldly walked into the concrete building.

Anne peeked in the museum entry, which only seemed to be illuminated by outdoor lighting. Alex's silhouette was the only sign of movement. "It feels dead inside."

Alex turned to Anne behind her. "You shouldn't be here." Anne just held up the modernized Dark Text in front of Alex's face. "I hate you." Alex teased. "Don't get killed." Alex stepped into the entryway of the museum. She motioned for Anne to join her.

Anne made the sign of the cross on her body before joining the Lite Sentry. "Ditto." Anne carefully stepped into the lobby of the entryway. Meanwhile, Alex strolled on like she didn't have a care in the world. The museum seemed black, quiet with a hint of death. There was a suit of armor to the left of them with traditional Native American garments to the left.

"Do you believe in ghosts?" Alex peeked into a display case of an old Bible and chalice.

"I have to. A person can't believe in the Holy Ghost if they don't believe in spirits." Anne was trying to keep quiet. "Do you?"

"Right now, I believe in everything; stories just altered from the truth; vampires are probably Demons; werewolves are Infiltrators; and ghosts are the Dark Mysts." Alex went to admire a sword hanging from the wall.

"What does that make us?" Anne was studying an angelic tapestry hung on the wall.

Alex grabbed the sword. "In trouble." She swung it around and nailed an Infiltrator in the body. It howled in pain as it stepped back. Alex dropped the sword and lit her fists along with her eyes. She punched and kicked the creature a few times before decapitating the black bearlike creature with her Lite-formed blade.

"Why do you come home all bloodied and broken if it's that easy to kill one of those?" Anne watched the Infiltrator melt into the ground.

Alex turned her head to her best friend. "Do you want the next one?" She scanned the room. "Where is this stone thing?"

"Downstairs." Anne pointed to the doorway in the corner.

They took a couple of steps. "Weird that only one Infiltrator was here." Alex didn't like the feeling within the darkened room. It was just a quiet sense of staleness to the air.

Anne tapped Alex on the shoulder. "Sweetie."

"What?" Alex saw Anne point over by the museum's front door.

Anne carefully secured her satchel with the modernized Dark Texts.

Gron was there with a Dark Angel in the entryway. "Hello, Alex."

***

Tristan shut the car off in the parking lot down the street from city hall. He took in a deep breath as he stared at the building.

"What is the matter, Sentry?" Dinah cautiously let go of the car door. She steadied herself to make sure they weren't moving. "Are we done moving in this death carriage?"

Tristan saw the imprint from her hands on the door handle. "Is this your first time in a car?"

"No, Zeke took me, he took me..." She sat there to think about it for a second. "What did he call it?"

"Off-roading?" Father Richard guessed.

"Yes, that was it," Dinah sat there to think about it. She had never realized how much life meant to Zeke. He was always taking life as a big gift that he wanted to use and not regret missing out on anything. "He laughed at my panic."

"We're all afraid of certain particular things, particular to each of us," Tristan unzipped his coat. He had a feeling he was going to need to be able to move quickly on this night.

"What is it you fear?" Dinah studied Tristan as he stared out of the car windshield.

Julian leaned over Misluna to point to the roof. "Look, it seems to be an Infiltrator on the roof."

Both Dinah and Tristan moved forward to stare out the front windshield. "When you see one, there are sure to be more." Dinah pointed out the Infiltrator to Tristan.

"I see it." The rookie Lite Sentry was trying to think of what Alex would do in this situation.

"How do you think we should do this?" Julian put his hand on Dinah's shoulder.

She was about to answer but then Father Richard spoke, "What do you think, Tristan?"

"A diversion would work, then sneak in the back with the witch, right over where we went last time." Tristan motioned with his thumb.

Megan rolled her eyes as he called her that.

"Not a bad idea. Who's going to do what?" Father Richards could feel the sweat start to form on top of his head.

"It would make sense for the Sentry and myself to attack from the front," Dinah suggested. "We are the warriors among us."

Tristan felt good as she called him a warrior. He turned around to Julian. "No offense, but can you handle her?"

"Even though I am a writer, I am still an angel," Julian pointed out. "I do not have a problem disposing of this primate."

Dinah glanced back at Julian in confusion. She knew he did not like to raise his fists. In fact, she only knew of one time when she saw him fight. It was when Azrael abandoned his posts away from the Conduit of Lite. The former Guardian of the Conduit was able to open the Conduit himself to bring the Dark forces into a battle within Heaven.

He was not the strongest of the warriors, but he fought with bravery. She could tell he was bluffing on disposing of the primate. He believed in the potential of the primates. The evidence pointed out that the Dark Harridan didn't believe his false statement either.

Father Richard turned to Misluna, who was giving him fake puppy dog eyes, begging for help. Father Richard took his hand and pushed her head away. "We should go; the longer we keep her out, the more dangerous it is."

"We should really get this over with," Tristan put the keys in his pocket.

Father Richard put his hand on Tristan's shoulder. "We should pray before we go through with this." Misluna's eye roll did not miss Father Richard's attention. They started to pray, but Misluna kept interrupting by flailing about.

Dinah got upset and grabbed her by the throat. "You interrupt this prayer again, and I will decapitate you so fast you will be able to see your headless body before you rot in Hell. Do you understand me?" Misluna saw the determination in her eyes. She meant what she spoke. "We have an understanding. Father Richard, you may continue." The angel of the Lite bowed her head while keeping her hand on Misluna's throat.

***

"Anne, stay behind me." Alex pushed her off to the side. "Roger, last time we met, it didn't really go well for you."

"I could say the same. Mine just didn't go to plan." Roger's eyes glowed as he confidentially marched with the Dark Angel.

Alex met them in the middle of the lobby. She eyed the Dark Angel, who had a weapon generated in his hand, an axe blade on one side and a blunt hammer opposite it. He held a large shield in the other hand. It had a curved top and bottom with two spikes at the end of each curve. Alex was not looking forward to this fight. Alex tried to play like she didn't know where Misluna was currently, "Where's your girl at?"

Roger smiled, "Ah, you found out about Misluna. Nice. What tipped you off?"

"Wasn't hard, plus she was just a horrible, nasty-ass person, Roger. Even you could do better than her." Alex peeked around to ensure there were no other Infiltrators or Demons that would sneak up on them.

"You know, Alex. You lost your chance. You have no idea what we could have brought into this world together." Roger eyed her up like a juicy piece of meat. "Something like the world had never seen; something more powerful than me, Azrael, or even Vandor. You blew it."

"I'll live," Alex rolled her eyes. "Roger, all this hate, evil, darkness, was this just because of that one night?"

"Don't flatter yourself. My life was nothing before I fully accepted the Dark. I have power, I have the privilege to do whatever I want, and most importantly, people respect me as I approach." Roger stood proud.

Alex didn't back down. "Roger, they don't respect you, they fear you. It's not the same thing. Because you don't know that it still makes you the pathetic little loser from high school."

Roger got visibly upset when he noticed something about Alex was missing. "Where's your dog anyways? Did something happen to old scrappy?"

Alex knew he had just emotionally jabbed at her. She swallowed hard before answering, "Tit for tat; I lost my dog, and you lost yours."

"My Leader," the angel spoke in a deep voice. "I hate to interrupt this banter, but the Pure of Heart is no longer in the room."

Roger realized what Alex was doing. She gave him a quick wink. "You bitch," he went to swing at the Lite Sentry.

Alex shot a Lite Beam into Roger, sending him clear outside the museum. The Dark Angel swung his weapon down at Alex, but she moved out of the way. She was able to land a punch on the angel's jaw.

He shook it off with a smile. "No sentry has ever killed an angel. I hope you have your spot picked out within the sky."

Alex centered her focus. "Since my first night of accepting my duties, you traitorous piece of shit." Out of anger, the angel swung around with his shield. It collided with Alex, sending her into a display case. She picked debris out of her braided hair. "This is going to be a long night."

***

375

Anne ran down the spiral staircase to see Devine just standing at the masonic structure in front of her. The purple-haired angel stared forward with the cross in her hand. "Devine!"

"Do not try to stop me, Pure of Heart. I must do this." Devine continued to have that blank stare as she was stuck in contemplation.

"What are you going to do?" Anne was relieved that she saw the halo and misty wings on her back.

"The Dark is so powerful. This world is in a darkened quicksand with no hope of escape." Devine had hopelessness in her eyes. "How can the primates accept it with such ease?"

"False promises with hidden agendas." Anne knew she could not physically stop Devine from doing whatever she was planning. The best she could do was stall her until Alex got down here. She continued forward, hoping to find out what she was planning to do.

Devine turned to Anne with angelic tears falling. "I could not do it. I had a chance, but I could not do it." The angel felt ashamed. "I am no longer worthy to guard the Conduit because I am a failure. I failed to protect Ariel. I failed to protect my..." Then she stopped herself from talking. "I must do this."

"Do what? What are you planning on doing?" Anne sat down on a bench, wanting to show Devine she was not a threat. There was a crash upstairs. Both Anne and Devine looked to the ceiling.

"The Sentry is here," Devine knew the truth to her next statement. "The Dark is here as well."

Devine held up the inverted cross with the black center piece. "I was there…"

"Why would you want to open the portal?" Anne grabbed the edge of the bench out of fear. "This is not a good idea."

Devine just stared at the artifact. "The best rewards for actions often do not have a good idea to start with."

"What reward could you have by opening the portal to the Dark?" Anne was almost in begging mode.

Devine put her head down. "My failure will not go unpunished." Devine slowly slid her hand below her stomach. "…I have even failed to protect myself from the evil the Dark puts into this world." She closed her eyes as her tears were now blue. "Bringing the Sentry's love back, might bring some good into this world. I failed in the first part of my mission; I will not fail again."

"It's not worth the Conduit from being open. It's too dangerous." Anne slowly got up to make her way towards her, but Devine put her finger up, telling her to stop. "What mission did you fail?"

Devine had tears drop from her eyes as she turned to Anne. "I failed to destroy the very spawn of evil that was ripped from me."

"What do you mean?" Then Anne's eyes got big. "You were going to throw your children into the Dark."

"They are evil, but I could not do it," Devine told her story. "I have failed my duties as an Angel of the Lite. Please forgive me. I could not destroy my children. I need you to forgive me." She gripped the cross and closed her eyes before turning to the Conduit. "I have to do something right." Devine looked to the ceiling. "Father, forgive my betrayal. This is something I must do."

Anne screamed, "No!" as the angel of Lite placed the inverted cross onto the Conduit.

***

Tristan easily broke into the City Hall doors. He took a minute before entering to scout the area, as if waiting for something.

"What is it?" Dinah stood on her toes to look over Tristan's shoulders. "There is obviously Dark present."

"I know, it's that there is no alarm." Tristan walked into the hallway leading into the massive lobby area, where the metal detector was the only barrier.

Dinah flew over the small blockade while Tristan just went through the machine. He halfway expected it to go off, but it was silent. The two of them met in the center of the room. Dinah stopped in her tracks as Infiltrators and security guards looked down at them from the second-floor railing.

"I'm starting to think this wasn't a good idea." Tristan lit his fists as he assessed the situation.

"Do not use your powers if you think you will fall." Dinah was waiting for the first one to attack.

"I accepted the fact I will be a star one day," Tristan motioned to one of the Infiltrators to come at him with his hand. The Infiltrator gladly obliged as the two of them started to fight for the distraction Julian needed.

***

Father Richard could hear the ruckus beginning inside the building. Faint flashes of light caught his eyes. "The distraction seems to be working."

Julian kept his hand on the back of Misluna's neck. Her feet were tied just enough to make her move slightly. Her hands were bound in the front while her mouth was gagged. He was eyeing the roof. "Hold her, let me scout."

Father Richard took control of Megan. The angel took off to the top of the second floor of city hall. Father Richard could feel Megan try to get away, but the priest held on tight. "Why did you do it, Megan?" He untied her gag. "You know if you scream, he'll come down here and kill you."

Megan had a hate that Father Richard had never seen before. It almost frightened him.

The newly discovered Harridan seemed to have a slight rasp in her voice. "The Lite is just full of hypocritical fascists. The Dark will control humans, and I will sit near the throne of the Fallen. You know I'm right. You are losing your faith. I can see it, sense it."

"A constant struggle of faith is expected in all of us. You are blind, Megan. I really hope you will be able to see it before it's too late." Father Richard watched as the angel returned. "What's it look like?"

"It seems to be working." The angel put the gag back on Misluna. "You cannot trust her. I can bring one of you up, but not both at the same time."

"Just push down the fire escape. I'll climb up." He pointed to the ladder.

Julian grabbed a hold of Misluna to fly up to the fire escape. On his way up, he flicked the lever that held the ladder. The big man was panting heavily once he got to the top of the roof. "You have much weight to lose, primate."

"Thanks for noticing," he responded. "I did just get a–"

"Quiet," Julian covered Misluna's mouth as he moved against the wall. He pointed to the sky to see his former brother Azrael flying above. If he were to see any of them, this night would fall to a victory for the Dark.

***

Tristan got hit by an Infiltrator across the face. It spun him into a Demon dressed in a security guard outfit. He butted his head into the Demon's face, sending black blood dripping from the mouth of evil as he spit out his teeth. The Demon grabbed Tristan by the throat and lifted him off the ground. Dinah's short blue sword came out through the chest of the Demon, who dropped Tristan as the possessed man melted into the ground.

Dinah quickly picked Tristan up. "Watch yourself, Sentry."

Tristan swept Dinah's legs, causing her to crash to the ground so he could punch the Infiltrator that almost clawed the angel's back. He, in turn, quickly picked her up, and the two of them locked eyes. "Careful, you're not seeing what's coming."

The two of them continued to fight the Demons and Infiltrators in the lobby. Dinah turned her head to see Azrael slowly approach the balcony to overlook the battle. The fact he was here now meant they were in some serious trouble. It would not take long for him to kill them both, but she needed to worry about the task at hand. She quickly killed an Infiltrator Tristan had weakened so they could move on to the next one.

**

Father Richard was pleasantly surprised the window was unlocked. "Small favors." But then he realized that he could barely make it through the window. He eventually made it into the mayor's office. Julian pushed Megan onto the floor before he entered. Father Richard could tell that hurt her. "She doesn't deserve that."

"Yes, she does." Julian surveyed the room. "The book must be here somewhere. The whole room smells of Dark."

Father Richard went to the desk. "The wardrobe in the corner." He pointed where the book was located. "There is something that I'm curious about." He started to search the drawers while Julian went to the wardrobe.

Julian brought Megan to the front of the wardrobe. "Open it." Misluna motioned with her tied hands that she could not with her gagged mouth. Julian hesitated before he flipped her around to remove her gag. "You scream for help, and I will not hesitate to destroy you."

"Don't worry, I got you, baby," Misluna stood in front the ancient coat closet. She was about to open it but stopped. "Oops, forgot the ancient context before opening." She thought about it for a minute. "Ancient forces of evil, transform this decrepit body into mum…Misluna, the ever-living!"

Father Richard looked up as she said that. He had heard that before.

Misluna opened the wardrobe with her hands still tightly entwined together. Inside was the evil book, that was just staring at the both of them. "Pretty sexy, isn't it?" Misluna picked up the book. The lock on it automatically opened with her Dark touch. "Wanna see what's in it?"

"I am Lite. I cannot read the texts," Julian was a little disappointed. "I do not even wish to touch the filthy thing."

"I wrote it with Lite Sentry blood. You should be able to see it. Here, I'll hold it for you," Misluna tried to open the book. She motioned her hands were tied. There was hesitation in the angel's eyes. "Look, what am I going to do? Everyone is downstairs trying to kill Tristan and that angel." Julian untied her hands.

"What are you doing?" Father Richard saw that the angel was about to untie the hands of the Dark Harridan.

"If the Lite is able to read the texts of the Dark, we can gain an advantage to put the Balance back into place." Julian turned to Misluna. "Let me see them."

Misluna held the book in front of the angel's face. "Are you ready to see what the Dark can do?"

Her eyes focused upwards at the ceiling. On a surprise, she threw the book at the angel's face. Simultaneously, a small creature dug its claws into the top of Father Richard's bald head. He screamed in pain, flailing about, trying to get the monster of evil off of his head. The claws remained latched onto his skull as he flailed about.

Misluna reached into the side of the inside wall of the wardrobe to grab a small dagger covered in Darkness. She stabbed the Angel of Lite in the stomach. He screamed in pain as he dropped to the ground, blue blood spilled onto the floor. Misluna swiped the knife to cut the ropes tied around her feet. Then she knelt down to stab him again. She grabbed the book from floor with one hand while licking the Lite blood off her fingers on the other. As she was leaving, she stepped on the top of the knife as she walked over the screaming angel lying on the floor.

***

Tristan turned to rip an Infiltrator off Dinah's back, who was now bleeding from the base of her neck. He slammed the Infiltrator to the ground; he was pounding it relentlessly. The creature was now weak enough to dispose. Just before he thrust his Lite Blade into the Infiltrator, a Demon came behind him and tried twisting his neck. Tristan immediately dug his chin into his chest as he elbowed the Demon. The Infiltrator angrily got off the floor, and he swung his massive claw for a death blow.

Dinah was able to grab the Demon, who was still attached to Tristan, and pull back the Sentry from joining her siblings in the sky. It was enough to save him, but not far enough from the creature's claws scratching the Sentry's chest. Dinah spun the two around while she sliced the Infiltrator with her Lite Sword.

Tristan jumped up into the air and slammed himself to the floor. The Demon was sandwiched between the marble floor and the Lite Sentry. The Demon let go of his grasp on the Sentry. Tristan rolled off the Demon, got to knees, and formed a knife with his Lite. Dinah and Tristan stabbed the Demon together. Their eyes met while the Demon was melting into the ground. Tristan was bleeding from his nose, lip, and a cut under his eye, but the wound on his chest was the cut that needed attention. Dinah was bleeding profusely from the base of her neck with a couple of cuts on her face. They both smiled at each other before standing up to look around for the next wave of attacks.

Azrael watched the two of them, as if he was in deep thought. There was no emotion from him. He just continued to stare. There were no more Demons or Infiltrators, just the Dark Angel who was glaring at them. For a second, it didn't seem like contempt, but more like reflection.

"Not that I'm complaining, but what's he waiting for?" Tristan was trying to catch his breath, but it hurt his chest every time he inhaled.

"I do not know," Dinah was just as confused as Tristan. "We should be dead by his hands well into this fight." Dinah softly spoke to herself. There was no reason she could think of on why he had not finished them off yet. "What is on your mind, brother?"

Azrael just stared at the two of them. Tristan could have been mistaken, but there seemed to be a moment of sadness in his dark eyes. The sound of Misluna screaming for Azrael broke his trance. He covered his body with his black wings, and slowly turned towards Misluna, who carrying the Dark Texts.

A small Demon creature flew above Misluna as she was running with the Dark Texts. Azrael motioned for her. She was carried off with the Dark Angel as the two of them flew over the lobby. Dinah and Tristan watched as the Dark Texts flew away with the witch and Dark Angel over their heads out of the building.

"We have failed," Dinah got up as she helped Tristan stay on his feet.

"We're alive; they didn't take that from us." Tristan nodded to her that he was able to stand by himself.

Dinah turned her attention to Tristan from watching Azrael fly away with the Dark Texts. "You are in need of a healer."

Father Richard came stumbling from the office to the balcony. He had spots from claw marks bleeding on top of his head. "Julian is badly hurt." Dinah instantly grabbed Tristan to fly to the second floor over the balcony barrier to get to her injured brother.

***

Alex's fight stayed in the in the middle of the museum lobby floor. She laid one of her hardest punches across his face. A quick feeling of accomplishment overfilled Alex as it was enough force to knock him down. The Dark Angel used his hammer axe as a tool to get himself up. She took this opportunity to kick the hammer out from under him, sending him back to the ground. She made sure Roger wasn't going to sneak up on her, but that was a mistake. The Dark Angel picked her up from the back and twisted in the air, driving her down to the ground onto her stomach.

"You fight like no Sentry I've seen." He started to push her head into the cemented floor.

Alex started to grunt from the pain of her head being squished. She elbowed him in the head right after he finished whispering that in her ear. "And I'm going to make sure I'm the last one you'll see." She rolled out of the way from a punch onto the floor. She went to kick him, but he grabbed her leg and swung her across the room. She slid on the floor but stopped herself using her Lite that formed a knife in the ground. Her eyes were glowing a neon blue.

The angel grabbed his hammer from the other side of the room. Alex generated a Lite Beam to shoot it at the angel. He rose his shield to block the beam, causing a sea spray of light to bounce off the shield as the angel trudged forward to Alex. She was pushing so hard to keep him away that her nose started to bleed. With all his strength, the angel swung his weapon with the blunt side. Just before it connected with Alex, her body was covered in blue neon mist. Her body still went flying across the other side of the room.

There was no doubt she had some broken ribs as she peeled herself off the indented wall. She fell face-first onto the floor. The angel put down his hammer as he, too, was bleeding from the fight. "You are strong." He took his shield off his arm to hold with both hands. The Dark Angel lifted up the shield and struck it down on Alex as she flipped herself over. Now, the shield was on her neck as the two points were embedded into the floor.

Alex was trying to lift it up but couldn't do it. The angel slowly got up to grab his weapon that he had put down. He spit out black blood as he strutted over to the Lite Sentry as she tried to lift the shield off her neck. "I truly hope you don't use your powers when I kill you." He rubbed his thumb across the blade of the axe. "I would like your head as a prize for all to see." He went to swing the axe down, but she was able to lift the shield with part of the floor still attached.

The Dark Angel's axe was stuck in the floor. Alex went on the offensive with multiple punches and kicks. In the corner of her eye, she saw Roger run downstairs. She shot another Beam at him but missed him as he went into the entryway. She turned back to the Dark Angel as he went to punch her, but she blocked it. She was able to flip him over her own body on the ground. She picked him up and kneed him in the stomach twice before grabbing his head. With all her strength, she jumped into the air and smashed his head into the floor. She stood up, huffing and puffing; she formed a blade as her eyes were a continuous glow of blue. With one swing, she decapitated the Dark Angel's head from his body.

She picked up the angel's head to lift it in front of hers. "I hope the last thing you see is me walking away." She dropped his head to the ground next to his body as what was left of the former angel of Lite melted into the ground.

***

Anne got a sense of fear as she saw Roger stopping in the middle of the stairs. She turned to Devine. "Devine, what did you do?"

"She forever tipped the Balance!" Roger couldn't help but laugh as he gripped the stair railing with anticipation. "You know what you did was right. Now we just sit back and wait."

Alex came rushing down the stairs. She pushed Roger out of the way, flipping him over the railing. Her only focus was to get to Devine as she stood in front of the opened portal. "Oh shit." She quickly said to herself. "Devine, what were you thinking?" Alex went to approach her, but Roger shot a Dark Beam at the Sentry as he was getting off the floor. That blast sent Alex flying into the wall.

The structure was starting to shake. The center of the cross had a black liquid inside that started to move around. The mirror in the center started to get encompassed by blackness.

"He's coming!" Roger started to get excited from the portal opening.

Alex got up to see Devine about to jump into the portal. The Lite Sentry ran full force to tackle the angel before she jumped into the Dark. "What the hell do you think you are doing?"

Devine just cried on the ground, with Alex on top of her. "Sentry, let me do this."

"I will not let you sacrifice yourself," Alex kept her to the ground.

"I need to do some good in this world," Devine cried out in pain.

Roger sneered as he approached the structure. It was so close now. Vandor was coming.

Alex peeked over at Anne who was frantically reading the text to find out if she would be able to close it from this side. "Devine, you want to do some good. Help me kill Roger. Where he is leading this town, is somewhere far worse than anything these people have seen." Alex stared at her surrogate sister. "You are Devine, the strongest of them all. Former Guardian to the Conduit of Lite." Alex helped her off the floor. "Help me kill him."

Devine wiped a tear as she nodded.

Roger heard what they said. He turned around to see Devine with her generated Lite Bo, a bloodied Alex had her eyes glowing, and fists Lit; behind them, was Anne who was frantically reading

389

the Dark Texts. He turned his head behind him, expecting to see Vandor, but for some reason, the Conduit of the Dark had not arrived. The Dark Sentry had no choice; he ran off up the stairs.

"Chicken shit!" Alex yelled to him. She then turned to Anne. "Please tell me you know how to close this thing."

Anne was frantically reading. "This is all about opening, nothing about closing."

"What did I do?" Devine's eyes were huge. "Once Vandor realizes the portal is open."

"We'll close it by then. Anne, we need options," Alex pleaded to the Historian as she read over the texts.

"As far as I know, what I can tell, it's powered by that inverted cross. We just need to wait until that small globe in the center runs out of that black stuff." She showed a picture of the center of the cross.

"So, we kill anything that comes out of it." Alex and Devine stood ready in front of the portal. Alex and the angel sat there for a bit waiting for the imminent attack. Devine and Alex looked at each other, not knowing what to say at the surprised lack of combatants to fight. Then Alex turned to her sister-in-law. "Anne, not that I'm complaining, but nothing is happening." Anne was frantically reading over the Dark Texts.

Anne just looked up to Alex and shrugged her shoulders. "I don't know."

***

Kameron stepped outside to a hostile group of people screaming with anger at Alex. He was amazed at how quickly they all congregated. Garbage was being thrown at Alex; somehow, even a dead dove got thrown at her, hitting her on the side of the face. Kameron stepped to her side to protect her from the crowd. He didn't miss that Anne and Kale just stood in front with a disappointed expression. They weren't really doing anything; they were just disappointed in both Kameron and Alex.

Alex, to her credit, held her head up high as she boldly continued up to the stairs, where she stopped before going up to her execution. She turned to Kameron. "Well, this sucks."

Kameron smiled at her, trying to make light of the situation. "Maybe if you give up your sister's location."

"I'm not going to do that, Kameron." Alex tried to give a sense of security. "I'm okay with this. Really, I'm fine."

Kameron fought back his tears. "I wish there was a way out of this."

Alex leaned to the side to view the hostile crowd. "There's always a way."

Roger was up on the execution stand with the two nooses behind them. Kameron was trying to figure out why there were two of them up on the block. Perhaps they were going to execute him with Alex. Roger quieted the crowd. "Tonight, we deliver you a leader in the Lite." The crowd angrily jeered at Alex. "With the Trinity of the Fallen is the only way of absolute Power. The Power to properly guide those who are weak," Roger pointed to Alex. "The Lite Followers, send you off course, to lead you to a faulty destination!"

"Kill her!" A lady in the background screamed.

"Patience," Roger chuckled. "We have something to settle first." Roger's grin turned scary. "Dedication to the Trinity must be always promoted. We must properly expose those who do not properly show their oath." Roger lectured to the crowd.

Kameron knew it. The second noose was for him.

"We must publicly show the cost of those hiding any information on the whereabouts of these domestic terrorists!" Roger explained as the crowd started to cheer.

Kameron took a deep breath as he knew his fate, which was about to get thrust onto him.

Roger continued to yell, "Someone in this crowd failed to report the Lite to the proper authorities. Tonight, that punishment will be an example for all to see!" The crowd cheered louder. Roger pointed to a specific member in the crowd. "Anne Moler! You failed to report a member of the Lite to the authorities!"

Anne's face was of shock. "What?" She was grabbed by other members of the Sentinels.

Kale stepped out in front of Anne, screaming, "No she didn't!"

A rather tall Sentinel with blonde hair escorted Anne to her final destination. She began crying as she looked towards Alex and Kameron. Alex screamed, "No!" She turned her attention to Roger. "You red-headed bastard!"

The rope slipped over Anne's head and tightened around her neck. She started breathing heavily as the feeble platform below her feet was now her countdown clock. Anne locked eyes with Kale with fear in her eyes. Kale broke free of the Sentinel holding him. "That's my wife, you son of bitch!" He started running towards the stage.

Roger pulled out a gun and shot Kale in the chest. He dropped instantly as the crowd applauded. He handed the gun to Megan as she came onto the stage to grab it. He whispered to her, "That felt good for some reason." He nonchalantly gave the signal to commence. The executioner pushed Anne off the box sitting on the stage. The sound of her neck snapping could only be heard by those on the stage. Anne's body twitched for a couple of moments before finally stopping. Her dead body just hung there for all to see. Roger turned to Alex. "You're up."

Alex and Kameron kept their eyes on each other before being forced to separate. Alex took it upon herself to walk up to the noose. She even helped the executioner put the rope around her neck…and then she head-butted him.

Kameron turned to the crowd as they screamed for her death. There was a girl in the crowd that caught Kameron's attention. She made eye contact with him. It was Alex's sister. What was she doing here? He looked to Alex, who was awaiting her execution, and then back to Cara, who pointed to her own chest. Kameron turned to Roger. "Wait!"

393

Roger turned to Kameron. "The execution will commence."

"Yes, but I knew she was a Lite Follower. I kept it to myself." The crowd fell quiet as Kameron hopped on stage with Alex behind him.

Roger came up to him with contentment. "I thought we had a deal?"

"We did. I just chose to tell everyone. Now I'm ready for you to fulfill your end." He confidentially told him. "And Roger tried to cover it up to save this horrific practice. I hope you all find comfort in the Lite." He turned to Alex. "I know I did."

Alex smiled at him. "We'll be together."

"Get her down," Roger pointed to Anne's dead body.

The executioner got Anne's limp body down and kicked it off the stage onto the ground, where it fell on top of Kale's body. Kameron turned to Alex as the executioner got the rope ready.

"Don't let them have the privilege, Kameron." Alex could see Kameron was getting nervous. "I couldn't think of a more fitting end."

Kameron maintained his composure in front of the crowd; but he lost it bit when he turned to Alex. "I love you."

"I love you, too." She gave him a loving smile. Kameron and Alex maintained eye contact before they both felt a push from behind, along with a quick, sharp pain to their necks.

Blackness was all he could see. There was no sound, nothing to see; he couldn't even feel the ground below him. He didn't know how long he was there until he saw flashes of blue in the distance. The movement of light showed a young lady fighting black creatures with glowing red eyes.

"Pure of Heart!" She yelled. "Look for the sliver of white light." She continued to fight off the black creatures.

Kameron was frantically looking, and a massive number of glowing red eyes surrounded him. Behind the creatures was a small amount of light. "I see it!"

The woman continued to fight the creatures fighting towards the light. She was slowly gaining ground but was starting to slow down. Her light was fading. "We are not going to make it."

Kameron started to help fight the creatures, but it was a futile effort as the creatures were starting to come in mass. "I'm sorry, Alex."

Chapter Sixteen

"Here they come!" From the depths of the portal, a bunch of red eyes started to come closer. Alex stepped back. She turned to Devine, who had nothing but guilt written on her face.

"What have I done?" Devine was starting to droop her wings. "Humanity, His wish for them…what did I do?"

"Devine, listen to me. I'm a Sentry. My job is to protect the Balance; that is what I plan to do." Alex saw over her shoulder, the eyes getting closer. "You were a Guardian to the Conduit of Lite, a damn good one. The best, actually. We both excel at protecting. Now, sister, that is what I need you to do." Alex was thinking of a way to motivate Devine. Then, she pointed to Anne. "Protect Anne. No harm must come to her. She is the only one who can close this. Do you understand? She cannot die."

Devine saw the helpless primate trying to find a way to close the portal. Devine nodded as Anne was starting to read the Dark Texts. The Angel of Lite showed her skills with her bo staff. Then she said with unprecedented confidence, "She will not fall."

"Nice, that's good to hear," Alex was now paying attention to the red eyes getting closer. "Talk to me, Anne."

Anne was rustling through the papers, before she just gave up. "I don't know, Alex. What I got out of this was just, I guess, we just let it just…run out."

"You guess?" Alex watched the cross slowly losing the black liquid. "So, we've got a few minutes of fighting."

"That is plenty of time for them to perish," Devine spoke with pride.

Alex smiled, "Nice to have you back." Alex Lite Beamed the group of Infiltrators that morphed from the black mist before them, pushing them back into the Dark. Then they swarmed into the room.

Devine seemed to be in her element as she focused on protecting Anne. She was fending off any Infiltrator with deadly grace. It seemed as if Anne appreciated the gesture. On the other hand, Alex was much more physical in her battle, as she was on the front line of defense, and Devine was handling the ones that got by her. They weren't perfect, as some of the Infiltrators were leaving the building.

***

Tristan and Dinah carried Julian between them as they exited City Hall. All three of them were sore and bloodied. Even Father Richard was checking his head as it continued to bleed. The priest knew he was going to have a massive headache in morning. It seemed like just a long distance to see the car was just on the other end of the parking lot.

"Come, my brother," Dinah encouraged him as she adjusted him back up. "You will not join the stars tonight."

The knife was still in Julian's stomach. They had no bandages to secure the wound, so they decided it would be best just to leave it in. It just meant more pain with every move for the angel. He let them know it hurt.

Before they got to the final door, Tristan stopped. He motioned to Father Richard. "My keys are inside my pocket." Tristan moved, but he, too, was bleeding quite extensively.

"I got them," Father Richard reached into his pocket to grab them. Blood got onto his hands from when he pulled them out of the pocket. "We need to get you looked at," he whispered.

"I'm fine." Tristan knew that Father Richard was not amused by his trying to hide his true state of health. "Okay, once we get Julian to the doorway."

The group stepped out of City Hall to see black mists leaving the area where the museum stood. The four of them watched as more Dark entered CopperTop. They could only fear the worst.

"The portal is open," Julian barely got out.

"This is bad," Tristan watched the Balance shifting even more.

Dinah seemed relatively unfazed. "Would there not be more than that, if it were open?"

***

Alex turned her head to Anne as she screeched from getting cut by an Infiltrator. Devine had her hands full with three others to notice. Alex hurried over to her friend to kill the beast that scratched her. "You, okay?"

Anne quickly nodded. "I'm fine." She pointed behind her. "Alex!"

Alex instinctively kicked the Infiltrator in the air. Once it hit the ground, Alex stabbed it in the chest with her Lite. It quickly melted into the ground. Alex then jumped into a group of four more. Surprisingly, she ended their existence in a short bit of time. Alex had a bit of blood dripping from her body, but nothing to be worried about.

Devine had just finished her last Infiltrator. They both convened near Anne, awaiting the second wave of the Dark soldiers. "Devine, how are you feeling?" Alex checked her wounds. She flicked some of the blood off her hand.

"I have felt better, Sentry," Devine halfway mused.

"Great, we are going to die. Devine made a joke: it's the end of the world." Alex flinched at her side. The structure's cross had very little black left in it. "Looks like we won't have that much longer."

Devine was relieved. "I will have to answer for my actions. Once the portal closes, I will go to face my punishment."

"Devine, what will happen to you?" Anne was concerned.

"I do not know, but I will accept it." Devine checked on Anne's wound. "I am sorry for causing you both harm."

Alex helped Anne up from the ground. "Come on. Once this thing closes, we're calling it a night." Alex verified if the cross still had black liquid in it. "I wanna go home, take a hot shower…" Then Alex stopped and turned to the portal. "Kameron," she softly spoke. Alex shoved Anne into Devine. "Watch her."

"Alex, what are you doing?!" Anne screamed.

"Alexandria, you will not be able to come back…" Devine went to chase her.

The Lite Sentry had a face of determination. Alex gently Lite Beamed Devine to push her back. Alex's body burst into a pure blue neon mist as she ran towards the portal. With no hesitation or remorse, she jumped into the doorway of the Darkness, leaving her two friends in shock as they stared at the structure.

It was darkness that surrounded Alex. The Lite generating from her body wasn't reflecting off anything, just the cold stone that acted as the floor. "Alexandria," a cold, familiar voice was heard in the distance. She heard screams a bit closer, but they weren't sounds of people or tortured souls. It was of the Dark diminishing.

Alex turned to the sound. Behind her was the light from the portal. Alex heard a woman scream. Then she heard the scream of a man, a man that she knew and loved. Her body burst a flash of a little more neon blue mist. She ran towards the voices as she saw a faint glow of two small balls of blue light moving about. It was another Lite Sentry, here, in Hell.

Alex rushed over and jumped in the middle of the group of Infiltrators. Alex easily defended them off the woman who seemed oddly familiar. The woman could barely keep her eyes open as she seemed to be grabbing onto Alex.

"Please, I beg of you, do not let me fall," she pleaded.

"Not on my watch," Alex promised her. She was carrying this Lite Sentry to the portal. With all her might, she threw the woman into the light leading back home. The mysterious Lite Sentry was rescued from the depths of the Dark. Hopefully, Devine and Anne were able to help her.

"Alexandria," Vandor's voice was getting louder. "Your soul shall not escape."

Alex turned to the portal, where she knew she could make it out. Kameron was her priority. The reflection of her light barely silhouetted a man in tactical gear, wavering on his feet. He was just about to drop to the floor when Alex caught him. He was hot to the touch, but shivering. "Kameron!" Alex kissed him. It was a relief as she felt him kiss her back. "Come on, Kameron. I got you."

She started to carry him to the light. He had little energy left as he was trying to stand. Alex limped him along to the white light representing freedom from this Hell. A group of red eyes separated Alex and Kameron from escape. She didn't even hesitate as she attacked the Infiltrators with one arm, as the other held up Kameron. She was not letting him go.

The Infiltrators were starting to overpower her as she needed her second arm. To fight them off.

She had a moment before they attacked again. She pulled Kameron in and kissed him as she threw him into the white light. Then she continued her battle as Vandor's voice calling her name got closer.

***

Anne continued to give aid to the mysterious woman who got flung from the portal. The girl's body was steaming, but her body was freezing to the touch. Devine's face was in shock. "Do you know this woman?"

"This is Cara," Devine watched as the Pure of Heart shook her hand after touching her.

"As in, Osiah's first Sentry he trained?" Anne noticed her body start to shiver. She ran over to the wall and ripped down a tapestry to cover her up with.

"Yes," Devine turned to the portal. "We do not have much time. I am going to get her out."

Anne knew there was no stopping her. Devine got up to run when another body came flying through the portal. This was a male in tactical police gear. The steam from his clothes and skin emitted off his body. Then, a blue light was seen in the Dark, and a glowing Alex jumped out of the portal. She had cuts on her face, and her clothes were ripped from battle. There were portions where blood was soaked into her outfit.

Alex immediately stood up and turned to the portal as the final bit of the black matter disappeared. It caused an impenetrable glass to form. Alex tapped on the glass. Vandor instantly appeared in front of Alex. The Lite Sentry didn't budge. She stared at his black eyes, barely visible through his greasy hair. The Lite Sentry knocked on the glass and blew him a kiss. Vandor punched the glass in anger as he disappeared into the Dark. The glass immediately turned back into a wall of a mixture of stone and metal. The Lite that surrounded her slowly diminished. "Is Kameron alive?"

"Yes, sweetie. He's breathing." Anne had her hand on Kameron's face.

"Good," Alex started wavery. "That's … good." Then she dropped to the ground.

"We must get them to the church," Devine picked up Cara over her shoulder.

Anne gave her the keys to the car. "Just push this button, and the car will open. Carry them out, and I need to find a way to get that cross off of there."

Devine started to carry Cara back to the car but stopped. "Just push this?"

"It will make a sound, and lights will flash; don't get scared." Anne gathered the Dark Texts.

"I am Devine. I know no fear." Devine carried Cara to the car.

Anne read the text as she stood in front of the portal. This cross was much too dangerous to leave for the Dark. She tried to pry it off, but it wouldn't budge. She frantically searched the papers for a way to get it off.

Devine returned from carrying Kameron to the car. Only Alex was left. Anne turned to her, "Can you try to get this thing off?"

Devine grabbed the cross but could not budge it. "It seems to be stuck. This is not moving. Come, Pure of Heart, we must go." Devine grabbed Alex over her shoulder and headed for the car.

Anne took one last look at the Dark texts. "Ugh, why won't this thing come off?" She frantically searched the texts. Then, the upside-down cross fell onto the ground. Anne looked around for a moment. She was a little hesitant to pick up the cross. After a few moments, the texts and cross went into the satchel to head upstairs. She got through the doorway, where a man was standing admiring the old needlepoint on the wall. He turned around to look at Anne.

"Scotty?" Anne was confused.

"Hey, Anne." He approached her.

"We thought you died," Anne was hoping Devine was coming back.

"No, I was under witness protection. Weston couldn't tell anyone. I'm going to testify with Scarlett Roberts about the F.O.R." He approached Anne. "He just asked me to receive and protect the clavis." He pointed to the satchel.

Anne put her hand on the satchel that held the cross. "Why?"

"To separate it far from the Ianua." Scotty motioned to Anne that he would walk out with her.

Anne started walking towards the door of the museum. "Makes sense. I was just going to give it to the Council."

"That is our plan as well, but the Sentry doesn't look like she is up to its protection. He just sent me because I won't be detected. No Lite in this body." He thumped his chest.

"Makes sense." Anne took the cross out of the satchel off her body and gave it to him. For some reason, she didn't think the Dark Texts should be known about.

He placed the satchel over his body. "Thanks for that."

"Are you going to go see Midnight?" Anne flinched from her scratch.

"I'm heading over to the hospital tonight," Scotty took a peek in the satchel.

Anne stopped in her tracks. "Hospital?"

Scotty turned to her. "Yah, to go see Midnight."

Anne started to back up. "Weston knows she's not at the hospital."

Scotty got irritated as his eyes glowed red and his teeth sharpened. "Thanks, I needed to get this." Then, he slowly started to approach her. "And now, as a bonus, I will bring Gron your head." He began to make his way towards her.

"Devine!" Anne screamed as she had no place to go.

The angel came crashing in through the door with her bo staff ready to fight. She saw the Demon heading towards Anne. She immediately took to the air and landed in front of Anne to protect her. "Give her back that cross."

"Let's see," Scotty gave an evil chuckle. "You have two Sentries and a Pure of Heart passed out in a car unprotected, with all that Dark out there; or you can come chase me." The Dark possessed man snickered.

Anne put her hand on Devine, "We need to get them out of here."

Devine protected Anne as they both ran to the car. Scotty silently laughed as he turned to go deliver the cross to his Leader.

***

Once everything calmed down, Gron ended up back at the museum. He wasn't happy that his plan to get Drazon, formerly known as Scotty, into the government was now compromised. It wasn't even set in motion before it was thwarted. There's no doubt that Alex already elevated up to the Council. They got their nasty Lite into everything. Gron was sitting in the museum, holding the cross, studying it. He couldn't help but try to open the portal to get Vandor back.

He placed the cross back in the holder. It was a dead effort. Gron just stared at the portal not opening. He turned to Misluna. "Thoughts?"

"It's not working." It was all she could come up with.

"No shit." Gron flashed his eyes. The cross fell out of the placement, hitting Gron in the head.

Misluna bit her lip while Azrael just stared at the structure in deep thought. The Dark Angel approached Gron so only he could hear him. "I should have been here. Your arrogance cost us our master to return."

"I needed you to rescue Misluna, to protect the book." Gron defended his position.

"You convince yourself of that lie. You wanted all the glory for his return for yourself, and when he returns, you will pay for your failure." Azrael coldly stated.

"Please, there is so much Dark in this town; we are so secured in this, it's not even funny." He turned to Azrael and put his finger on his chest. "The question is, why didn't you kill that angel and sentry? They would have been no match for you." He looked over at Misluna, who was holding the twins' hands. "It was opened before this last time. There's gotta be a way to open it again."

***

The feeling of waking up from a sleep wasn't something Alex had felt for quite some time. For a split second, she thought she had died. Especially when she opened her eyes to see Celestial sitting on the foot of her bed. "Good morning, Alexandria."

"Morning. I thought I was dead." Alex started to stretch, and then she instantly sat up. "Kameron."

Celestial put her hand on Alex's chest. "Relax. He is healing in this church."

"And the other Lite Sentry?" Alex was trying to get out of bed, but Celestial was keeping her calm.

"She is resting in a separate room as well," Celestial eased her mind.

Arome and Omeila approached Celestial. "The NEWS." They both said.

407

Celestial took in a deep breath from nerves before nodding to her guardians. "You need to rest. The Balance is tipped far to the Dark."

"I know." Alex slowly got out of the bed. "I can feel it."

Celestial placed her hand on the Lite Sentry's cheek. "I have to go."

Alex got up from the little bed that was set up in her office. There was no doubt it had a little of Anne's touch to the setup, as a can of Apollo was sitting in a cooler next to her bed. Alex opened the sweet nectar. A quick shower was needed because there was no question about it: a foul smell was coming off of her. Almost like burnt flesh.

It was a fast shower, and then she got dressed. She put on a pair of white jogging pants and a pink t-shirt she had gotten from Michelle's closet. Harold and Beth let her pick whatever she wanted out of Michelle's room when she died. There were a couple of clothes that reminded her of Michelle that she picked out. Over the pink t-shirt, she put Kameron's Secret Service sweatshirt.

She went downstairs to see Father Richard, who was in jeans and flannel. Alex never realized she hardly saw him without his priest garment while in the church. The baseball cap on his head had see through mesh, Alex could see bandages on his head. She felt terrible as such a good man got hurt. He was on the phone with Cardinal Joe about the events. Tristan slowly came down the hallway. Alex was glad to see he survived the night, even though it was evident he was a little sore.

"Morning, Alex," he said as he tried to hide his pain.

"Tell me about it?" She touched his arm in support.

"We failed to obtain the Dark Texts. Megan escaped to the F.O.R., and Julian got injured pretty badly, but he is still with us." Tristan couldn't bring himself to look at Alex in shame. "I failed."

"We failed." Dinah came up from behind him. "All..." she emphasized. "...fought bravely and valiantly. There is no shame from that night." She gave him a shy, reassuring smile.

Alex just moved her eyes from Dinah back to Tristan. "Really, that's all that happened last night?"

Dinah shook her head, "No." She pointed over to Devine, sitting in the congregation on the pew, staring at the stained-glass window. She had a sadness to her, almost like a teenager looking to the future with little hope.

Alex slowly made it over to her friend. "You, okay?"

"I have been better." The angel stared ahead. "My arrogance and inability to see the big picture almost caused the destruction of His creation."

"Well, we humans are doing a fine job of that without your help." Alex sat down next to her.

"My actions were selfish," Devine reminded her. "There is so much Dark out there, and you sacrifice so much; it is not fair."

Alex quickly raised her eyebrows up and down. "I got my fiancé back. Even though it was a mistake on your intentions; it's a debt I will owe you forever."

Devine dropped a tear. "What is the saying the primates use, 'The roadway to Hell is often paved with good intentions.' I am afraid I cleared the way for the Dark."

"Vandor came close, but he is still trapped in the Dark. I'm not too worried." Alex saw Dinah approach from behind them.

"Sister, it will not be that bad. It just takes a bit longer to heal and get to places." The orange-haired angel assured her. "But it is manageable."

Alex was confused. "What happened?"

Devine turned to her. "I have been banished until the Balance is put back into alignment."

Alex's eyes got huge as Devine got up. "I have nowhere to go." Devine went outside to get some time alone.

"He banished her?" Alex verified with Dinah.

"She is not the first," she pointed to herself. "Will not be the last." Dinah looked around as if to make sure no one was listening. "You will never hear me repeat these words. We angels may act as if we are perfect, but we are not. We have just enough free will in us to see trouble. Remember, we too, are also his children."

"You are almost just like us?" Alex adjusted herself, realizing how sore she actually was.

"No, we are much better," Dinah shook her head as if she said something completely stupid.

"And there it is." Alex smirked. "What did you do to get banished?" Alex's curiosity was intrigued.

Dinah hesitated. "My allegiance to the Lite is strong, and my love for my Father will never falter."

"What did you do?" Alex pushed again.

Dinah smirked. "I told Him I thought He was completely nuts and thought He left His mind back in the kitchen."

Alex couldn't help but snort from laughter. "You didn't? What about?"

Dinah smirked, "Some things are better not told."

Father Richard peeked his head into the congregation room. "Alex, Dinah. Can you join Tristan and me downstairs with Anne?"

They all joined together in the dining area of the church. Anne was sitting on the table as if she made a horrible mistake. "What's going on?" Alex sat next to Anne, knowing she needed support.

"I willingly gave the cross to a Demon." Anne just shook her head in disbelief.

"What? Who?" Alex was shocked.

"Scotty."

"Kameron's friend?"

Anne nodded. "His eyes glowed, and his teeth were those of a Demon."

"I really don't want to kill him, considering all he did for us." Alex thought about it even though she knew she would have to.

Father Richard made sure all were present before speaking. "I just got off the phone with the Council. They want us to prepare for the testimony of Scarlett Roberts." Everyone's eyes got big.

Alex was the first to speak. "We're setting up an offensive?"

"In a way," Father Richard stated. "Cardinal Joe will be here the day after tomorrow. He will be in charge of the direction. We're hoping having a full-out Cardinal will start bringing people into the church."

"What about you?" Anne lifted her head out of her hands.

"I've been sent on special tasking." Father Richard made eye contact with Tristan.

Alex got up. "Where are we going?"

"You are staying here. You're going to set up protection for Ms. Roberts." Father Richard could see the pride on Alex's face.

"I got this," she winked.

Tristan got a nervous feeling in his stomach. "Any news on my next assignment?"

"Yes, actually. You and me. We are being sent to escort Ms. Roberts back." Father Richard studied Tristan. "Are you up for this?"

"When do we leave?" Tristan adjusted his stance. He immediately made eye contact with Dinah, who, in turn, seemed a bit distraught.

"A couple of weeks before the trial." Father Richard stood up. "So, we have time to get things ready before we go." Father Richard looked at his watch. "Any news on when Carl is supposed to be back?"

Alex shook her head.

"What do I need to be ready for?" Tristan was trying to piece this all together by returning the conversation to his mission.

412

Father Richard addressed the whole group. "The Council said the trial is scheduled for late November."

Alex stood up. "Once the trial starts, the F.O.R. will be exposed for what they are. It will be a big step to putting Balance back."

"I guess I'll have some time before I have to pack." Tristan was nervous about his special assignment.

Alex studied Tristan's reaction. "You're going to be okay, Tristan. I will have you ready by then. Protect Father Richard."

Dinah stood up as if she just made up her mind from a decision. "I shall go with you. It does not hurt to have another warrior on this mission."

Tristan smiled, "You're going to have to ride in a car."

Dinah's face turned to fear. "That does not bother me." Her voice cracked a little.

Alex smirked at the two of them, "Yah, I'm sure it will be an interesting drive."

After the meeting was conveyed, Alex quietly walked up the stairs to the hallway. The urge just to get to Kameron was pulling her towards his room, but she knew once she went to the room, she wouldn't leave. There was something else she needed to do first. Alex slowly opened the door to check in on the poor Lite Sentry that had been trapped in Hell.

They tried to make her room look as old as possible so she wouldn't be too shocked upon her waking. Alex quietly peeked in on Cara. The room was too dark to see her, so Alex lit one finger with

413

lite. Cara was sweating under the covers, mumbling something to herself. Alex turned to the door where Dr. Smithon and his nurse were dressed in renaissance clothing. They just put up their hands and shook their heads, telling her not to say anything. Alex just smirked as she tucked the blankets on her. The Lite Sentry turned to Dr. Smithon.

"We'll take care of her," was all he said.

Alex nodded as she was looking forward but scared as her next stop was just right next door. She poked her head into the room that was as dark as it could get. The mattress was on the floor, and the bed flipped over, acting almost like a barricade. Alex didn't see her fiancé. She came up to the makeshift barrier to peek over it. Kameron was in the far corner, shivering from the light, mumbling nonsense. Alex tried everything not to cry to see what was mentally left of her man, who was once so strong.

"Kameron," she softly said. She carefully went into the room. "It's me, Alex."

"Alex," he peeked through his arms. "No, get away." He tried to bury himself deeper into the corner of the room.

"It's okay, I'm not going to hurt you," she knelt down as she slowly approached him.

"Alex, no, not Alex. It's not. Alex can't be. Head, water, lead, all of it, false, fake, no." Kameron hid his head in his arms as he tried to get away from her, screaming. "Baby dark, blue eyes, death. Not again, you can have it. Take it from me."

Alex wiped a tear from her eyes then over covered her to prevent herself from crying. "Baby, what did they do to you?" She slowly approached him.

"Get away!" He screamed. "Not again!" He pushed her away. "Burning coldness." He shivered in the corner, before finally passing out.

Alex carefully crawled up to him. She placed her arm around him as he continued as he mumbled nonsense in his sleep. She put her cheek on top of head as he passed out as she held the man she loved. Only the hand of God could pry her away from this spot. She remained in the dark, holding Kameron, with only a sliver of light from the door showing.

Post End

The sun was setting over the town of CopperTop Mountain. Celestial closed her eyes to enjoy the warmth of the sun before it retired for the day. This planet was so pretty, so full of potential, until the primates became more willing to accept the Dark. Dinah might have been crude in her comment to the Father, but she did have a point. The amount of Dark in this town was devastating. People openly accepting the Dark into their lives was disheartening. The evil influence over the humans was just too tantalizing for them not to accept. It was going to come at a cost, a cost that Celestial could not allow.

Arome and Omeila approached their mistress. "The NEWS is here." They backed away as Celestial nodded. She heard the rustling of the air being blown from the steel horse. North always loved to ride, no matter the method. Her brother took off the helmet, showing his dark skin and braided short hair. He was wearing his signature white colors as he approached Celestial.

"Hey, sis, what's going on?" He annoyingly put his helmet away. "If it wasn't the human's law, I'd get rid of that thing. Messes up my hair." He placed the helmet on the bike.

"I wish you were not here." Celestial continued to watch over the town. Then she faced him. "But it is good to see you again." The two of them hugged each other. "It makes me nervous every time the NEWS is about to report."

"We only collect the stories, Celes," North reminded her. "Our opinion doesn't make it in the message."

The Conduit of Lite reminded him of the reality. "He takes your word as the truth. You cannot dilute it or exaggerate."

"I never do. You know what would happen if the NEWS did that." He continued to look over the town. "There is a lot of the Dark here, though."

"There is, but the Sentry, she will put the Balance back." Celestial joined in, staring over the town.

"I met her. She's a nice kid. I can see Osiah in her." North hesitated as if he wanted to tell her something but stopped himself. "I am sorry about his passing."

"He died the hero he was always meant to be." Celestial gave a forced smile.

North put his hand on her shoulder in support. "He was more of a hero than you would ever know."

Celestial was about to ask if he meant anything about that until a car came racing toward them. Celestial turned to see East and West coming out of a car with very loud music. West was the skinnier one with long hair. He was wearing a black leather jacket with a dark green silk shirt. East was in a dark green polo. He was bald with a combover. The overweight angel was finishing up food as the remaining sunlight glistened off his head.

"Hey, sis," West raised his fist in the air. "One second." He started swinging his hair around to the beat of the music. "Sorry...love that part..." He went into the car to turn the music off.

"It is bittersweet to see you all again." She gave West a hug as he swung her around. Celestial couldn't help but laugh. It was East's turn for a hug as his stomach bumped into the blonde angel.

"Sorry about that, sis." East gave her a hug.

"Ah, you got a little pizza sauce on your face." He took his finger to wipe it off. Celestial admired all three of her brothers. "I am happy to see you all."

East grabbed a candy bar from his back pocket. "Good to see you too, Celes."

West grabbed a hold of East's stomach. "Looks like someone got a little jelly in the belly."

"Stop it, you are making me cry." East playfully slapped West's hand.

Omeila and Arome approached Celestial. "My lady."

Celestial nodded. "Where is South?" She scanned the area but couldn't find him.

North thought about it for a quick second before finally answering. "He needed to clean up a little mess, nothing serious."

"Give him my love," Celestial gave them all a hug again. "Please ensure accuracy."

"That's what the NEWS is," North assured his important sister. "Report the facts."

Celestial smiled, "I will be sure to see you before you leave."

"Of course, sis," North crossed his heart.

East and West both gave her hugs before she left.

"Please make sure I get to see South before you disperse," Celestial asked of her brothers.

"Cross our lite," West made a symbol on his chest. They waited until Celestial left before all three of them went to the cliff to oversee the town. "It truly is beautiful." West admired the view.

"It is," East saw a beautiful woman below them. She turned to smile at him as he waved. "We going to be long? I need to congregate with the locals."

North just shook his head at this brother. "Look, I'm sure this report will go just like all the rest."

West gave him a look of disbelief, "Really? This town has the same feeling as Sodom and Gomorrah?"

"Okay, maybe like the rest after that," North admitted. "Just try to enjoy yourselves. It's easy to see the negative in the primates but remember the rule."

"With every negative we witness, we look or promote a positive." East and West both said in annoyance. Then they started play fighting with North.

They laughed until they saw an F.O.R. van below them, picking up a group of people, including the girl East was admiring. East sighed, "It may be harder than we thought."

They were all staring over the cliff when the fourth brother arrived. "South," North acknowledged.

Their brother was all dressed in a black hooded robe, and he seemed to glide as he walked. Not

419

even his brothers could see his face. Just the hood covering his face seemed to nod.

The leader of the NEWS checked back over the darkening horizon. "I'm glad it's all cleaned up. We can't install judgment; we are only reporters. No judgment."

South tilted his head to North.

West stepped in, "I know it's sad to see the children in situations like that, but we are carriers of the message. That's it. Plus, we get all the benefits of experiencing human pleasures. Just enjoy it, be like me, keep a low profile."

South pointed in the direction of the park with his gloved hand under his long black robe.

West smiled. "You have to admit, it was a good song."

East stomach was growling. "Come on, let's go get something to eat."

North agreed, as he emphasized. "Accurate reporting. The NEWS cannot push an agenda, just report all sides of the story. Our Father will be the judge." He put up his finger. "When He sees fit."

A sudden wall of Dark hit their senses. They all turned to South, realizing what he just said had the potential to be the scary truth of the matter.